STAR TREK®

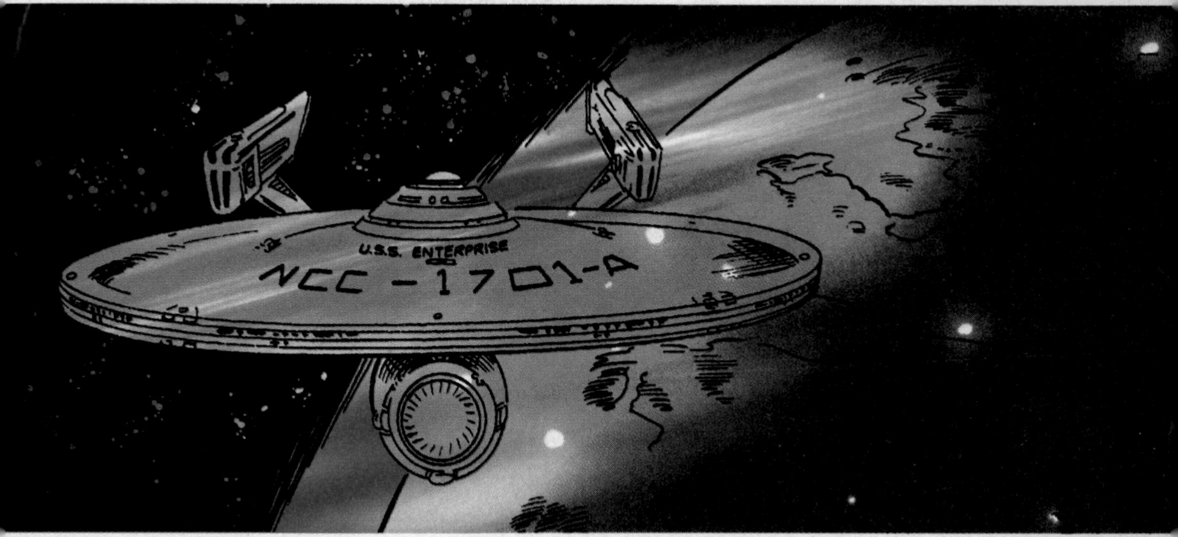
U.S.S. ENTERPRISE
NCC-1701-A

REVISITATIONS

HOWARD WEINSTEIN
WRITER

GORDON PURCELL
ROD WHIGHAM
PENCILLERS

ARNE STARR
CARLOS GARZON
ROMEO TANGHAL
INKERS

BOB PINAHA
LETTERER

TOM McCRAW
COLORIST

INTRODUCTION BY DAVID GERROLD
BASED ON STAR TREK CREATED BY GENE RODDENBERRY

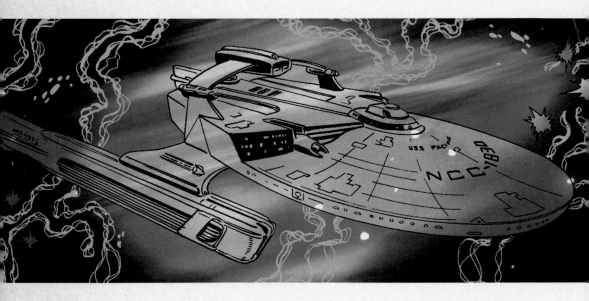

Jenette Kahn
President & Editor-in-Chief

Paul Levitz
Executive VP & Publisher

Martin Pasko
Group Editor

Robert Greenberger
Alan Gold
Editors, Original Series

Bob Kahan
Editor, Collected Edition

Margaret Clark
Robert Greenberger
Consulting Editors, Collected Edition

Robbin Brosterman
Art Director

Joe Orlando
VP-Creative Director

Bruce Bristow
VP-Sales & Marketing

Patrick Caldon
VP-Finance & Operations

Terri Cunningham
Managing Editor

Chantal d'Aulnis
VP-Business Affairs

Lillian Laserson
VP & General Counsel

Bob Rozakis
Executive Director - Production

STAR TREK: REVISITATIONS

DC COMICS, 1700 BROADWAY, NEW
YORK, NY 10019
A DIVISION OF WARNER BROS. - A TIME
WARNER ENTERTAINMENT COMPANY
PRINTED IN CANADA. FIRST PRINTING.
ISBN # 1-56389-223-5

COVER PAINTING BY SONIA R. HILLIOS

"Howard Weinstein, Howard Weinstein, Howard Weinstein..."

AN APPRECIATION BY DAVID GERROLD

Whenever I hear the name Howard Weinstein, I am reminded of the melancholy image of Barbra Streisand in *Funny Girl*, plaintively singing the name of the man she loves. Only instead of Nicki Arnstein (played by Omar Sharif), she's warbling, *"Howard Weinstein, Howard Weinstein, Howard Weinstein..."* (played by Howard Weinstein). I can't help it. It's the alliteration of the name.

Yes, it's a bizarre image. Barbra Streisand mooning over Howard Weinstein. It's especially bizarre if you've met either one of them. Now, in all truth, I have to admit that I have absolutely no idea if Barbra Streisand is a *Star Trek* fan, or even if she's a *Star Trek* FAN. It's possible that she's never heard of Howard Weinstein. In fact, it's more than possible, it's probable. In fact, it's more than probable that even if she had heard of Howard Weinstein, she probably wouldn't care. Let's face it, in the real world, it is extremely unlikely that Barbra Streisand will ever croon a single melancholy lovestruck note like this: *"Howard Weinstein, Howard Weinstein, Howard Weinstein..."*

This is probably one of the great tragedies in Howard Weinstein's prolific career — that he will never know Barbra Streisand. And, of course, it is equally one of the great tragedies in Barbra Streisand's life — that she will never meet Howard Weinstein. (Unless of course

the two of them are so successful at covering up their secret dalliances that the rest of us will never suspect a thing. In which case, this casual speculation on my part will have blown their carefully constructed cover. But let us not pursue this thought any further. That way lies madness and libel suits.) And besides, the state of Howard Weinstein's love life is not really a suitable topic for a publication that is likely to find its way into the hands of impressionable children. Let us then skip lightly over this whole squalid subject.

But...if we were to spend some time spelunking into the sordid details of Howard Weinstein's life, we would find that his non-relationship with *La Streisand* is an unimportant ripple in the stream compared to his much more telling character failures. Because if truth be told, the unpleasant fact of the matter is that Howard Weinstein's biggest character failure is that he has no character failures. Howard Weinstein is a nice man.

Now most people, upon hearing this news, would assume that this is a compliment. On the contrary. A writer must be known for his quirks and foibles. His eccentricities must be legendary. His phobias must be the source of fear and wonder. Because it is out of his most grandiose deviations from the norm that the most interesting insights and perspectives will flow.

Think about all the great writers in the world. Ernest Hemingway was an adventurer — he was overcompensating for his formative years when he was pampered and dressed like a girl; but he gave us the most marvelous stories of risk and courage. In the end, he sucked the bullets out of his shotgun.

Edgar Allan Poe was a laudanum freak (a mixture of rum and cocaine); he drowned in a Baltimore gutter — do you realize how drunk you have to be to drown in a gutter? Poe was obsessed with the death of his young wife Lenore, so he gave us terrifying visions of premature burial and plagues and people being walled up alive in the wine cellar.

Howard Philip Lovecraft was sickly, feeble and self-absorbed; he lived with his mother all of his life — and he ended up creating one of the most enduring mythos of evil in modern fantasy.

In other words, great writers come from dysfunctional circumstances, and their best writing is the excess of that dysfunction expressed in words. They live on the borderline of sanity and send us back images that are twisted and bizarre and ultimately so disturbing that they shift our perceptions of reality. Very often, the most astonishing work of a writer is the baroque invention of his or her own identity as a certifiable loony toon.

Which brings me — unfortunately — back to Howard Weinstein and his biggest character flaw. Howard Weinstein is a normal human being. He is a nice man. If you hold him up to the light, there is no secret message. What you see is what you get. Howard Weinstein, Howard Weinstein, Howard Weinstein — Howard Weinstein is as healthy as cottage cheese. (I'll get back to this thought in a moment.) While you and I might find this an admirable trait, it is an extraordinarily debilitating burden for any professional storyteller to endure.

Surely, you say, Howard Weinstein must have some endearing quirk.

No, I say. He does not.

Howard Weinstein has no major character flaws. There is simply nothing at all that you can point to that would distinguish him as unfit for polite society. He bathes regularly. He brushes his teeth

after every meal. He combs his hair neatly. He takes off his hat in the presence of ladies. He offers his seat on the subway to pregnant women and the elderly. He holds the door open for editors. He always gives a quarter to the panhandler on the corner. He signs autographs graciously. He doesn't pick his nose in public (anymore). And he remembers the names of people he meets. He remembers to call his mother and he dresses warm when he goes outside. He colors inside the lines. He is, without a doubt, his mother's pride and joy. If you look up *shayneh punim* in a Yiddish-to-English dictionary, you will find Howard Weinstein's picture.

While this is no doubt a source of unending pride to all of the elderly Weinsteins, assorted grandparents, aunts, uncles, and kibitzers, it is not much of a source of anything else to anyone who has the unfortunate task of having to write something about Howard Weinstein. Lacking any significant character flaws, he is simply hell to write about.

Howard Weinstein does not throw his more enthusiastic fans down elevator shafts. He never smuggled a baby elephant into his hotel room. He was never caught naked in the bedroom of the Chilean ambassador's daughter. He does not ride a motorcycle with a gang of genetically-challenged sociopaths. He does not sky-dive into volcanoes. He does not scuba-dive for sunken treasures in the Bermuda Triangle. He has never fought sharks in a day-long battle over the custody of a marlin. He has never walled up anybody alive in his wine cellar. He does not routinely summon elder evils.

Howard Weinstein never wrestled a pig, an octopus, an alligator, or an angry water buffalo. He has never been thrown out of a restaurant — or anywhere else for that matter. His name has never been romantically linked with Barbra Streisand — or anyone else famous enough to guarantee him significant column inches in a supermarket tabloid. He doesn't even pick his nose in public (anymore).

In short, the job of describing Howard Weinstein is roughly the same as describing cottage cheese.

"It's white. It's lumpy. It's sort of good for you."

Yes, it is probably unkind of me to say all of these terrible things about Howard Weinstein — that he's a nice man — in front of an audience whose continued support he depends upon for his rent, an audience who would probably much prefer to hear me tell tales of Howard Weinstein's fortnightly visitations with UFOs and demonic visigoths. Nevertheless, I feel it is imperative to demonstrate just what kind of a handicap Howard Weinstein works under, because it makes the resultant high quality of his writing even more amazing.

Writing without any great or significant personal traumas in his history to draw upon for source material, Howard Weinstein still continues to turn out work that stands as a standard of excellence for other storytellers to match. In other words, this is a man who works on pure imagination alone.

I've known Howard Weinstein since the Cretaceous (actually, it's the Mesozoic, but I couldn't remember how to spell Mesozoic), when he was found wandering around the first New York *Star Trek* convention with a dazed expression and a hand-embroidered tribble. Stunned by the discovery that he was *not* the only *Star Trek* fan in the world, he had to have his eyebrows surgically reattached; he had to be continually reminded that it was all right to blink; and every so often, a helpful member of the convention committee would wander by and wipe the spittle from his lips. He was young and innocent at the time. Amazingly, more than twenty years later, he is *still* young and innocent. I would suspect that he has a picture in his attic that ages horribly, except that he has no attic. (It's probably his driver's license photo that looks terrible instead.)

At that time there were those who came to *Star Trek* as a place to escape the real world, who used it as a domain in which they could reinvent themselves as Starfleet Admirals and Vulcans and Klingons and priestesses of far-off worlds. Well, yeah, okay; fun is fun — but there were also those who not only went to the edge of eccentricity, but leapt happily off into the domains of dysfunction and madness. While there don't seem to be as many of the truly crazy fanatics wandering around anymore, they have left a lasting impression of ~~Trekkies~~ Trekkers as socially retarded primates who have not yet finished climbing up the evolutionary ladder and remain stuck somewhere between lawyer and chimpanzee (with chimpanzee representing the higher end of the scale). This culminated in the enduring, but not endearing, image of William Shatner appearing on *Saturday Night Live*, telling a group of gawky, geeky fans to "Get a life!"

As funny as that image was at the time, even to ~~Trekkies~~ Trekkers, it was also very unfair to the larger universe of fans who came to *Star Trek* as a vision of a place where human beings could learn to resolve their differences without having to put their hands on the hilts of their swords.

Like many other fans, Howard Weinstein came to *Star Trek* not as a television show, but as a marvelous realm of adventure. But *unlike* many other fans, Howard saw *Star Trek* not just as a realm of adventures to be enjoyed, but as adventures to be *created* as well. In 1974, he sold his first *Star Trek* story to Filmation Studios, a script for a *Star Trek Animated* episode, the title of which eludes me at the moment (and which I am too lazy to go look up, because all of my files and laser discs and tapes have been in storage since the earthquake, and maybe some kindly editor who has that information closer to hand will footnote the information here[1]).

Although there are those who insist that the *Star Trek Animated* series is non-canonical —

Excuse me a minute. *Non-canonical?!!* Just how seriously are we going to take this? Okay, let's everybody stop for a minute and take three big deep breaths and repeat slowly, "It's only a TV show, it's only a TV show, it's only a TV show..."

— Okay, back to work. Although there are those who insist that *Star Trek Animated* is not part of the **real** *Star Trek,* let me tell you that the cast and crew of that series took it very seriously, and brought the same dedication and skill to their work as if they were creating a live

[1] "The Pirates of Orion"

action show. Howard Weinstein's first script was of the same high professional caliber as those turned in by the other screenwriters for the animated series. It was an auspicious debut.

Not too many years after that, Howard Weinstein wrote one of the first of Pocket Books' *Star Trek* novels, *The Covenant of the Crown,* the title of which I do remember because I was asked to write the introduction for the book. (Now, two decades later, he has forgiven me enough for that introduction to allow me a second chance at defaming what's left of his character.) Like his animated script, his first novel demonstrated long-lasting enthusiasm for *Star Trek.*

In the years since then, Howard Weinstein has not only established himself as part of the *Star Trek* family of storytellers, he has established himself as one of the story- tellers who upholds the standards set by the original TV series that started it all. He has done this by turning himself into a veritable cornucopia of novels and comic books that have provided *Star Trek* enthusiasts with hours and hours of enjoyment.

Howard has also been a frequent guest at many *Star Trek* and science-fiction conventions, where he has demonstrated again and again his enthusiasm for *Star Trek* — as well as the previously mentioned fact of his terminal niceness. He doesn't even charge for his autograph. He's a popular guest, the fans like his considerate manner, his soft- spoken knowledgeability, and his gentle sense of humor.

And if that weren't enough of a threat to the sanity of his colleagues on the panels he participates on, he's also prolific. He has never in his life had a writer's block — at least, never one that he's admitted to in public. He just writes and writes and writes and writes. And he is consistently readable, thoughtful, and entertaining.

Personally, I think it's in the comic-book format that Howard Weinstein's best work can be found. There's an enthusiasm and vitality in comic books that exists in no other art form. Comics are a compelling medium. They propel you from page to page with much the same energy as a movie; but unlike movies, comic books leave room for your imagi- nation to supply details and actions that far surpass what any special effects man will ever be able to build, blow up, or synthesize in a computer. It has been said elsewhere, but it's worth repeating here, that comic books are the true American art form.

In the fifties, comic books were viewed as an unhealthy occupation, and many parents tried to limit their children's exposure to Superman and Batman. But comic books represented then — and still do today — an escape into alternative possibilities. They expand the event horizon of the reader's imagination. They allow us to shift our percep- tion of the way the universe works. The way things are is not necessarily the way they have to be. And this was always the strength and message of the original *Star Trek* series, too; so the comic book is one of the most suitable expressions of *Star Trek* possible. It serves as a hook for the reader's own ability to be inspired, and it provides a launching pad for his or her own capability to dream.

(If I may be so immodest as to insert a personal note here, now that I have a son of my own, I have encouraged him to read comic books, even to the point of nagging. I do not want him to suffer from a blighted childhood. I want him exposed to all of the marvelous realms of fear and wonder to be found in comic books. Unfortunately, my child continues to demonstrate a disturbing attraction to hardcover books with serious stories in them, but I remain hopeful that he can yet be trained to appreciate the beauties of this classic art form.)

And that brings me back, yet again, to Howard Weinstein.

If writing *Star Trek* is a particularly rigorous challenge — and I believe I know whereof I speak — and if writing comic books is also a particularly rigorous challenge, then the writing of a *Star Trek* comic book should be a par- ticularly rigorous challenge **squared.** Or **cubed.** That Howard Weinstein has established himself as one of the most skilled practitioners of this art is a demonstration of his ability as a storyteller as well as his extensive experience with *Star Trek.* Consider yourself lucky. You hold in your hands a handsome piece of quintessential *Star Trek* storytelling.

You'll just have to overlook the fact that the guy who wrote it, Howard Weinstein, is a very nice man. (And that's Barbra Streisand's loss.)

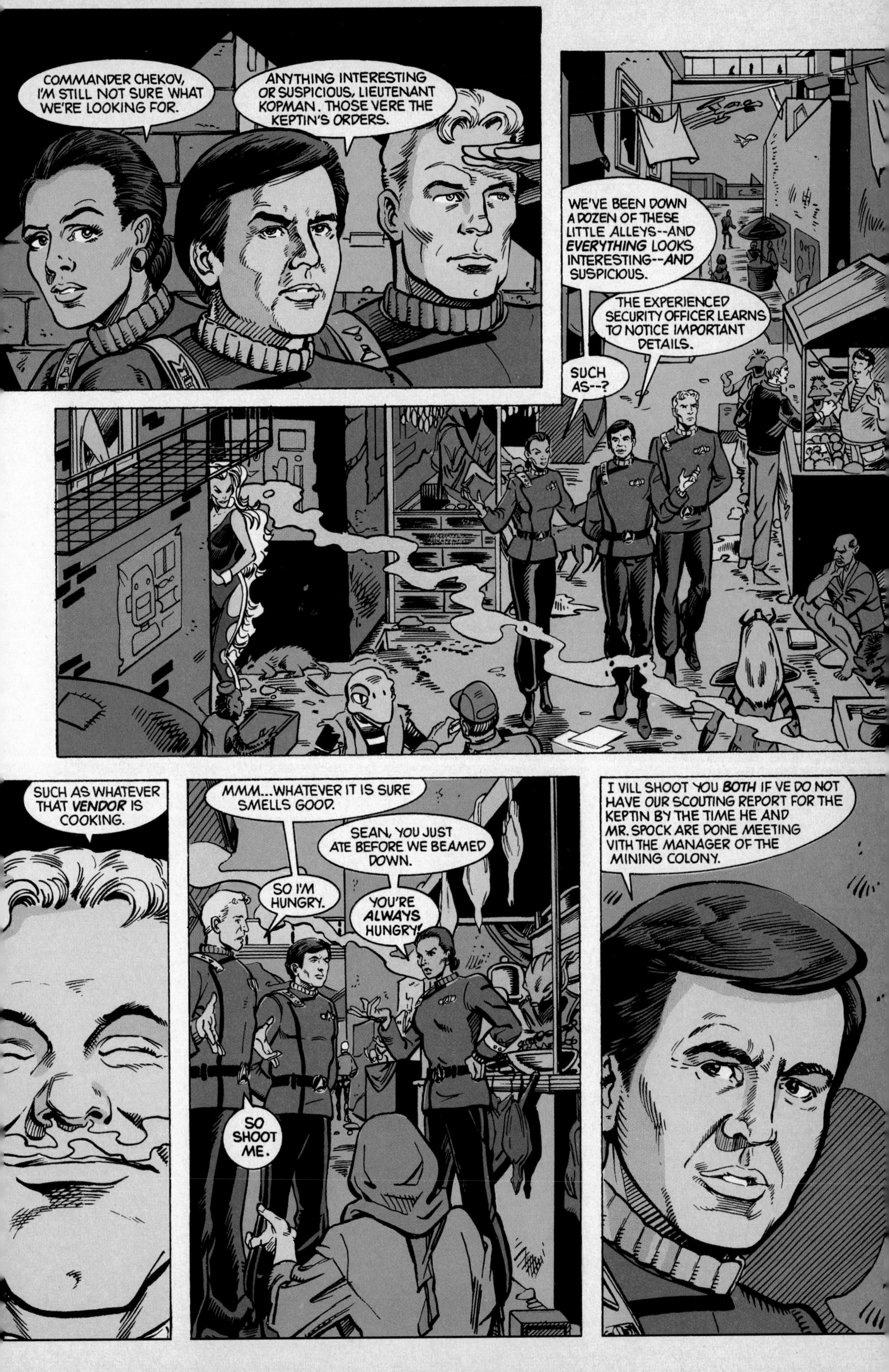
COMMANDER CHEKOV, I'M STILL NOT SURE WHAT WE'RE LOOKING FOR.
ANYTHING INTERESTING OR SUSPICIOUS, LIEUTENANT KOPMAN. THOSE VERE THE KEPTIN'S ORDERS.
WE'VE BEEN DOWN A DOZEN OF THESE LITTLE ALLEYS--AND EVERYTHING LOOKS INTERESTING--AND SUSPICIOUS.
THE EXPERIENCED SECURITY OFFICER LEARNS TO NOTICE IMPORTANT DETAILS.
SUCH AS--?
SUCH AS WHATEVER THAT VENDOR IS COOKING.
MMM...WHATEVER IT IS SURE SMELLS GOOD.
SEAN, YOU JUST ATE BEFORE WE BEAMED DOWN.
SO I'M HUNGRY.
YOU'RE ALWAYS HUNGRY!
SO SHOOT ME.
I VILL SHOOT YOU BOTH IF VE DO NOT HAVE OUR SCOUTING REPORT FOR THE KEPTIN BY THE TIME HE AND MR. SPOCK ARE DONE MEETING VITH THE MANAGER OF THE MINING COLONY.

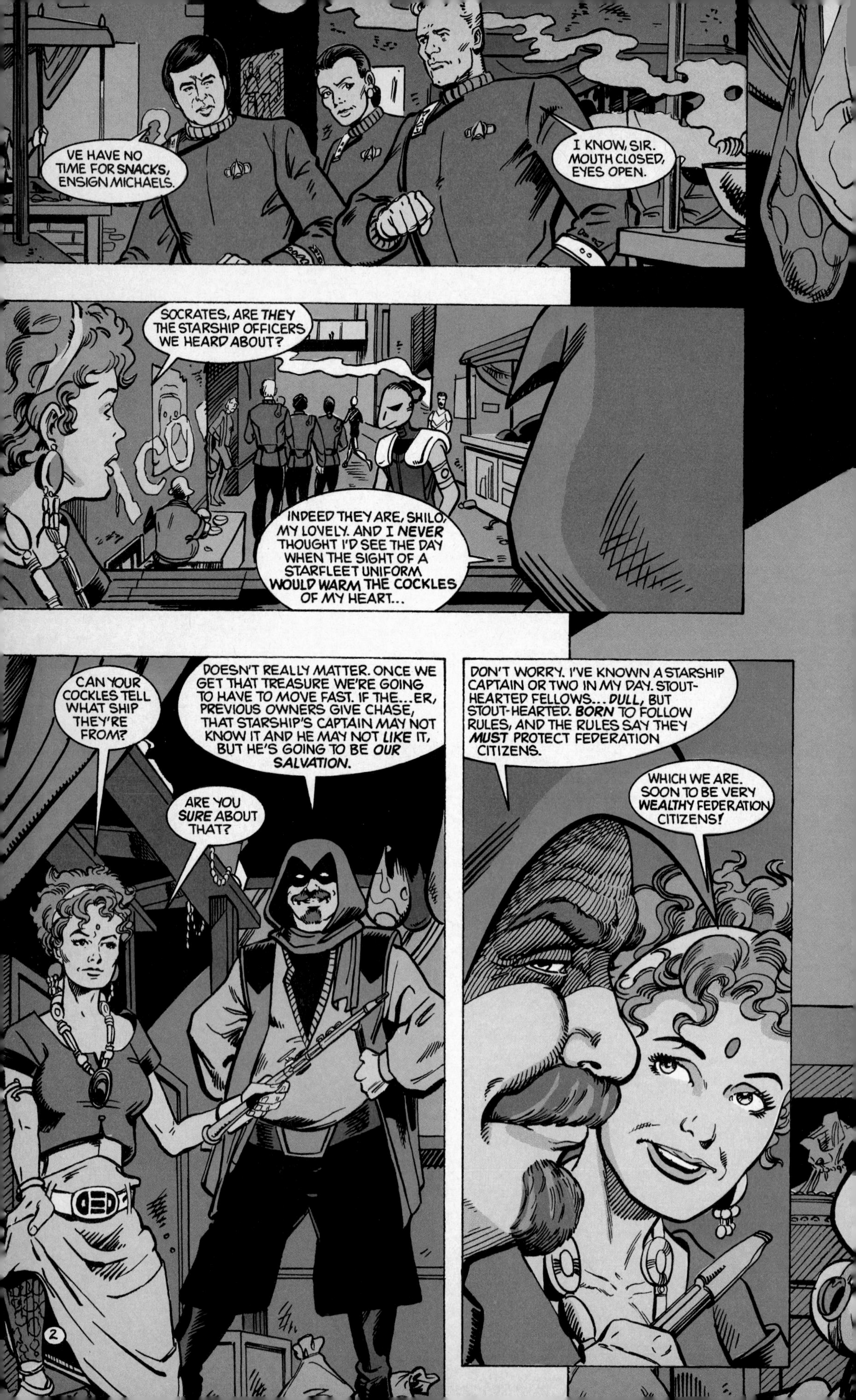
VE HAVE NO TIME FOR SNACKS, ENSIGN MICHAELS.
I KNOW, SIR. MOUTH CLOSED, EYES OPEN.
SOCRATES, ARE THEY THE STARSHIP OFFICERS WE HEARD ABOUT?
INDEED THEY ARE, SHILO, MY LOVELY. AND I NEVER THOUGHT I'D SEE THE DAY WHEN THE SIGHT OF A STARFLEET UNIFORM WOULD WARM THE COCKLES OF MY HEART...
CAN YOUR COCKLES TELL WHAT SHIP THEY'RE FROM?
DOESN'T REALLY MATTER. ONCE WE GET THAT TREASURE WE'RE GOING TO HAVE TO MOVE FAST. IF THE...ER, PREVIOUS OWNERS GIVE CHASE, THAT STARSHIP'S CAPTAIN MAY NOT KNOW IT AND HE MAY NOT LIKE IT, BUT HE'S GOING TO BE OUR SALVATION.
ARE YOU SURE ABOUT THAT?
DON'T WORRY. I'VE KNOWN A STARSHIP CAPTAIN OR TWO IN MY DAY. STOUT-HEARTED FELLOWS... DULL, BUT STOUT-HEARTED. BORN TO FOLLOW RULES, AND THE RULES SAY THEY MUST PROTECT FEDERATION CITIZENS.
WHICH WE ARE. SOON TO BE VERY WEALTHY FEDERATION CITIZENS!
2

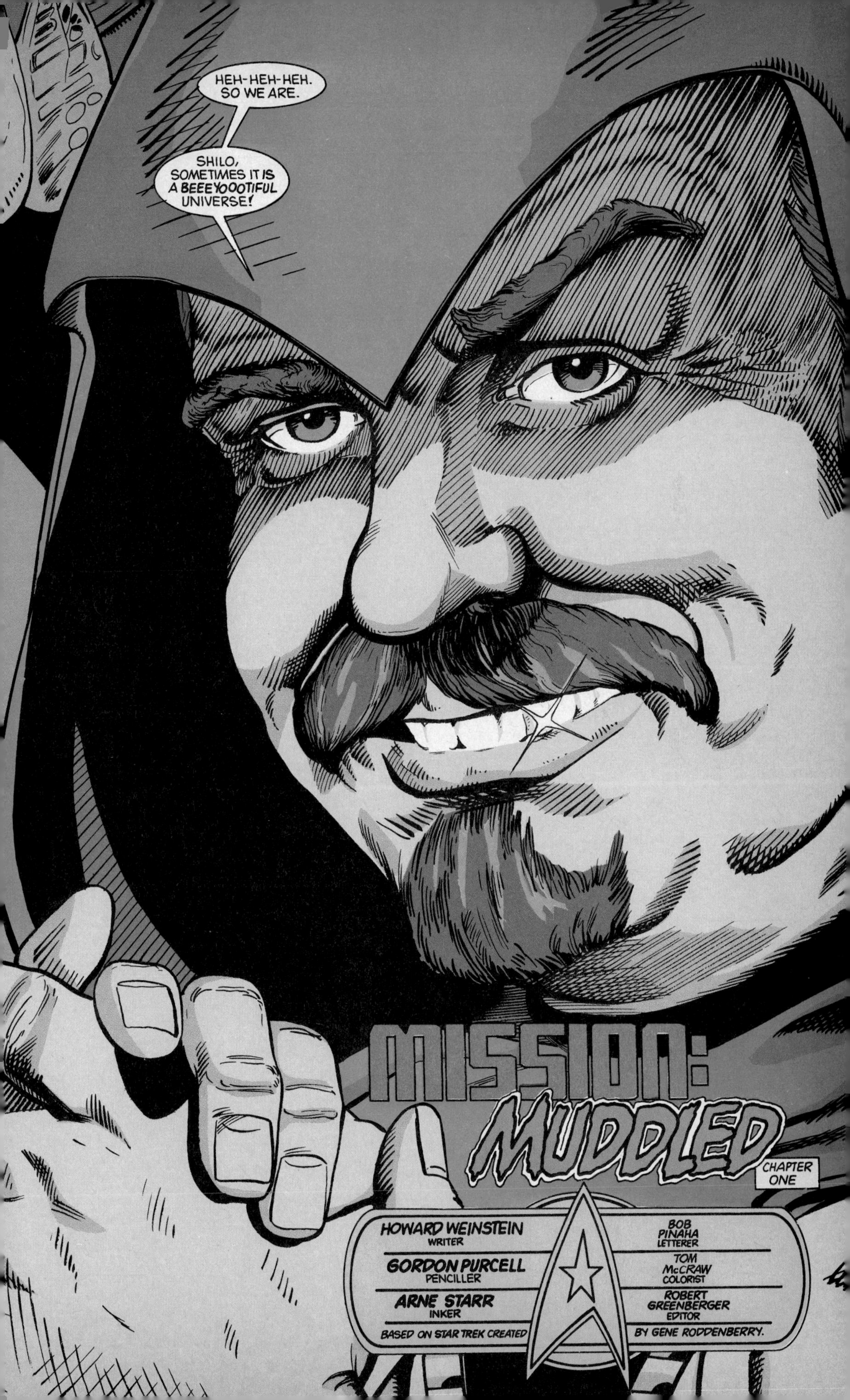
HEH-HEH-HEH. SO WE ARE.
SHILO, SOMETIMES IT IS A BEEEYOOOTIFUL UNIVERSE!
MISSION: MUDDLED
CHAPTER ONE
HOWARD WEINSTEIN WRITER
GORDON PURCELL PENCILLER
ARNE STARR INKER
BOB PINAHA LETTERER
TOM McCRAW COLORIST
ROBERT GREENBERGER EDITOR
BASED ON STAR TREK CREATED BY GENE RODDENBERRY.

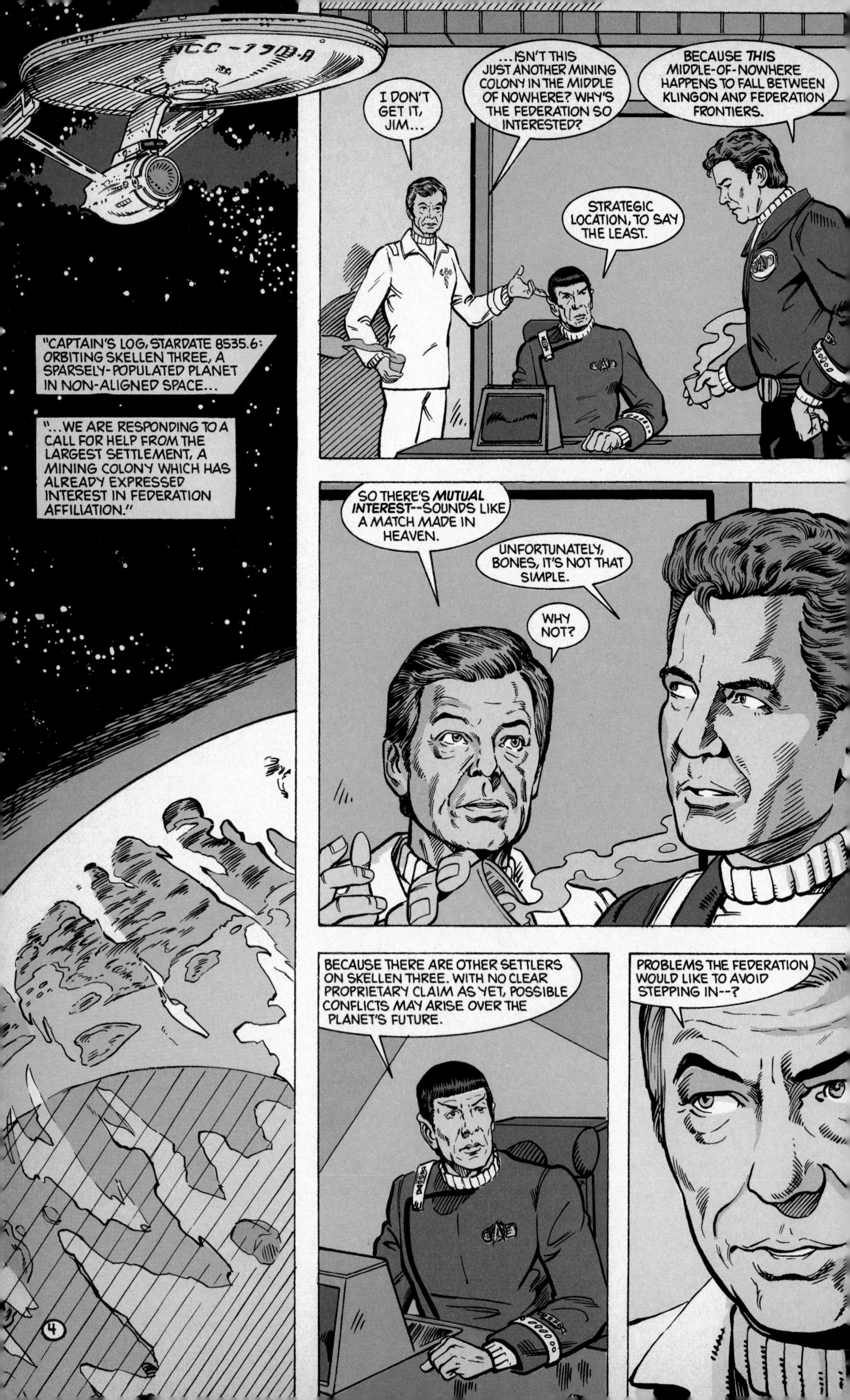
NCC-1701-A
"CAPTAIN'S LOG, STARDATE 8535.6: ORBITING SKELLEN THREE, A SPARSELY-POPULATED PLANET IN NON-ALIGNED SPACE...
"...WE ARE RESPONDING TO A CALL FOR HELP FROM THE LARGEST SETTLEMENT, A MINING COLONY WHICH HAS ALREADY EXPRESSED INTEREST IN FEDERATION AFFILIATION."
I DON'T GET IT, JIM...
...ISN'T THIS JUST ANOTHER MINING COLONY IN THE MIDDLE OF NOWHERE? WHY'S THE FEDERATION SO INTERESTED?
BECAUSE *THIS* MIDDLE-OF-NOWHERE HAPPENS TO FALL BETWEEN KLINGON AND FEDERATION FRONTIERS.
STRATEGIC LOCATION, TO SAY THE LEAST.
SO THERE'S ***MUTUAL INTEREST***--SOUNDS LIKE A MATCH MADE IN HEAVEN.
UNFORTUNATELY, BONES, IT'S NOT THAT SIMPLE.
WHY NOT?
BECAUSE THERE ARE OTHER SETTLERS ON SKELLEN THREE. WITH NO CLEAR PROPRIETARY CLAIM AS YET, POSSIBLE CONFLICTS *MAY* ARISE OVER THE PLANET'S FUTURE.
PROBLEMS THE FEDERATION WOULD LIKE TO AVOID STEPPING IN--?

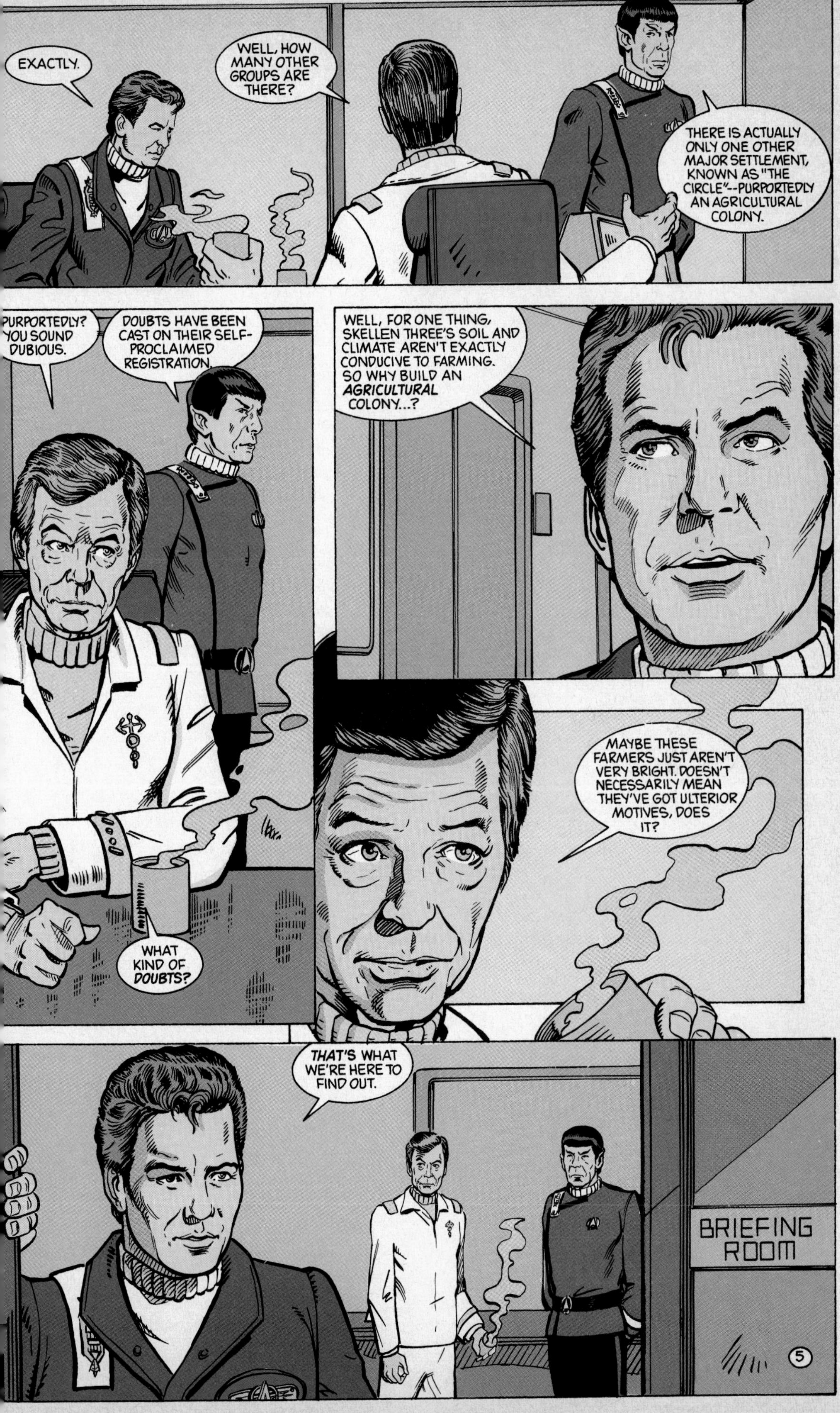

EXACTLY.
WELL, HOW MANY OTHER GROUPS ARE THERE?
THERE IS ACTUALLY ONLY ONE OTHER MAJOR SETTLEMENT, KNOWN AS "THE CIRCLE"--PURPORTEDLY AN AGRICULTURAL COLONY.
PURPORTEDLY? YOU SOUND DUBIOUS.
DOUBTS HAVE BEEN CAST ON THEIR SELF-PROCLAIMED REGISTRATION.
WHAT KIND OF DOUBTS?
WELL, FOR ONE THING, SKELLEN THREE'S SOIL AND CLIMATE AREN'T EXACTLY CONDUCIVE TO FARMING. SO WHY BUILD AN AGRICULTURAL COLONY...?
MAYBE THESE FARMERS JUST AREN'T VERY BRIGHT. DOESN'T NECESSARILY MEAN THEY'VE GOT ULTERIOR MOTIVES, DOES IT?
THAT'S WHAT WE'RE HERE TO FIND OUT.
BRIEFING ROOM

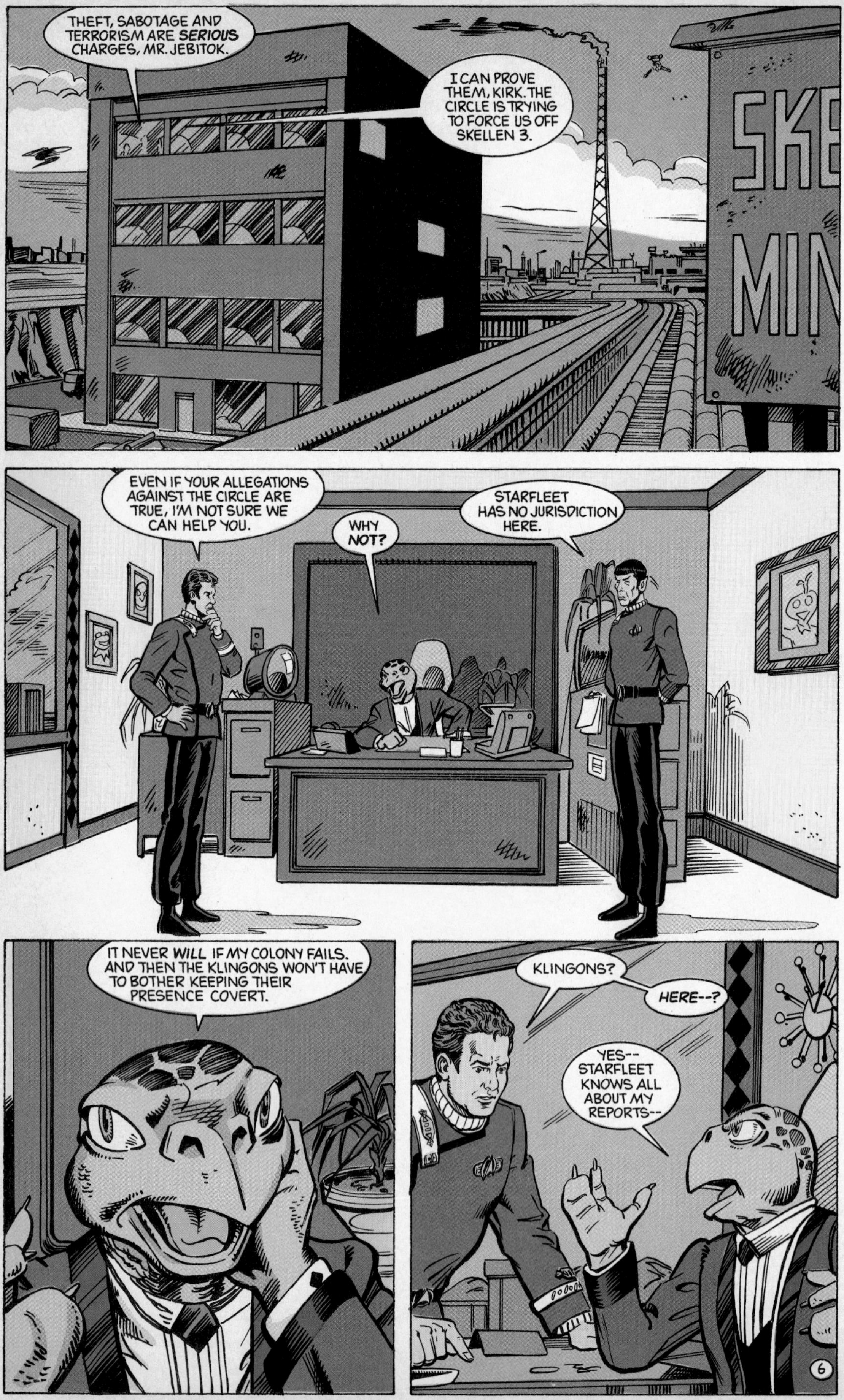
THEFT, SABOTAGE AND TERRORISM ARE SERIOUS CHARGES, MR. JEBITOK.
I CAN PROVE THEM, KIRK. THE CIRCLE IS TRYING TO FORCE US OFF SKELLEN 3.
EVEN IF YOUR ALLEGATIONS AGAINST THE CIRCLE ARE TRUE, I'M NOT SURE WE CAN HELP YOU.
WHY NOT?
STARFLEET HAS NO JURISDICTION HERE.
IT NEVER WILL IF MY COLONY FAILS. AND THEN THE KLINGONS WON'T HAVE TO BOTHER KEEPING THEIR PRESENCE COVERT.
KLINGONS?
HERE--?
YES-- STARFLEET KNOWS ALL ABOUT MY REPORTS--

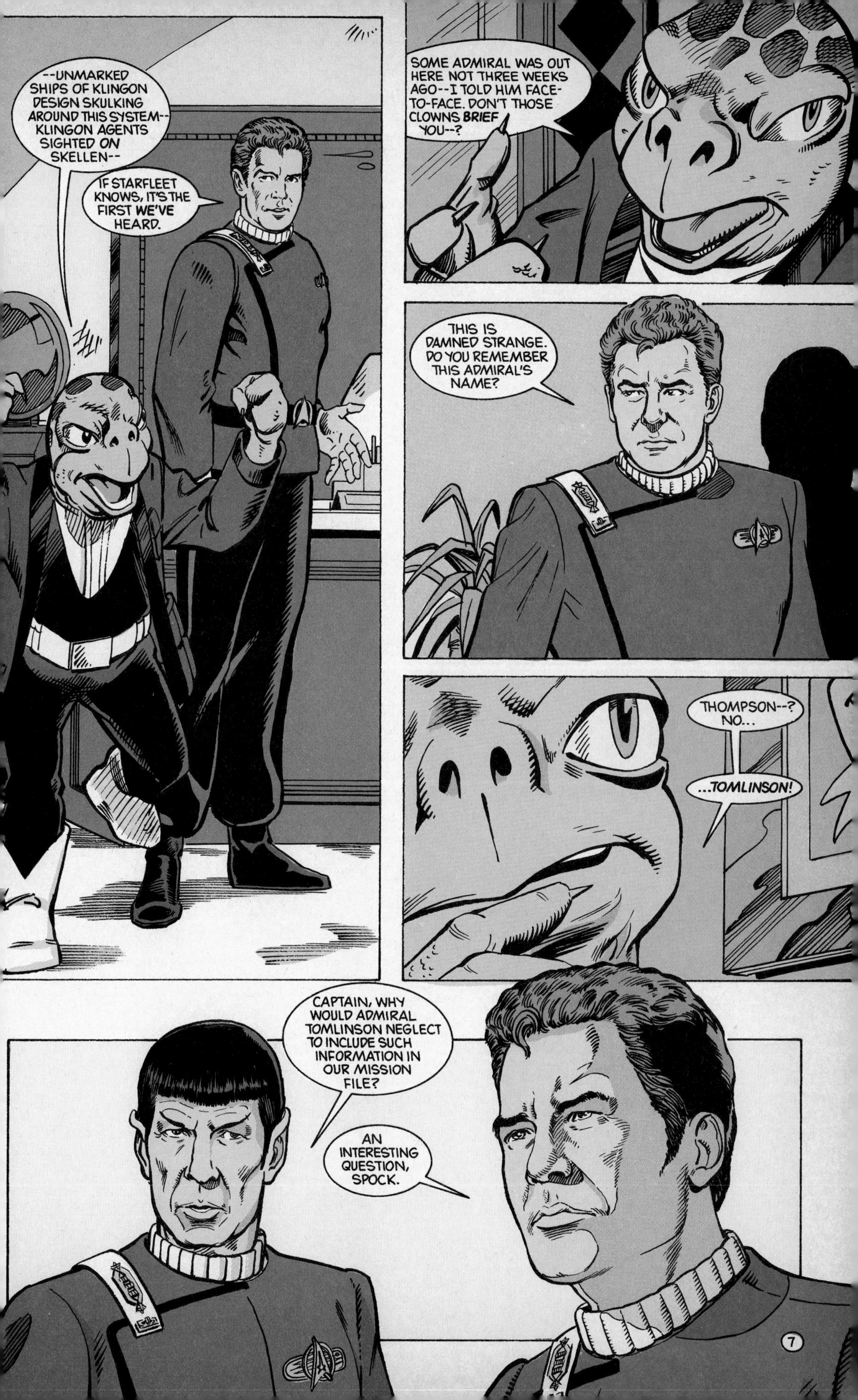
--UNMARKED SHIPS OF KLINGON DESIGN SKULKING AROUND THIS SYSTEM--KLINGON AGENTS SIGHTED ON SKELLEN--
IF STARFLEET KNOWS, IT'S THE FIRST WE'VE HEARD.
SOME ADMIRAL WAS OUT HERE NOT THREE WEEKS AGO--I TOLD HIM FACE-TO-FACE. DON'T THOSE CLOWNS BRIEF YOU--?
THIS IS DAMNED STRANGE. DO YOU REMEMBER THIS ADMIRAL'S NAME?
THOMPSON--? NO...
...TOMLINSON!
CAPTAIN, WHY WOULD ADMIRAL TOMLINSON NEGLECT TO INCLUDE SUCH INFORMATION IN OUR MISSION FILE?
AN INTERESTING QUESTION, SPOCK.

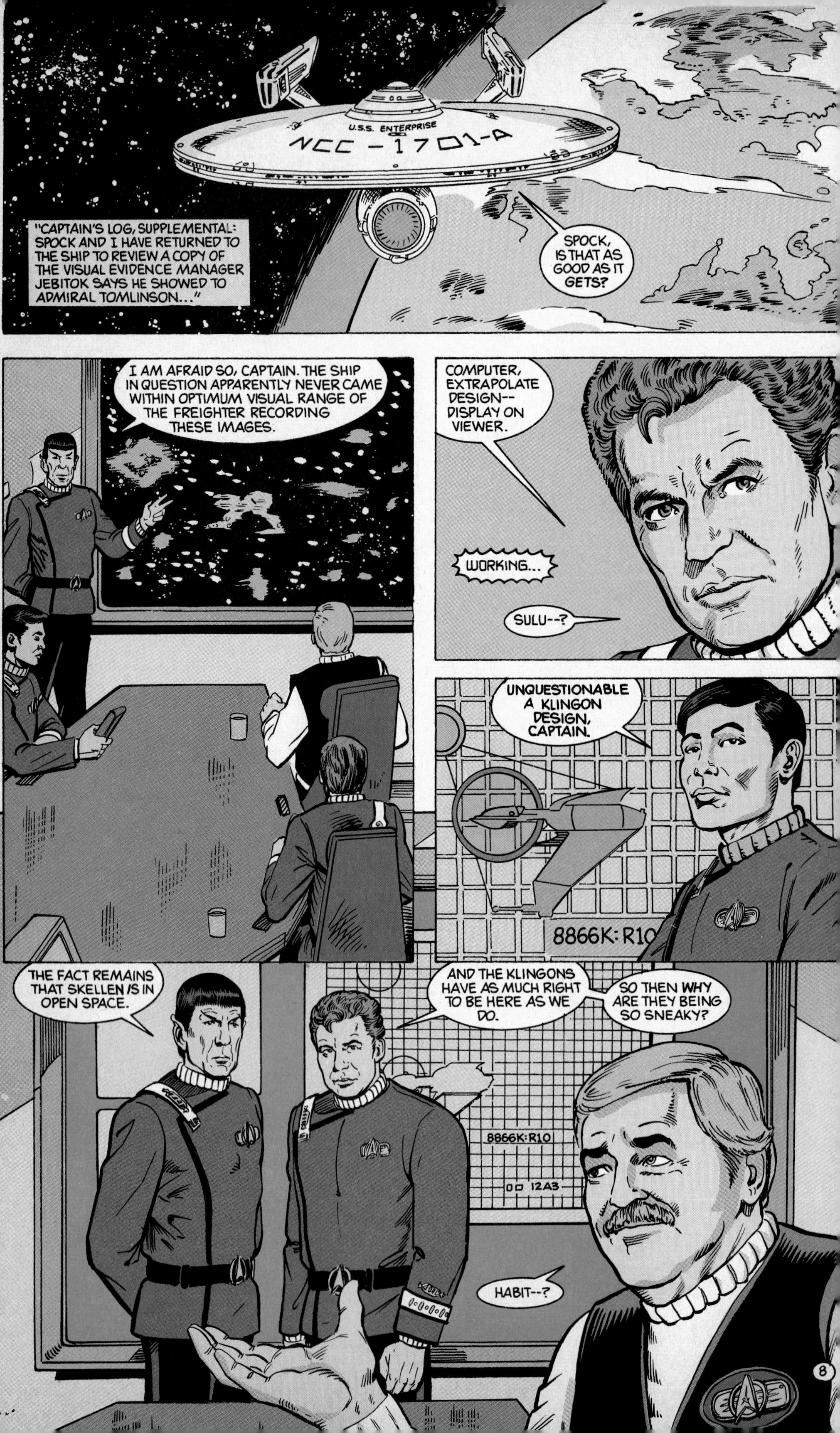

U.S.S. ENTERPRISE
NCC-1701-A
"CAPTAIN'S LOG, SUPPLEMENTAL: SPOCK AND I HAVE RETURNED TO THE SHIP TO REVIEW A COPY OF THE VISUAL EVIDENCE MANAGER JEBITOK SAYS HE SHOWED TO ADMIRAL TOMLINSON..."
SPOCK, IS THAT AS GOOD AS IT GETS?
I AM AFRAID SO, CAPTAIN. THE SHIP IN QUESTION APPARENTLY NEVER CAME WITHIN OPTIMUM VISUAL RANGE OF THE FREIGHTER RECORDING THESE IMAGES.
COMPUTER, EXTRAPOLATE DESIGN-- DISPLAY ON VIEWER.
WORKING...
SULU--?
UNQUESTIONABLE A KLINGON DESIGN, CAPTAIN.
8866K:R10
THE FACT REMAINS THAT SKELLEN IS IN OPEN SPACE.
AND THE KLINGONS HAVE AS MUCH RIGHT TO BE HERE AS WE DO.
SO THEN WHY ARE THEY BEING SO SNEAKY?
8866K:R10
12A3
HABIT--?

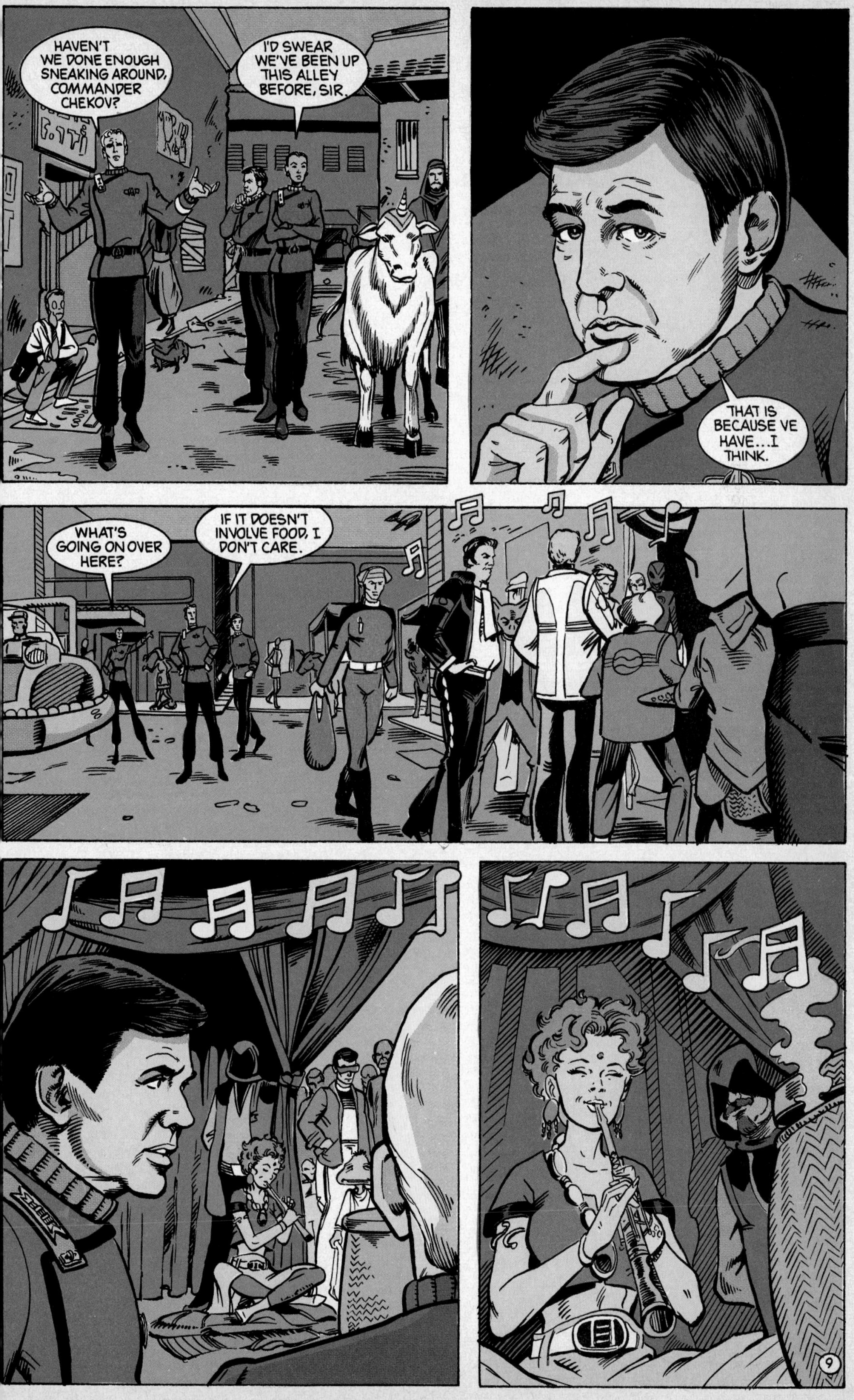
HAVEN'T WE DONE ENOUGH SNEAKING AROUND, COMMANDER CHEKOV?
I'D SWEAR WE'VE BEEN UP THIS ALLEY BEFORE, SIR.
THAT IS BECAUSE VE HAVE...I THINK.
WHAT'S GOING ON OVER HERE?
IF IT DOESN'T INVOLVE FOOD, I DON'T CARE.

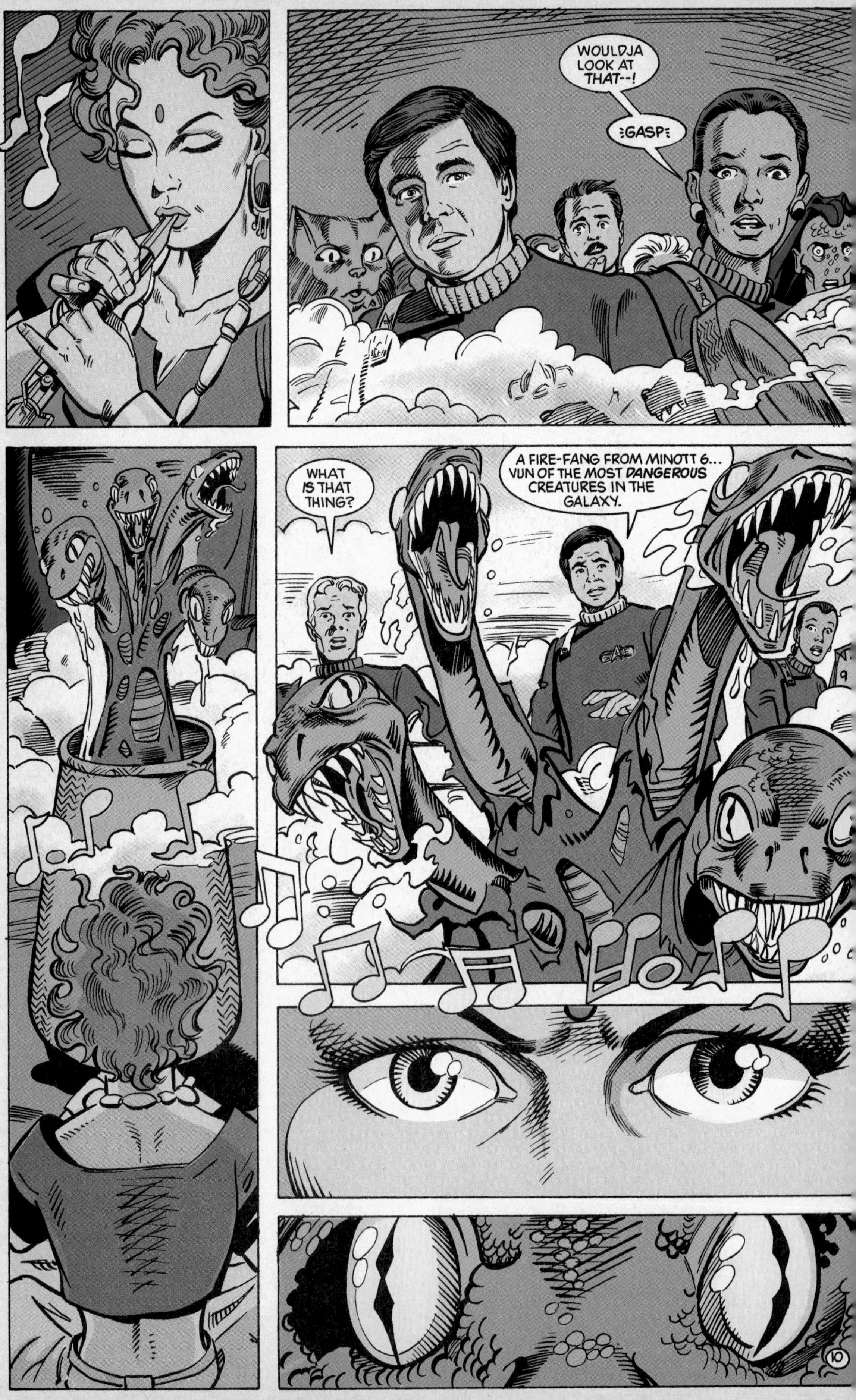

WOULDJA LOOK AT THAT--!
GASP
WHAT IS THAT THING?
A FIRE-FANG FROM MINOTT 6... VUN OF THE MOST DANGEROUS CREATURES IN THE GALAXY.

CLAP CLAP

CLAP CLAP
BRAVO!   AMAZING

ALL DONATIONS APPRECIATED--!

THANK YOU, THANK YOU VERY MUCH. COME SEE US AGAIN...

LANDING PARTY TO ENTERPRISE-- SECURITY CHECK-IN...

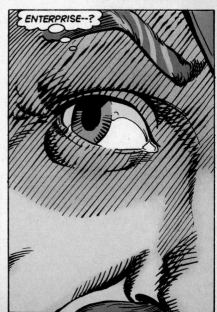

ENTERPRISE--?

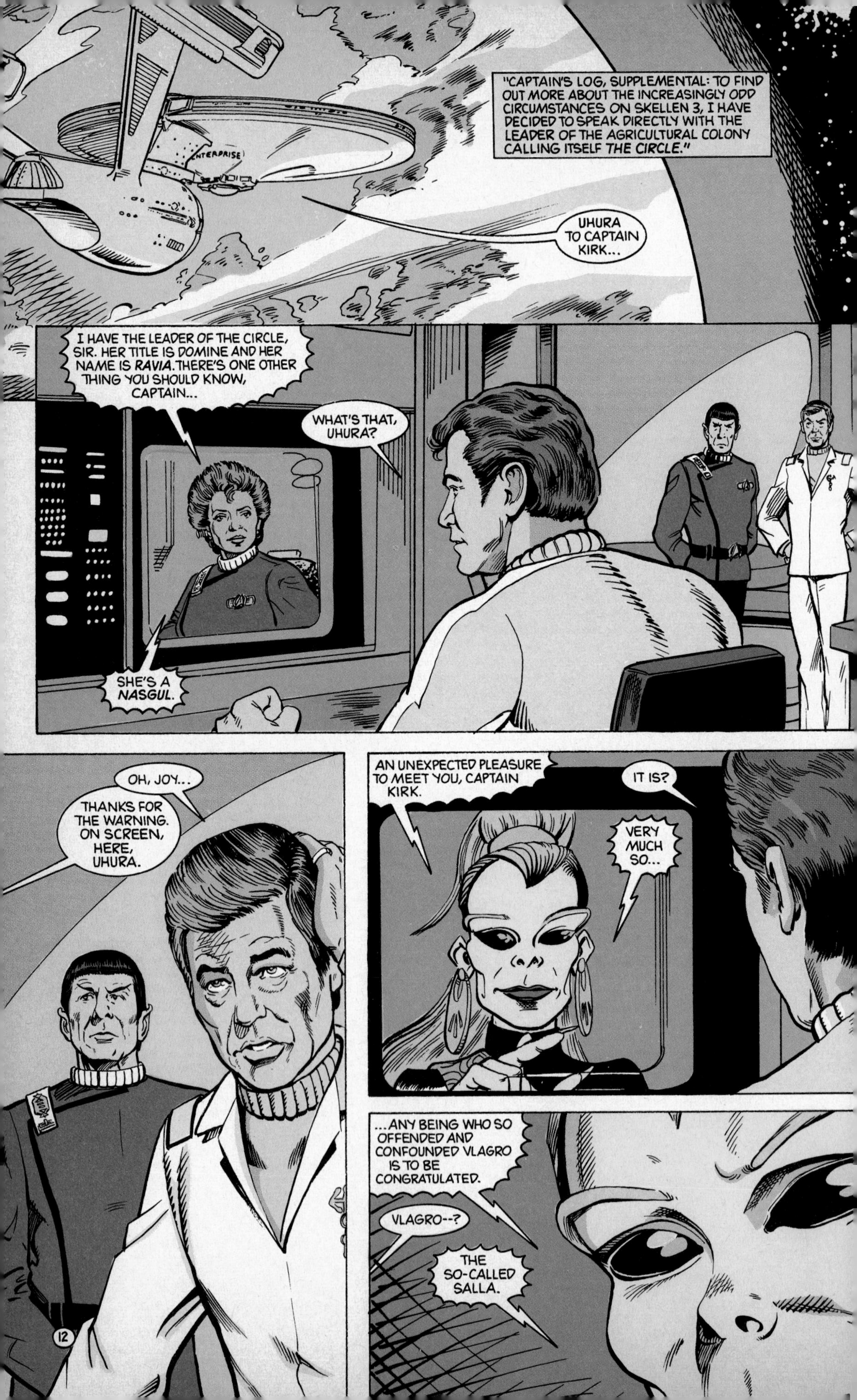
"CAPTAIN'S LOG, SUPPLEMENTAL: TO FIND OUT MORE ABOUT THE INCREASINGLY ODD CIRCUMSTANCES ON SKELLEN 3, I HAVE DECIDED TO SPEAK DIRECTLY WITH THE LEADER OF THE AGRICULTURAL COLONY CALLING ITSELF THE CIRCLE."
UHURA TO CAPTAIN KIRK...
I HAVE THE LEADER OF THE CIRCLE, SIR. HER TITLE IS DOMINE AND HER NAME IS RAVIA. THERE'S ONE OTHER THING YOU SHOULD KNOW, CAPTAIN...
WHAT'S THAT, UHURA?
SHE'S A NASGUL.
OH, JOY...
THANKS FOR THE WARNING. ON SCREEN, HERE, UHURA.
AN UNEXPECTED PLEASURE TO MEET YOU, CAPTAIN KIRK.
IT IS?
VERY MUCH SO...
...ANY BEING WHO SO OFFENDED AND CONFOUNDED VLAGRO IS TO BE CONGRATULATED.
VLAGRO--?
THE SO-CALLED SALLA.

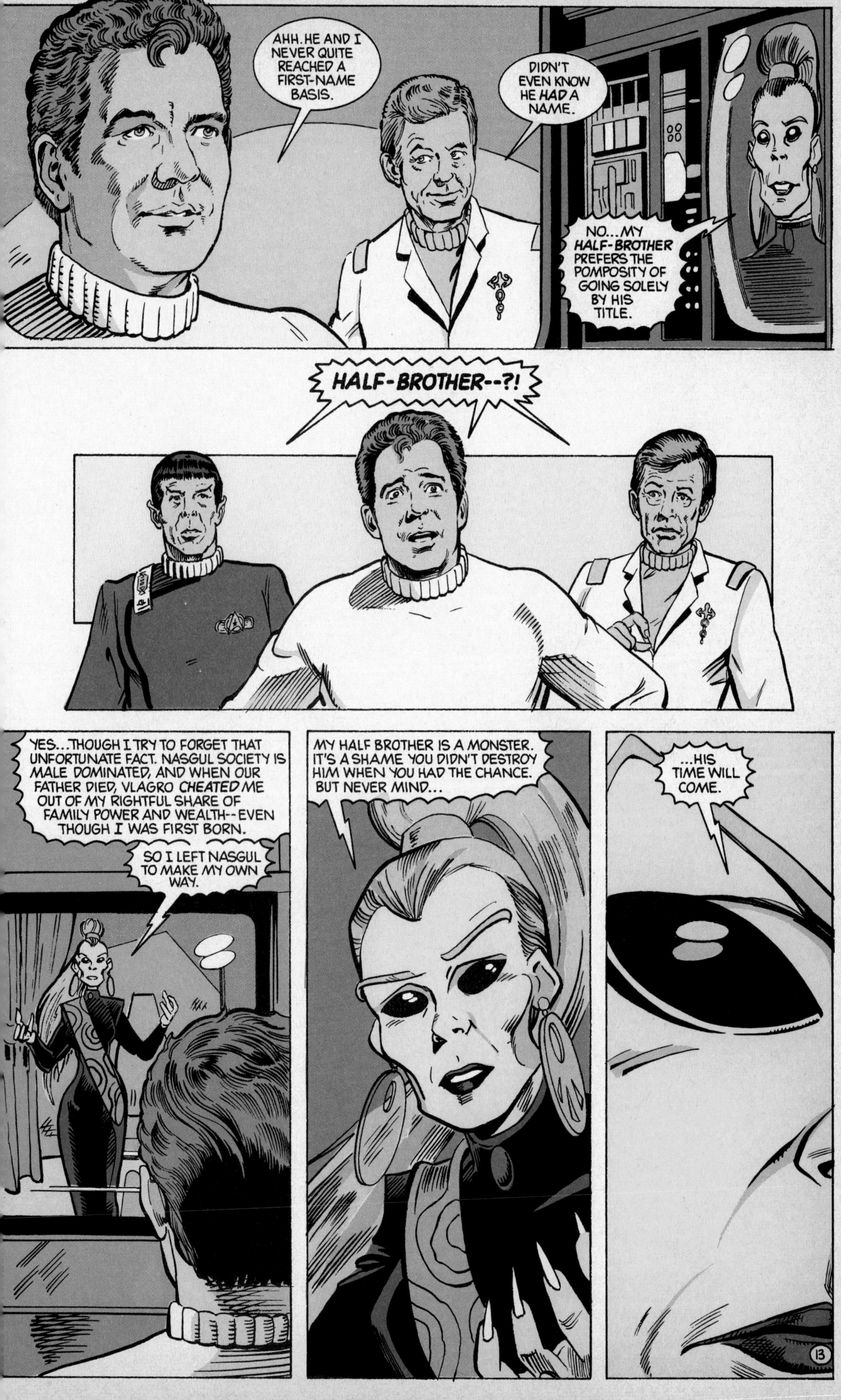
AHH. HE AND I NEVER QUITE REACHED A FIRST-NAME BASIS.
DIDN'T EVEN KNOW HE *HAD* A NAME.
NO... MY *HALF-BROTHER* PREFERS THE POMPOSITY OF GOING SOLELY BY HIS TITLE.
HALF-BROTHER--?!
YES... THOUGH I TRY TO FORGET THAT UNFORTUNATE FACT. NASGUL SOCIETY IS MALE DOMINATED, AND WHEN OUR FATHER DIED, VLAGRO *CHEATED* ME OUT OF MY RIGHTFUL SHARE OF FAMILY POWER AND WEALTH--EVEN THOUGH I WAS FIRST BORN.
SO I LEFT NASGUL TO MAKE MY OWN WAY.
MY HALF BROTHER IS A MONSTER. IT'S A SHAME YOU DIDN'T DESTROY HIM WHEN YOU HAD THE CHANCE. BUT NEVER MIND...
...HIS TIME WILL COME.

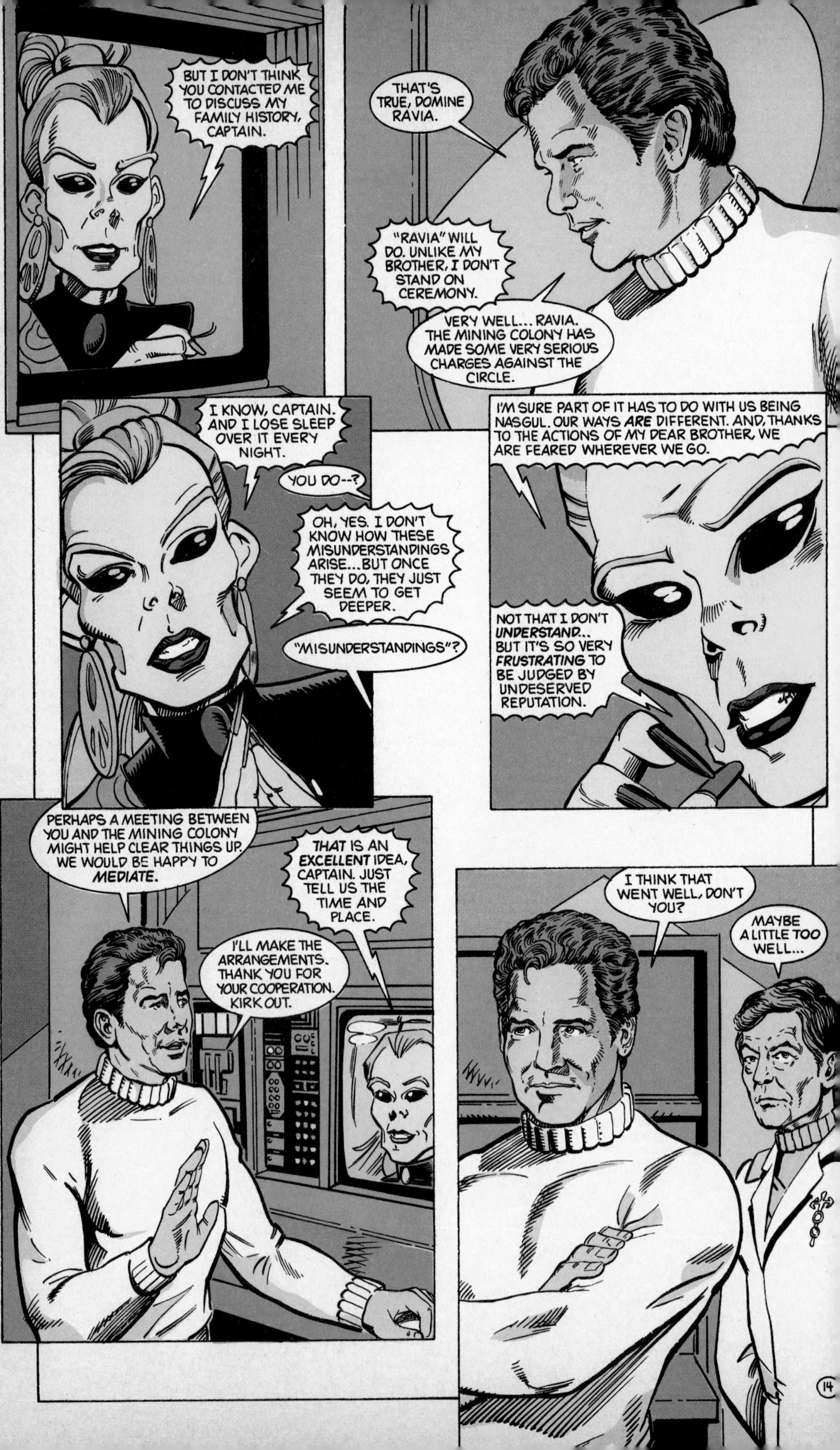
BUT I DON'T THINK YOU CONTACTED ME TO DISCUSS MY FAMILY HISTORY, CAPTAIN.
THAT'S TRUE, DOMINE RAVIA.
"RAVIA" WILL DO. UNLIKE MY BROTHER, I DON'T STAND ON CEREMONY.
VERY WELL... RAVIA. THE MINING COLONY HAS MADE SOME VERY SERIOUS CHARGES AGAINST THE CIRCLE.
I KNOW, CAPTAIN. AND I LOSE SLEEP OVER IT EVERY NIGHT.
YOU DO--?
OH, YES. I DON'T KNOW HOW THESE MISUNDERSTANDINGS ARISE... BUT ONCE THEY DO, THEY JUST SEEM TO GET DEEPER.
"MISUNDERSTANDINGS"?
I'M SURE PART OF IT HAS TO DO WITH US BEING NASGUL. OUR WAYS *ARE* DIFFERENT. AND, THANKS TO THE ACTIONS OF MY DEAR BROTHER, WE ARE FEARED WHEREVER WE GO.
NOT THAT I DON'T ***UNDERSTAND***... BUT IT'S SO VERY ***FRUSTRATING*** TO BE JUDGED BY UNDESERVED REPUTATION.
PERHAPS A MEETING BETWEEN YOU AND THE MINING COLONY MIGHT HELP CLEAR THINGS UP. WE WOULD BE HAPPY TO ***MEDIATE***.
THAT IS AN ***EXCELLENT*** IDEA, CAPTAIN. JUST TELL US THE TIME AND PLACE.
I'LL MAKE THE ARRANGEMENTS. THANK YOU FOR YOUR COOPERATION. KIRK OUT.
I THINK THAT WENT WELL, DON'T YOU?
MAYBE A LITTLE ***TOO*** WELL...

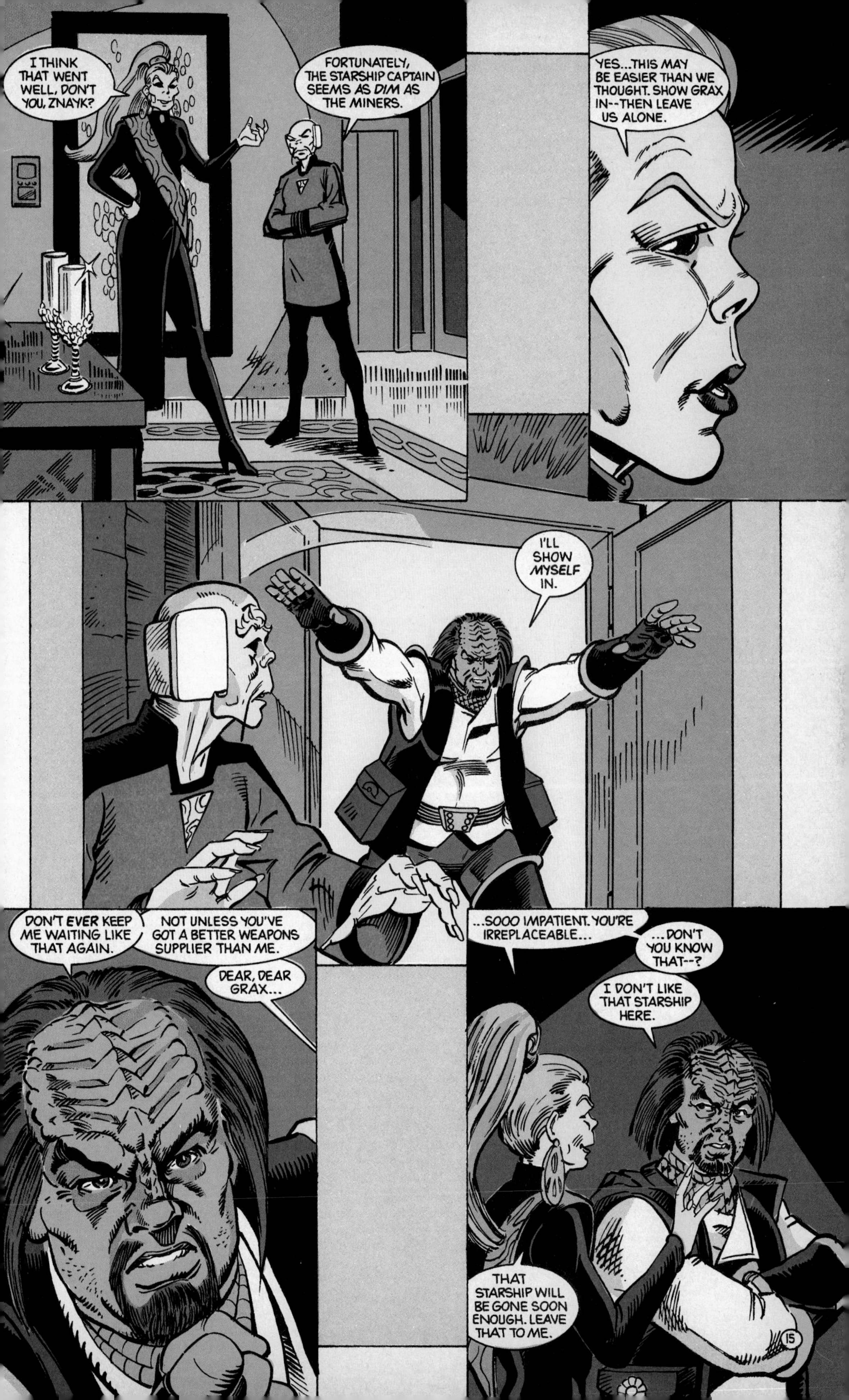
I THINK THAT WENT WELL, DON'T YOU, ZNAYK?
FORTUNATELY, THE STARSHIP CAPTAIN SEEMS AS *DIM* AS THE MINERS.
YES...THIS MAY BE EASIER THAN WE THOUGHT. SHOW GRAX IN--THEN LEAVE US ALONE.
I'LL SHOW *MYSELF* IN.
DON'T **EVER** KEEP ME WAITING LIKE THAT AGAIN.
NOT UNLESS YOU'VE GOT A BETTER WEAPONS SUPPLIER THAN ME.
DEAR, DEAR GRAX...
...SOOO IMPATIENT. YOU'RE IRREPLACEABLE...
...DON'T YOU KNOW THAT--?
I DON'T LIKE THAT STARSHIP HERE.
THAT STARSHIP WILL BE GONE SOON ENOUGH. LEAVE THAT TO ME.

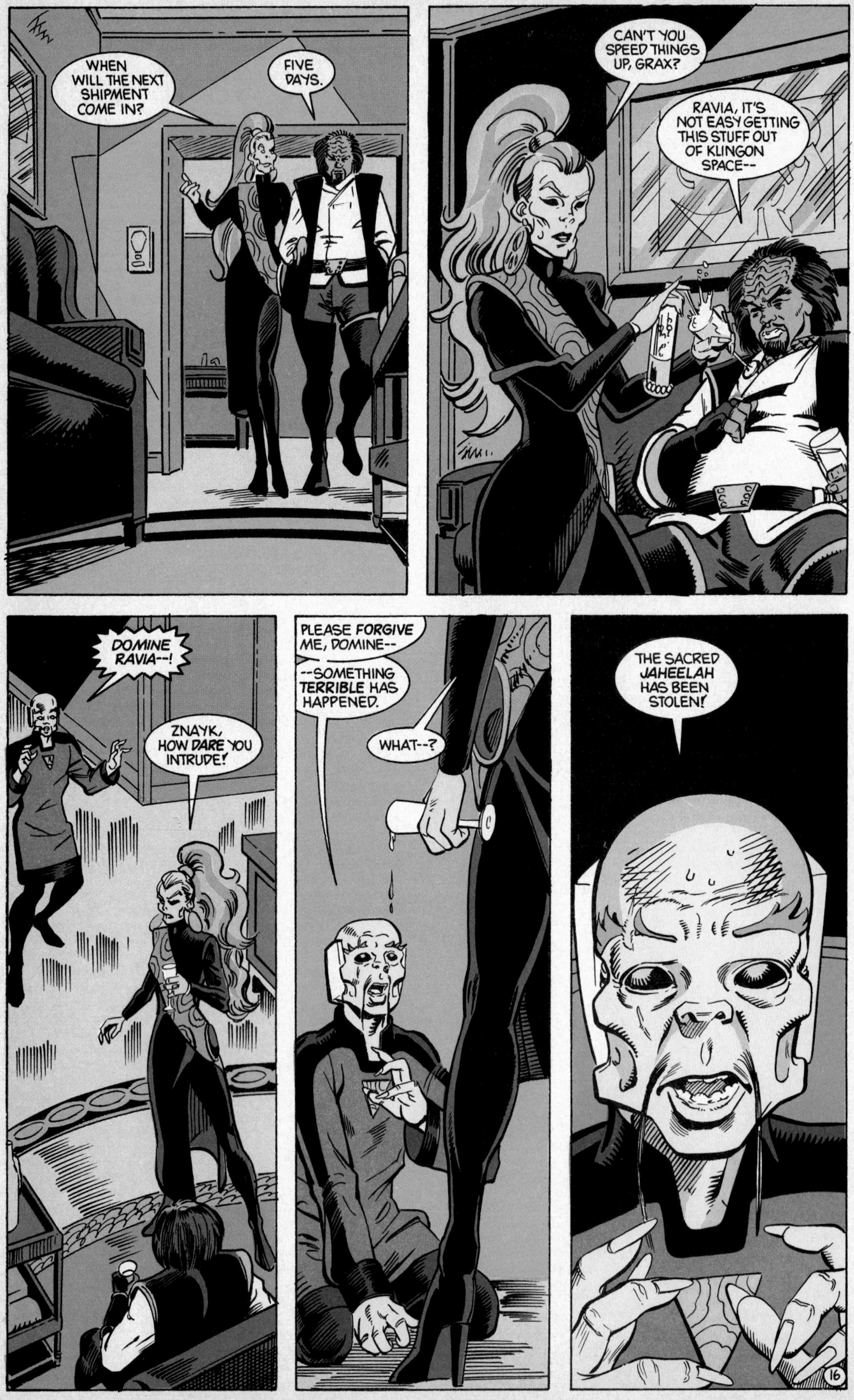
WHEN WILL THE NEXT SHIPMENT COME IN?
FIVE DAYS.
CAN'T YOU SPEED THINGS UP, GRAX?
RAVIA, IT'S NOT EASY GETTING THIS STUFF OUT OF KLINGON SPACE--
DOMINE RAVIA--!
ZNAYK, HOW DARE YOU INTRUDE!
PLEASE FORGIVE ME, DOMINE--
--SOMETHING TERRIBLE HAS HAPPENED.
WHAT--?
THE SACRED JAHEELAH HAS BEEN STOLEN!
16

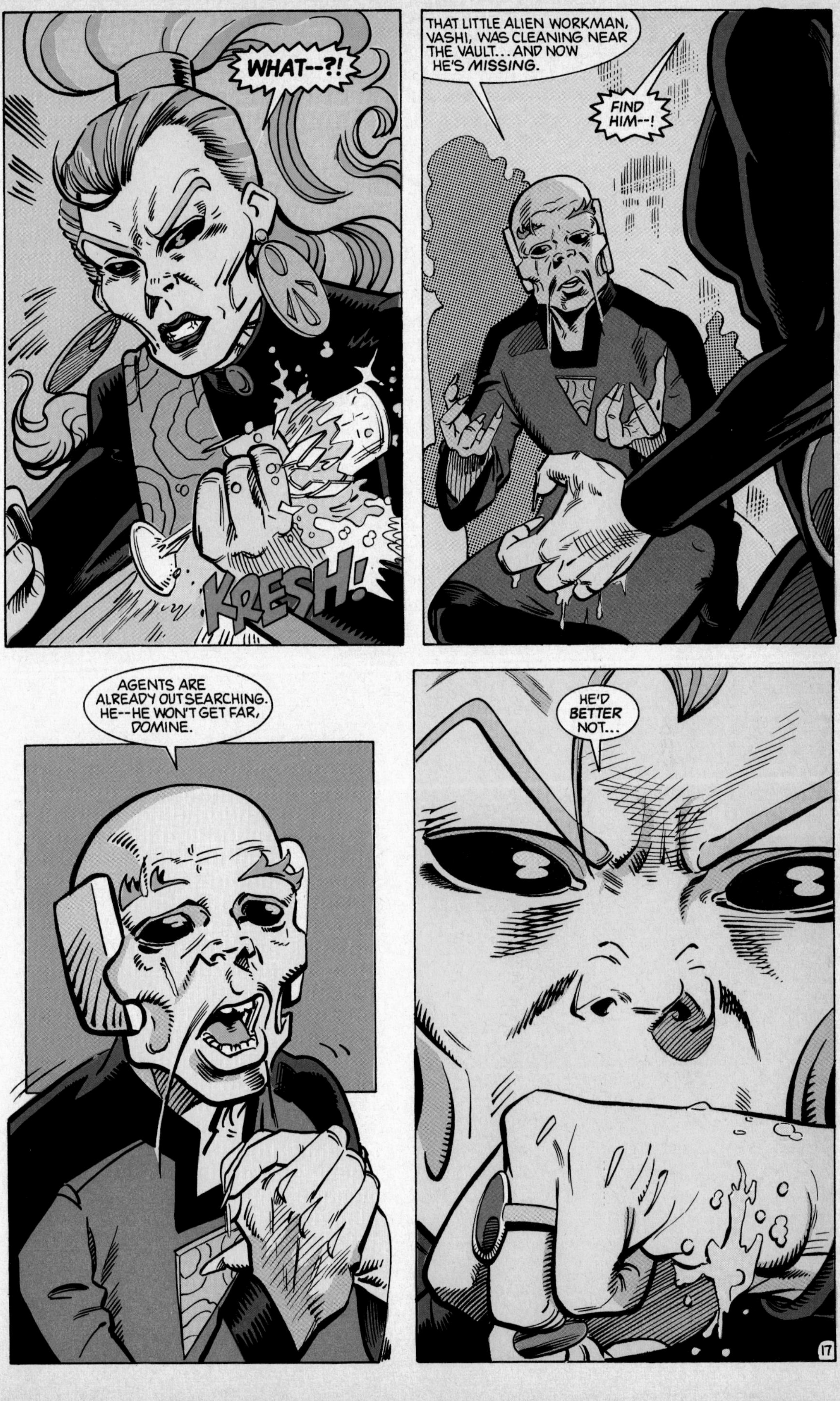
WHAT--?!
KRESH!
THAT LITTLE ALIEN WORKMAN, VASHI, WAS CLEANING NEAR THE VAULT... AND NOW HE'S MISSING.
FIND HIM--!
AGENTS ARE ALREADY OUT SEARCHING. HE--HE WON'T GET FAR, DOMINE.
HE'D BETTER NOT...
17

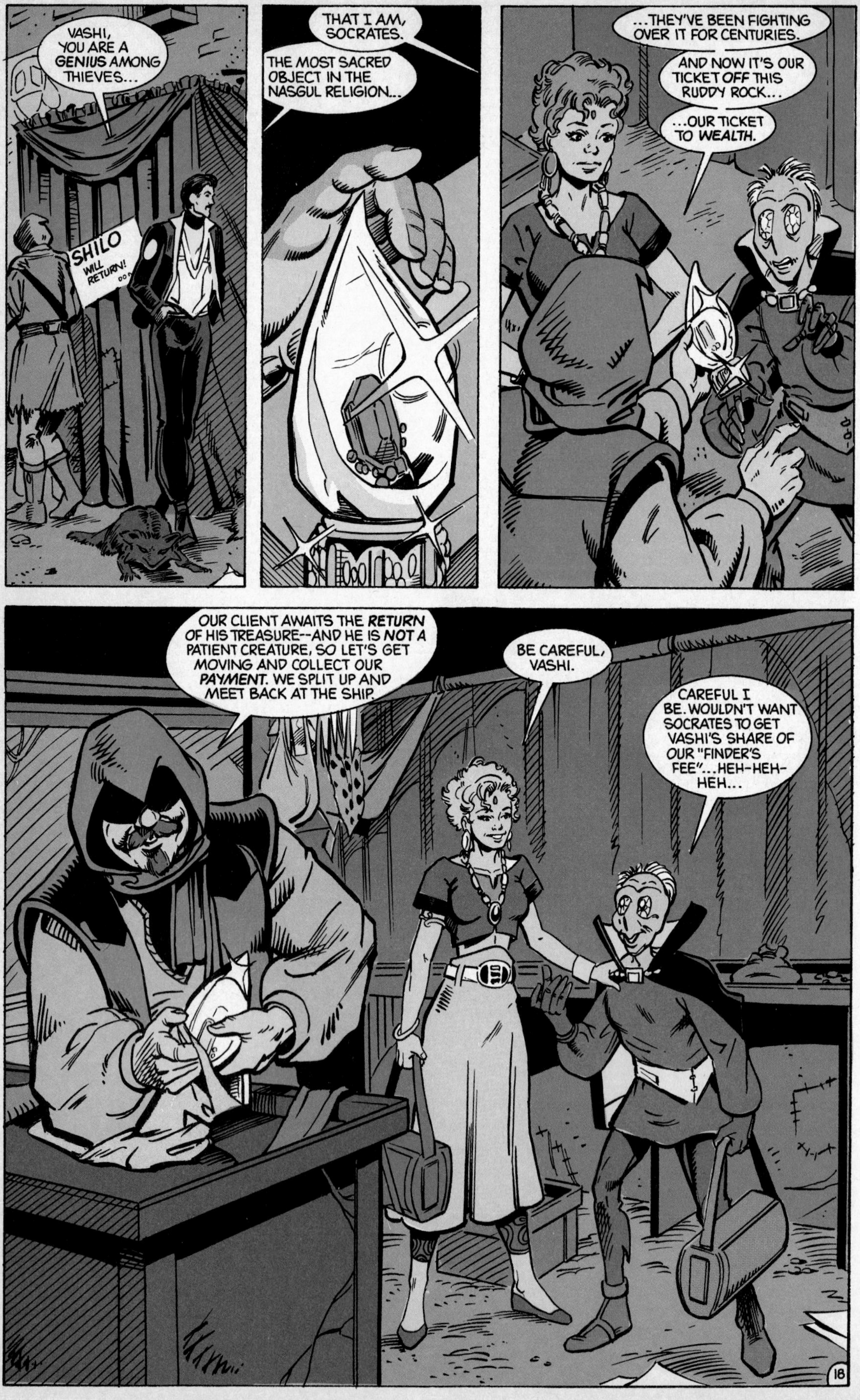
VASHI, YOU ARE A GENIUS AMONG THIEVES...
SHILO WILL RETURN!
THAT I AM, SOCRATES.
THE MOST SACRED OBJECT IN THE NASGUL RELIGION...
...THEY'VE BEEN FIGHTING OVER IT FOR CENTURIES.
AND NOW IT'S OUR TICKET OFF THIS RUDDY ROCK...
...OUR TICKET TO WEALTH.
OUR CLIENT AWAITS THE RETURN OF HIS TREASURE--AND HE IS NOT A PATIENT CREATURE, SO LET'S GET MOVING AND COLLECT OUR PAYMENT. WE SPLIT UP AND MEET BACK AT THE SHIP.
BE CAREFUL, VASHI.
CAREFUL I BE. WOULDN'T WANT SOCRATES TO GET VASHI'S SHARE OF OUR "FINDER'S FEE"...HEH-HEH-HEH...
18

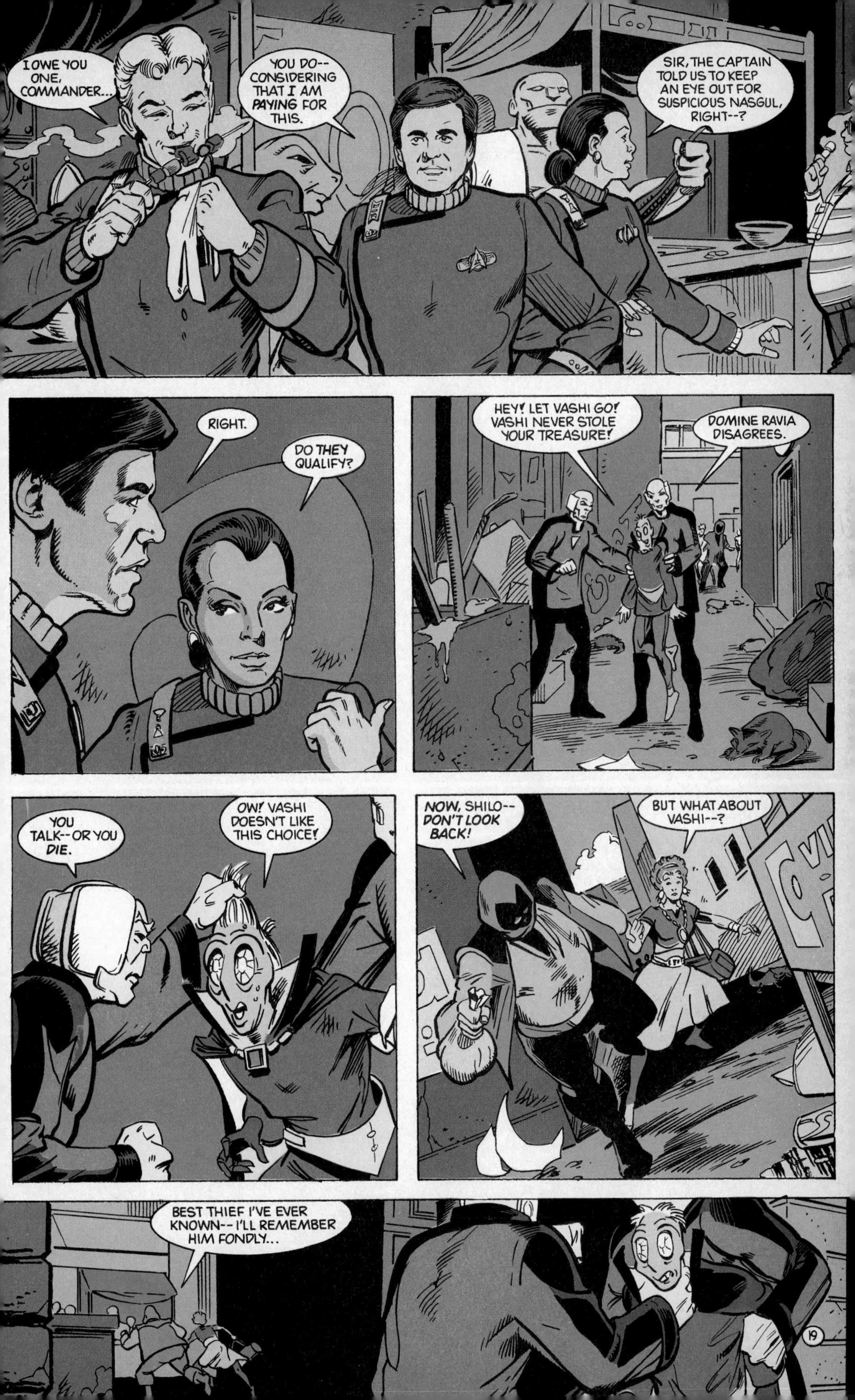

I OWE YOU ONE, COMMANDER...
YOU DO--CONSIDERING THAT I AM PAYING FOR THIS.
SIR, THE CAPTAIN TOLD US TO KEEP AN EYE OUT FOR SUSPICIOUS NASGUL, RIGHT--?
RIGHT.
DO THEY QUALIFY?
HEY! LET VASHI GO! VASHI NEVER STOLE YOUR TREASURE!
DOMINE RAVIA DISAGREES.
YOU TALK--OR YOU DIE.
OW! VASHI DOESN'T LIKE THIS CHOICE!
NOW, SHILO--DON'T LOOK BACK!
BUT WHAT ABOUT VASHI--?
BEST THIEF I'VE EVER KNOWN--I'LL REMEMBER HIM FONDLY...

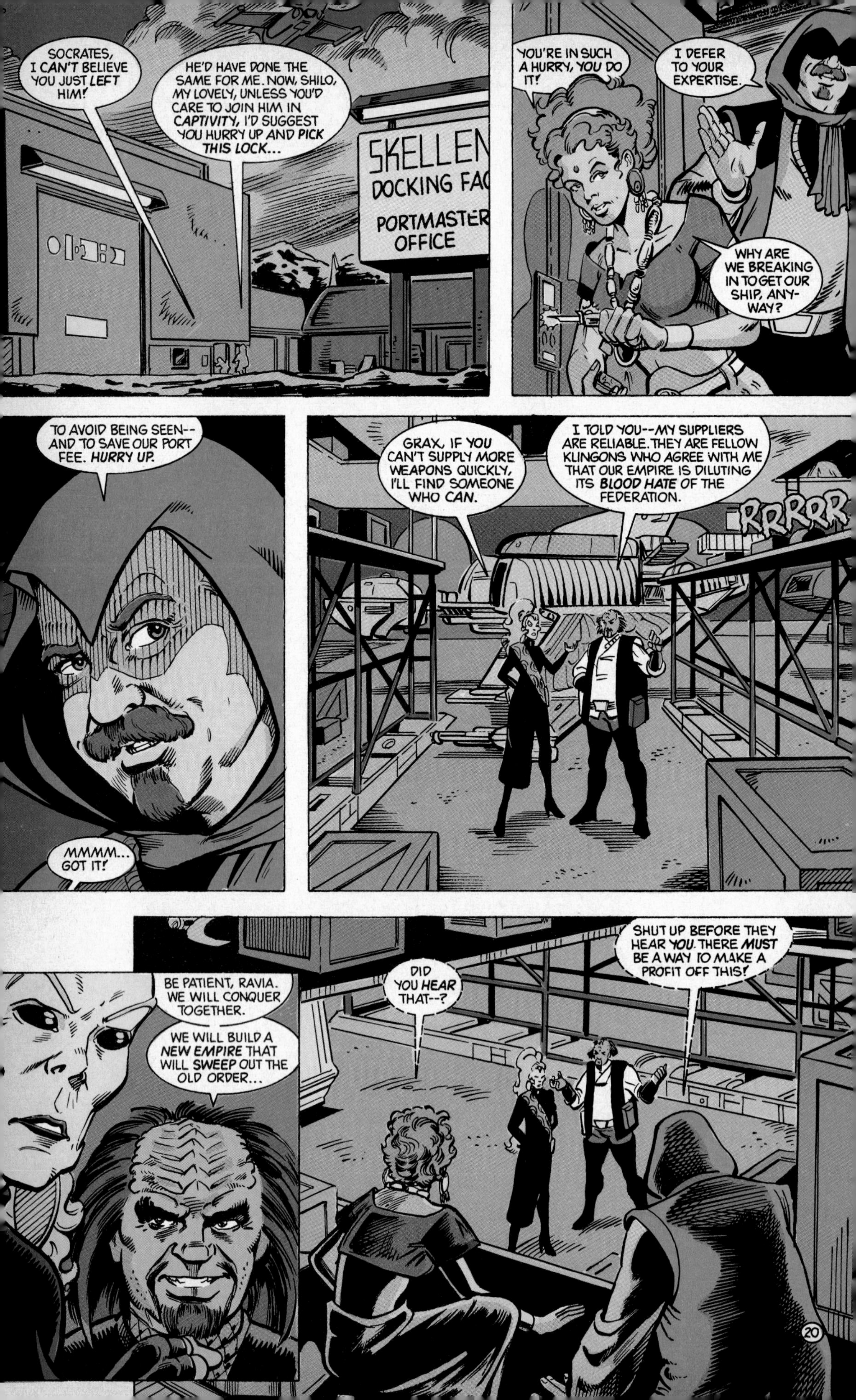
SOCRATES, I CAN'T BELIEVE YOU JUST LEFT HIM!
HE'D HAVE DONE THE SAME FOR ME. NOW, SHILO, MY LOVELY, UNLESS YOU'D CARE TO JOIN HIM IN CAPTIVITY, I'D SUGGEST YOU HURRY UP AND PICK THIS LOCK...
SKELLEN
DOCKING FAC
PORTMASTER OFFICE
YOU'RE IN SUCH A HURRY, YOU DO IT!
I DEFER TO YOUR EXPERTISE.
WHY ARE WE BREAKING IN TO GET OUR SHIP, ANYWAY?
TO AVOID BEING SEEN-- AND TO SAVE OUR PORT FEE. HURRY UP.
MMMM... GOT IT!
GRAX, IF YOU CAN'T SUPPLY MORE WEAPONS QUICKLY, I'LL FIND SOMEONE WHO CAN.
I TOLD YOU--MY SUPPLIERS ARE RELIABLE. THEY ARE FELLOW KLINGONS WHO AGREE WITH ME THAT OUR EMPIRE IS DILUTING ITS BLOOD HATE OF THE FEDERATION.
RRRRR
BE PATIENT, RAVIA. WE WILL CONQUER TOGETHER.
WE WILL BUILD A NEW EMPIRE THAT WILL SWEEP OUT THE OLD ORDER...
DID YOU HEAR THAT--?
SHUT UP BEFORE THEY HEAR YOU. THERE MUST BE A WAY TO MAKE A PROFIT OFF THIS!
20

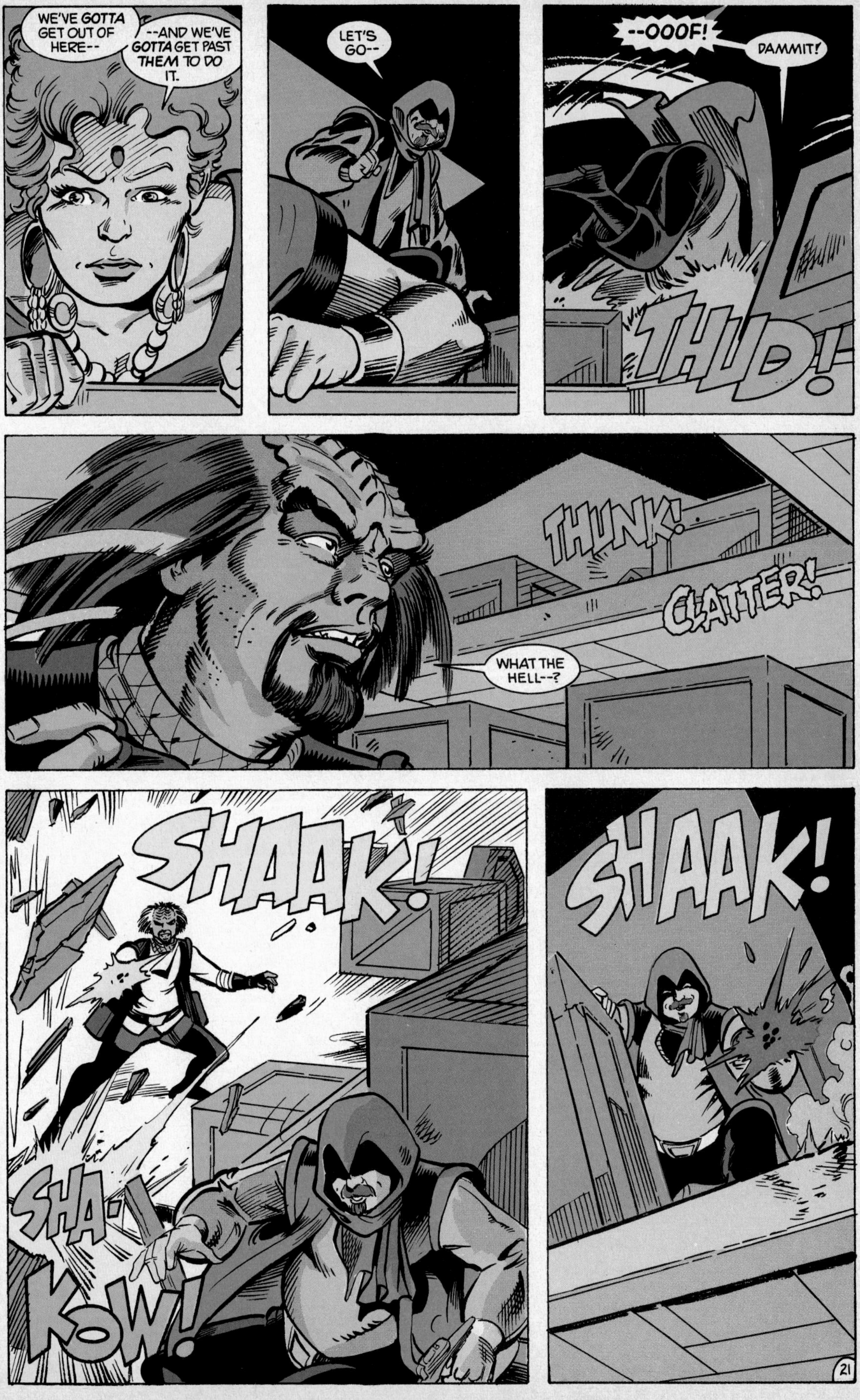
WE'VE GOTTA GET OUT OF HERE--
--AND WE'VE GOTTA GET PAST THEM TO DO IT.
LET'S GO--
--OOOF!
DAMMIT!
THUD!
THUNK!
CLATTER!
WHAT THE HELL--?
SHAAK!
SHA-KOW!
SHAAK!
21

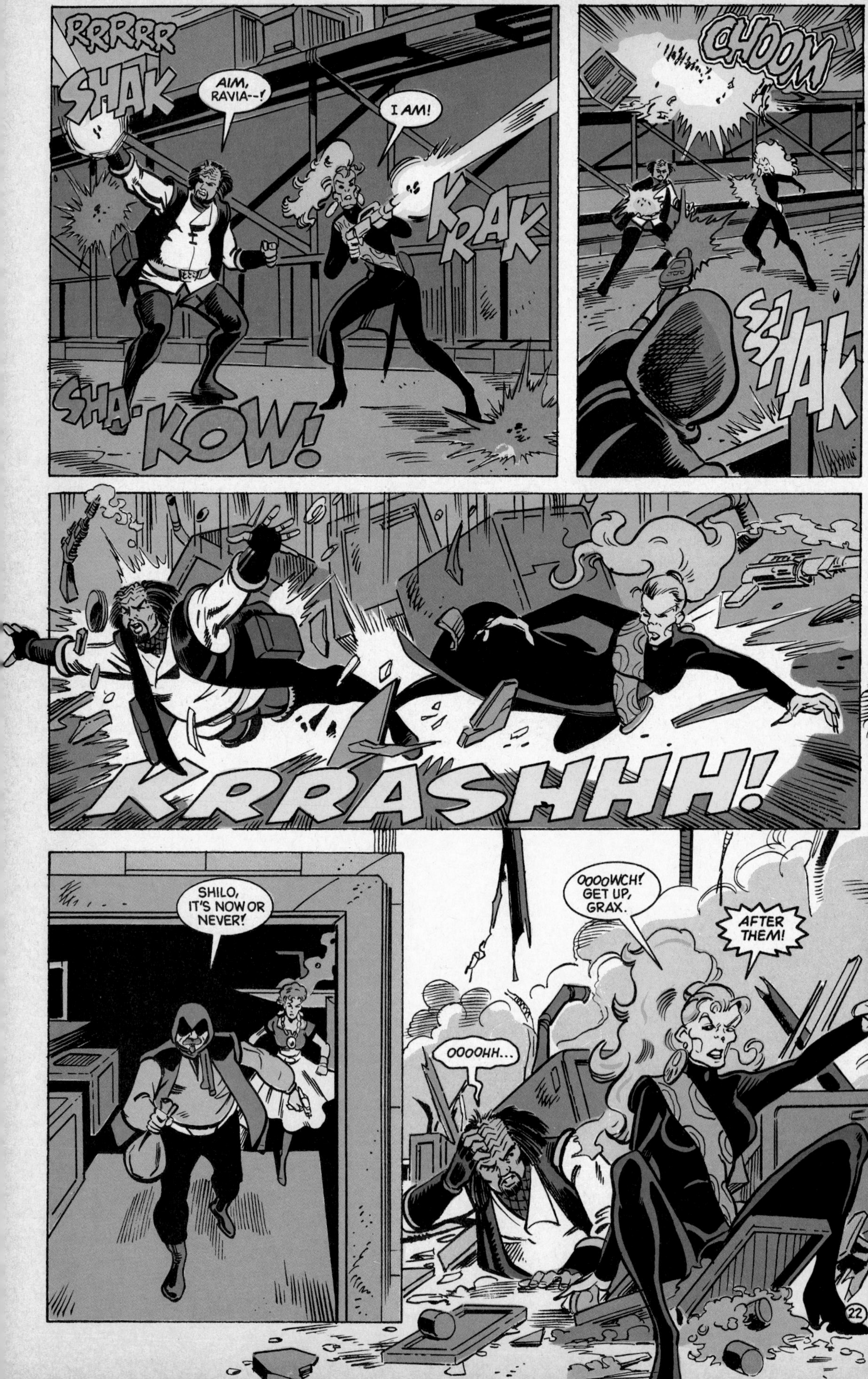
RRRRR
SHAK
AIM, RAVIA--!
I AM!
KRAK
SHA-KOW!
CHOOM
SSHAK
KRRASHHH!
SHILO, IT'S NOW OR NEVER!
OOOOWCH! GET UP, GRAX.
AFTER THEM!
OOOOHH...

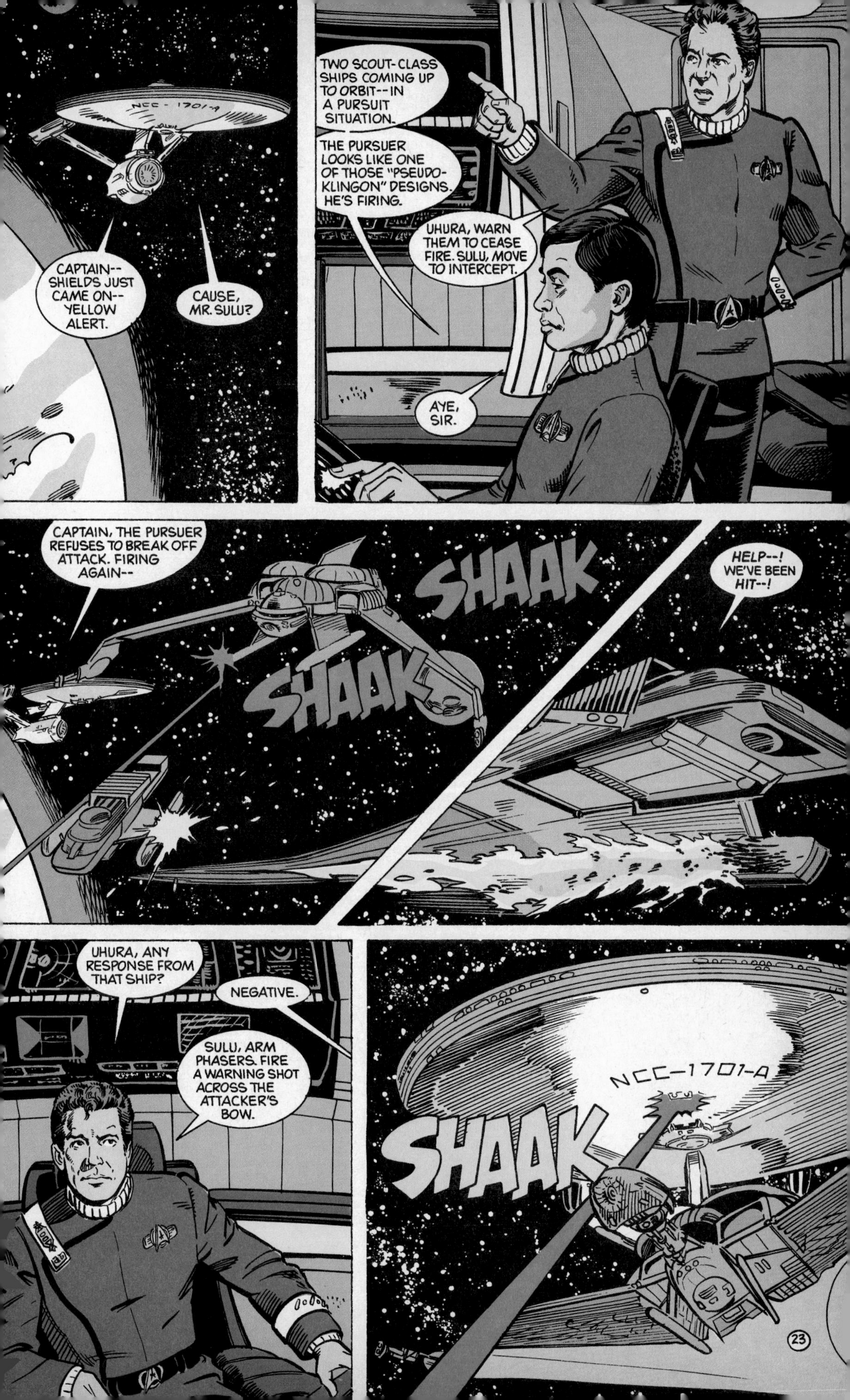
NCC-1701-A
CAPTAIN-- SHIELDS JUST CAME ON-- YELLOW ALERT.
CAUSE, MR. SULU?
TWO SCOUT-CLASS SHIPS COMING UP TO ORBIT--IN A PURSUIT SITUATION.
THE PURSUER LOOKS LIKE ONE OF THOSE "PSEUDO-KLINGON" DESIGNS. HE'S FIRING.
UHURA, WARN THEM TO CEASE FIRE. SULU, MOVE TO INTERCEPT.
AYE, SIR.
CAPTAIN, THE PURSUER REFUSES TO BREAK OFF ATTACK. FIRING AGAIN--
SHAAK
SHAAK
HELP--! WE'VE BEEN HIT--!
UHURA, ANY RESPONSE FROM THAT SHIP?
NEGATIVE.
SULU, ARM PHASERS. FIRE A WARNING SHOT ACROSS THE ATTACKER'S BOW.
NCC-1701-A
SHAAK

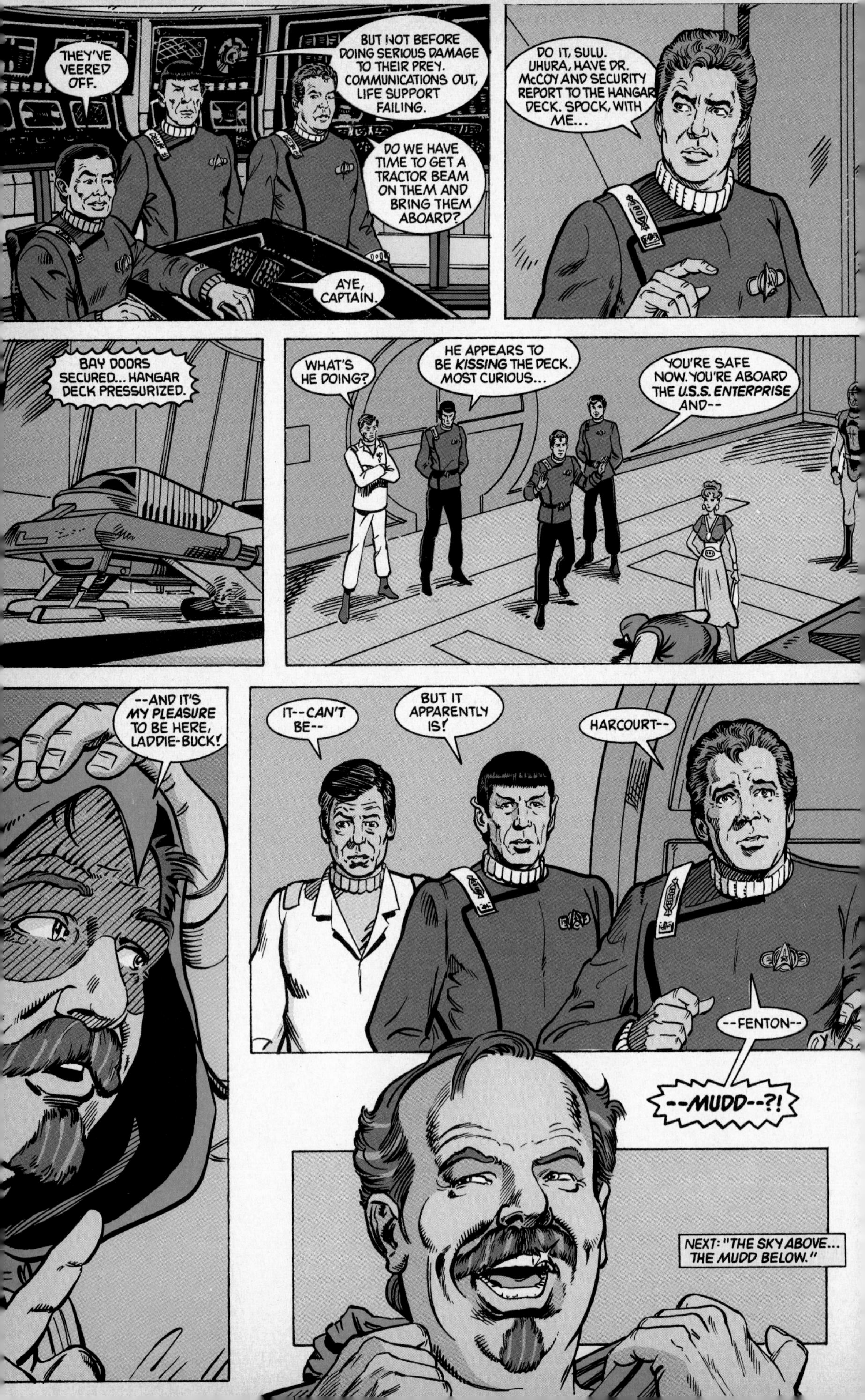
THEY'VE VEERED OFF.
BUT NOT BEFORE DOING SERIOUS DAMAGE TO THEIR PREY. COMMUNICATIONS OUT, LIFE SUPPORT FAILING.
DO WE HAVE TIME TO GET A TRACTOR BEAM ON THEM AND BRING THEM ABOARD?
AYE, CAPTAIN.
DO IT, SULU. UHURA, HAVE DR. McCOY AND SECURITY REPORT TO THE HANGAR DECK. SPOCK, WITH ME...
BAY DOORS SECURED... HANGAR DECK PRESSURIZED.
WHAT'S HE DOING?
HE APPEARS TO BE KISSING THE DECK. MOST CURIOUS...
YOU'RE SAFE NOW. YOU'RE ABOARD THE U.S.S. ENTERPRISE AND--
--AND IT'S MY PLEASURE TO BE HERE, LADDIE-BUCK!
IT--CAN'T BE--
BUT IT APPARENTLY IS!
HARCOURT--
--FENTON--
--MUDD--?!
NEXT: "THE SKY ABOVE... THE MUDD BELOW."

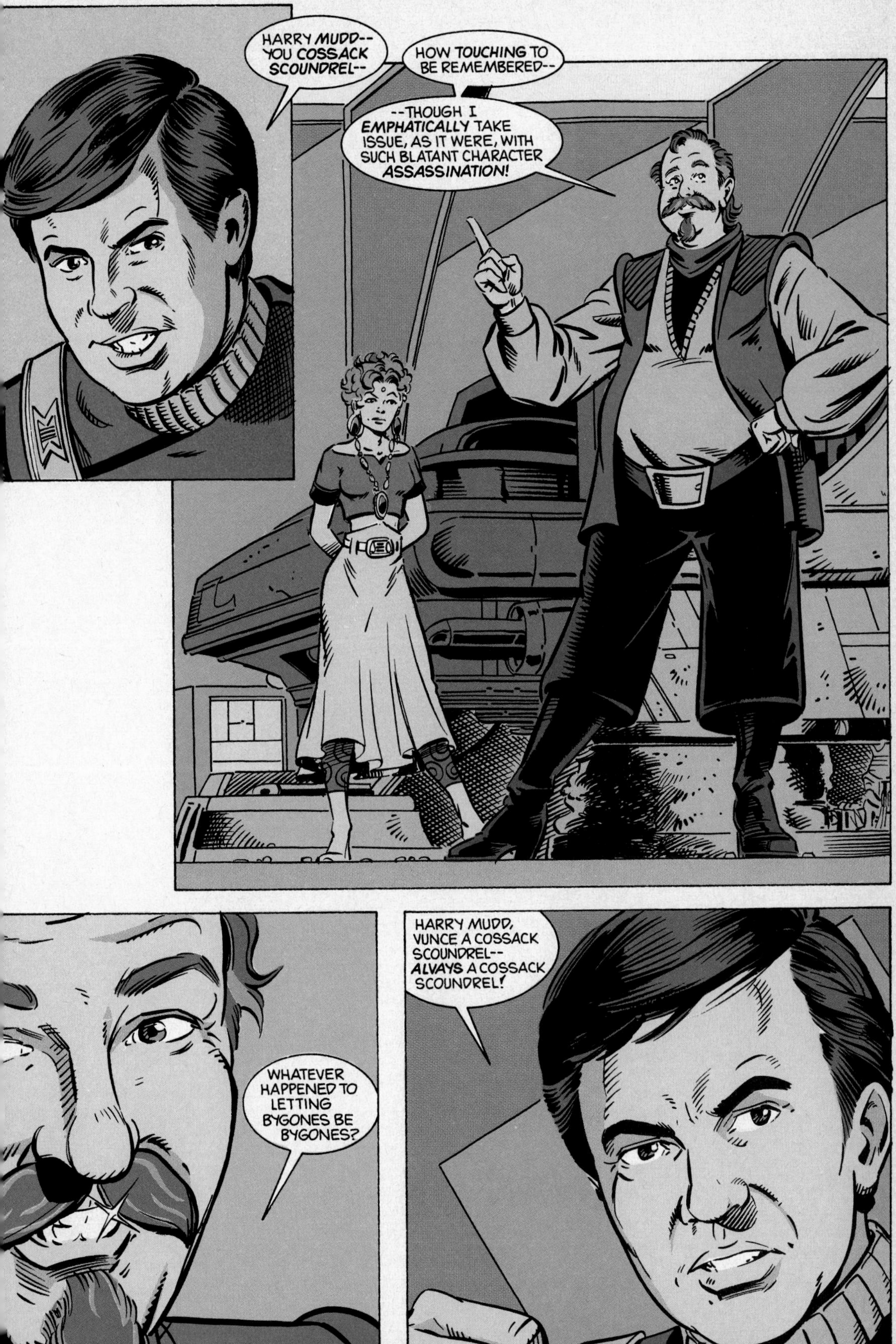
HARRY MUDD-- YOU COSSACK SCOUNDREL--
HOW TOUCHING TO BE REMEMBERED--
--THOUGH I EMPHATICALLY TAKE ISSUE, AS IT WERE, WITH SUCH BLATANT CHARACTER ASSASSINATION!
WHATEVER HAPPENED TO LETTING BYGONES BE BYGONES?
HARRY MUDD, VUNCE A COSSACK SCOUNDREL-- ALVAYS A COSSACK SCOUNDREL!

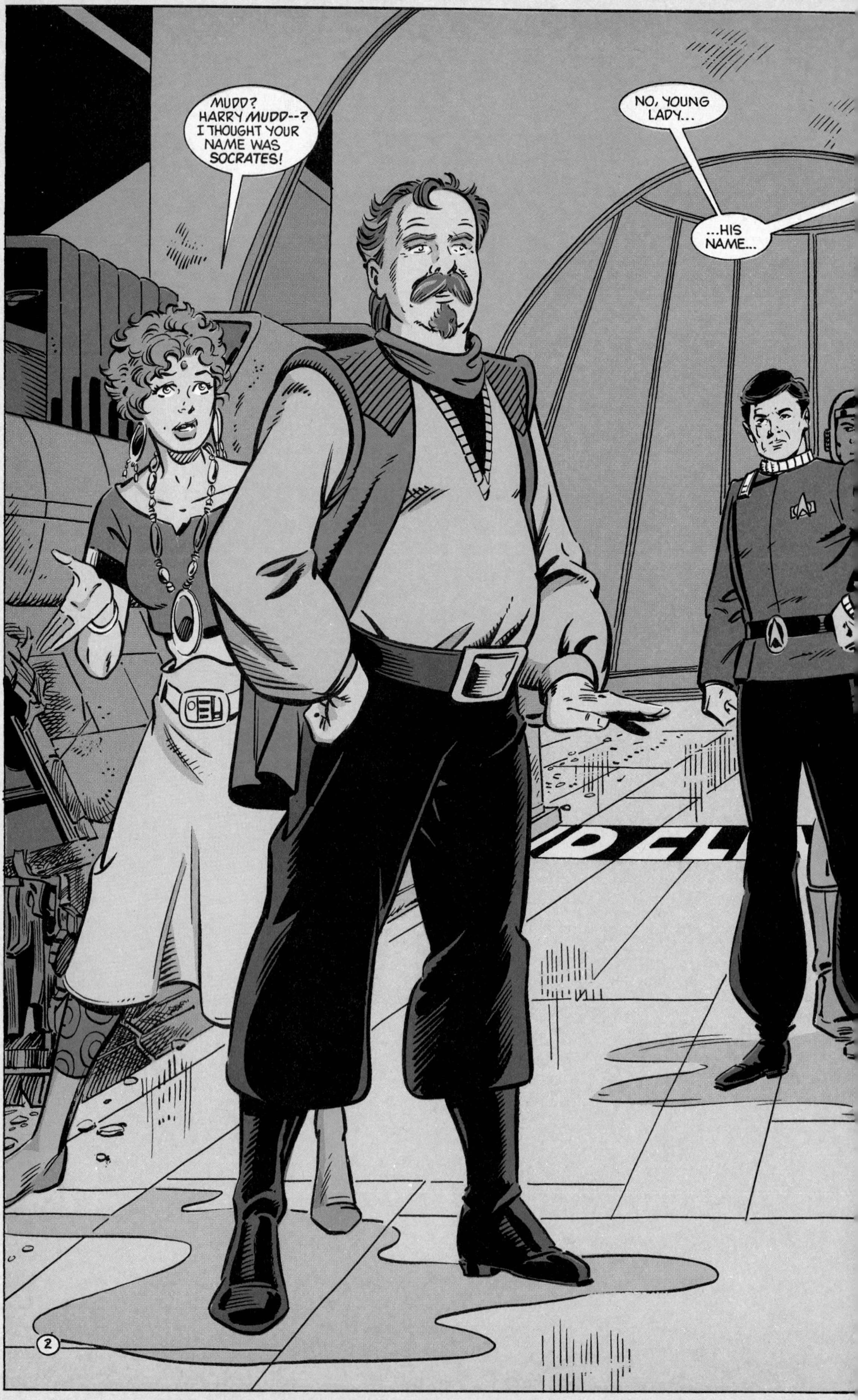

MUDD? HARRY MUDD--? I THOUGHT YOUR NAME WAS SOCRATES!
NO, YOUNG LADY...
...HIS NAME...

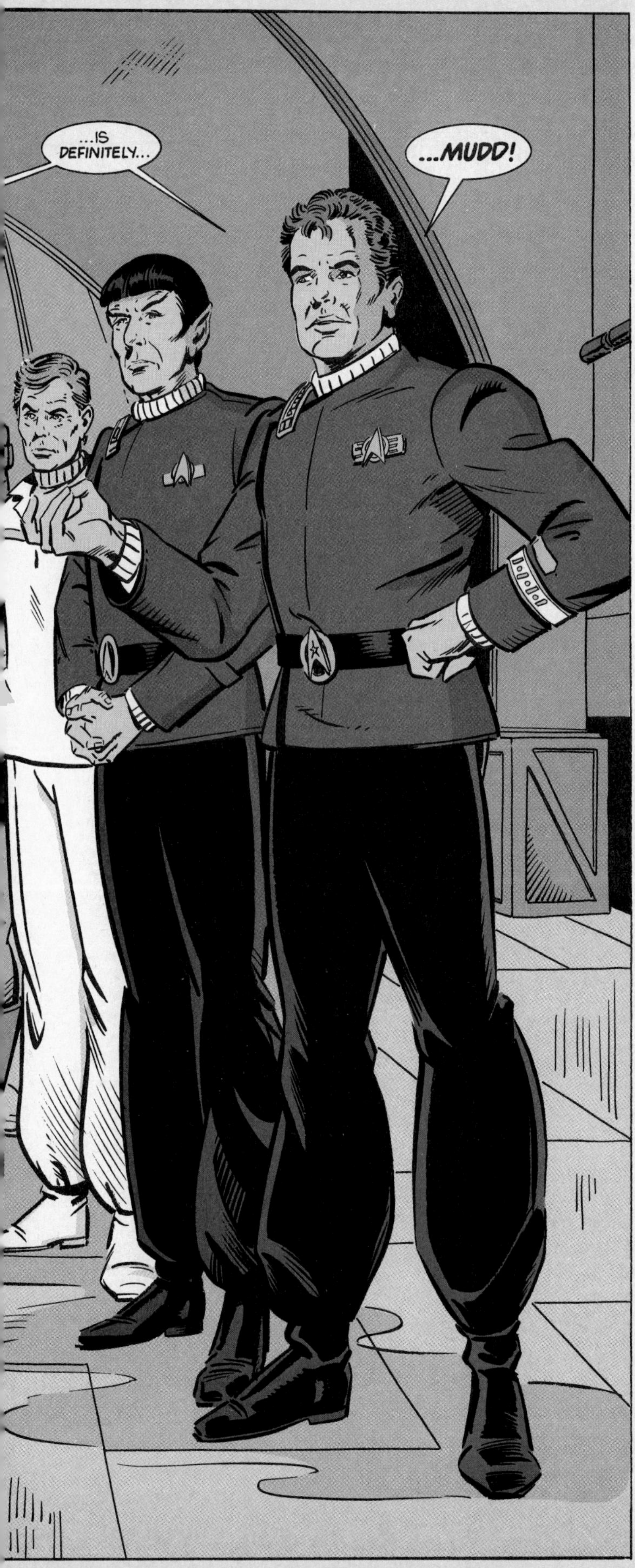
...IS DEFINITELY...
...MUDD!

THE SKY ABOVE ••• THE MUDD BELOW

CHAPTER TWO

HOWARD WEINSTEIN
WRITER

GORDON PURCELL
PENCILLER

CARLOS GARZON
INKER

BOB PINAHA
LETTERER

TOM McCRAW
COLORIST

ROBERT GREENBERGER
EDITOR

BASED ON STAR TREK CREATED BY GENE RODDENBERRY

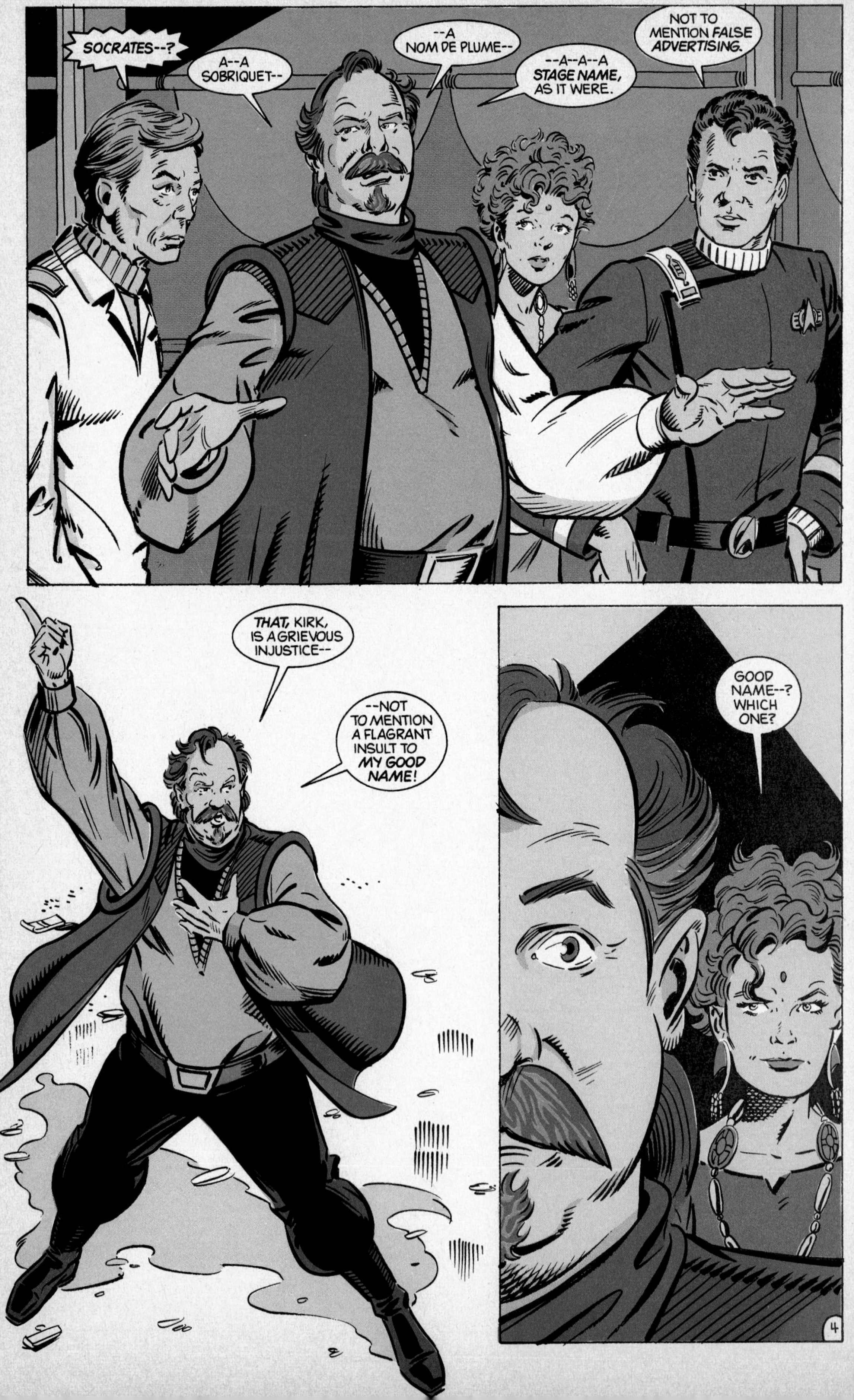
SOCRATES--?
A--A SOBRIQUET--
--A NOM DE PLUME--
--A--A--A STAGE NAME, AS IT WERE.
NOT TO MENTION FALSE ADVERTISING.
THAT, KIRK, IS A GRIEVOUS INJUSTICE--
--NOT TO MENTION A FLAGRANT INSULT TO MY GOOD NAME!
GOOD NAME--? WHICH ONE?
4

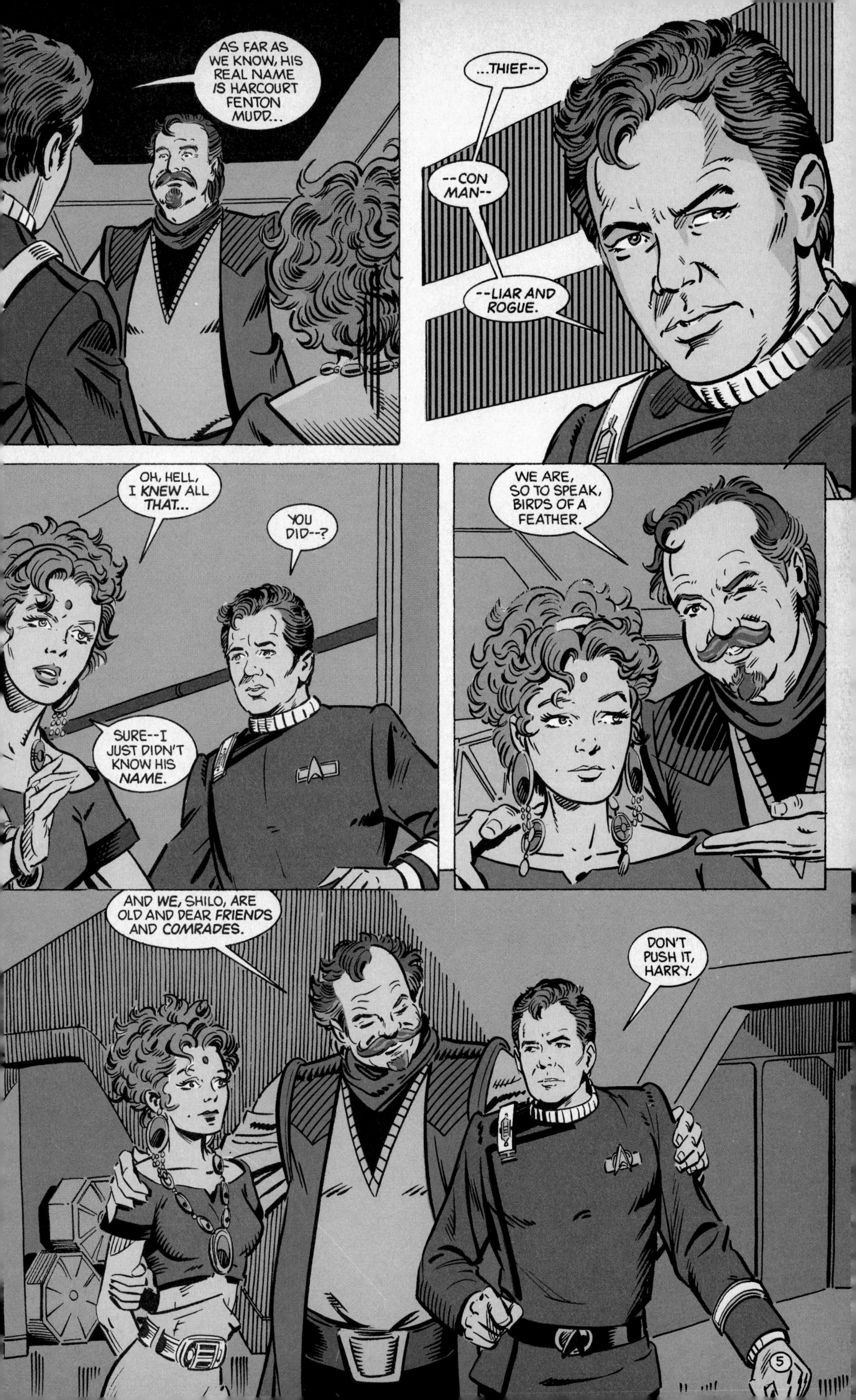
AS FAR AS WE KNOW, HIS REAL NAME IS HARCOURT FENTON MUDD...
...THIEF--
--CON MAN--
--LIAR AND ROGUE.
OH, HELL, I KNEW ALL THAT...
YOU DID--?
SURE--I JUST DIDN'T KNOW HIS NAME.
WE ARE, SO TO SPEAK, BIRDS OF A FEATHER.
AND WE, SHILO, ARE OLD AND DEAR FRIENDS AND COMRADES.
DON'T PUSH IT, HARRY.
5

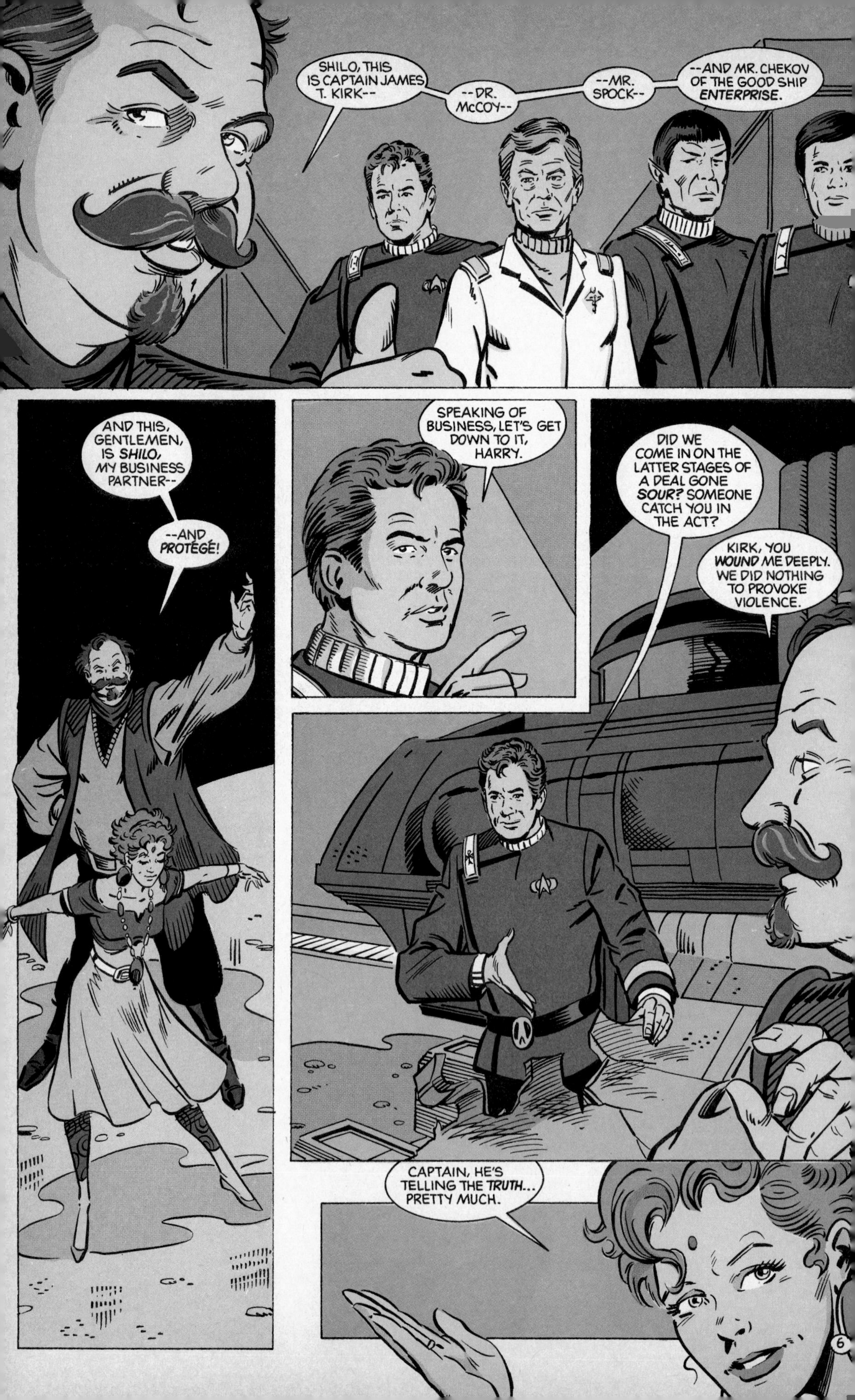
SHILO, THIS IS CAPTAIN JAMES T. KIRK--
--DR. McCOY--
--MR. SPOCK--
--AND MR. CHEKOV OF THE GOOD SHIP *ENTERPRISE*.
AND THIS, GENTLEMEN, IS *SHILO*, MY BUSINESS PARTNER--
--AND *PROTÉGÉ*!
SPEAKING OF BUSINESS, LET'S GET DOWN TO IT, HARRY.
DID WE COME IN ON THE LATTER STAGES OF A DEAL GONE *SOUR?* SOMEONE CATCH YOU IN THE ACT?
KIRK, YOU *WOUND* ME DEEPLY. WE DID NOTHING TO PROVOKE VIOLENCE.
CAPTAIN, HE'S TELLING THE *TRUTH*... PRETTY MUCH.
6

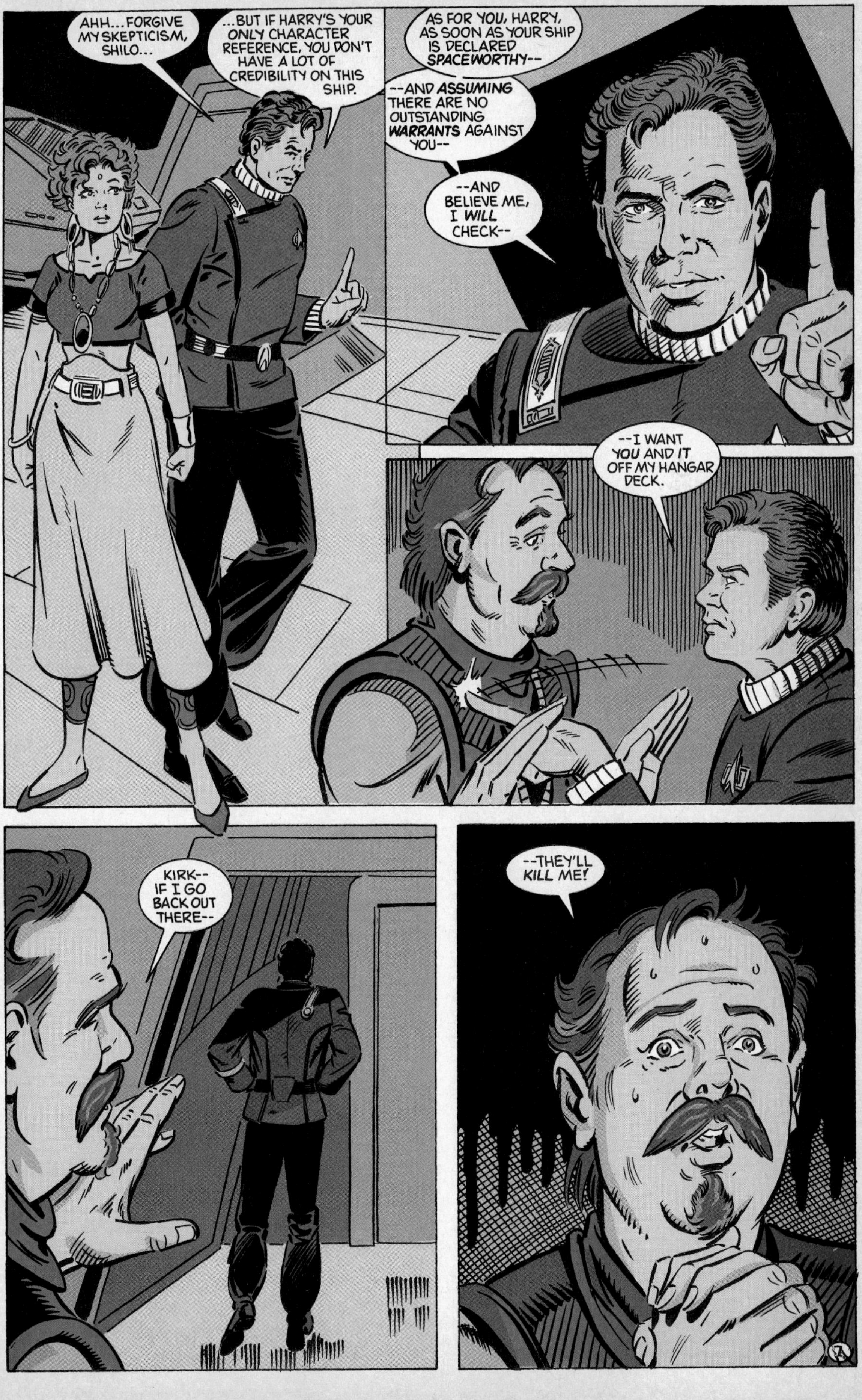
AHH...FORGIVE MY SKEPTICISM, SHILO...
...BUT IF HARRY'S YOUR ONLY CHARACTER REFERENCE, YOU DON'T HAVE A LOT OF CREDIBILITY ON THIS SHIP.
AS FOR YOU, HARRY, AS SOON AS YOUR SHIP IS DECLARED SPACEWORTHY--
--AND ASSUMING THERE ARE NO OUTSTANDING WARRANTS AGAINST YOU--
--AND BELIEVE ME, I WILL CHECK--
--I WANT YOU AND IT OFF MY HANGAR DECK.
KIRK-- IF I GO BACK OUT THERE--
--THEY'LL KILL ME!

THAT'S THE WHOLE TRUTH, CAPTAIN-- I *SWEAR* ON MY WIFE'S GRAVE...

DEAR OLD STELLA PASSED AWAY--?

HOPE SPRINGS ETERNAL, DOCTOR...BUT I'M SURE THE OLD BATTLE-AX IS STILL ALIVE AND KICKING...SOMEONE.

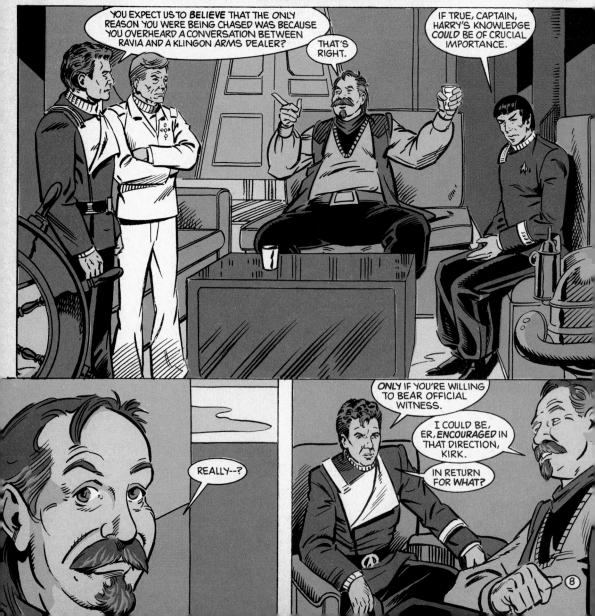

YOU EXPECT US TO *BELIEVE* THAT THE ONLY REASON YOU WERE BEING CHASED WAS BECAUSE YOU OVERHEARD A CONVERSATION BETWEEN RAVIA AND A KLINGON ARMS DEALER?

THAT'S RIGHT.

IF TRUE, CAPTAIN, HARRY'S KNOWLEDGE *COULD* BE OF CRUCIAL IMPORTANCE.

REALLY--?

ONLY IF YOU'RE WILLING TO BEAR OFFICIAL WITNESS.

I COULD BE, ER, *ENCOURAGED* IN THAT DIRECTION, KIRK.

IN RETURN FOR *WHAT?*

8

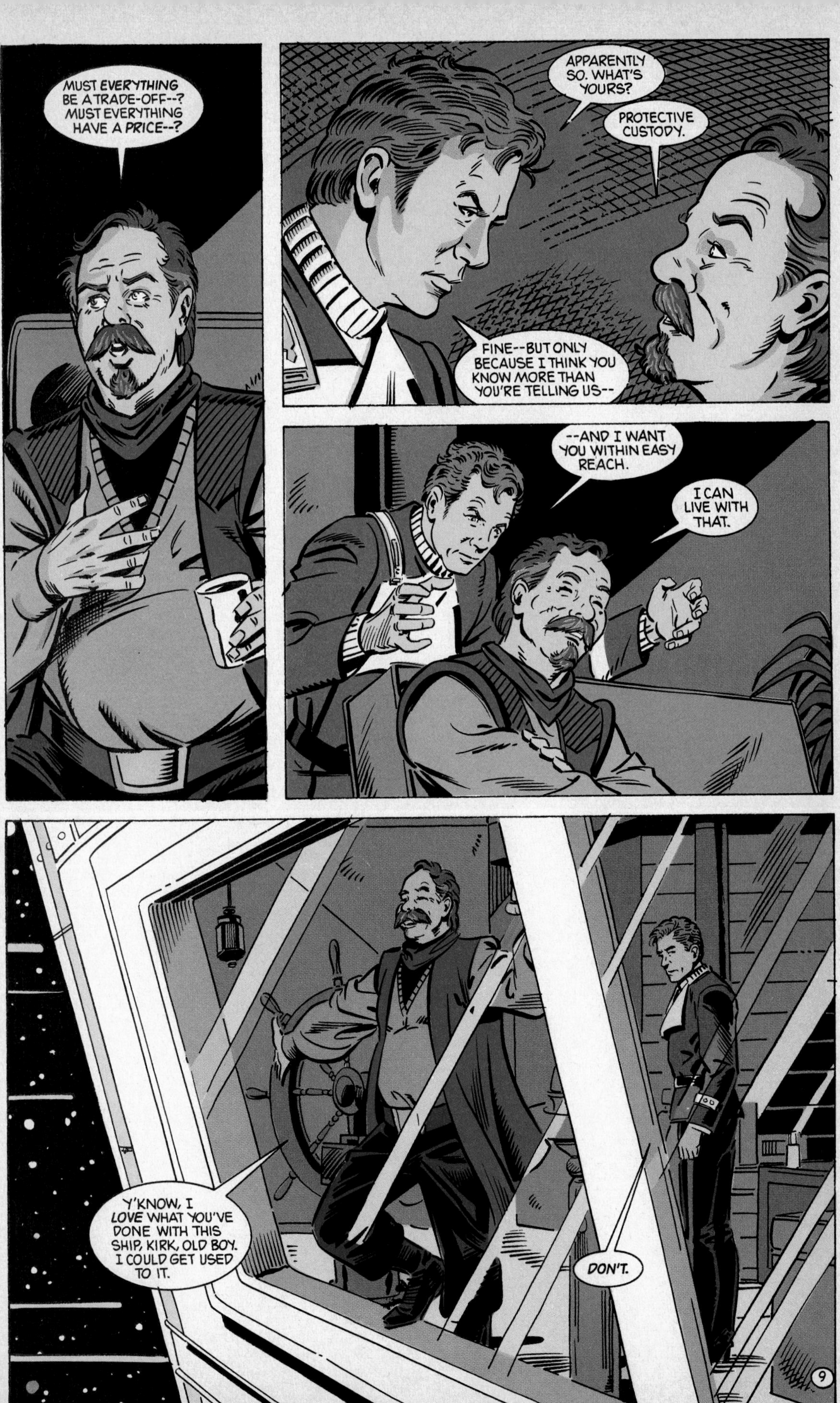
MUST *EVERYTHING* BE A TRADE-OFF--? MUST EVERYTHING HAVE A *PRICE*--?
APPARENTLY SO. WHAT'S YOURS?
PROTECTIVE CUSTODY.
FINE--BUT ONLY BECAUSE I THINK YOU KNOW MORE THAN YOU'RE TELLING US--
--AND I WANT YOU WITHIN EASY REACH.
I CAN LIVE WITH THAT.
Y'KNOW, I *LOVE* WHAT YOU'VE DONE WITH THIS SHIP, KIRK, OLD BOY. I COULD GET USED TO IT.
DON'T.
9

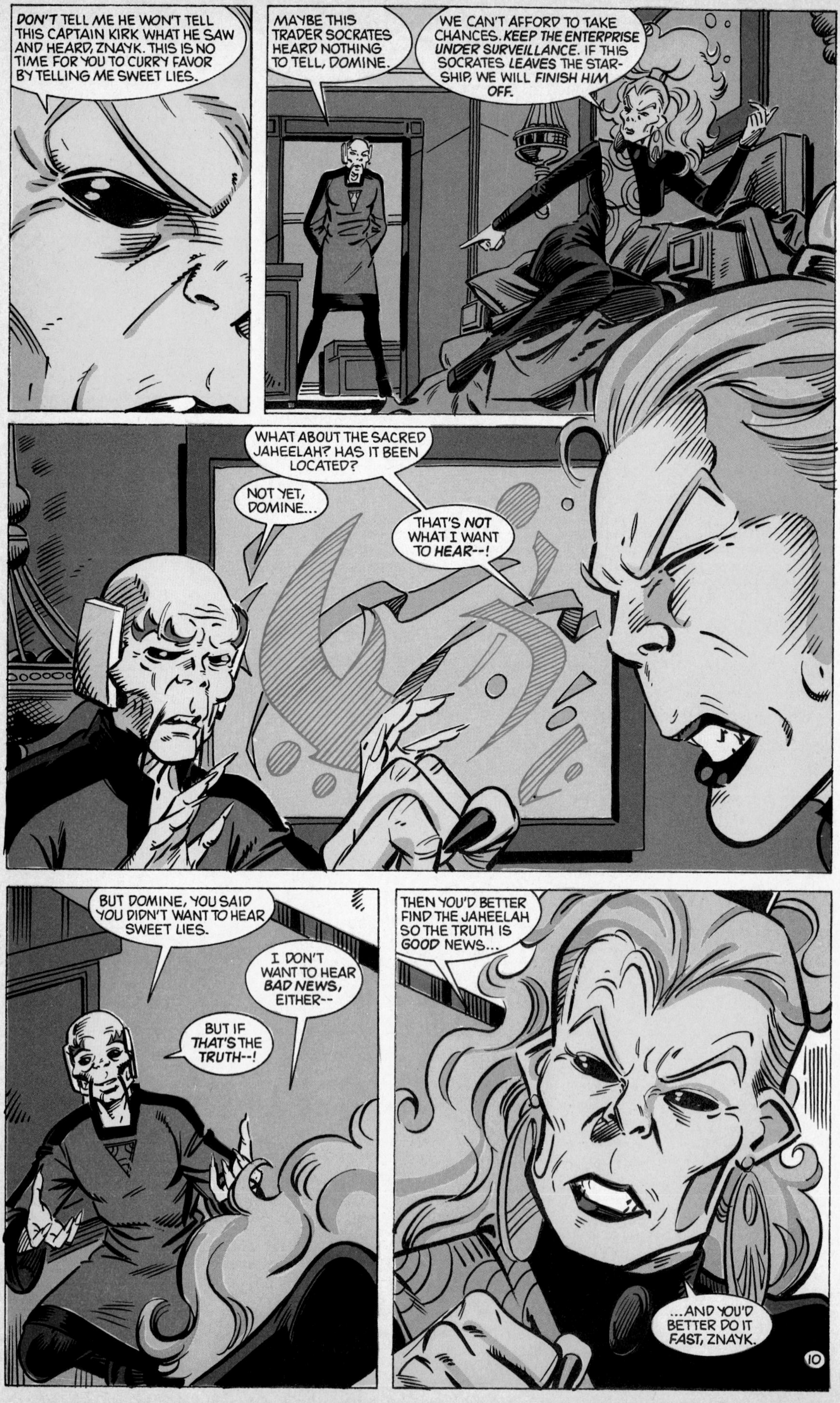
DON'T TELL ME HE WON'T TELL THIS CAPTAIN KIRK WHAT HE SAW AND HEARD, ZNAYK. THIS IS NO TIME FOR YOU TO CURRY FAVOR BY TELLING ME SWEET LIES.
MAYBE THIS TRADER SOCRATES HEARD NOTHING TO TELL, DOMINE.
WE CAN'T AFFORD TO TAKE CHANCES. KEEP THE ENTERPRISE UNDER SURVEILLANCE. IF THIS SOCRATES LEAVES THE STAR-SHIP, WE WILL FINISH HIM OFF.
WHAT ABOUT THE SACRED JAHEELAH? HAS IT BEEN LOCATED?
NOT YET, DOMINE...
THAT'S NOT WHAT I WANT TO HEAR--!
BUT DOMINE, YOU SAID YOU DIDN'T WANT TO HEAR SWEET LIES.
I DON'T WANT TO HEAR BAD NEWS, EITHER--
BUT IF THAT'S THE TRUTH--!
THEN YOU'D BETTER FIND THE JAHEELAH SO THE TRUTH IS GOOD NEWS...
...AND YOU'D BETTER DO IT FAST, ZNAYK.
10

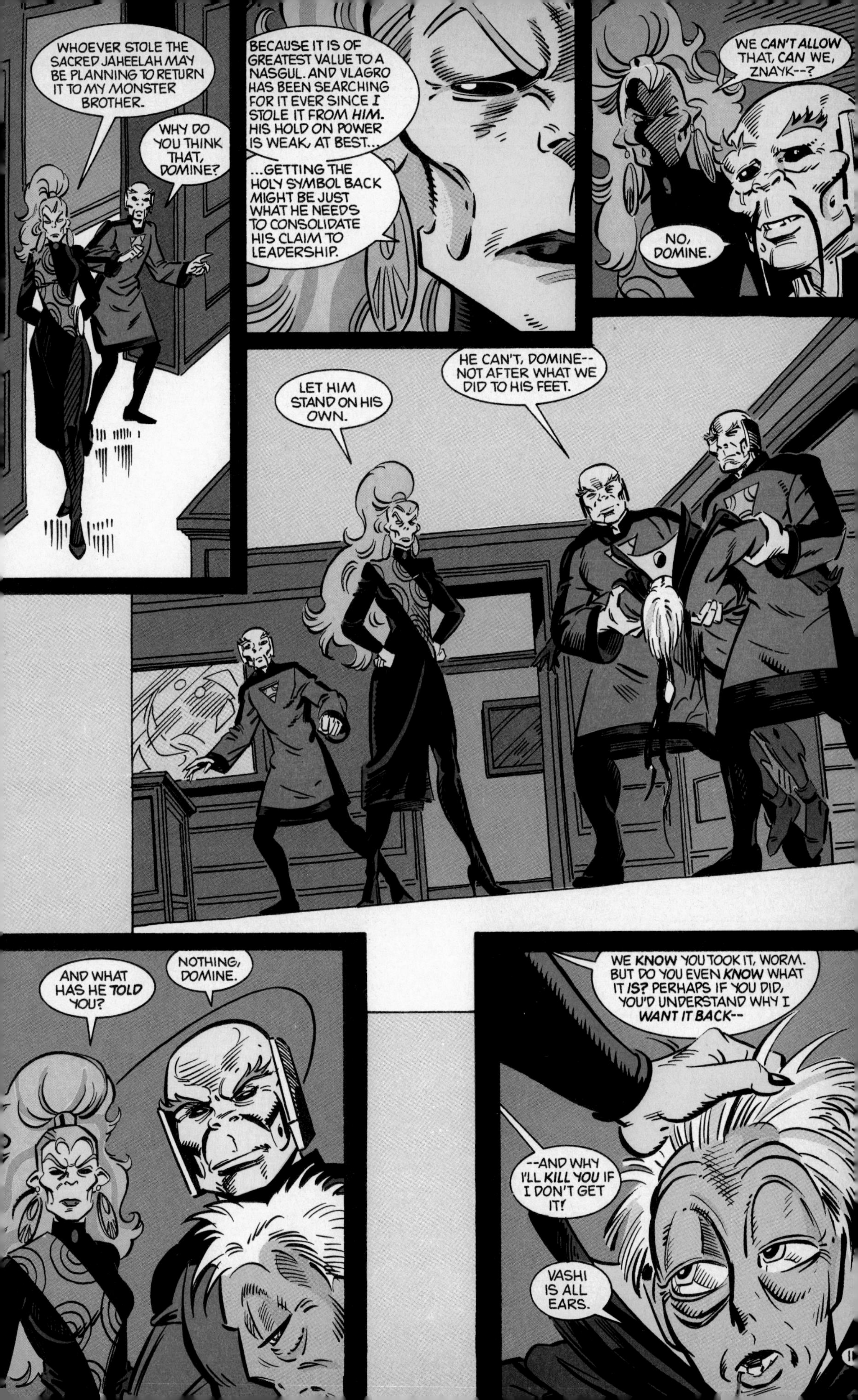
WHOEVER STOLE THE SACRED JAHEELAH MAY BE PLANNING TO RETURN IT TO MY MONSTER BROTHER.
WHY DO YOU THINK THAT, DOMINE?
BECAUSE IT IS OF GREATEST VALUE TO A NASGUL. AND VLAGRO HAS BEEN SEARCHING FOR IT EVER SINCE I STOLE IT FROM HIM. HIS HOLD ON POWER IS WEAK, AT BEST...
...GETTING THE HOLY SYMBOL BACK MIGHT BE JUST WHAT HE NEEDS TO CONSOLIDATE HIS CLAIM TO LEADERSHIP.
WE CAN'T ALLOW THAT, CAN WE, ZNAYK--?
NO, DOMINE.
LET HIM STAND ON HIS OWN.
HE CAN'T, DOMINE-- NOT AFTER WHAT WE DID TO HIS FEET.
AND WHAT HAS HE TOLD YOU?
NOTHING, DOMINE.
WE KNOW YOU TOOK IT, WORM. BUT DO YOU EVEN KNOW WHAT IT IS? PERHAPS IF YOU DID, YOU'D UNDERSTAND WHY I WANT IT BACK--
--AND WHY I'LL KILL YOU IF I DON'T GET IT!
VASHI IS ALL EARS.

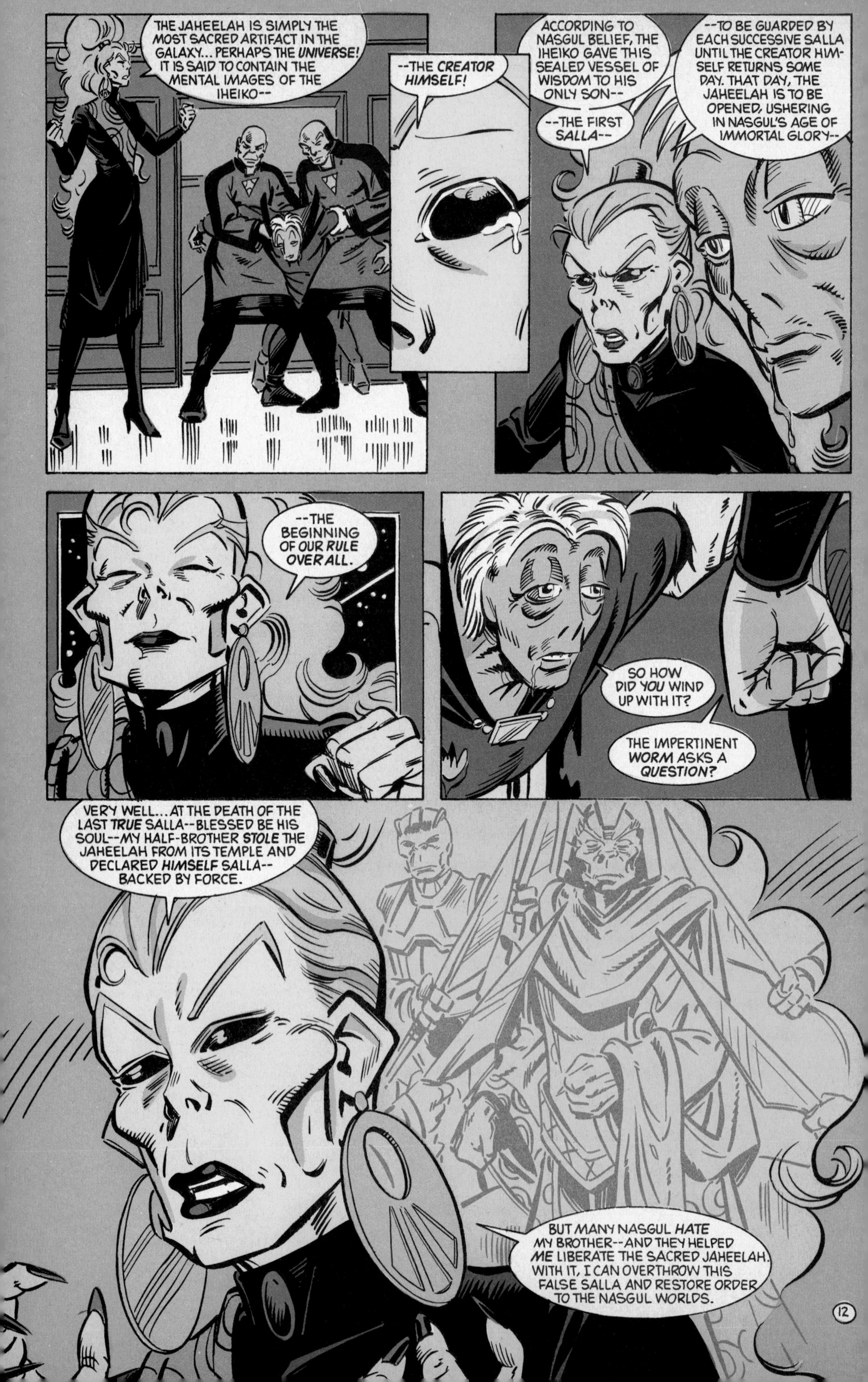
THE JAHEELAH IS SIMPLY THE MOST SACRED ARTIFACT IN THE GALAXY... PERHAPS THE UNIVERSE! IT IS SAID TO CONTAIN THE MENTAL IMAGES OF THE IHEIKO--
--THE CREATOR HIMSELF!
ACCORDING TO NASGUL BELIEF, THE IHEIKO GAVE THIS SEALED VESSEL OF WISDOM TO HIS ONLY SON--
--THE FIRST SALLA--
--TO BE GUARDED BY EACH SUCCESSIVE SALLA UNTIL THE CREATOR HIMSELF RETURNS SOME DAY. THAT DAY, THE JAHEELAH IS TO BE OPENED, USHERING IN NASGUL'S AGE OF IMMORTAL GLORY--
--THE BEGINNING OF OUR RULE OVER ALL.
SO HOW DID YOU WIND UP WITH IT?
THE IMPERTINENT WORM ASKS A QUESTION?
VERY WELL... AT THE DEATH OF THE LAST TRUE SALLA--BLESSED BE HIS SOUL--MY HALF-BROTHER STOLE THE JAHEELAH FROM ITS TEMPLE AND DECLARED HIMSELF SALLA--BACKED BY FORCE.
BUT MANY NASGUL HATE MY BROTHER--AND THEY HELPED ME LIBERATE THE SACRED JAHEELAH. WITH IT, I CAN OVERTHROW THIS FALSE SALLA AND RESTORE ORDER TO THE NASGUL WORLDS.

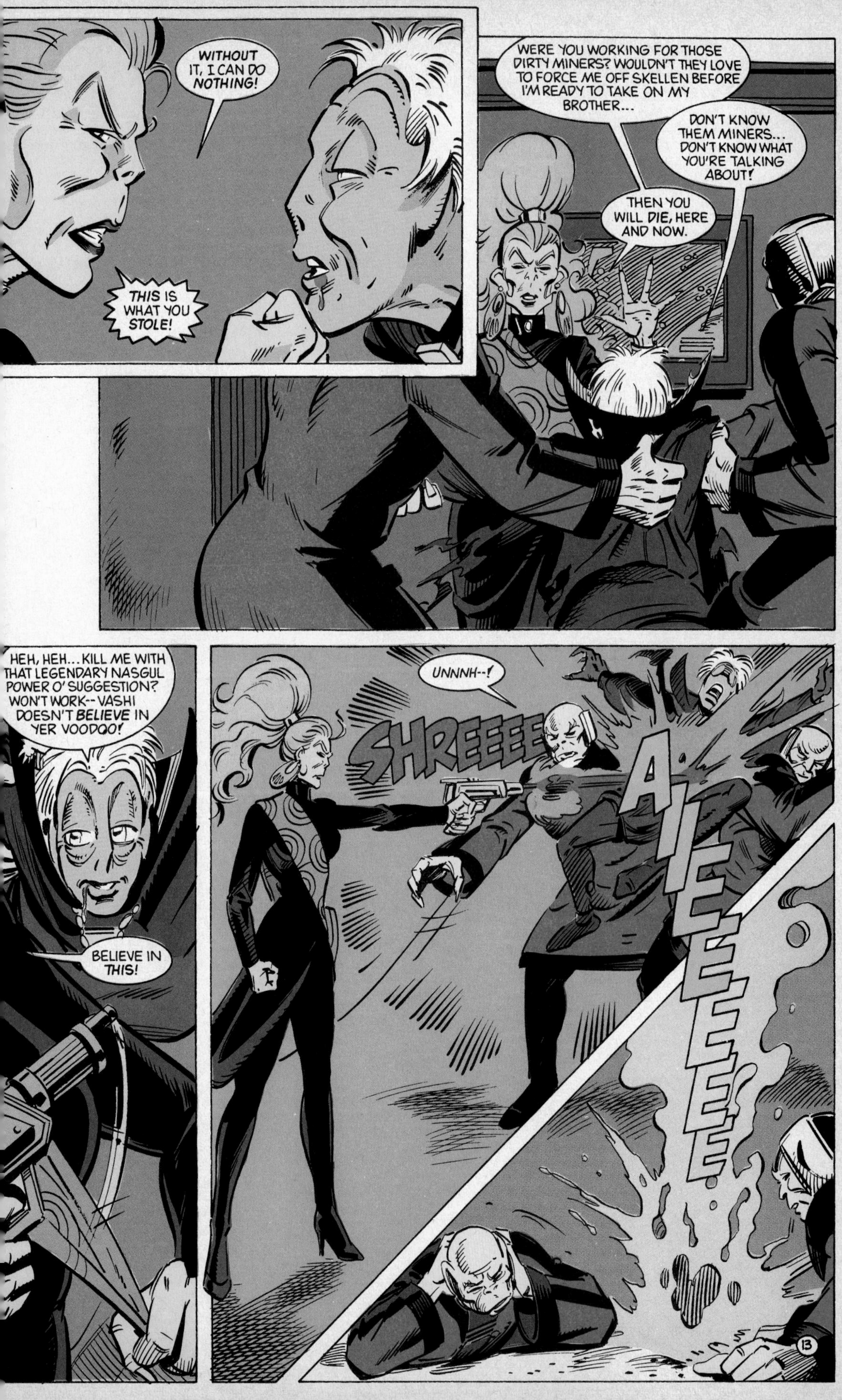
WITHOUT IT, I CAN DO NOTHING!
THIS IS WHAT YOU STOLE!
WERE YOU WORKING FOR THOSE DIRTY MINERS? WOULDN'T THEY LOVE TO FORCE ME OFF SKELLEN BEFORE I'M READY TO TAKE ON MY BROTHER...
DON'T KNOW THEM MINERS... DON'T KNOW WHAT YOU'RE TALKING ABOUT!
THEN YOU WILL DIE, HERE AND NOW.
HEH, HEH... KILL ME WITH THAT LEGENDARY NASGUL POWER O' SUGGESTION? WON'T WORK-- VASHI DOESN'T BELIEVE IN YER VOODOO!
BELIEVE IN THIS!
SHREEEEE
UNNNH--!
AIEEEEEEE

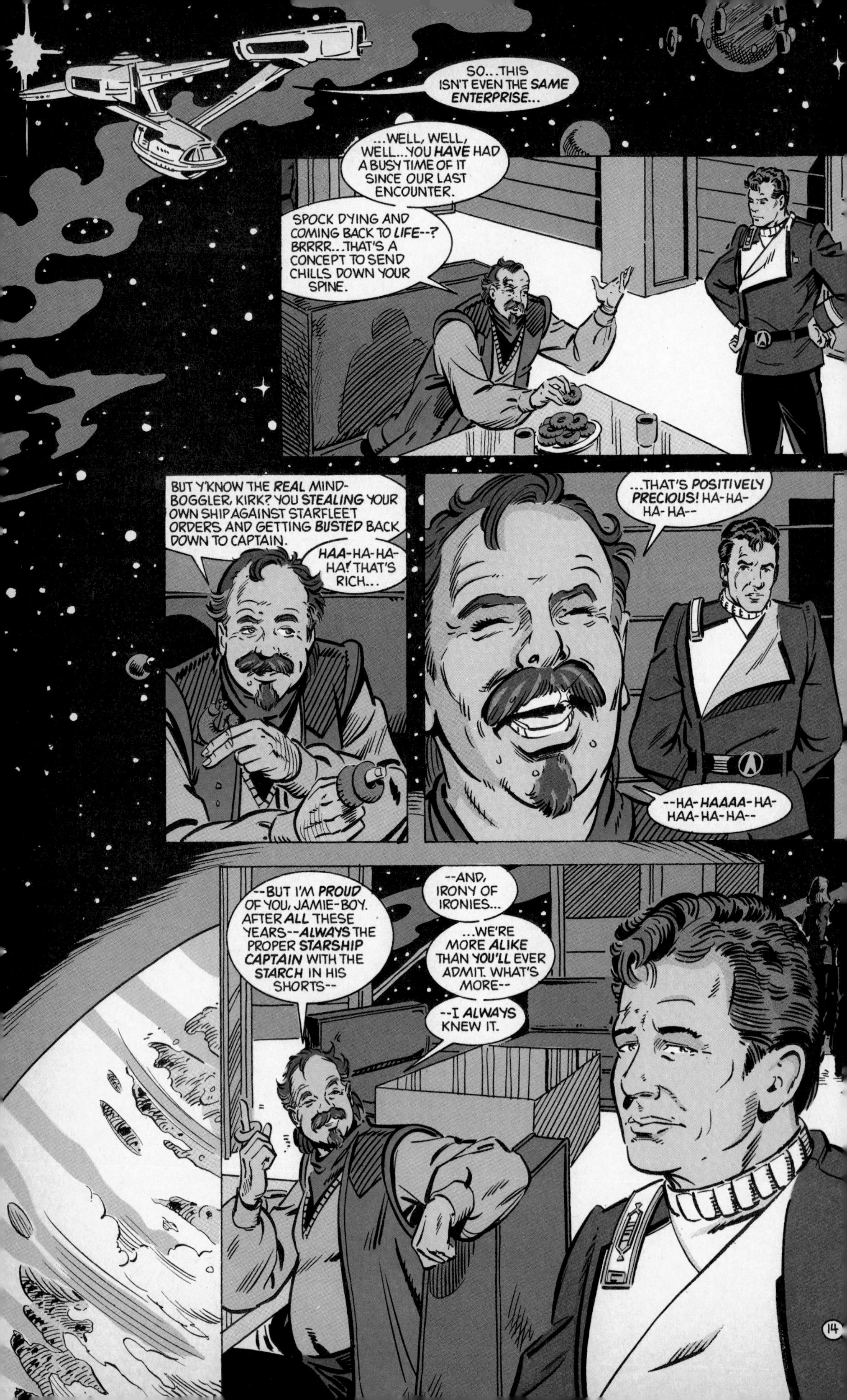
SO...THIS ISN'T EVEN THE SAME ENTERPRISE...
...WELL, WELL, WELL...YOU HAVE HAD A BUSY TIME OF IT SINCE OUR LAST ENCOUNTER.
SPOCK DYING AND COMING BACK TO LIFE--? BRRRR...THAT'S A CONCEPT TO SEND CHILLS DOWN YOUR SPINE.
BUT Y'KNOW THE REAL MIND-BOGGLER, KIRK? YOU STEALING YOUR OWN SHIP AGAINST STARFLEET ORDERS AND GETTING BUSTED BACK DOWN TO CAPTAIN.
HAA-HA-HA-HA! THAT'S RICH...
...THAT'S POSITIVELY PRECIOUS! HA-HA-HA-HA--
--HA-HAAAA-HA-HAA-HA-HA--
--BUT I'M PROUD OF YOU, JAMIE-BOY. AFTER ALL THESE YEARS--ALWAYS THE PROPER STARSHIP CAPTAIN WITH THE STARCH IN HIS SHORTS--
--AND, IRONY OF IRONIES...
...WE'RE MORE ALIKE THAN YOU'LL EVER ADMIT. WHAT'S MORE--
--I ALWAYS KNEW IT.

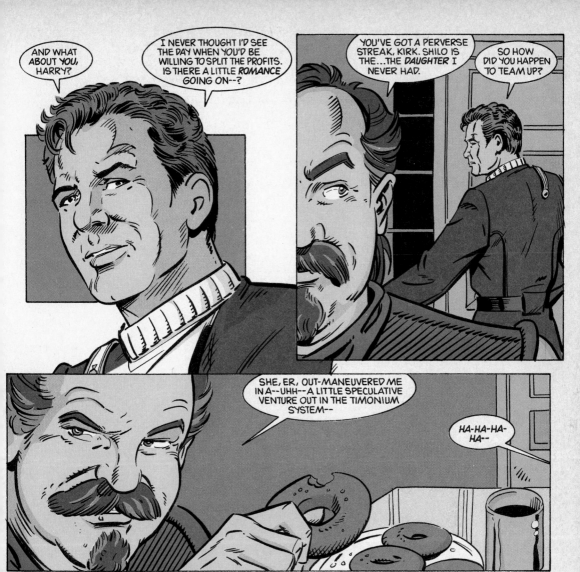

AND WHAT ABOUT *YOU*, HARRY?

I NEVER THOUGHT I'D SEE THE DAY WHEN YOU'D BE WILLING TO SPLIT THE PROFITS. IS THERE A LITTLE *ROMANCE* GOING ON--?

YOU'VE GOT A PERVERSE STREAK, KIRK. SHILO IS THE...THE *DAUGHTER* I NEVER HAD.

SO HOW DID YOU HAPPEN TO TEAM UP?

SHE, ER, OUT-MANEUVERED ME IN A--UHH--A LITTLE SPECULATIVE VENTURE OUT IN THE TIMONIUM SYSTEM--

HA-HA-HA-HA--

--SHE OUT-*SWINDLED* YOU!

YES... WELLLL...

...I SUPPOSE ONE COULD PUT IT THAT WAY... IF ONE *CHOSE* TO...

AND HOW WOULD *YOU* PUT IT?

SHE CAUGHT ME ON AN OFF-DAY--?

UH-HUH.

I *DID* MANAGE, AS IT WERE, TO RE-COUP SOME OF MY LOSSES...BUT I WAS IMPRESSED BY HER SPUNK--NOT TO MENTION HER WIZARDRY WITH ELECTRONIC GIZMOS--

--SHE COULD TEACH YOUR MR. SCOTT A THING OR TWO.

ANYWAY...SO I TOOK HER UNDER MY WING.

15

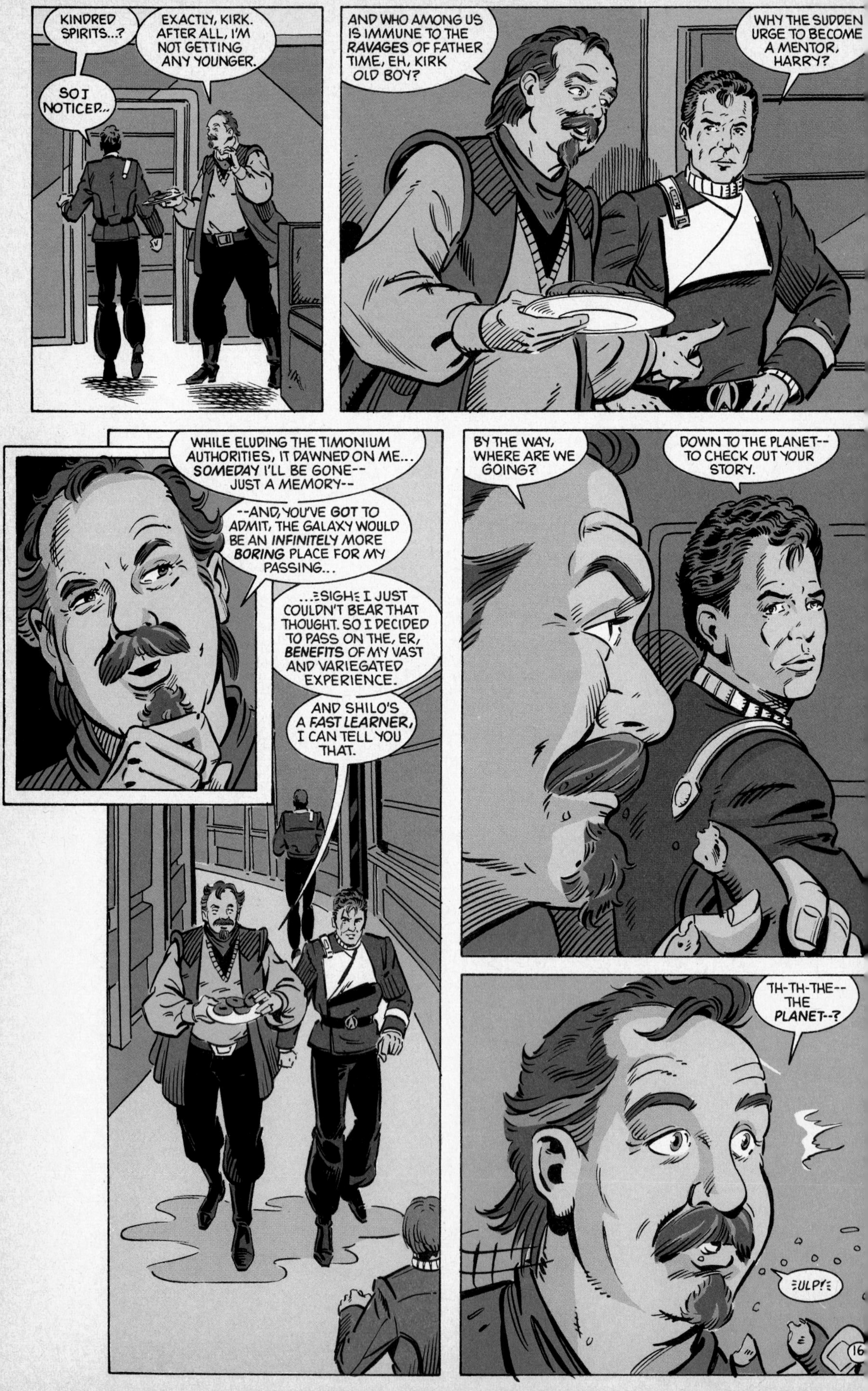
KINDRED SPIRITS...?
EXACTLY, KIRK. AFTER ALL, I'M NOT GETTING ANY YOUNGER.
SO I NOTICED...
AND WHO AMONG US IS IMMUNE TO THE RAVAGES OF FATHER TIME, EH, KIRK OLD BOY?
WHY THE SUDDEN URGE TO BECOME A MENTOR, HARRY?
WHILE ELUDING THE TIMONIUM AUTHORITIES, IT DAWNED ON ME... SOMEDAY I'LL BE GONE-- JUST A MEMORY--
--AND, YOU'VE GOT TO ADMIT, THE GALAXY WOULD BE AN INFINITELY MORE BORING PLACE FOR MY PASSING...
...SIGH I JUST COULDN'T BEAR THAT THOUGHT. SO I DECIDED TO PASS ON THE, ER, BENEFITS OF MY VAST AND VARIEGATED EXPERIENCE.
AND SHILO'S A FAST LEARNER, I CAN TELL YOU THAT.
BY THE WAY, WHERE ARE WE GOING?
DOWN TO THE PLANET-- TO CHECK OUT YOUR STORY.
TH-TH-THE-- THE PLANET--?
GULP!

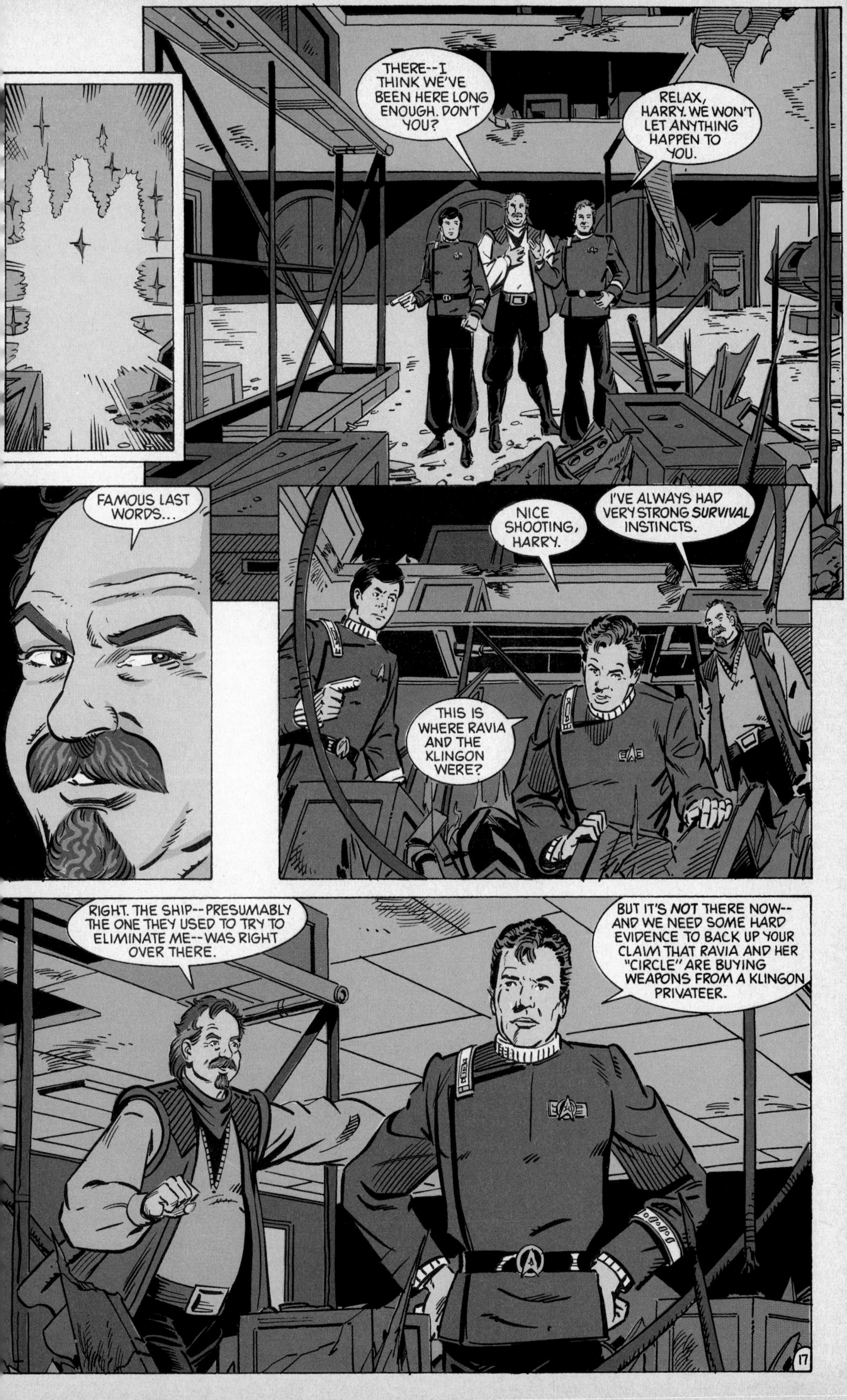

THERE--I THINK WE'VE BEEN HERE LONG ENOUGH. DON'T YOU?
RELAX, HARRY. WE WON'T LET ANYTHING HAPPEN TO YOU.
FAMOUS LAST WORDS...
NICE SHOOTING, HARRY.
I'VE ALWAYS HAD VERY STRONG SURVIVAL INSTINCTS.
THIS IS WHERE RAVIA AND THE KLINGON WERE?
RIGHT. THE SHIP--PRESUMABLY THE ONE THEY USED TO TRY TO ELIMINATE ME--WAS RIGHT OVER THERE.
BUT IT'S NOT THERE NOW--AND WE NEED SOME HARD EVIDENCE TO BACK UP YOUR CLAIM THAT RAVIA AND HER "CIRCLE" ARE BUYING WEAPONS FROM A KLINGON PRIVATEER.

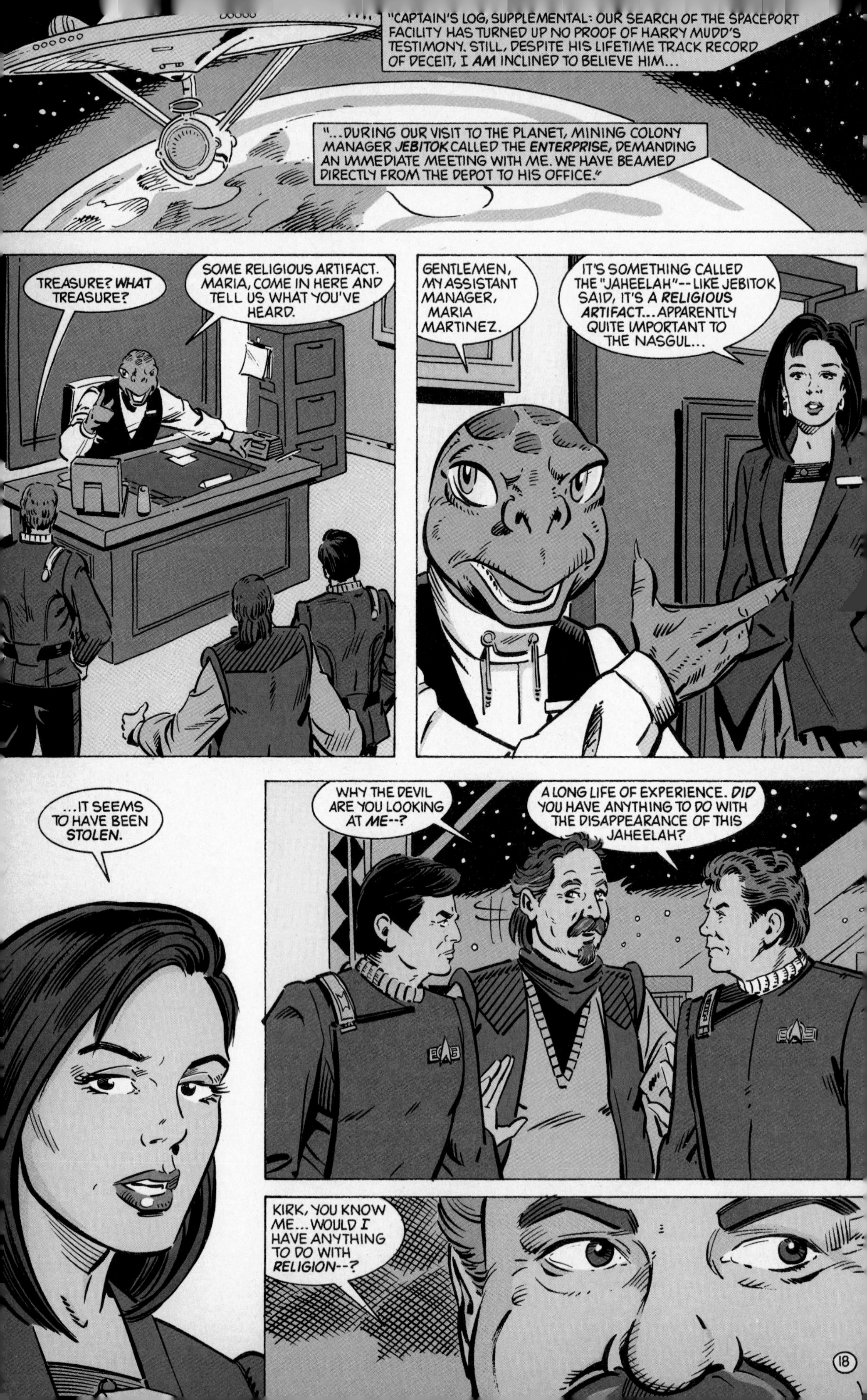
"CAPTAIN'S LOG, SUPPLEMENTAL: OUR SEARCH OF THE SPACEPORT FACILITY HAS TURNED UP NO PROOF OF HARRY MUDD'S TESTIMONY. STILL, DESPITE HIS LIFETIME TRACK RECORD OF DECEIT, I AM INCLINED TO BELIEVE HIM...
"...DURING OUR VISIT TO THE PLANET, MINING COLONY MANAGER JEBITOK CALLED THE ENTERPRISE, DEMANDING AN IMMEDIATE MEETING WITH ME. WE HAVE BEAMED DIRECTLY FROM THE DEPOT TO HIS OFFICE."
TREASURE? WHAT TREASURE?
SOME RELIGIOUS ARTIFACT. MARIA, COME IN HERE AND TELL US WHAT YOU'VE HEARD.
GENTLEMEN, MY ASSISTANT MANAGER, MARIA MARTINEZ.
IT'S SOMETHING CALLED THE "JAHEELAH"--LIKE JEBITOK SAID, IT'S A RELIGIOUS ARTIFACT... APPARENTLY QUITE IMPORTANT TO THE NASGUL...
...IT SEEMS TO HAVE BEEN STOLEN.
WHY THE DEVIL ARE YOU LOOKING AT ME--?
A LONG LIFE OF EXPERIENCE. DID YOU HAVE ANYTHING TO DO WITH THE DISAPPEARANCE OF THIS JAHEELAH?
KIRK, YOU KNOW ME... WOULD I HAVE ANYTHING TO DO WITH RELIGION--?
18

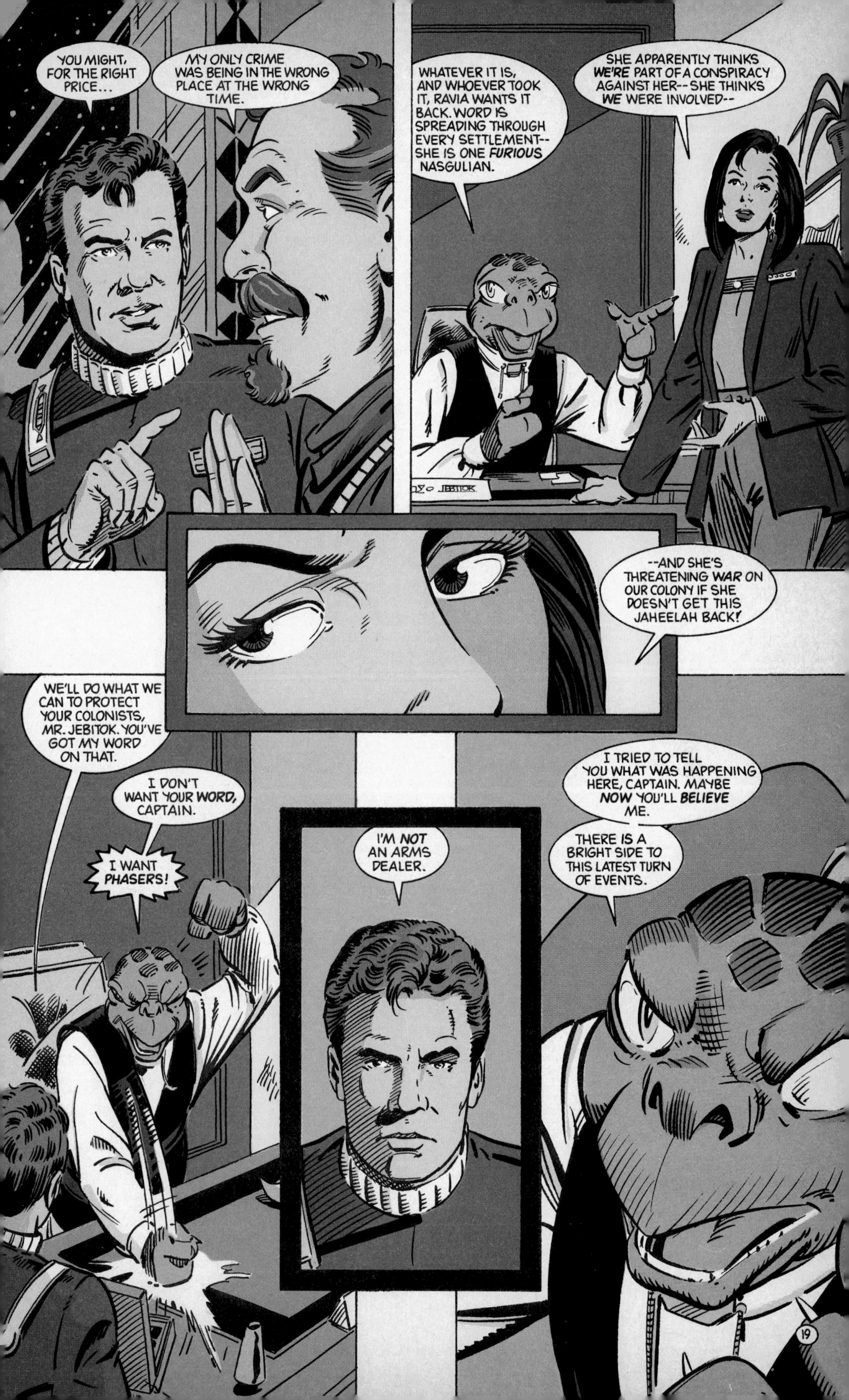
YOU MIGHT, FOR THE RIGHT PRICE...
MY ONLY CRIME WAS BEING IN THE WRONG PLACE AT THE WRONG TIME.
WHATEVER IT IS, AND WHOEVER TOOK IT, RAVIA WANTS IT BACK. WORD IS SPREADING THROUGH EVERY SETTLEMENT-- SHE IS ONE FURIOUS NASGULIAN.
SHE APPARENTLY THINKS WE'RE PART OF A CONSPIRACY AGAINST HER-- SHE THINKS WE WERE INVOLVED--
JEBITOK
--AND SHE'S THREATENING WAR ON OUR COLONY IF SHE DOESN'T GET THIS JAHEELAH BACK!
WE'LL DO WHAT WE CAN TO PROTECT YOUR COLONISTS, MR. JEBITOK. YOU'VE GOT MY WORD ON THAT.
I DON'T WANT YOUR WORD, CAPTAIN.
I WANT PHASERS!
I'M NOT AN ARMS DEALER.
I TRIED TO TELL YOU WHAT WAS HAPPENING HERE, CAPTAIN. MAYBE NOW YOU'LL BELIEVE ME.
THERE IS A BRIGHT SIDE TO THIS LATEST TURN OF EVENTS.

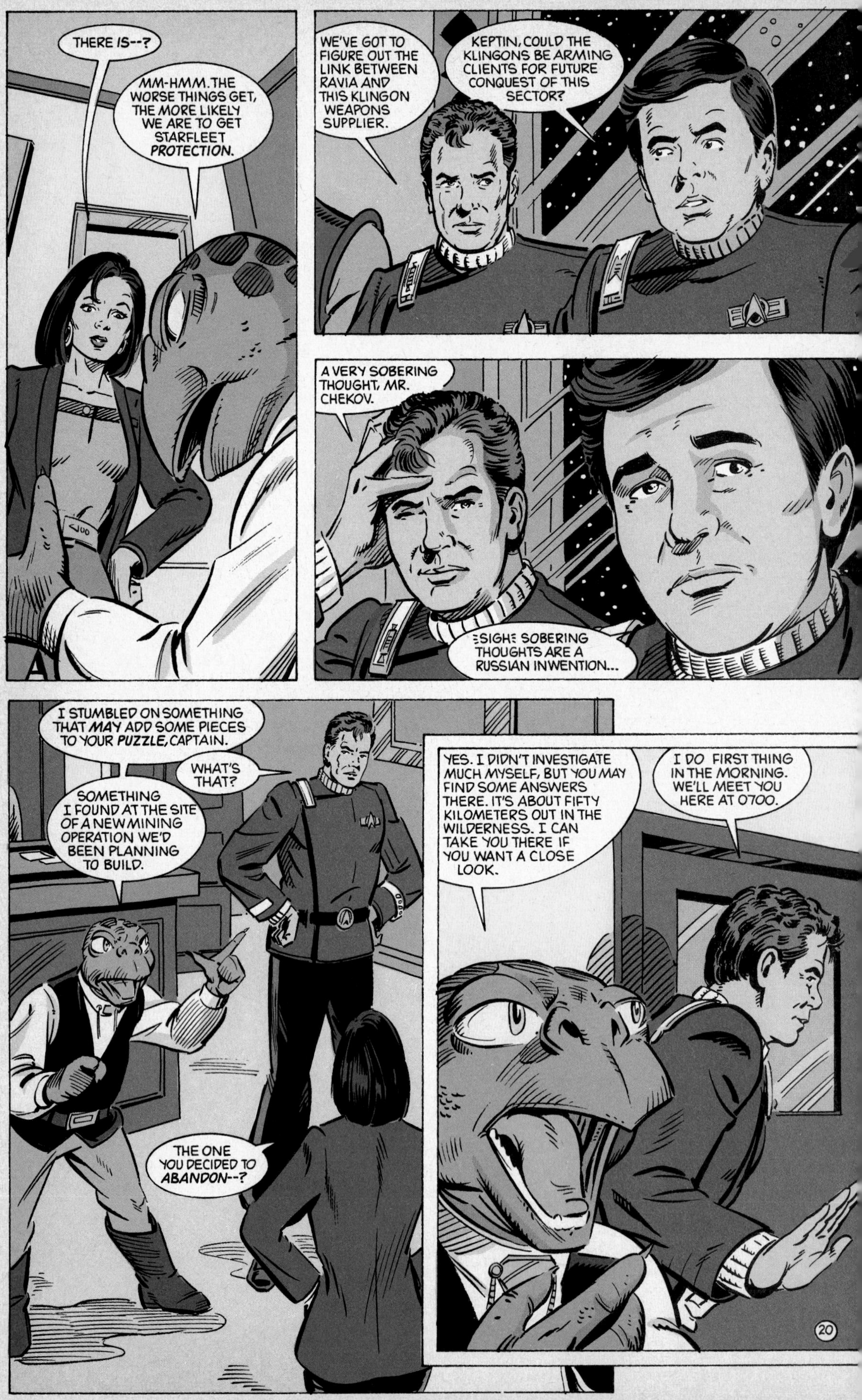

THERE IS--?
MM-HMM. THE WORSE THINGS GET, THE MORE LIKELY WE ARE TO GET STARFLEET *PROTECTION*.
WE'VE GOT TO FIGURE OUT THE LINK BETWEEN RAVIA AND THIS KLINGON WEAPONS SUPPLIER.
KEPTIN, COULD THE KLINGONS BE ARMING CLIENTS FOR FUTURE CONQUEST OF THIS SECTOR?
A VERY SOBERING THOUGHT, MR. CHEKOV.
=SIGH= SOBERING THOUGHTS ARE A RUSSIAN INWENTION...
I STUMBLED ON SOMETHING THAT *MAY* ADD SOME PIECES TO YOUR *PUZZLE*, CAPTAIN.
WHAT'S THAT?
SOMETHING I FOUND AT THE SITE OF A NEW MINING OPERATION WE'D BEEN PLANNING TO BUILD.
THE ONE YOU DECIDED TO *ABANDON*--?
YES. I DIDN'T INVESTIGATE MUCH MYSELF, BUT YOU MAY FIND SOME ANSWERS THERE. IT'S ABOUT FIFTY KILOMETERS OUT IN THE WILDERNESS. I CAN TAKE YOU THERE IF YOU WANT A CLOSE LOOK.
I DO FIRST THING IN THE MORNING. WE'LL MEET YOU HERE AT 0700.

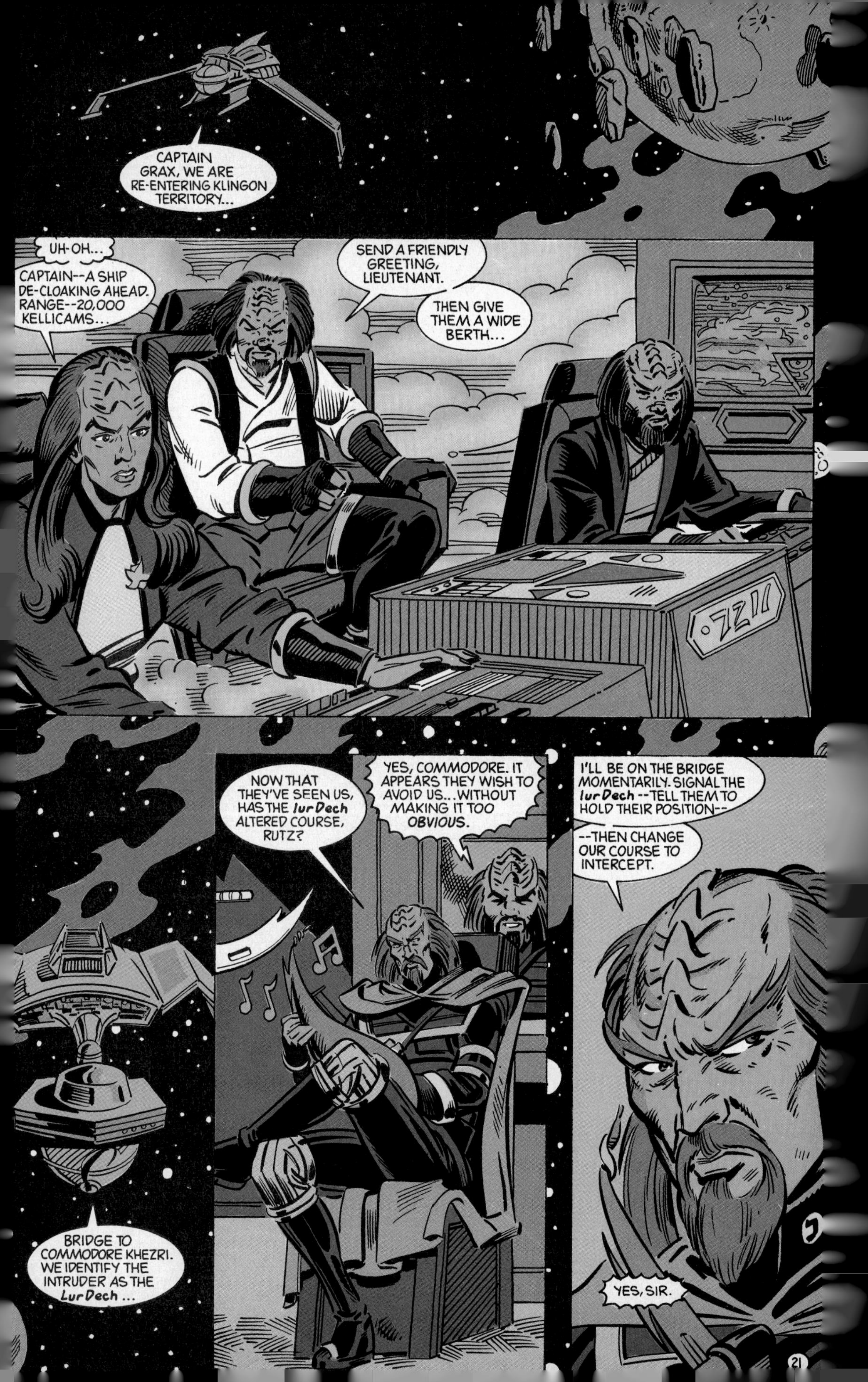

CAPTAIN GRAX, WE ARE RE-ENTERING KLINGON TERRITORY...
UH-OH...
CAPTAIN--A SHIP DE-CLOAKING AHEAD. RANGE--20,000 KELLICAMS...
SEND A FRIENDLY GREETING, LIEUTENANT.
THEN GIVE THEM A WIDE BERTH...
BRIDGE TO COMMODORE KHEZRI. WE IDENTIFY THE INTRUDER AS THE LurDech...
NOW THAT THEY'VE SEEN US, HAS THE lurDech ALTERED COURSE, RUTZ?
YES, COMMODORE. IT APPEARS THEY WISH TO AVOID US... WITHOUT MAKING IT TOO OBVIOUS.
I'LL BE ON THE BRIDGE MOMENTARILY. SIGNAL THE lurDech --TELL THEM TO HOLD THEIR POSITION--
--THEN CHANGE OUR COURSE TO INTERCEPT.
YES, SIR.

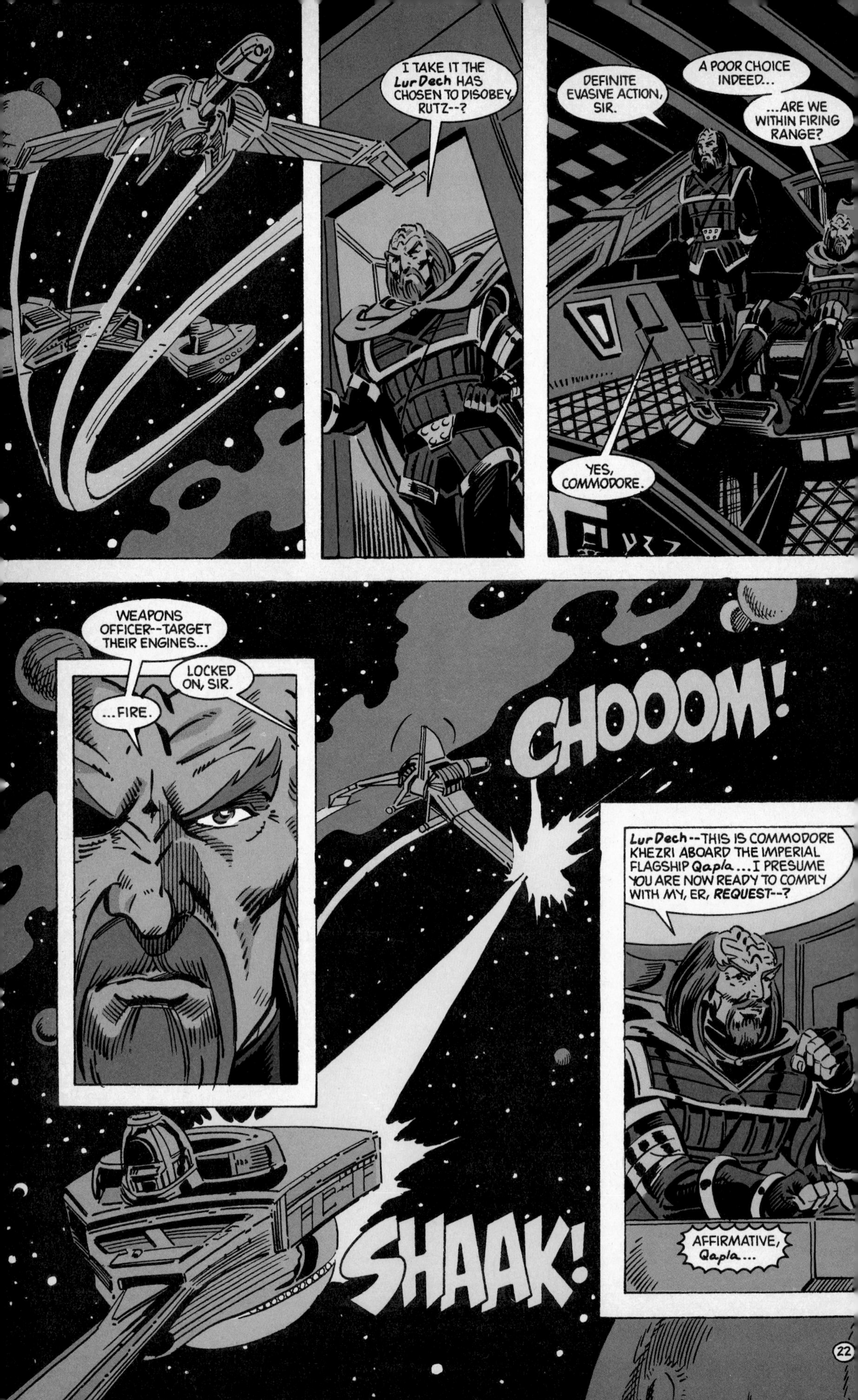
I TAKE IT THE *Lur Dech* HAS CHOSEN TO DISOBEY, RUTZ--?
DEFINITE EVASIVE ACTION, SIR.
A POOR CHOICE INDEED...
...ARE WE WITHIN FIRING RANGE?
YES, COMMODORE.
WEAPONS OFFICER--TARGET THEIR ENGINES...
LOCKED ON, SIR.
...FIRE.
CHOOOM!
SHAAK!
Lur Dech--THIS IS COMMODORE KHEZRI ABOARD THE IMPERIAL FLAGSHIP *Qapla*... I PRESUME YOU ARE NOW READY TO COMPLY WITH MY, ER, *REQUEST*--?
AFFIRMATIVE, *Qapla*...

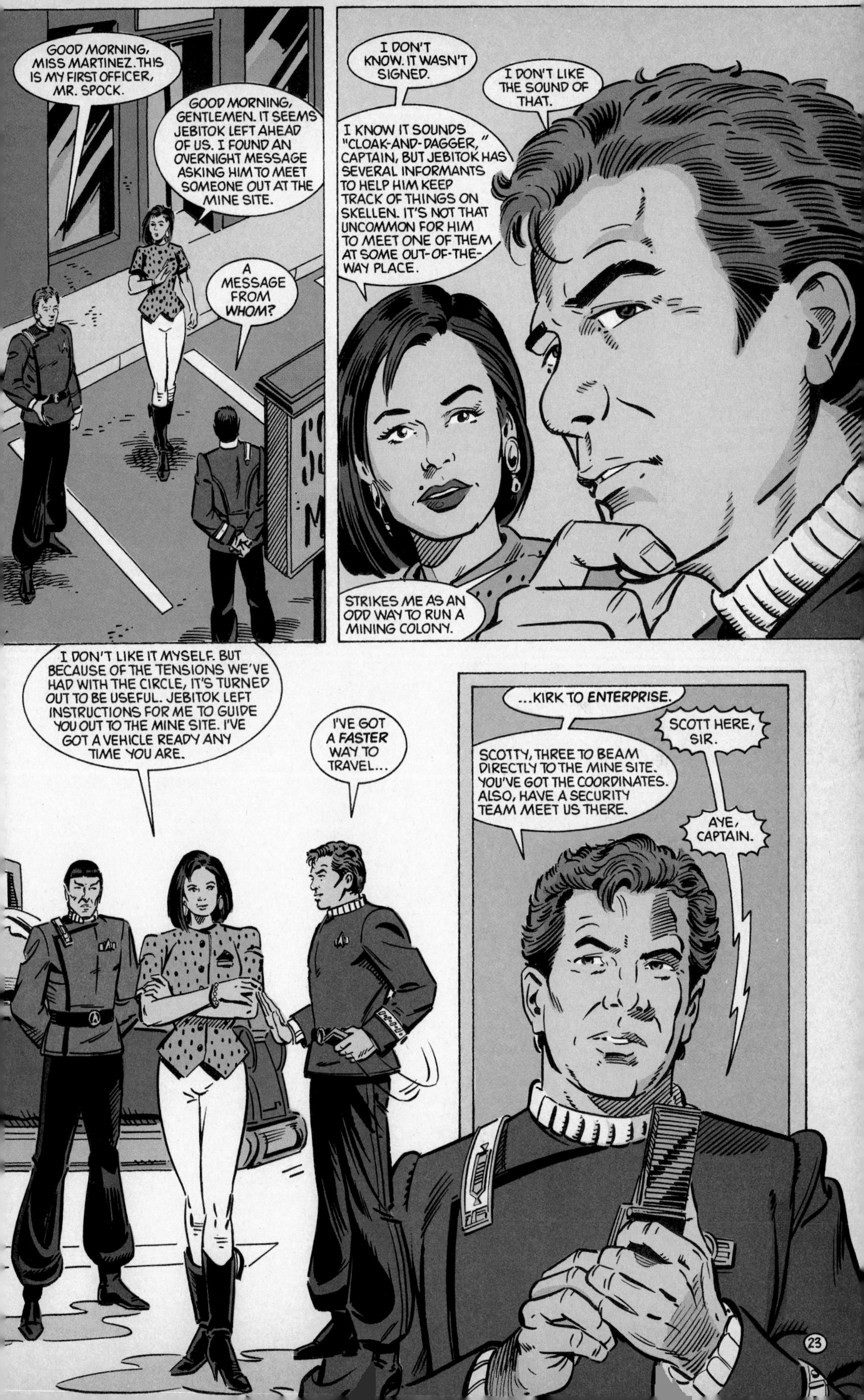
GOOD MORNING, MISS MARTINEZ. THIS IS MY FIRST OFFICER, MR. SPOCK.
GOOD MORNING, GENTLEMEN. IT SEEMS JEBITOK LEFT AHEAD OF US. I FOUND AN OVERNIGHT MESSAGE ASKING HIM TO MEET SOMEONE OUT AT THE MINE SITE.
A MESSAGE FROM WHOM?
I DON'T KNOW. IT WASN'T SIGNED.
I DON'T LIKE THE SOUND OF THAT.
I KNOW IT SOUNDS "CLOAK-AND-DAGGER," CAPTAIN, BUT JEBITOK HAS SEVERAL INFORMANTS TO HELP HIM KEEP TRACK OF THINGS ON SKELLEN. IT'S NOT THAT UNCOMMON FOR HIM TO MEET ONE OF THEM AT SOME OUT-OF-THE-WAY PLACE.
STRIKES ME AS AN ODD WAY TO RUN A MINING COLONY.
I DON'T LIKE IT MYSELF. BUT BECAUSE OF THE TENSIONS WE'VE HAD WITH THE CIRCLE, IT'S TURNED OUT TO BE USEFUL. JEBITOK LEFT INSTRUCTIONS FOR ME TO GUIDE YOU OUT TO THE MINE SITE. I'VE GOT A VEHICLE READY ANY TIME YOU ARE.
I'VE GOT A FASTER WAY TO TRAVEL...
...KIRK TO ENTERPRISE.
SCOTT HERE, SIR.
SCOTTY, THREE TO BEAM DIRECTLY TO THE MINE SITE. YOU'VE GOT THE COORDINATES. ALSO, HAVE A SECURITY TEAM MEET US THERE.
AYE, CAPTAIN.

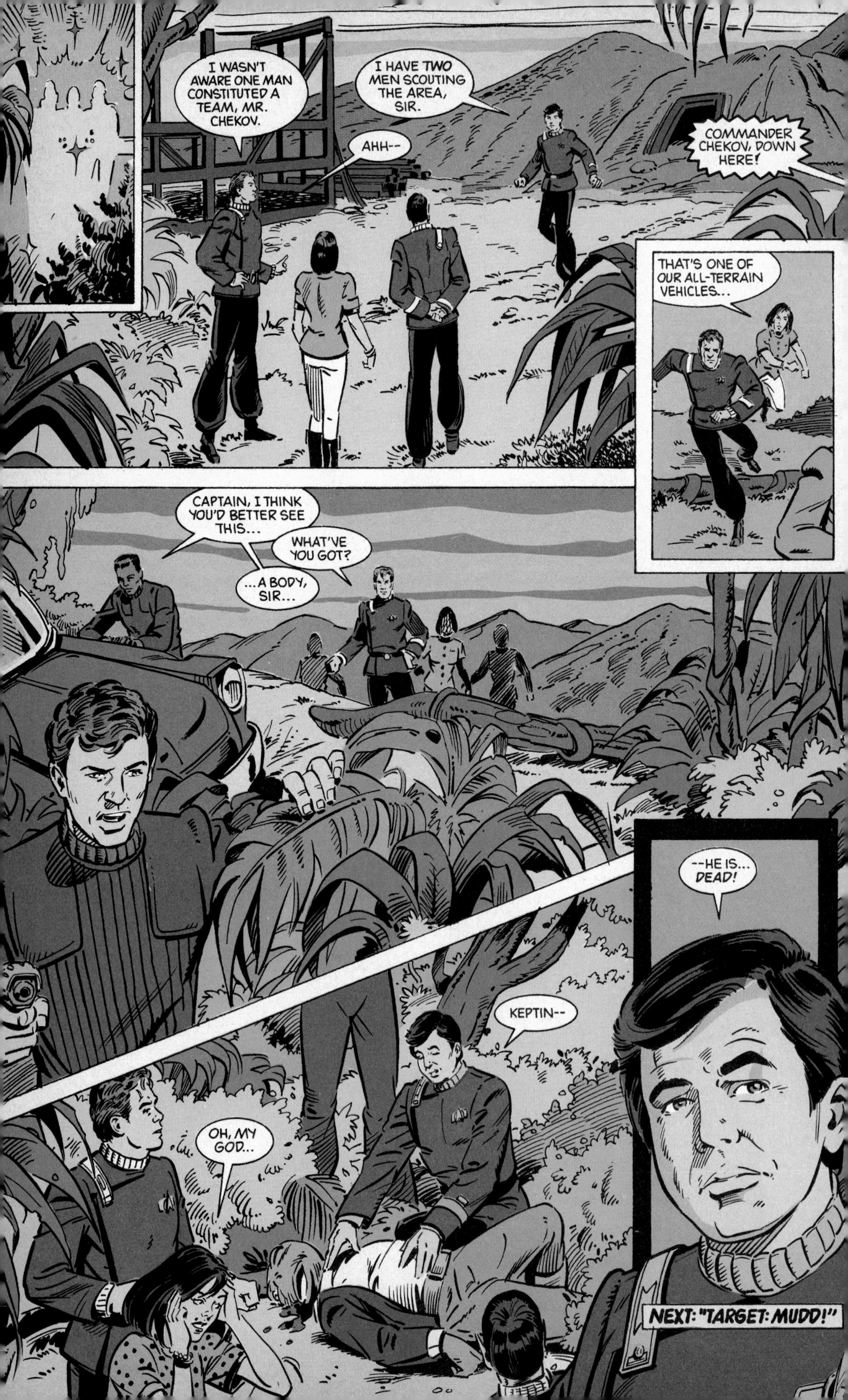
I WASN'T AWARE ONE MAN CONSTITUTED A TEAM, MR. CHEKOV.
I HAVE TWO MEN SCOUTING THE AREA, SIR.
AHH--
COMMANDER CHEKOV, DOWN HERE!
THAT'S ONE OF OUR ALL-TERRAIN VEHICLES...
CAPTAIN, I THINK YOU'D BETTER SEE THIS...
WHAT'VE YOU GOT?
...A BODY, SIR...
KEPTIN--
--HE IS... DEAD!
OH, MY GOD...
NEXT: "TARGET: MUDD!"

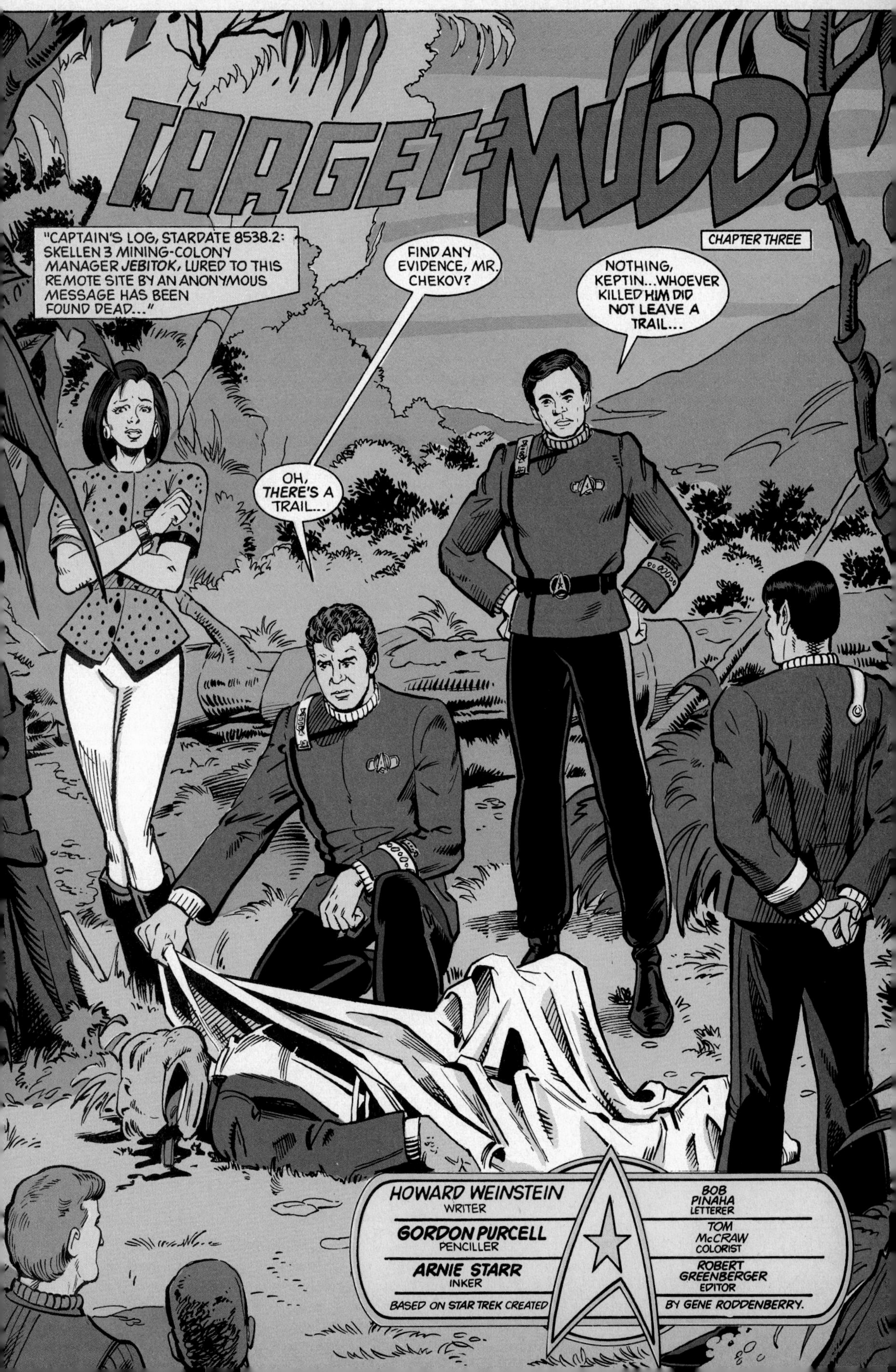
TARGET: MUDD!
CHAPTER THREE
"CAPTAIN'S LOG, STARDATE 8538.2: SKELLEN 3 MINING-COLONY MANAGER JEBITOK, LURED TO THIS REMOTE SITE BY AN ANONYMOUS MESSAGE HAS BEEN FOUND DEAD..."
FIND ANY EVIDENCE, MR. CHEKOV?
NOTHING, KEPTIN...WHOEVER KILLED HIM DID NOT LEAVE A TRAIL...
OH, THERE'S A TRAIL...
HOWARD WEINSTEIN WRITER
GORDON PURCELL PENCILLER
ARNIE STARR INKER
BOB PINAHA LETTERER
TOM McCRAW COLORIST
ROBERT GREENBERGER EDITOR
BASED ON STAR TREK CREATED BY GENE RODDENBERRY.

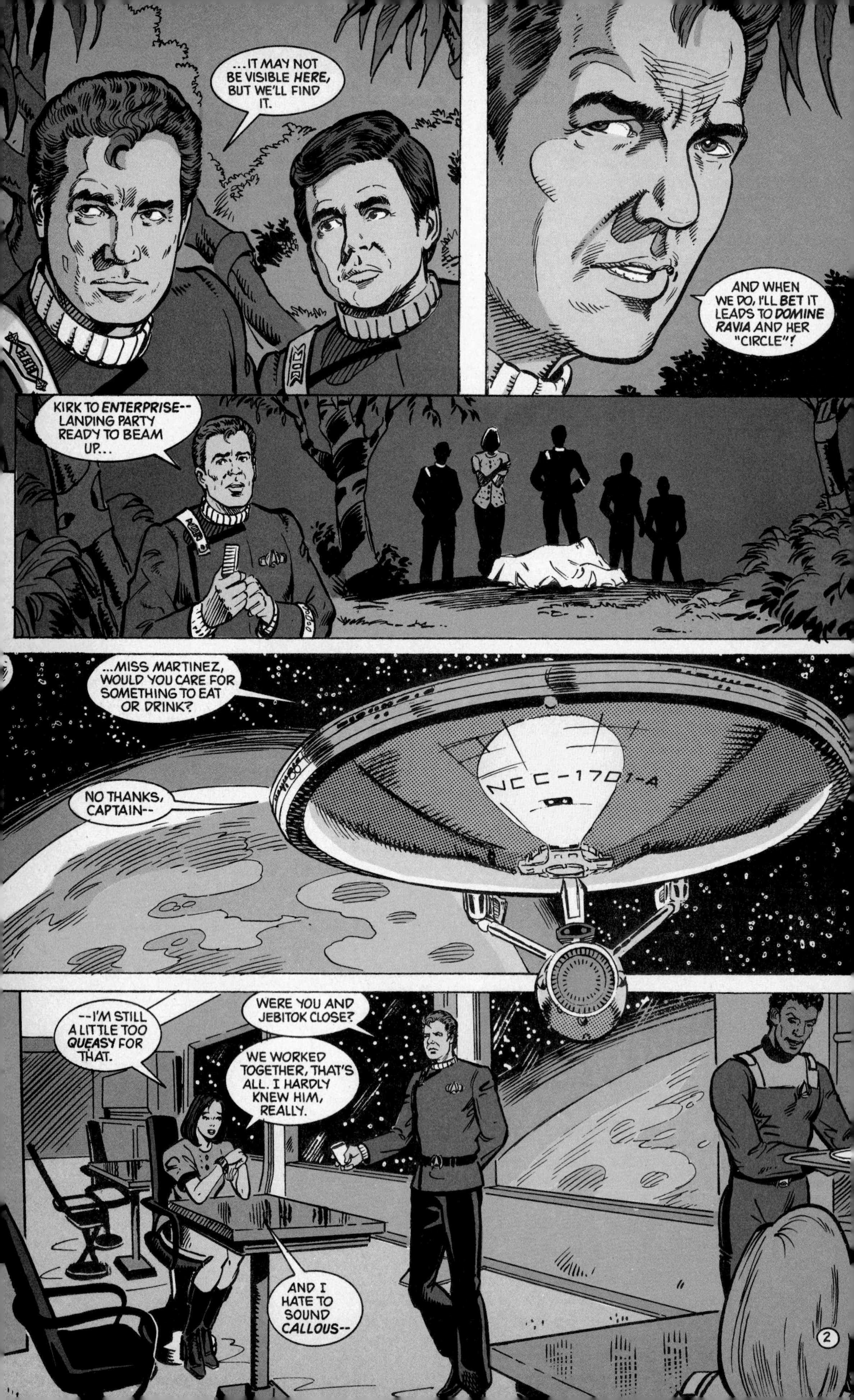
...IT MAY NOT BE VISIBLE HERE, BUT WE'LL FIND IT.
AND WHEN WE DO, I'LL BET IT LEADS TO DOMINE RAVIA AND HER "CIRCLE"!
KIRK TO ENTERPRISE-- LANDING PARTY READY TO BEAM UP...
...MISS MARTINEZ, WOULD YOU CARE FOR SOMETHING TO EAT OR DRINK?
NO THANKS, CAPTAIN--
NCC-1701-A
--I'M STILL A LITTLE TOO QUEASY FOR THAT.
WERE YOU AND JEBITOK CLOSE?
WE WORKED TOGETHER, THAT'S ALL. I HARDLY KNEW HIM, REALLY.
AND I HATE TO SOUND CALLOUS--

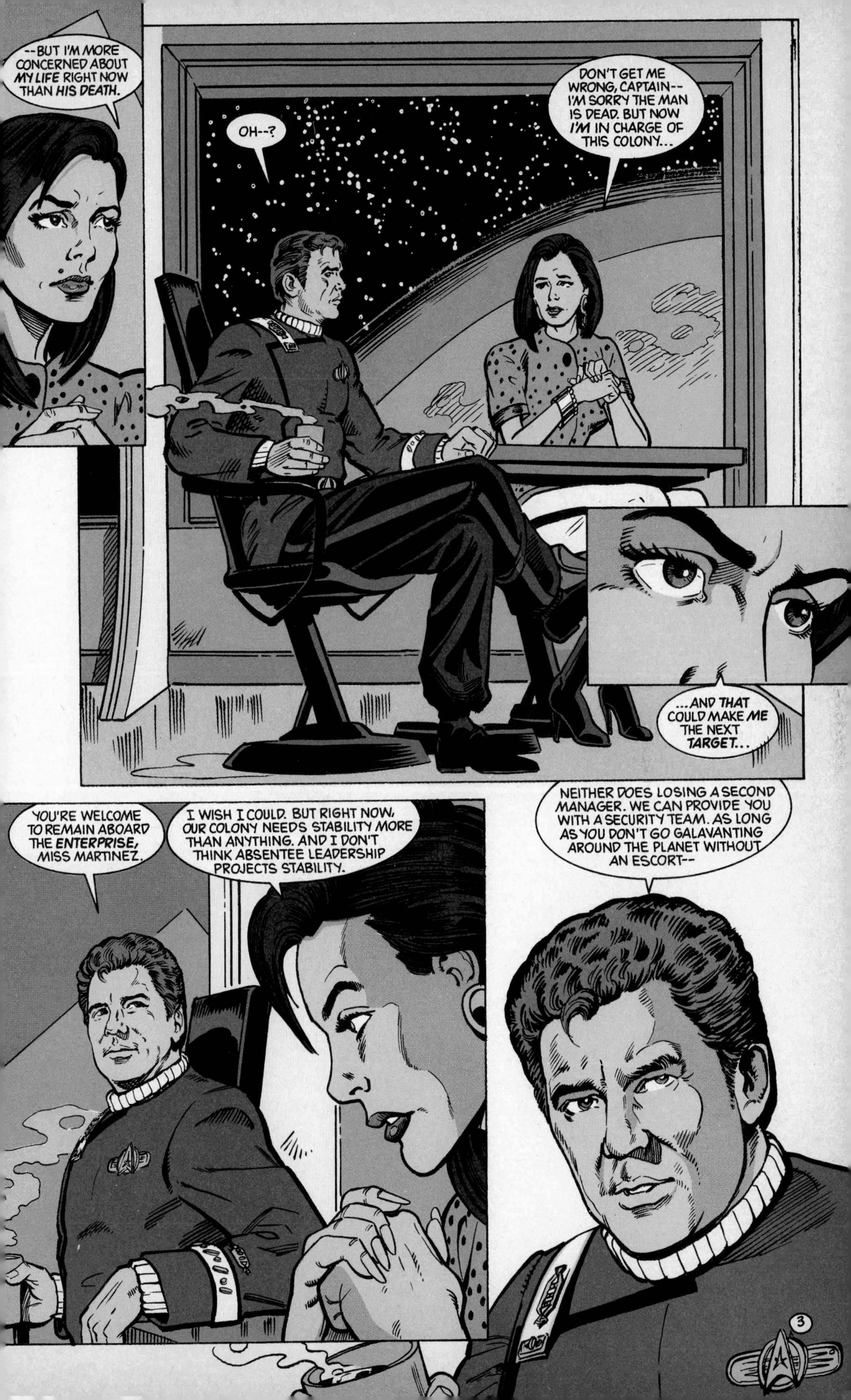
--BUT I'M MORE CONCERNED ABOUT MY LIFE RIGHT NOW THAN HIS DEATH.
OH--?
DON'T GET ME WRONG, CAPTAIN--I'M SORRY THE MAN IS DEAD. BUT NOW I'M IN CHARGE OF THIS COLONY...
...AND THAT COULD MAKE ME THE NEXT TARGET...
YOU'RE WELCOME TO REMAIN ABOARD THE ENTERPRISE, MISS MARTINEZ.
I WISH I COULD. BUT RIGHT NOW, OUR COLONY NEEDS STABILITY MORE THAN ANYTHING. AND I DON'T THINK ABSENTEE LEADERSHIP PROJECTS STABILITY.
NEITHER DOES LOSING A SECOND MANAGER. WE CAN PROVIDE YOU WITH A SECURITY TEAM. AS LONG AS YOU DON'T GO GALAVANTING AROUND THE PLANET WITHOUT AN ESCORT--

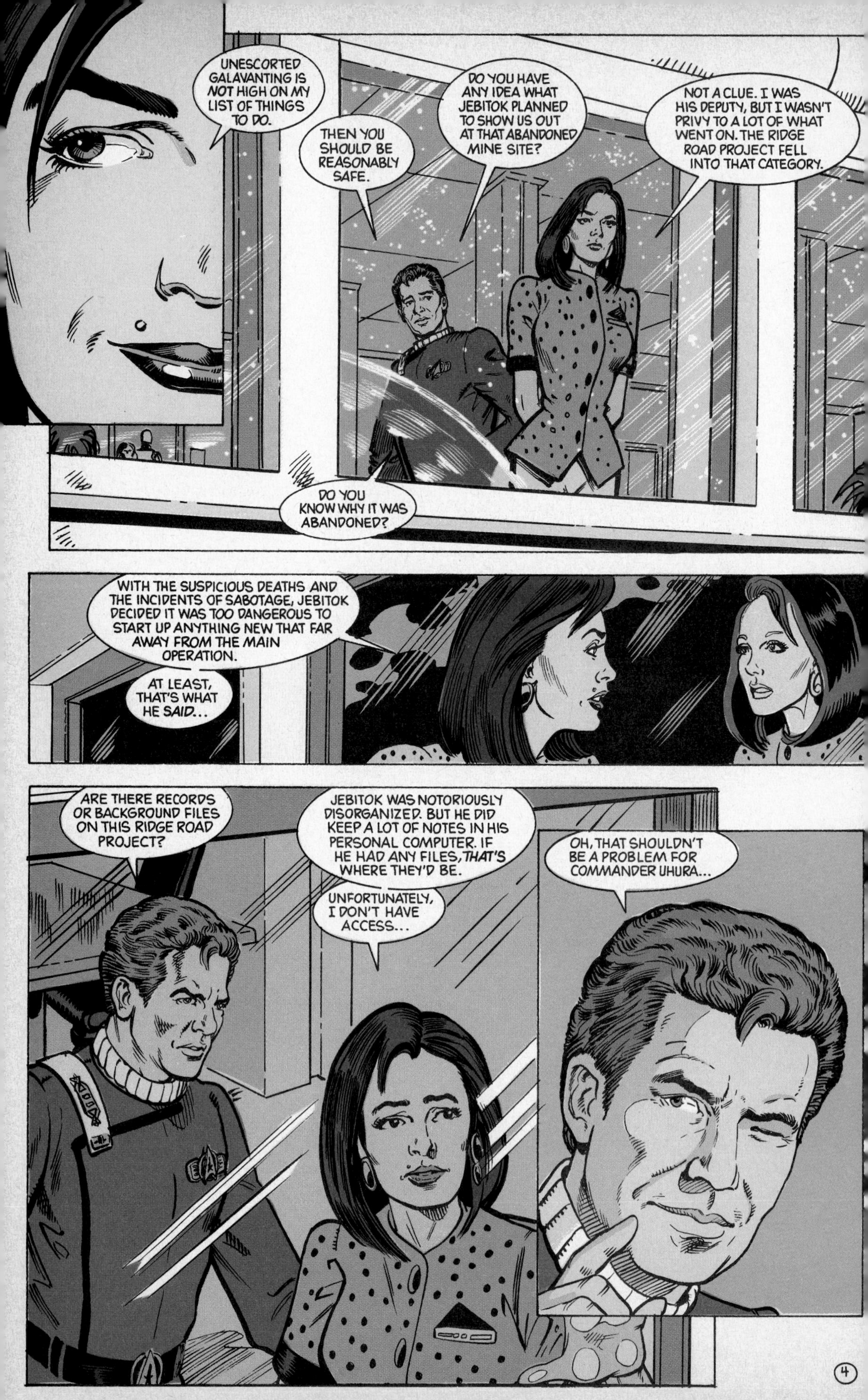
UNESCORTED GALAVANTING IS *NOT* HIGH ON MY LIST OF THINGS TO DO.
THEN YOU SHOULD BE REASONABLY SAFE.
DO YOU HAVE ANY IDEA WHAT JEBITOK PLANNED TO SHOW US OUT AT THAT ABANDONED MINE SITE?
NOT A CLUE. I WAS HIS DEPUTY, BUT I WASN'T PRIVY TO A LOT OF WHAT WENT ON. THE RIDGE ROAD PROJECT FELL INTO THAT CATEGORY.
DO YOU KNOW WHY IT WAS ABANDONED?
WITH THE SUSPICIOUS DEATHS AND THE INCIDENTS OF SABOTAGE, JEBITOK DECIDED IT WAS TOO DANGEROUS TO START UP ANYTHING NEW THAT FAR AWAY FROM THE MAIN OPERATION.
AT LEAST, THAT'S WHAT HE *SAID*...
ARE THERE RECORDS OR BACKGROUND FILES ON THIS RIDGE ROAD PROJECT?
JEBITOK WAS NOTORIOUSLY DISORGANIZED. BUT HE DID KEEP A LOT OF NOTES IN HIS PERSONAL COMPUTER. IF HE HAD ANY FILES, *THAT'S* WHERE THEY'D BE.
UNFORTUNATELY, I DON'T HAVE ACCESS...
OH, THAT SHOULDN'T BE A PROBLEM FOR COMMANDER UHURA...

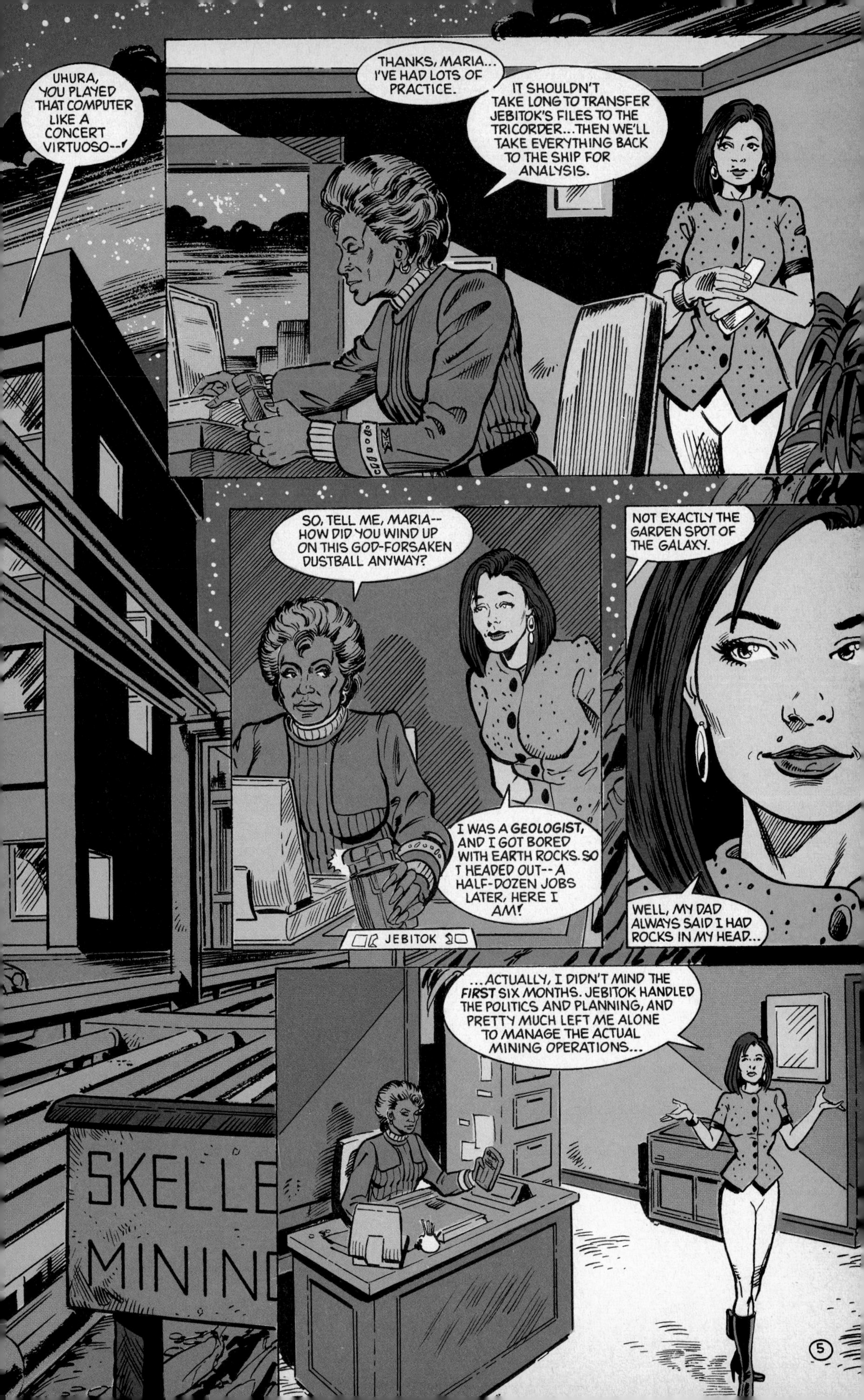

UHURA, YOU PLAYED THAT COMPUTER LIKE A CONCERT VIRTUOSO--!
THANKS, MARIA... I'VE HAD LOTS OF PRACTICE.
IT SHOULDN'T TAKE LONG TO TRANSFER JEBITOK'S FILES TO THE TRICORDER...THEN WE'LL TAKE EVERYTHING BACK TO THE SHIP FOR ANALYSIS.
SO, TELL ME, MARIA-- HOW DID YOU WIND UP ON THIS GOD-FORSAKEN DUSTBALL ANYWAY?
I WAS A GEOLOGIST, AND I GOT BORED WITH EARTH ROCKS. SO I HEADED OUT-- A HALF-DOZEN JOBS LATER, HERE I AM!
JEBITOK
NOT EXACTLY THE GARDEN SPOT OF THE GALAXY.
WELL, MY DAD ALWAYS SAID I HAD ROCKS IN MY HEAD...
...ACTUALLY, I DIDN'T MIND THE FIRST SIX MONTHS. JEBITOK HANDLED THE POLITICS AND PLANNING, AND PRETTY MUCH LEFT ME ALONE TO MANAGE THE ACTUAL MINING OPERATIONS...
SKELLE
MININ

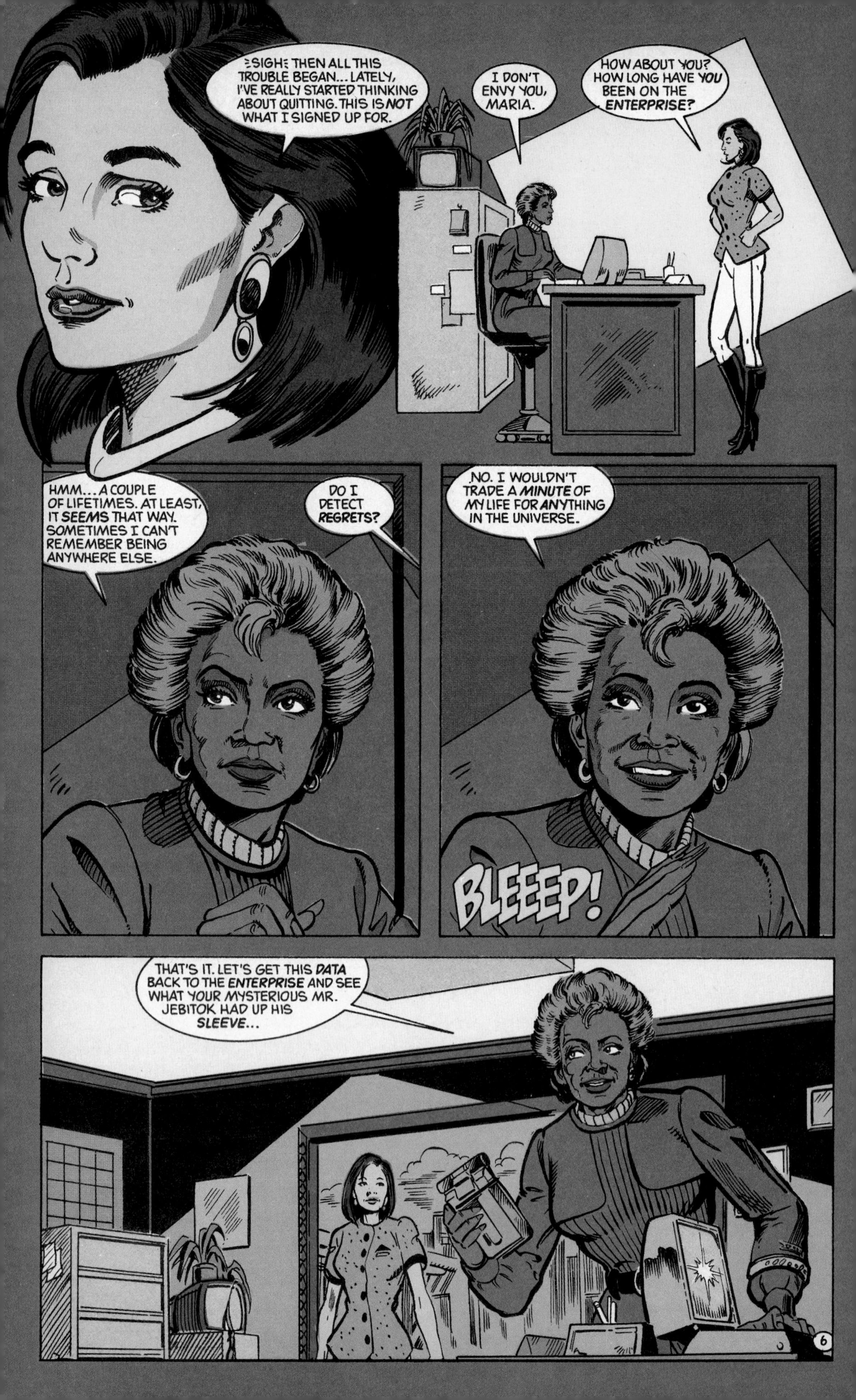

=SIGH= THEN ALL THIS TROUBLE BEGAN... LATELY, I'VE REALLY STARTED THINKING ABOUT QUITTING. THIS IS NOT WHAT I SIGNED UP FOR.
I DON'T ENVY YOU, MARIA.
HOW ABOUT YOU? HOW LONG HAVE YOU BEEN ON THE ENTERPRISE?
HMM... A COUPLE OF LIFETIMES. AT LEAST, IT SEEMS THAT WAY. SOMETIMES I CAN'T REMEMBER BEING ANYWHERE ELSE.
DO I DETECT REGRETS?
NO. I WOULDN'T TRADE A MINUTE OF MY LIFE FOR ANYTHING IN THE UNIVERSE.
BLEEEP!
THAT'S IT. LET'S GET THIS DATA BACK TO THE ENTERPRISE AND SEE WHAT YOUR MYSTERIOUS MR. JEBITOK HAD UP HIS SLEEVE...
6

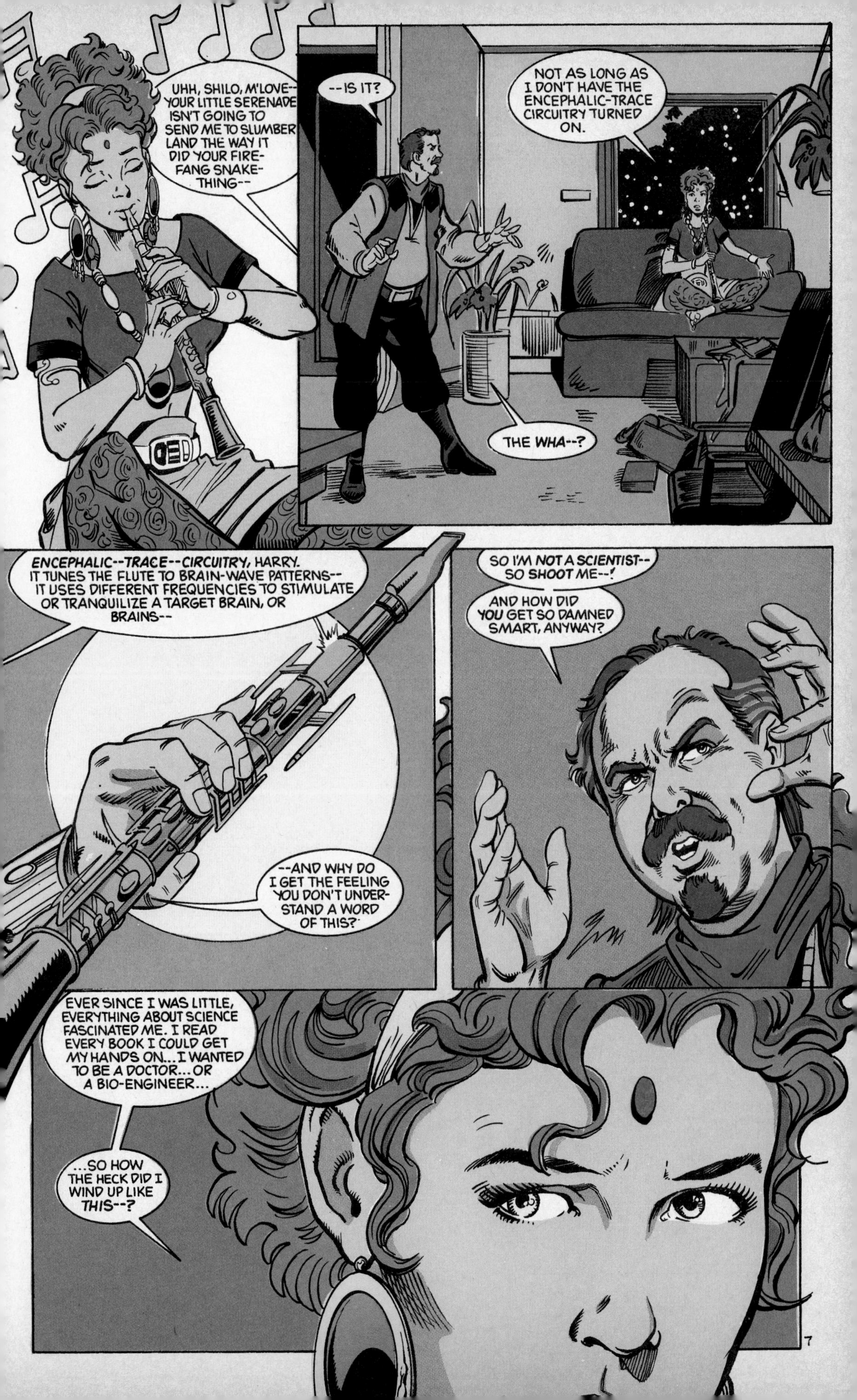

UHH, SHILO, M'LOVE--YOUR LITTLE SERENADE ISN'T GOING TO SEND ME TO SLUMBERLAND THE WAY IT DID YOUR FIRE-FANG SNAKE-THING--
--IS IT?
NOT AS LONG AS I DON'T HAVE THE ENCEPHALIC-TRACE CIRCUITRY TURNED ON.
THE WHA--?
ENCEPHALIC--TRACE--CIRCUITRY, HARRY. IT TUNES THE FLUTE TO BRAIN-WAVE PATTERNS--IT USES DIFFERENT FREQUENCIES TO STIMULATE OR TRANQUILIZE A TARGET BRAIN, OR BRAINS--
--AND WHY DO I GET THE FEELING YOU DON'T UNDERSTAND A WORD OF THIS?
SO I'M NOT A SCIENTIST--SO SHOOT ME--!
AND HOW DID YOU GET SO DAMNED SMART, ANYWAY?
EVER SINCE I WAS LITTLE, EVERYTHING ABOUT SCIENCE FASCINATED ME. I READ EVERY BOOK I COULD GET MY HANDS ON...I WANTED TO BE A DOCTOR...OR A BIO-ENGINEER...
...SO HOW THE HECK DID I WIND UP LIKE THIS--?

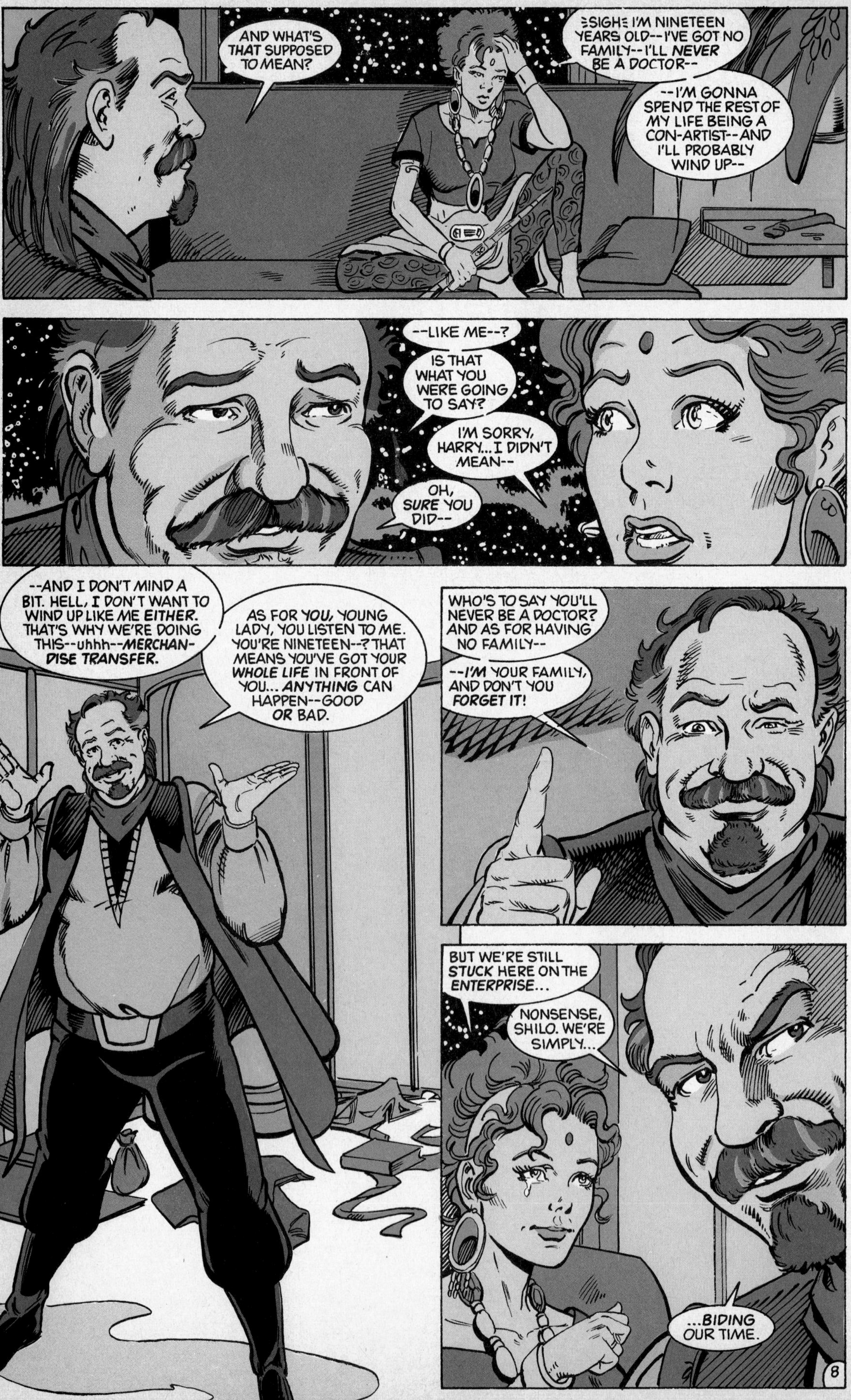
AND WHAT'S THAT SUPPOSED TO MEAN?
≡SIGH≡ I'M NINETEEN YEARS OLD--I'VE GOT NO FAMILY--I'LL NEVER BE A DOCTOR--
--I'M GONNA SPEND THE REST OF MY LIFE BEING A CON-ARTIST--AND I'LL PROBABLY WIND UP--
--LIKE ME--?
IS THAT WHAT YOU WERE GOING TO SAY?
I'M SORRY, HARRY... I DIDN'T MEAN--
OH, SURE YOU DID--
--AND I DON'T MIND A BIT. HELL, I DON'T WANT TO WIND UP LIKE ME EITHER. THAT'S WHY WE'RE DOING THIS--uhhh--MERCHANDISE TRANSFER.
AS FOR YOU, YOUNG LADY, YOU LISTEN TO ME. YOU'RE NINETEEN--? THAT MEANS YOU'VE GOT YOUR WHOLE LIFE IN FRONT OF YOU... ANYTHING CAN HAPPEN--GOOD OR BAD.
WHO'S TO SAY YOU'LL NEVER BE A DOCTOR? AND AS FOR HAVING NO FAMILY--
--I'M YOUR FAMILY, AND DON'T YOU FORGET IT!
BUT WE'RE STILL STUCK HERE ON THE ENTERPRISE...
NONSENSE, SHILO. WE'RE SIMPLY...
...BIDING OUR TIME.

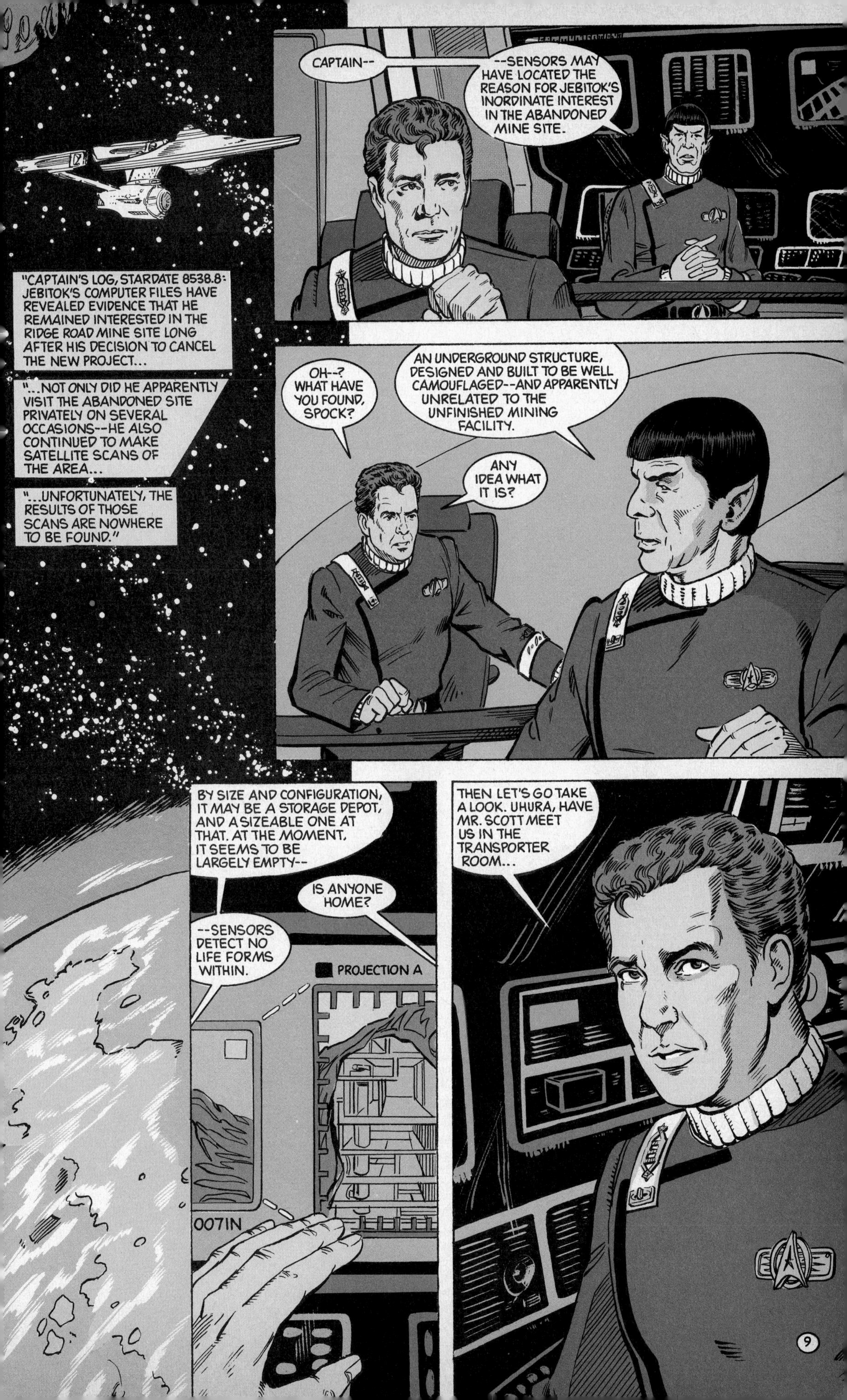
CAPTAIN--
--SENSORS MAY HAVE LOCATED THE REASON FOR JEBITOK'S INORDINATE INTEREST IN THE ABANDONED MINE SITE.
"CAPTAIN'S LOG, STARDATE 8538.8: JEBITOK'S COMPUTER FILES HAVE REVEALED EVIDENCE THAT HE REMAINED INTERESTED IN THE RIDGE ROAD MINE SITE LONG AFTER HIS DECISION TO CANCEL THE NEW PROJECT...
"...NOT ONLY DID HE APPARENTLY VISIT THE ABANDONED SITE PRIVATELY ON SEVERAL OCCASIONS--HE ALSO CONTINUED TO MAKE SATELLITE SCANS OF THE AREA...
"...UNFORTUNATELY, THE RESULTS OF THOSE SCANS ARE NOWHERE TO BE FOUND."
OH--? WHAT HAVE YOU FOUND, SPOCK?
AN UNDERGROUND STRUCTURE, DESIGNED AND BUILT TO BE WELL CAMOUFLAGED--AND APPARENTLY UNRELATED TO THE UNFINISHED MINING FACILITY.
ANY IDEA WHAT IT IS?
BY SIZE AND CONFIGURATION, IT MAY BE A STORAGE DEPOT, AND A SIZEABLE ONE AT THAT. AT THE MOMENT, IT SEEMS TO BE LARGELY EMPTY--
IS ANYONE HOME?
--SENSORS DETECT NO LIFE FORMS WITHIN.
PROJECTION A
007IN
THEN LET'S GO TAKE A LOOK. UHURA, HAVE MR. SCOTT MEET US IN THE TRANSPORTER ROOM...
9

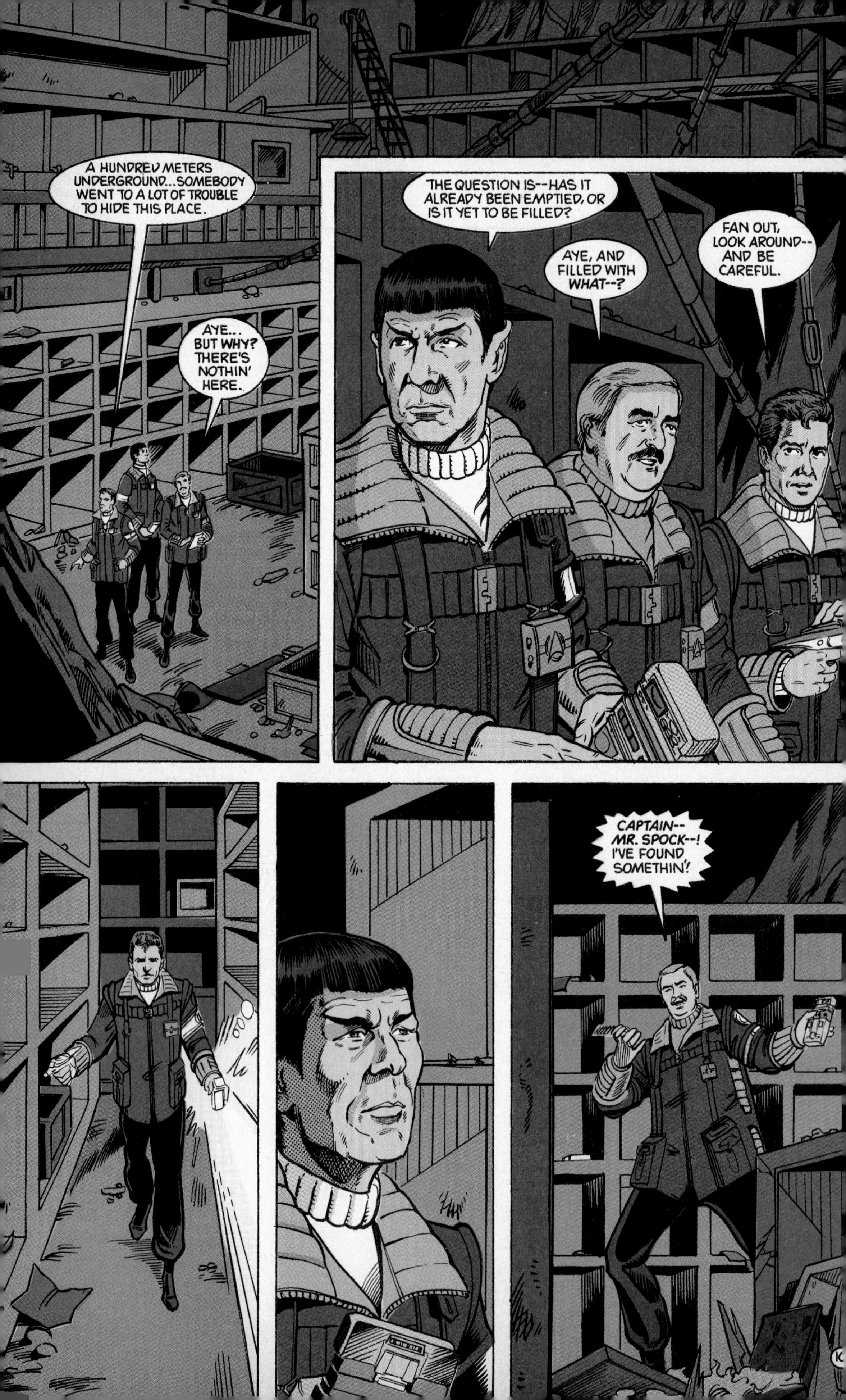
A HUNDRED METERS UNDERGROUND...SOMEBODY WENT TO A LOT OF TROUBLE TO HIDE THIS PLACE.
AYE... BUT WHY? THERE'S NOTHIN' HERE.
THE QUESTION IS--HAS IT ALREADY BEEN EMPTIED, OR IS IT YET TO BE FILLED?
AYE, AND FILLED WITH WHAT--?
FAN OUT, LOOK AROUND-- AND BE CAREFUL.
CAPTAIN-- MR. SPOCK--! I'VE FOUND SOMETHIN'!

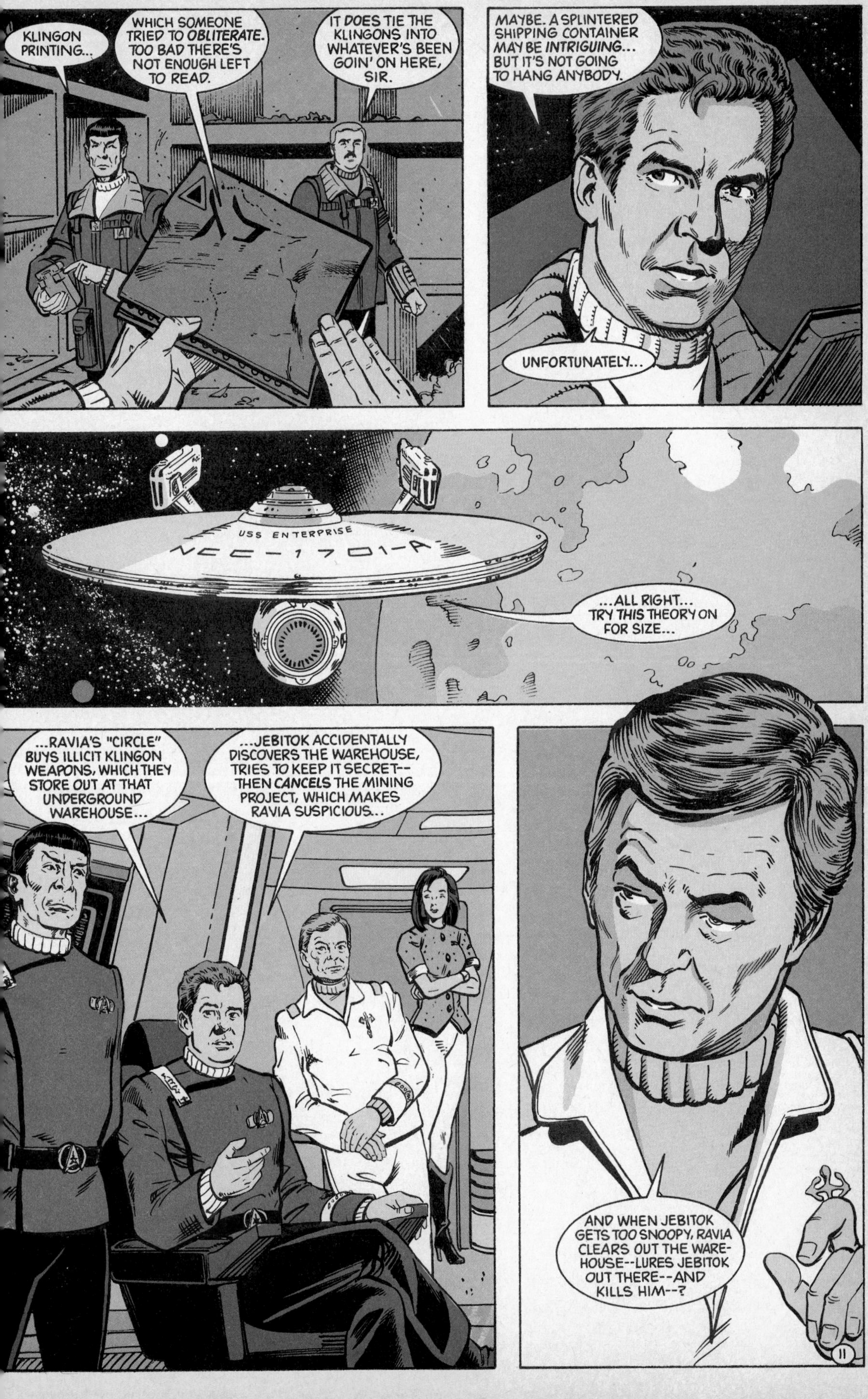
KLINGON PRINTING...
WHICH SOMEONE TRIED TO OBLITERATE. TOO BAD THERE'S NOT ENOUGH LEFT TO READ.
IT DOES TIE THE KLINGONS INTO WHATEVER'S BEEN GOIN' ON HERE, SIR.
MAYBE. A SPLINTERED SHIPPING CONTAINER MAY BE INTRIGUING... BUT IT'S NOT GOING TO HANG ANYBODY.
UNFORTUNATELY...
USS ENTERPRISE
NCC-1701-A
...ALL RIGHT... TRY THIS THEORY ON FOR SIZE...
...RAVIA'S "CIRCLE" BUYS ILLICIT KLINGON WEAPONS, WHICH THEY STORE OUT AT THAT UNDERGROUND WAREHOUSE...
...JEBITOK ACCIDENTALLY DISCOVERS THE WAREHOUSE, TRIES TO KEEP IT SECRET-- THEN CANCELS THE MINING PROJECT, WHICH MAKES RAVIA SUSPICIOUS...
AND WHEN JEBITOK GETS TOO SNOOPY, RAVIA CLEARS OUT THE WARE-HOUSE--LURES JEBITOK OUT THERE--AND KILLS HIM--?

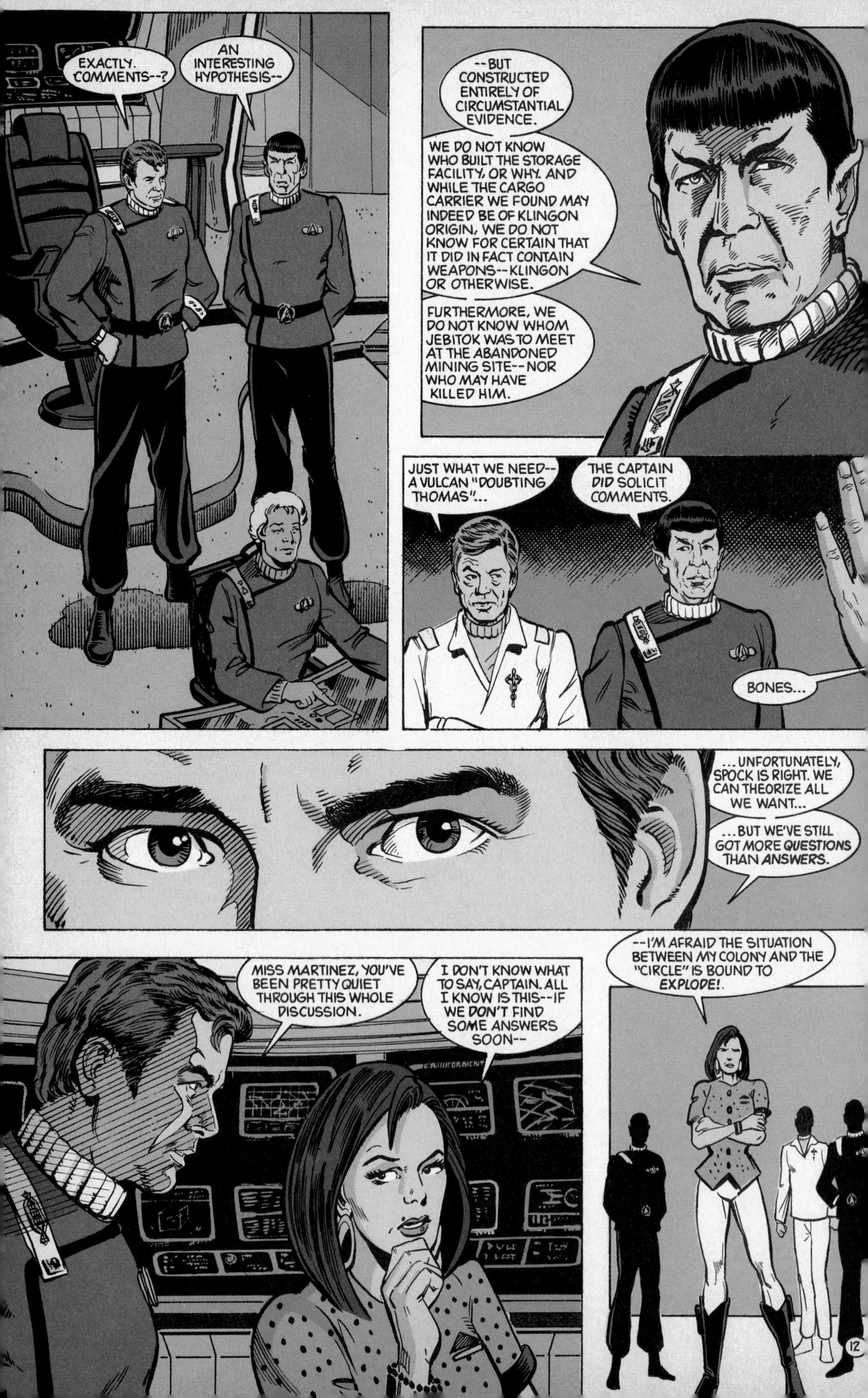
EXACTLY. COMMENTS--?
AN INTERESTING HYPOTHESIS--
--BUT CONSTRUCTED ENTIRELY OF CIRCUMSTANTIAL EVIDENCE.
WE DO NOT KNOW WHO BUILT THE STORAGE FACILITY, OR WHY. AND WHILE THE CARGO CARRIER WE FOUND MAY INDEED BE OF KLINGON ORIGIN, WE DO NOT KNOW FOR CERTAIN THAT IT DID IN FACT CONTAIN WEAPONS--KLINGON OR OTHERWISE.
FURTHERMORE, WE DO NOT KNOW WHOM JEBITOK WAS TO MEET AT THE ABANDONED MINING SITE--NOR WHO MAY HAVE KILLED HIM.
JUST WHAT WE NEED--A VULCAN "DOUBTING THOMAS"...
THE CAPTAIN DID SOLICIT COMMENTS.
BONES...
...UNFORTUNATELY, SPOCK IS RIGHT. WE CAN THEORIZE ALL WE WANT...
...BUT WE'VE STILL GOT MORE QUESTIONS THAN ANSWERS.
MISS MARTINEZ, YOU'VE BEEN PRETTY QUIET THROUGH THIS WHOLE DISCUSSION.
I DON'T KNOW WHAT TO SAY, CAPTAIN. ALL I KNOW IS THIS--IF WE DON'T FIND SOME ANSWERS SOON--
--I'M AFRAID THE SITUATION BETWEEN MY COLONY AND THE "CIRCLE" IS BOUND TO EXPLODE!
12

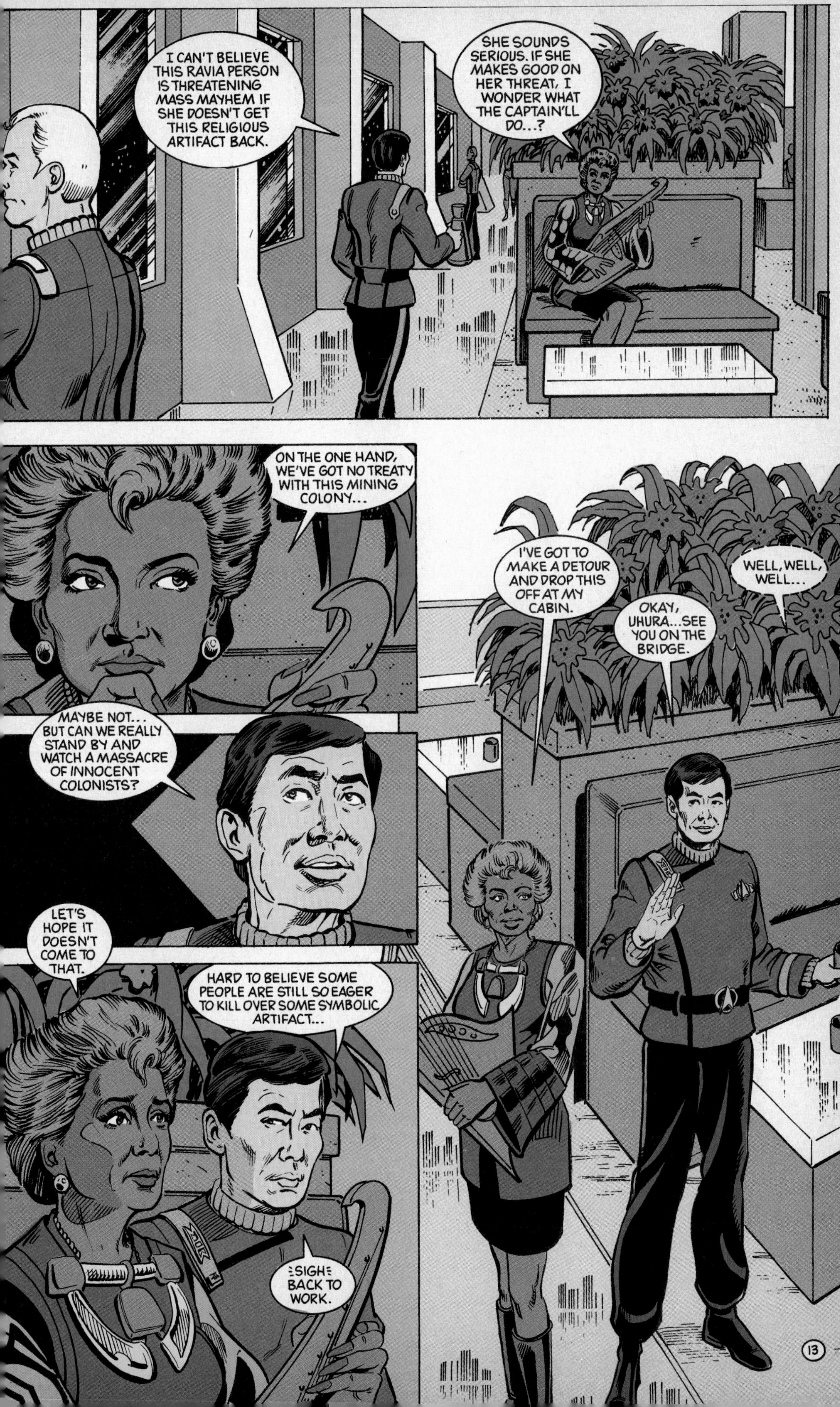

I CAN'T BELIEVE THIS RAVIA PERSON IS THREATENING MASS MAYHEM IF SHE DOESN'T GET THIS RELIGIOUS ARTIFACT BACK.
SHE SOUNDS SERIOUS. IF SHE MAKES GOOD ON HER THREAT, I WONDER WHAT THE CAPTAIN'LL DO...?
ON THE ONE HAND, WE'VE GOT NO TREATY WITH THIS MINING COLONY...
MAYBE NOT... BUT CAN WE REALLY STAND BY AND WATCH A MASSACRE OF INNOCENT COLONISTS?
LET'S HOPE IT DOESN'T COME TO THAT.
HARD TO BELIEVE SOME PEOPLE ARE STILL SO EAGER TO KILL OVER SOME SYMBOLIC ARTIFACT...
=SIGH= BACK TO WORK.
I'VE GOT TO MAKE A DETOUR AND DROP THIS OFF AT MY CABIN.
OKAY, UHURA...SEE YOU ON THE BRIDGE.
WELL, WELL, WELL...

...DOMINE RAVIA SEEMS WILLING TO MOVE HEAVEN AND EARTH TO RETRIEVE THIS JAHEELAH.

HMMMM...

I DON'T LIKE THE LOOK ON YOUR FACE, HARRY...

HEH-HEH-HEH... PERHAPS A CHANGE IN PLAN MIGHT BE IN ORDER.

HUH--?

IF RAVIA CAN BEAT THE SALLA'S OFFER--

--WHY NOT SELL THIS BLOODY JAHEELAH BACK TO HER INSTEAD--?

I DON'T LIKE IT. A DEAL'S A DEAL.

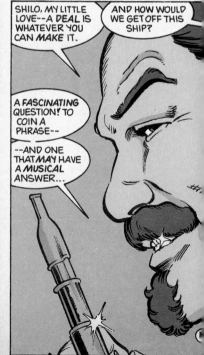

SHILO, MY LITTLE LOVE--A DEAL IS WHATEVER YOU CAN MAKE IT.

AND HOW WOULD WE GET OFF THIS SHIP?

A FASCINATING QUESTION! TO COIN A PHRASE--

--AND ONE THAT MAY HAVE A MUSICAL ANSWER...

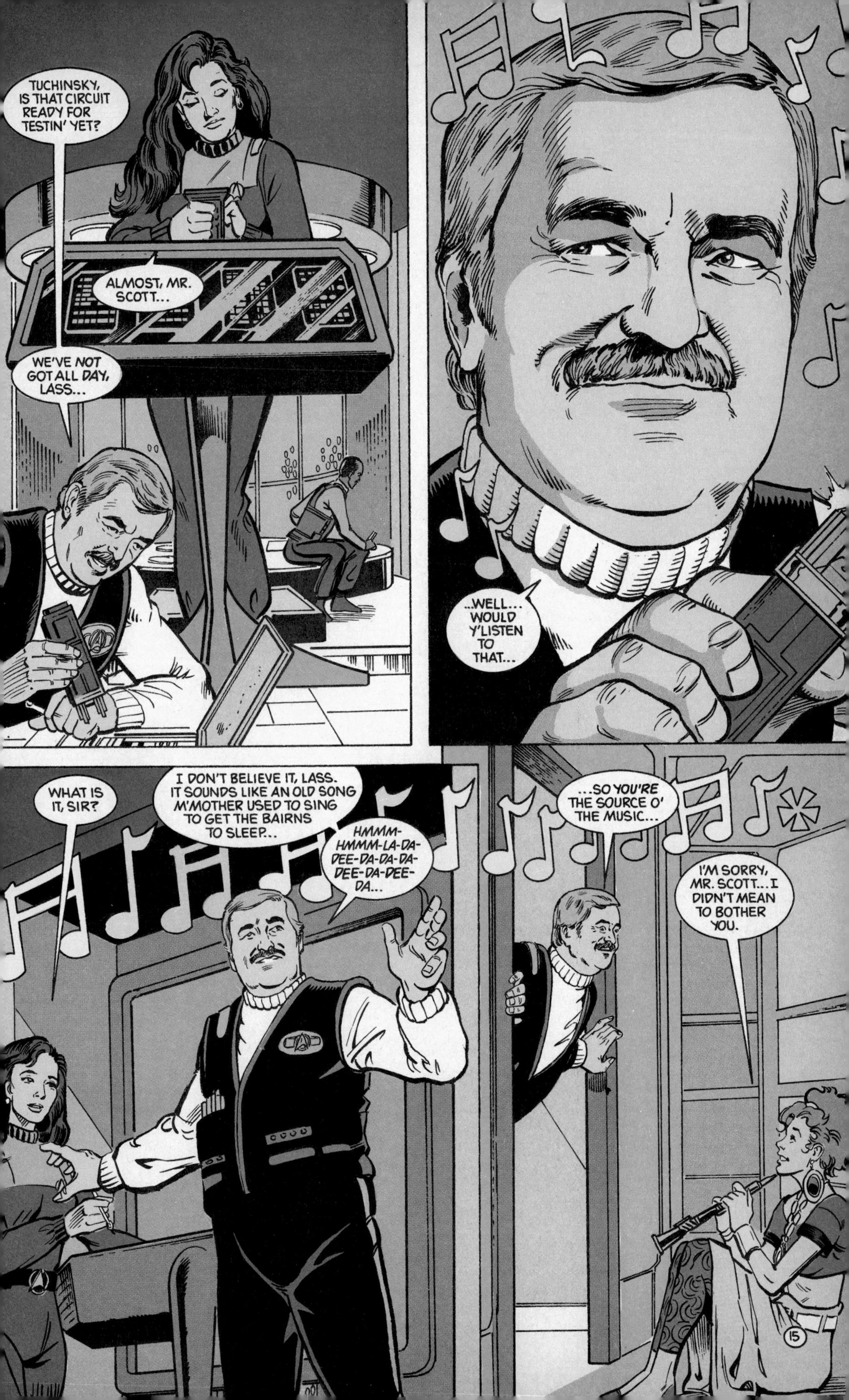
TUCHINSKY, IS THAT CIRCUIT READY FOR TESTIN' YET?
ALMOST, MR. SCOTT...
WE'VE NOT GOT ALL DAY, LASS...
...WELL... WOULD Y'LISTEN TO THAT...
WHAT IS IT, SIR?
I DON'T BELIEVE IT, LASS. IT SOUNDS LIKE AN OLD SONG M'MOTHER USED TO SING TO GET THE BAIRNS TO SLEEP...
HMMM-HMMM-LA-DA-DEE-DA-DA-DA-DEE-DA-DEE-DA...
...SO YOU'RE THE SOURCE O' THE MUSIC...
I'M SORRY, MR. SCOTT... I DIDN'T MEAN TO BOTHER YOU.
15

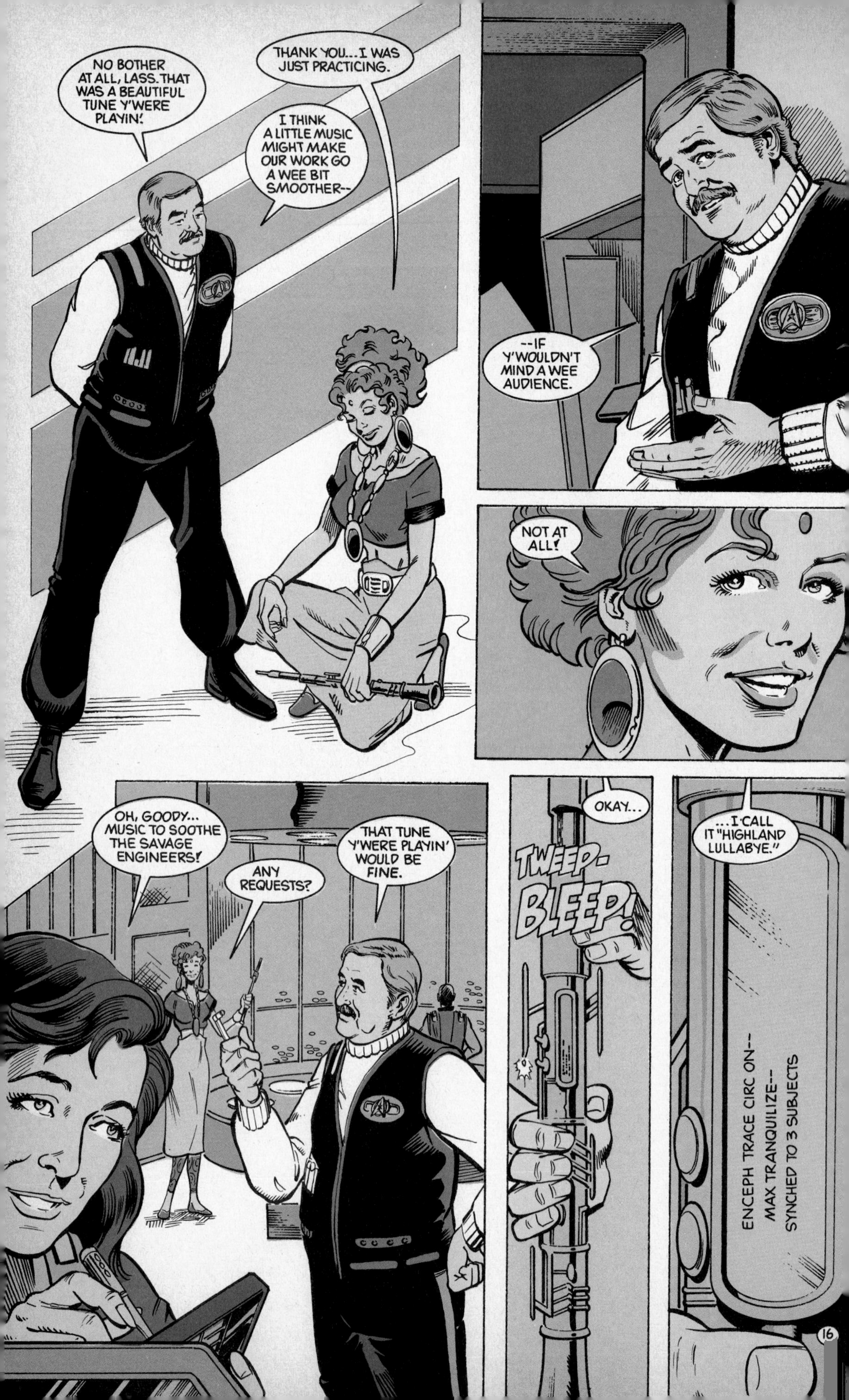
NO BOTHER AT ALL, LASS. THAT WAS A BEAUTIFUL TUNE Y'WERE PLAYIN'.
THANK YOU... I WAS JUST PRACTICING.
I THINK A LITTLE MUSIC MIGHT MAKE OUR WORK GO A WEE BIT SMOOTHER--
--IF Y'WOULDN'T MIND A WEE AUDIENCE.
NOT AT ALL!
OH, GOODY... MUSIC TO SOOTHE THE SAVAGE ENGINEERS!
ANY REQUESTS?
THAT TUNE Y'WERE PLAYIN' WOULD BE FINE.
OKAY...
TWEEP-BLEEP!
...I CALL IT "HIGHLAND LULLABYE."
ENCEPH TRACE CIRC ON--
MAX TRANQUILIZE--
SYNCHED TO 3 SUBJECTS

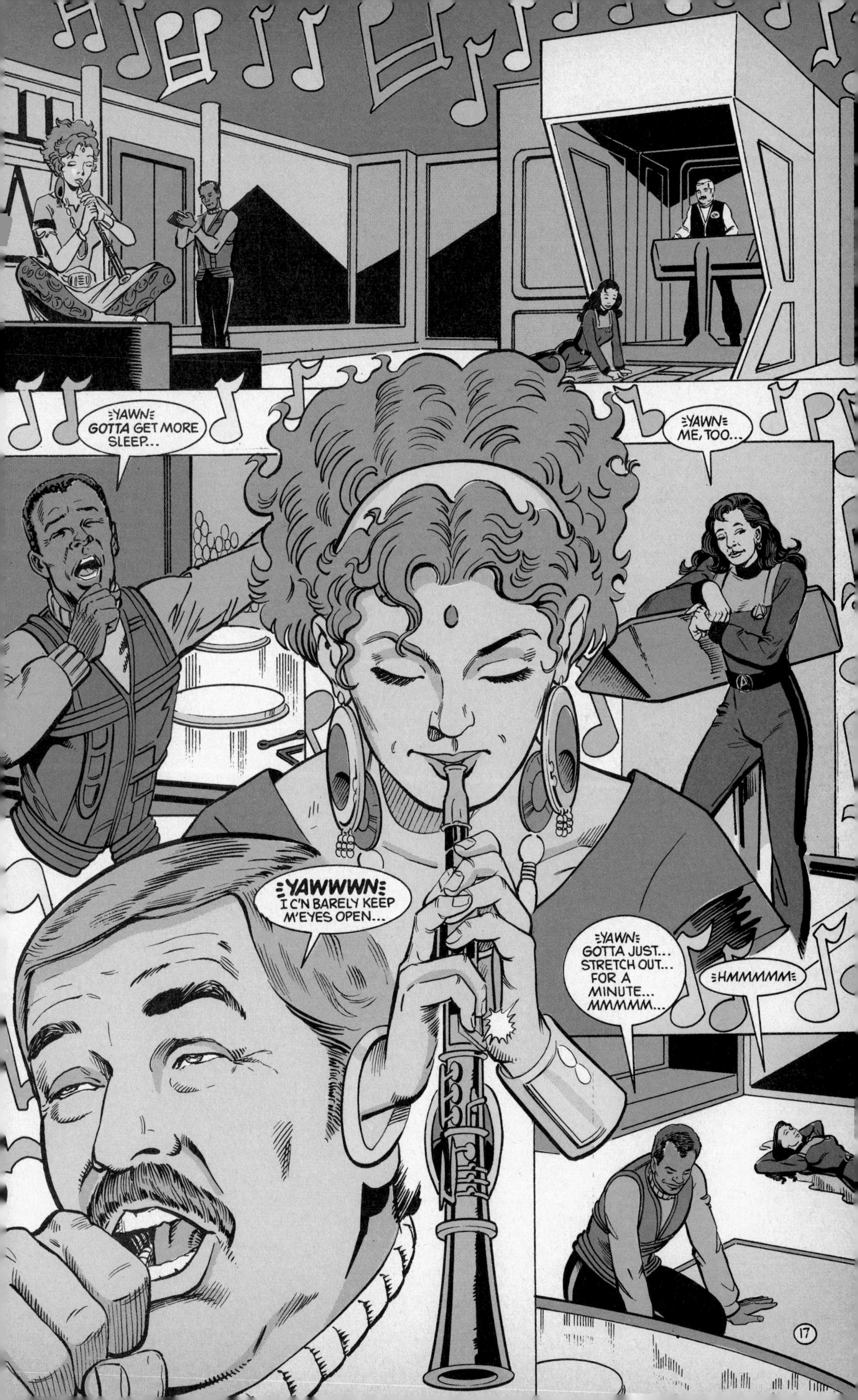

YAWN
GOTTA GET MORE SLEEP...
YAWN
ME, TOO...
YAWWWN
I C'N BARELY KEEP M'EYES OPEN...
YAWN
GOTTA JUST... STRETCH OUT... FOR A MINUTE... MMMMM...
HMMMMM

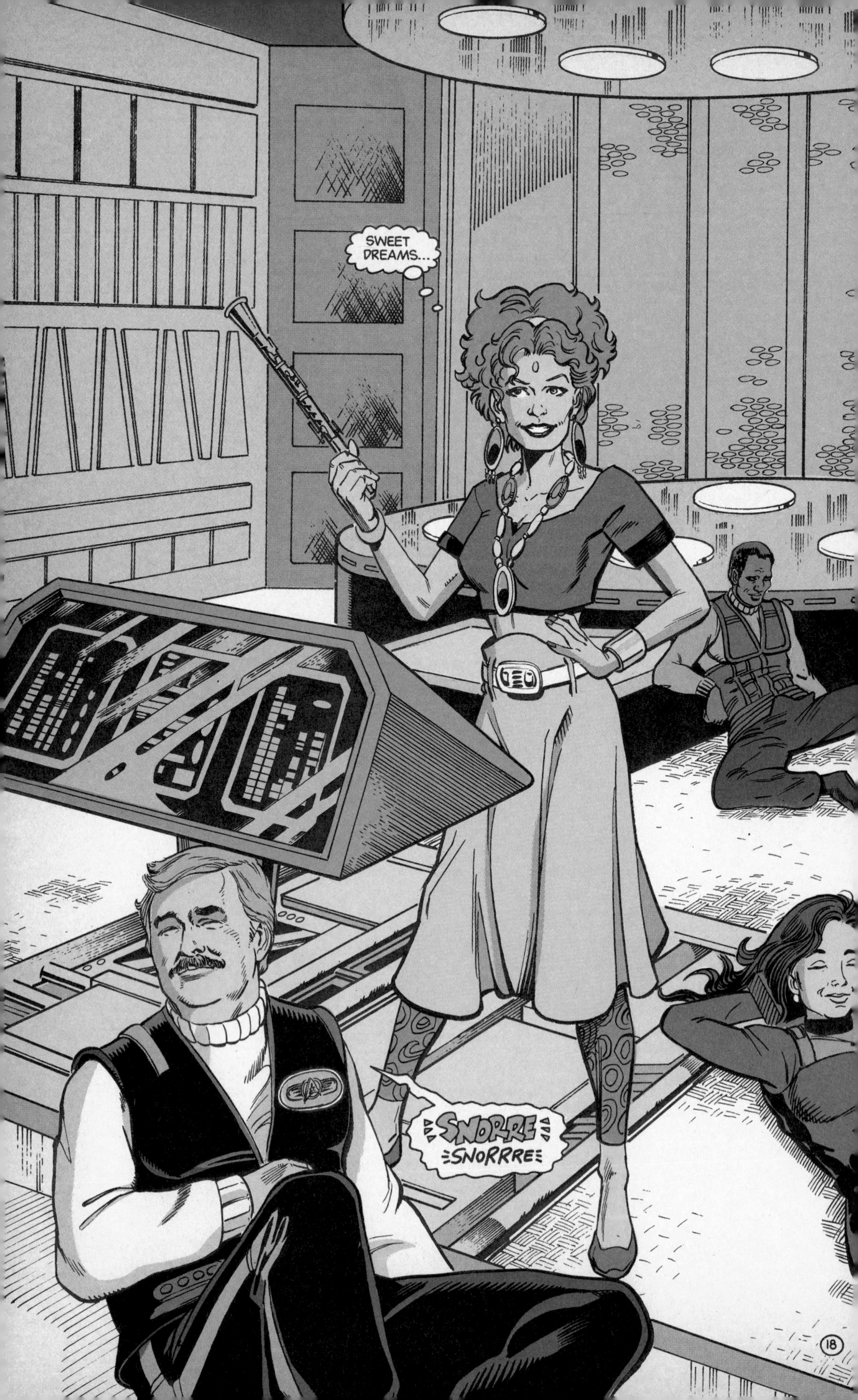
SWEET DREAMS...
SNORRE
SNORRRE

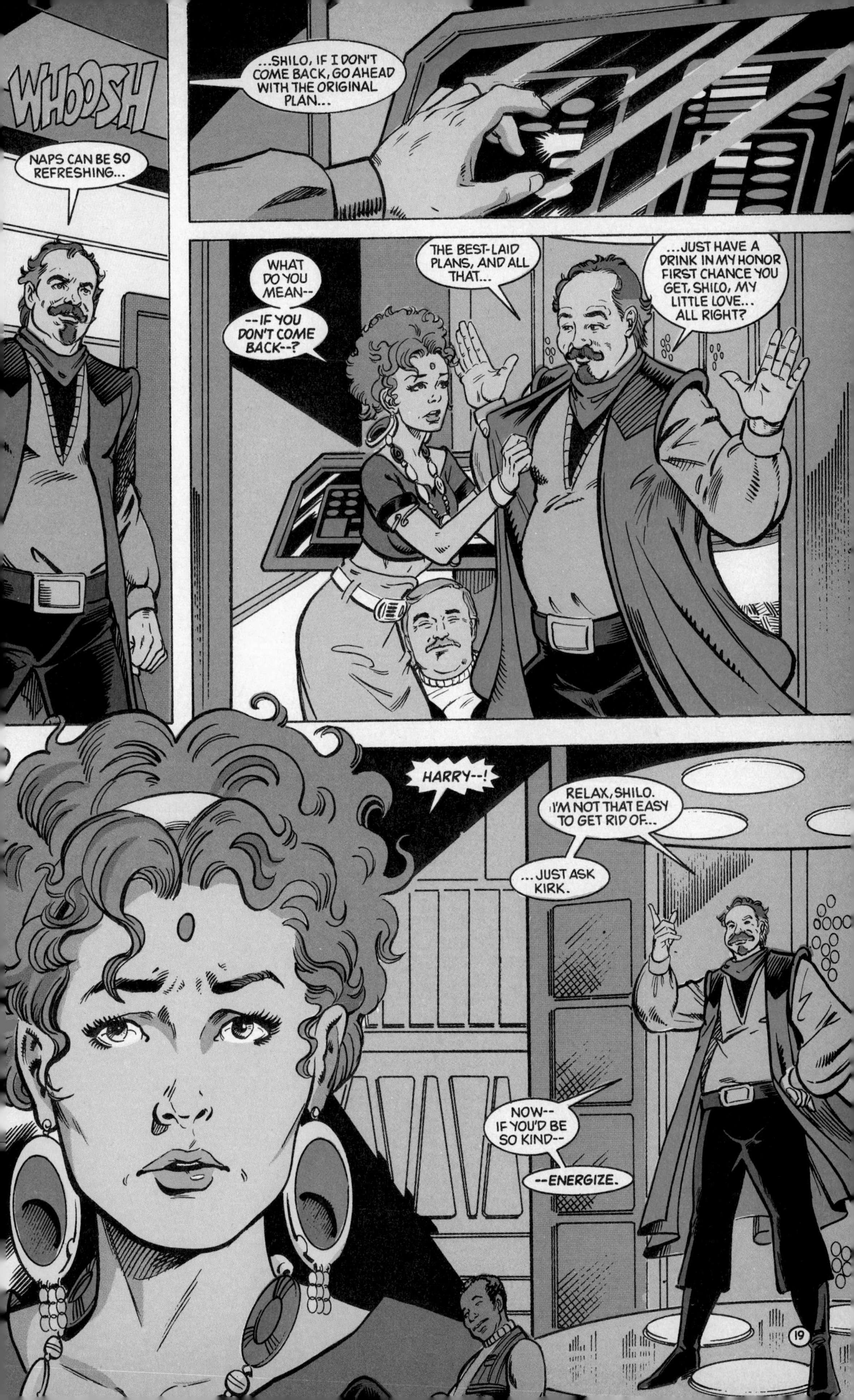
WHOOSH
NAPS CAN BE SO REFRESHING...
...SHILO, IF I DON'T COME BACK, GO AHEAD WITH THE ORIGINAL PLAN...
WHAT DO YOU MEAN--
--IF YOU DON'T COME BACK--?
THE BEST-LAID PLANS, AND ALL THAT...
...JUST HAVE A DRINK IN MY HONOR FIRST CHANCE YOU GET, SHILO, MY LITTLE LOVE... ALL RIGHT?
HARRY--!
RELAX, SHILO. I'M NOT THAT EASY TO GET RID OF...
...JUST ASK KIRK.
NOW-- IF YOU'D BE SO KIND--
--ENERGIZE.
19

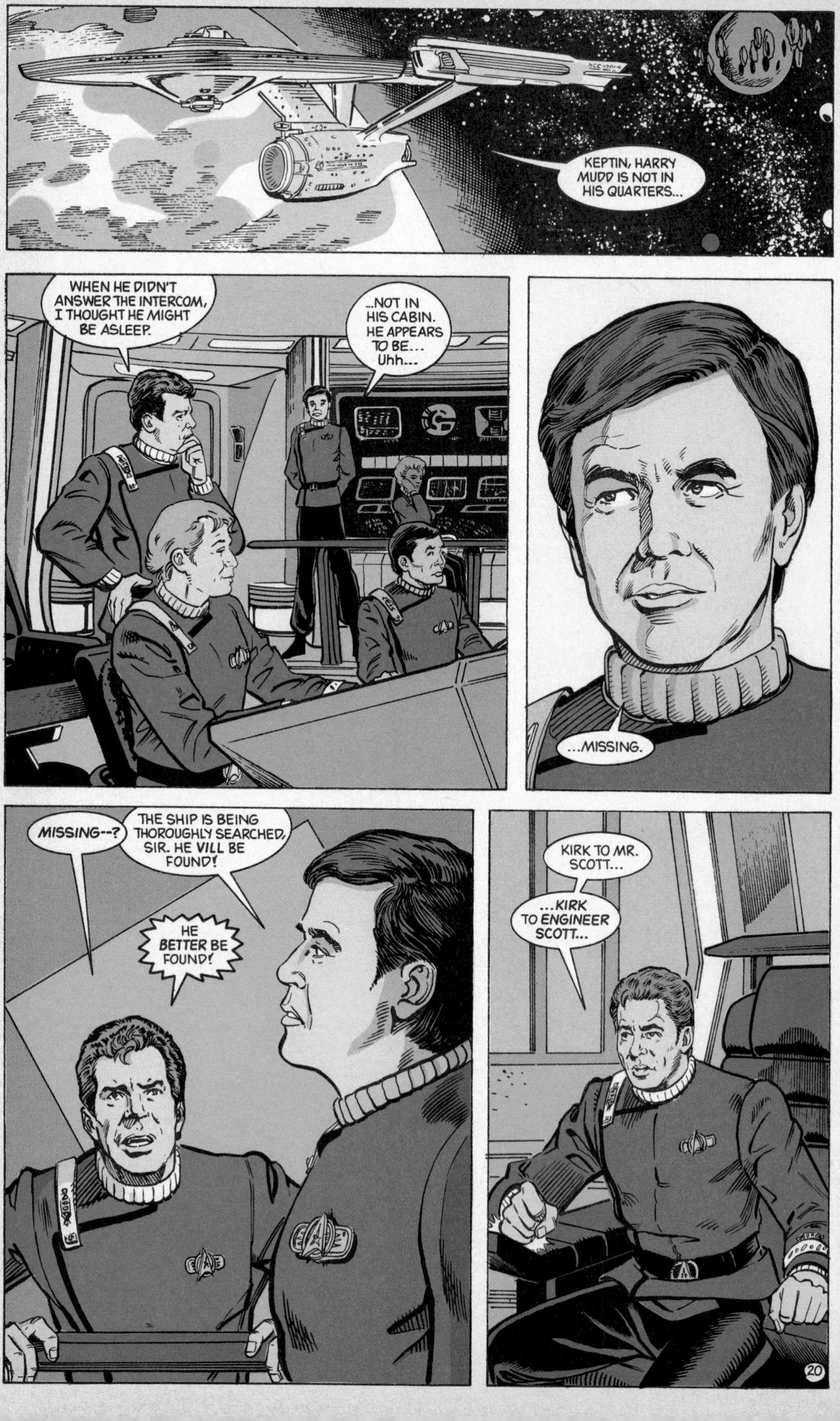
KEPTIN, HARRY MUDD IS NOT IN HIS QUARTERS...
WHEN HE DIDN'T ANSWER THE INTERCOM, I THOUGHT HE MIGHT BE ASLEEP.
...NOT IN HIS CABIN. HE APPEARS TO BE... Uhh...
...MISSING.
MISSING--?
THE SHIP IS BEING THOROUGHLY SEARCHED, SIR. HE VILL BE FOUND!
HE BETTER BE FOUND!
KIRK TO MR. SCOTT...
...KIRK TO ENGINEER SCOTT...
20

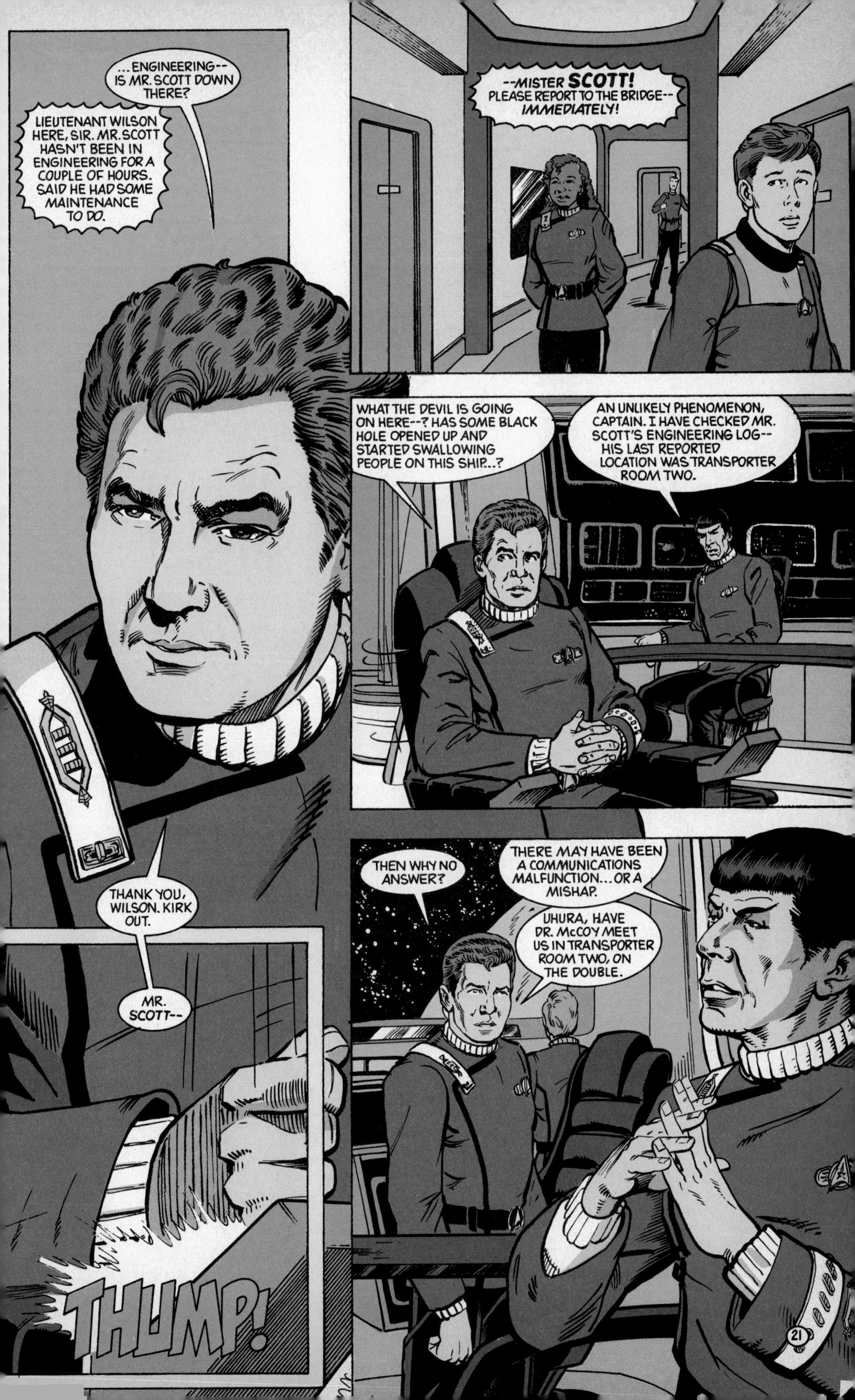

...ENGINEERING-- IS MR. SCOTT DOWN THERE?
LIEUTENANT WILSON HERE, SIR. MR. SCOTT HASN'T BEEN IN ENGINEERING FOR A COUPLE OF HOURS. SAID HE HAD SOME MAINTENANCE TO DO.
THANK YOU, WILSON. KIRK OUT.
--MISTER SCOTT! PLEASE REPORT TO THE BRIDGE-- IMMEDIATELY!
WHAT THE DEVIL IS GOING ON HERE--? HAS SOME BLACK HOLE OPENED UP AND STARTED SWALLOWING PEOPLE ON THIS SHIP...?
AN UNLIKELY PHENOMENON, CAPTAIN. I HAVE CHECKED MR. SCOTT'S ENGINEERING LOG-- HIS LAST REPORTED LOCATION WAS TRANSPORTER ROOM TWO.
THEN WHY NO ANSWER?
THERE MAY HAVE BEEN A COMMUNICATIONS MALFUNCTION...OR A MISHAP.
UHURA, HAVE DR. McCOY MEET US IN TRANSPORTER ROOM TWO, ON THE DOUBLE.
MR. SCOTT--
THUMP!

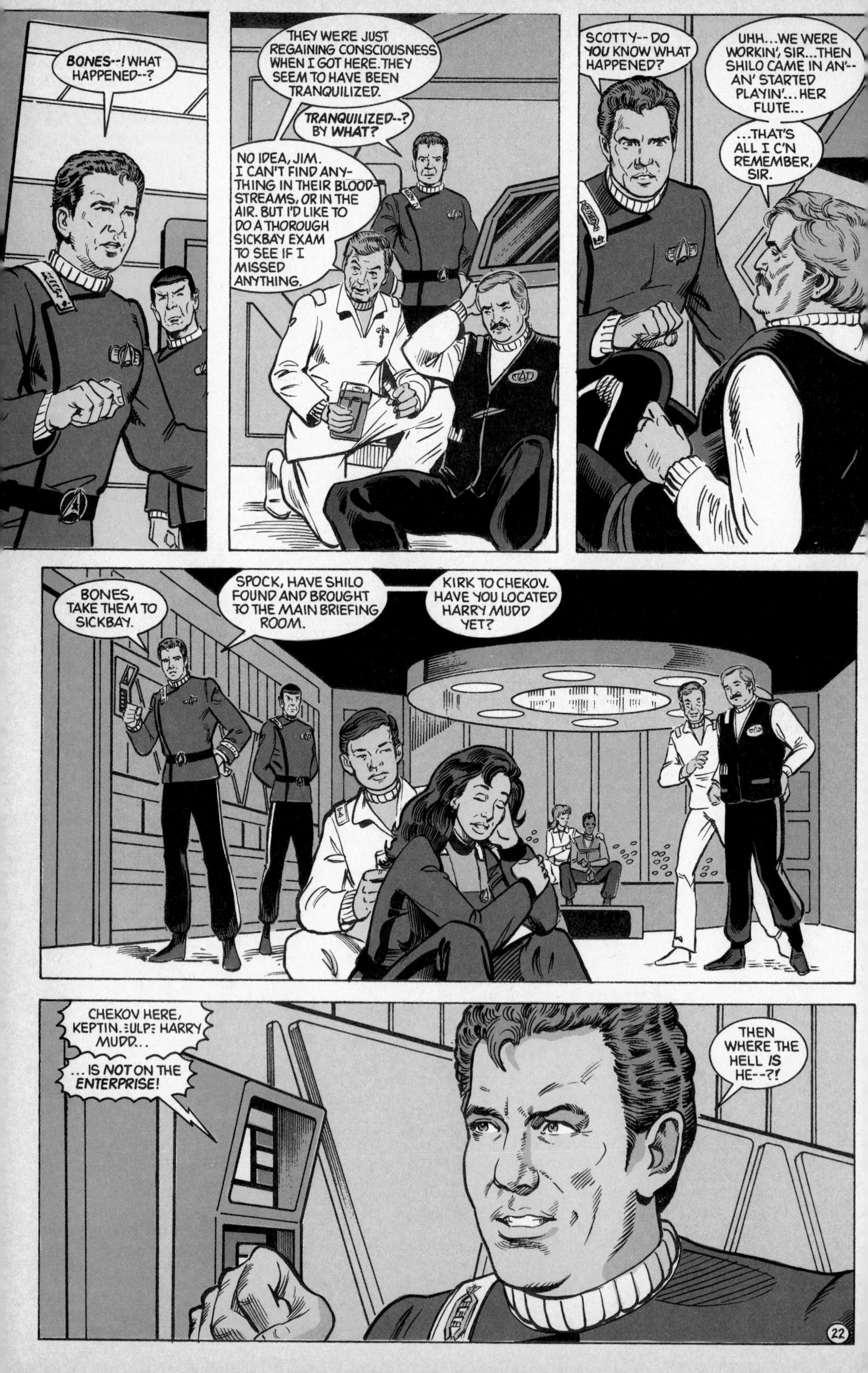
BONES--! WHAT HAPPENED--?
THEY WERE JUST REGAINING CONSCIOUSNESS WHEN I GOT HERE. THEY SEEM TO HAVE BEEN TRANQUILIZED.
TRANQUILIZED--? BY WHAT?
NO IDEA, JIM. I CAN'T FIND ANYTHING IN THEIR BLOODSTREAMS, OR IN THE AIR. BUT I'D LIKE TO DO A THOROUGH SICKBAY EXAM TO SEE IF I MISSED ANYTHING.
SCOTTY-- DO YOU KNOW WHAT HAPPENED?
UHH...WE WERE WORKIN', SIR...THEN SHILO CAME IN AN'-- AN' STARTED PLAYIN'... HER FLUTE...
...THAT'S ALL I C'N REMEMBER, SIR.
BONES, TAKE THEM TO SICKBAY.
SPOCK, HAVE SHILO FOUND AND BROUGHT TO THE MAIN BRIEFING ROOM.
KIRK TO CHEKOV. HAVE YOU LOCATED HARRY MUDD YET?
CHEKOV HERE, KEPTIN. =ULP= HARRY MUDD...
...IS NOT ON THE ENTERPRISE!
THEN WHERE THE HELL IS HE--?!

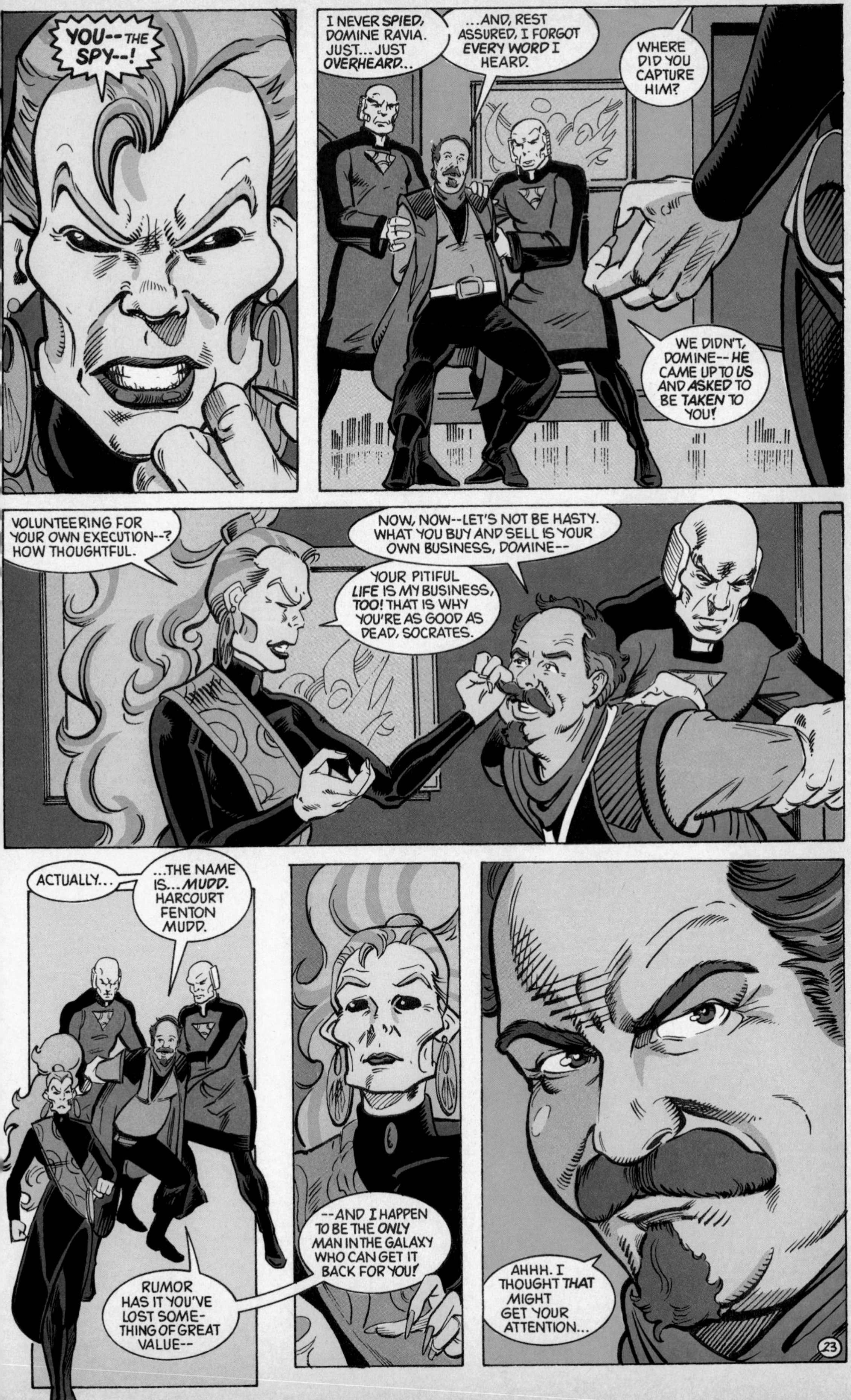

YOU--THE SPY--!
I NEVER SPIED, DOMINE RAVIA. JUST... JUST OVERHEARD...
...AND, REST ASSURED, I FORGOT EVERY WORD I HEARD.
WHERE DID YOU CAPTURE HIM?
WE DIDN'T, DOMINE--HE CAME UP TO US AND ASKED TO BE TAKEN TO YOU!
VOLUNTEERING FOR YOUR OWN EXECUTION--? HOW THOUGHTFUL.
NOW, NOW--LET'S NOT BE HASTY. WHAT YOU BUY AND SELL IS YOUR OWN BUSINESS, DOMINE--
YOUR PITIFUL LIFE IS MY BUSINESS, TOO! THAT IS WHY YOU'RE AS GOOD AS DEAD, SOCRATES.
ACTUALLY...
...THE NAME IS... MUDD. HARCOURT FENTON MUDD.
RUMOR HAS IT YOU'VE LOST SOMETHING OF GREAT VALUE--
--AND I HAPPEN TO BE THE ONLY MAN IN THE GALAXY WHO CAN GET IT BACK FOR YOU!
AHHH. I THOUGHT THAT MIGHT GET YOUR ATTENTION...

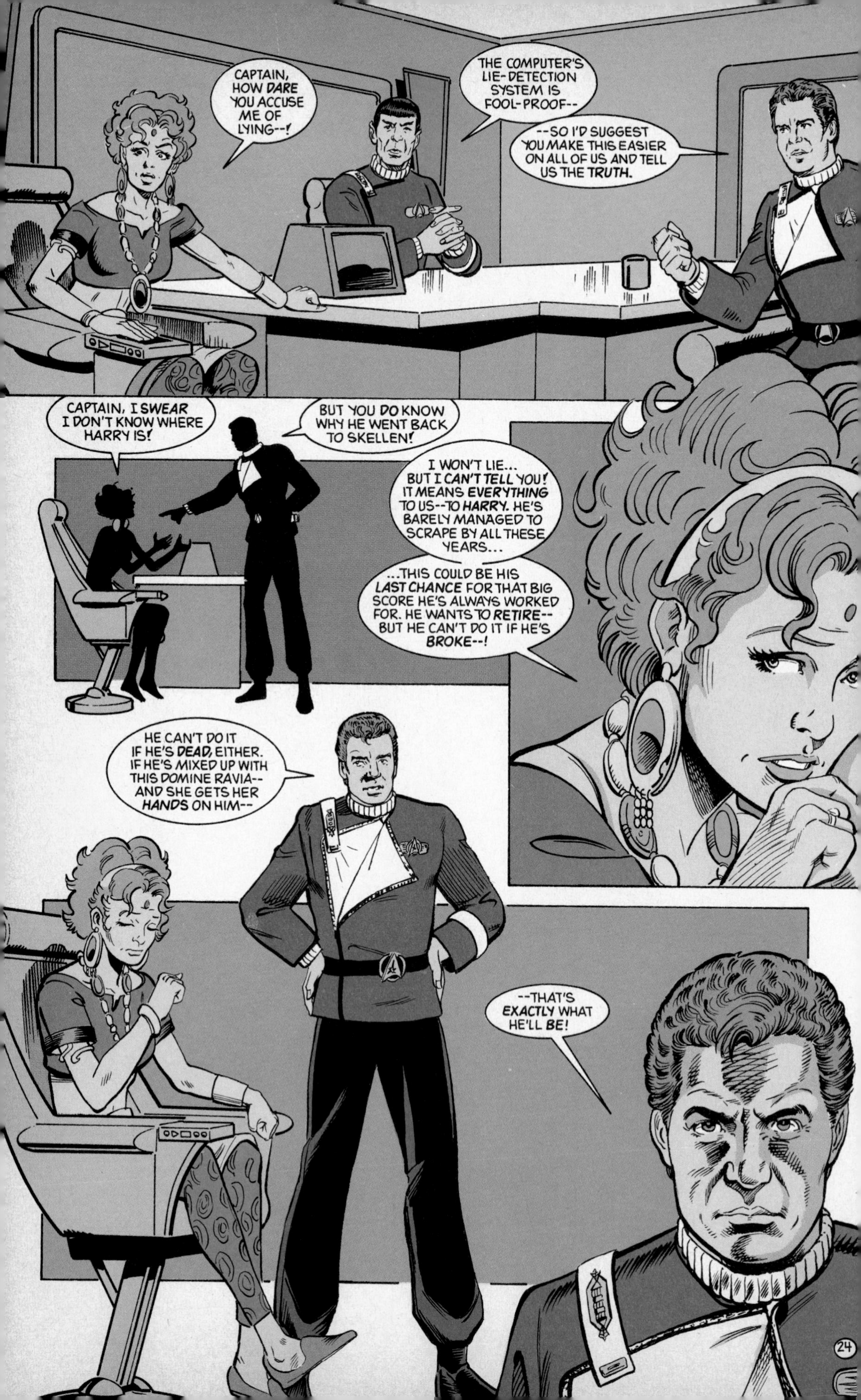

CAPTAIN, HOW DARE YOU ACCUSE ME OF LYING--!
THE COMPUTER'S LIE-DETECTION SYSTEM IS FOOL-PROOF--
--SO I'D SUGGEST YOU MAKE THIS EASIER ON ALL OF US AND TELL US THE TRUTH.
CAPTAIN, I SWEAR I DON'T KNOW WHERE HARRY IS!
BUT YOU DO KNOW WHY HE WENT BACK TO SKELLEN!
I WON'T LIE... BUT I CAN'T TELL YOU! IT MEANS EVERYTHING TO US--TO HARRY. HE'S BARELY MANAGED TO SCRAPE BY ALL THESE YEARS...
...THIS COULD BE HIS LAST CHANCE FOR THAT BIG SCORE HE'S ALWAYS WORKED FOR. HE WANTS TO RETIRE-- BUT HE CAN'T DO IT IF HE'S BROKE--!
HE CAN'T DO IT IF HE'S DEAD, EITHER. IF HE'S MIXED UP WITH THIS DOMINE RAVIA-- AND SHE GETS HER HANDS ON HIM--
--THAT'S EXACTLY WHAT HE'LL BE!

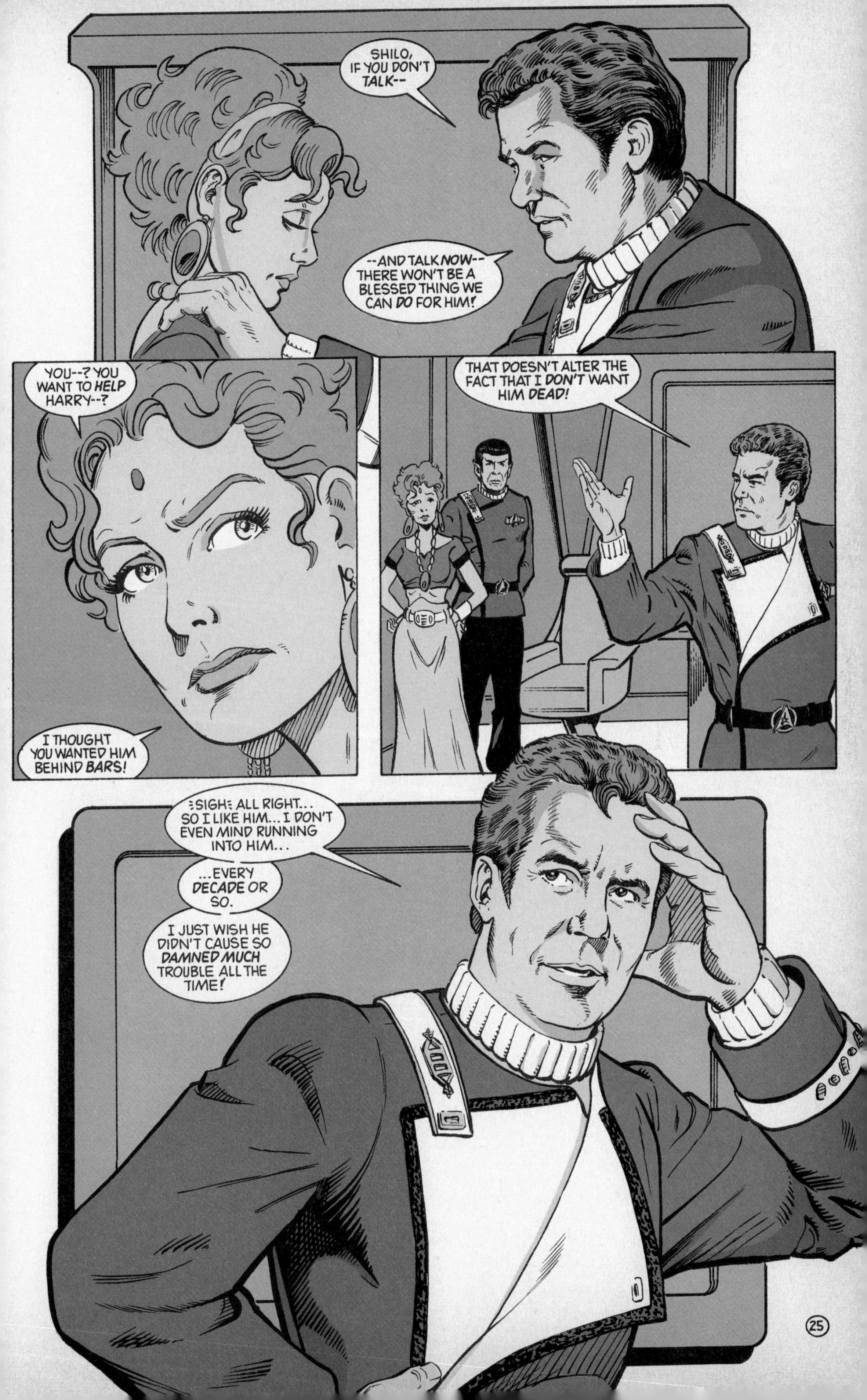
SHILO, IF YOU DON'T TALK--
--AND TALK NOW-- THERE WON'T BE A BLESSED THING WE CAN DO FOR HIM!
YOU--? YOU WANT TO HELP HARRY--?
I THOUGHT YOU WANTED HIM BEHIND BARS!
THAT DOESN'T ALTER THE FACT THAT I DON'T WANT HIM DEAD!
:SIGH: ALL RIGHT... SO I LIKE HIM... I DON'T EVEN MIND RUNNING INTO HIM...
...EVERY DECADE OR SO.
I JUST WISH HE DIDN'T CAUSE SO DAMNED MUCH TROUBLE ALL THE TIME!

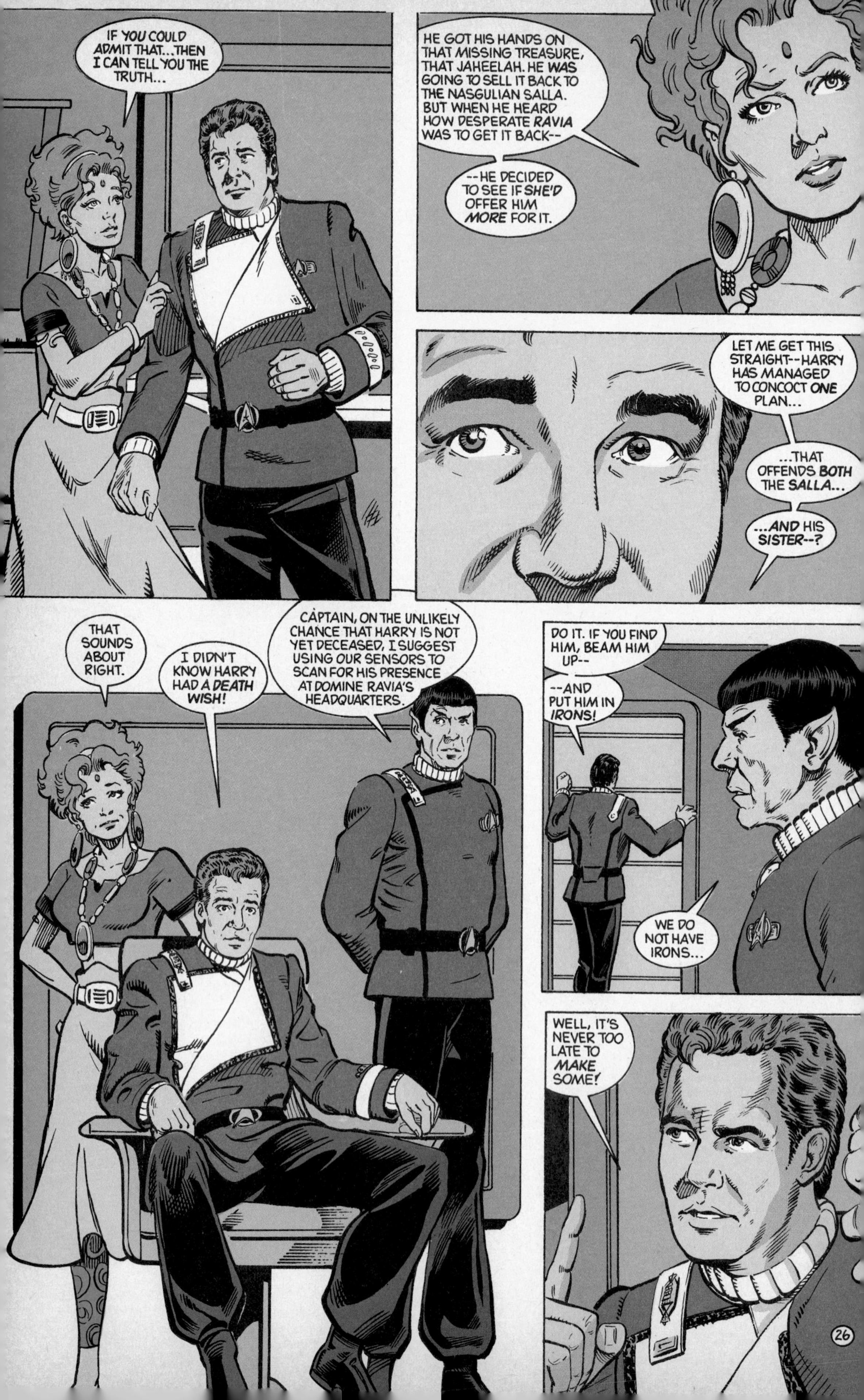
IF YOU COULD ADMIT THAT...THEN I CAN TELL YOU THE TRUTH...
HE GOT HIS HANDS ON THAT MISSING TREASURE, THAT JAHEELAH. HE WAS GOING TO SELL IT BACK TO THE NASGULIAN SALLA. BUT WHEN HE HEARD HOW DESPERATE RAVIA WAS TO GET IT BACK--
--HE DECIDED TO SEE IF SHE'D OFFER HIM MORE FOR IT.
LET ME GET THIS STRAIGHT--HARRY HAS MANAGED TO CONCOCT ONE PLAN...
...THAT OFFENDS BOTH THE SALLA...
...AND HIS SISTER--?
THAT SOUNDS ABOUT RIGHT.
I DIDN'T KNOW HARRY HAD A DEATH WISH!
CAPTAIN, ON THE UNLIKELY CHANCE THAT HARRY IS NOT YET DECEASED, I SUGGEST USING OUR SENSORS TO SCAN FOR HIS PRESENCE AT DOMINE RAVIA'S HEADQUARTERS.
DO IT. IF YOU FIND HIM, BEAM HIM UP--
--AND PUT HIM IN IRONS!
WE DO NOT HAVE IRONS...
WELL, IT'S NEVER TOO LATE TO MAKE SOME!
26

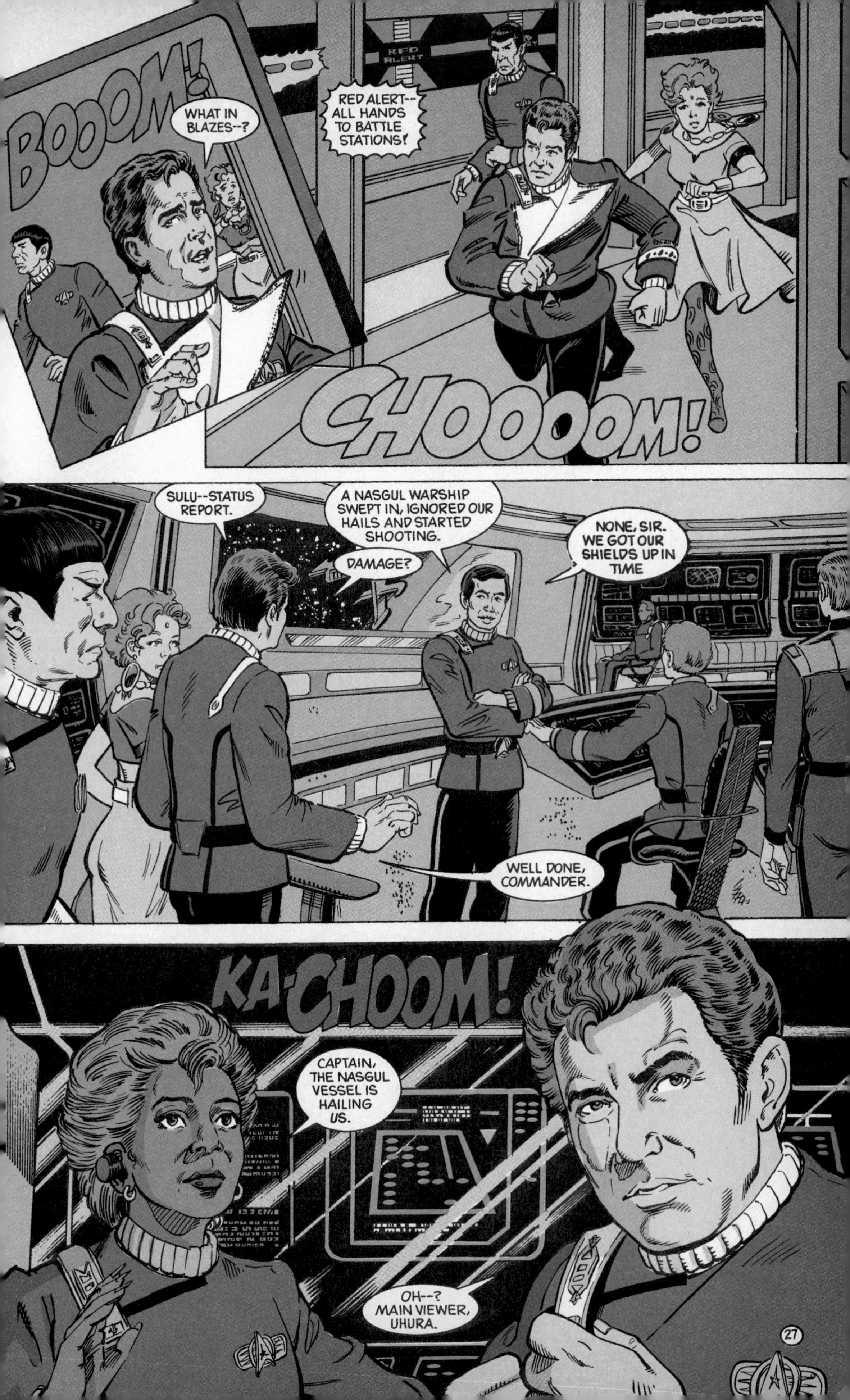
BOOOM!
WHAT IN BLAZES--?
RED ALERT
RED ALERT-- ALL HANDS TO BATTLE STATIONS!
CHOOOOM!
SULU--STATUS REPORT.
A NASGUL WARSHIP SWEPT IN, IGNORED OUR HAILS AND STARTED SHOOTING.
DAMAGE?
NONE, SIR. WE GOT OUR SHIELDS UP IN TIME
WELL DONE, COMMANDER.
KA-CHOOM!
CAPTAIN, THE NASGUL VESSEL IS HAILING US.
OH--? MAIN VIEWER, UHURA.

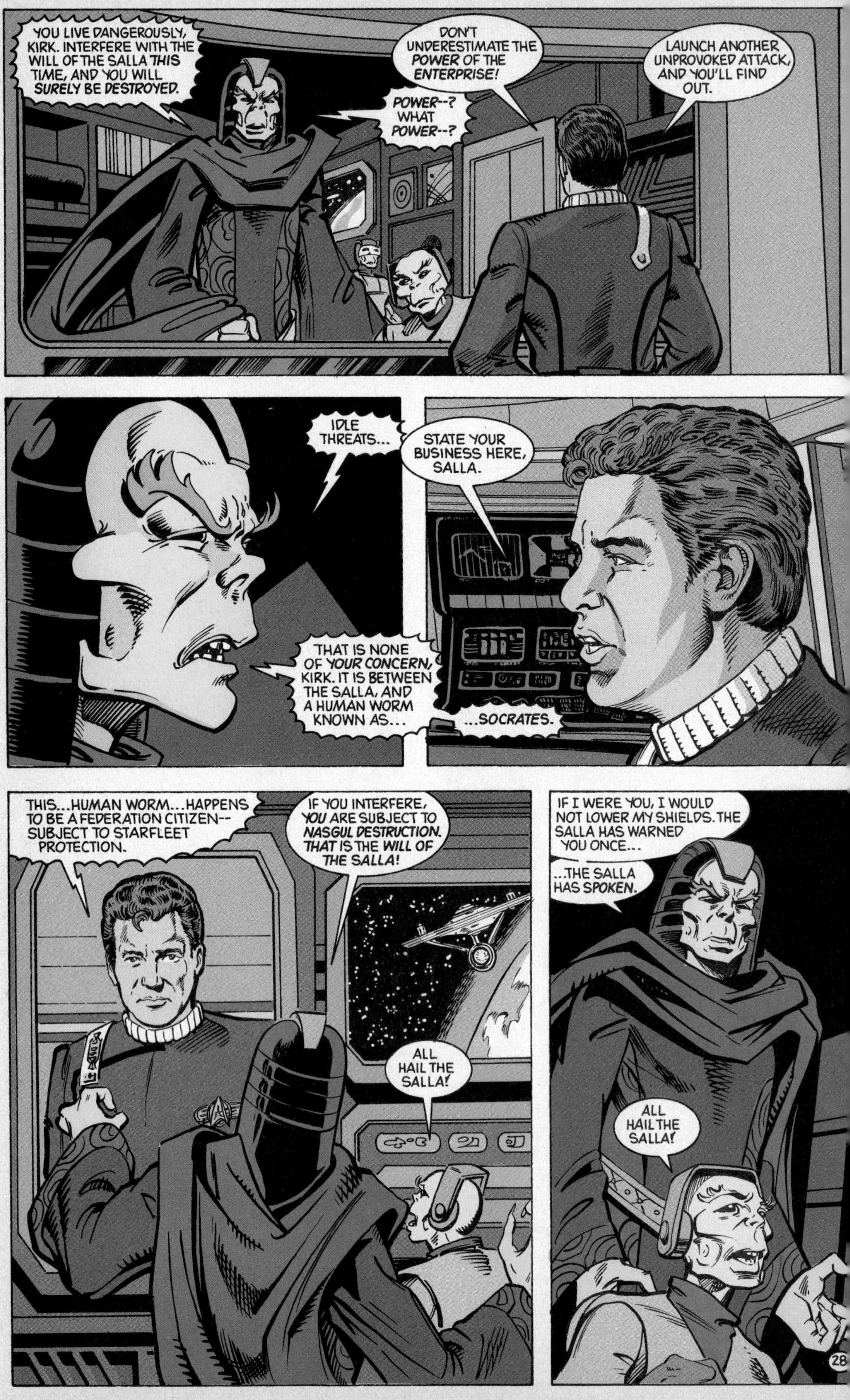
YOU LIVE DANGEROUSLY, KIRK. INTERFERE WITH THE WILL OF THE SALLA THIS TIME, AND YOU WILL SURELY BE DESTROYED.
DON'T UNDERESTIMATE THE POWER OF THE ENTERPRISE!
POWER--? WHAT POWER--?
LAUNCH ANOTHER UNPROVOKED ATTACK, AND YOU'LL FIND OUT.
IDLE THREATS...
STATE YOUR BUSINESS HERE, SALLA.
THAT IS NONE OF YOUR CONCERN, KIRK. IT IS BETWEEN THE SALLA, AND A HUMAN WORM KNOWN AS...
...SOCRATES.
THIS...HUMAN WORM...HAPPENS TO BE A FEDERATION CITIZEN--SUBJECT TO STARFLEET PROTECTION.
IF YOU INTERFERE, YOU ARE SUBJECT TO NASGUL DESTRUCTION. THAT IS THE WILL OF THE SALLA!
ALL HAIL THE SALLA!
IF I WERE YOU, I WOULD NOT LOWER MY SHIELDS. THE SALLA HAS WARNED YOU ONCE...
...THE SALLA HAS SPOKEN.
ALL HAIL THE SALLA!
28

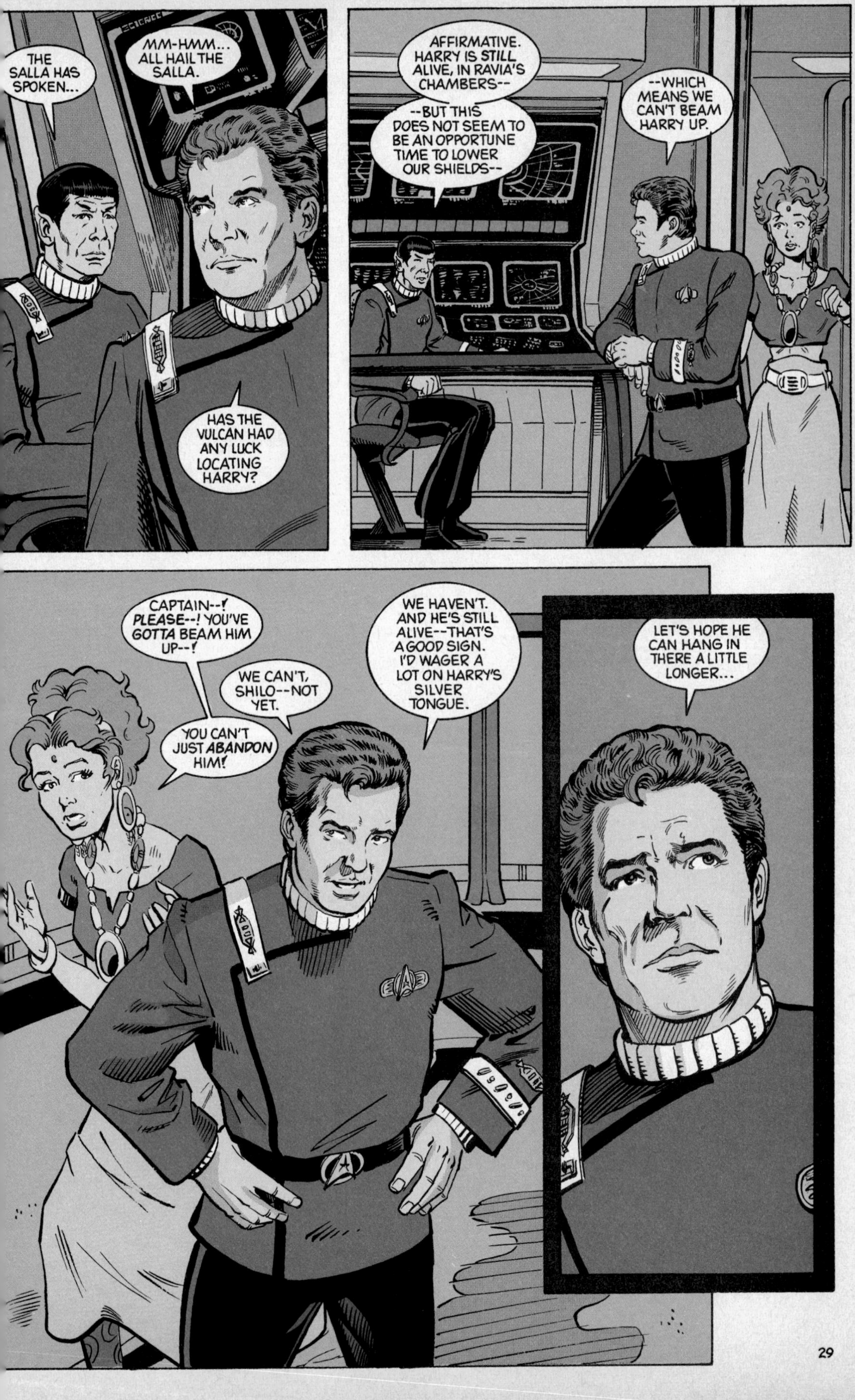
THE SALLA HAS SPOKEN...
MM-HMM... ALL HAIL THE SALLA.
HAS THE VULCAN HAD ANY LUCK LOCATING HARRY?
AFFIRMATIVE. HARRY IS STILL ALIVE, IN RAVIA'S CHAMBERS--
--BUT THIS DOES NOT SEEM TO BE AN OPPORTUNE TIME TO LOWER OUR SHIELDS--
--WHICH MEANS WE CAN'T BEAM HARRY UP.
CAPTAIN--! PLEASE--! YOU'VE GOTTA BEAM HIM UP--!
WE CAN'T, SHILO--NOT YET.
YOU CAN'T JUST ABANDON HIM!
WE HAVEN'T. AND HE'S STILL ALIVE--THAT'S A GOOD SIGN. I'D WAGER A LOT ON HARRY'S SILVER TONGUE.
LET'S HOPE HE CAN HANG IN THERE A LITTLE LONGER...

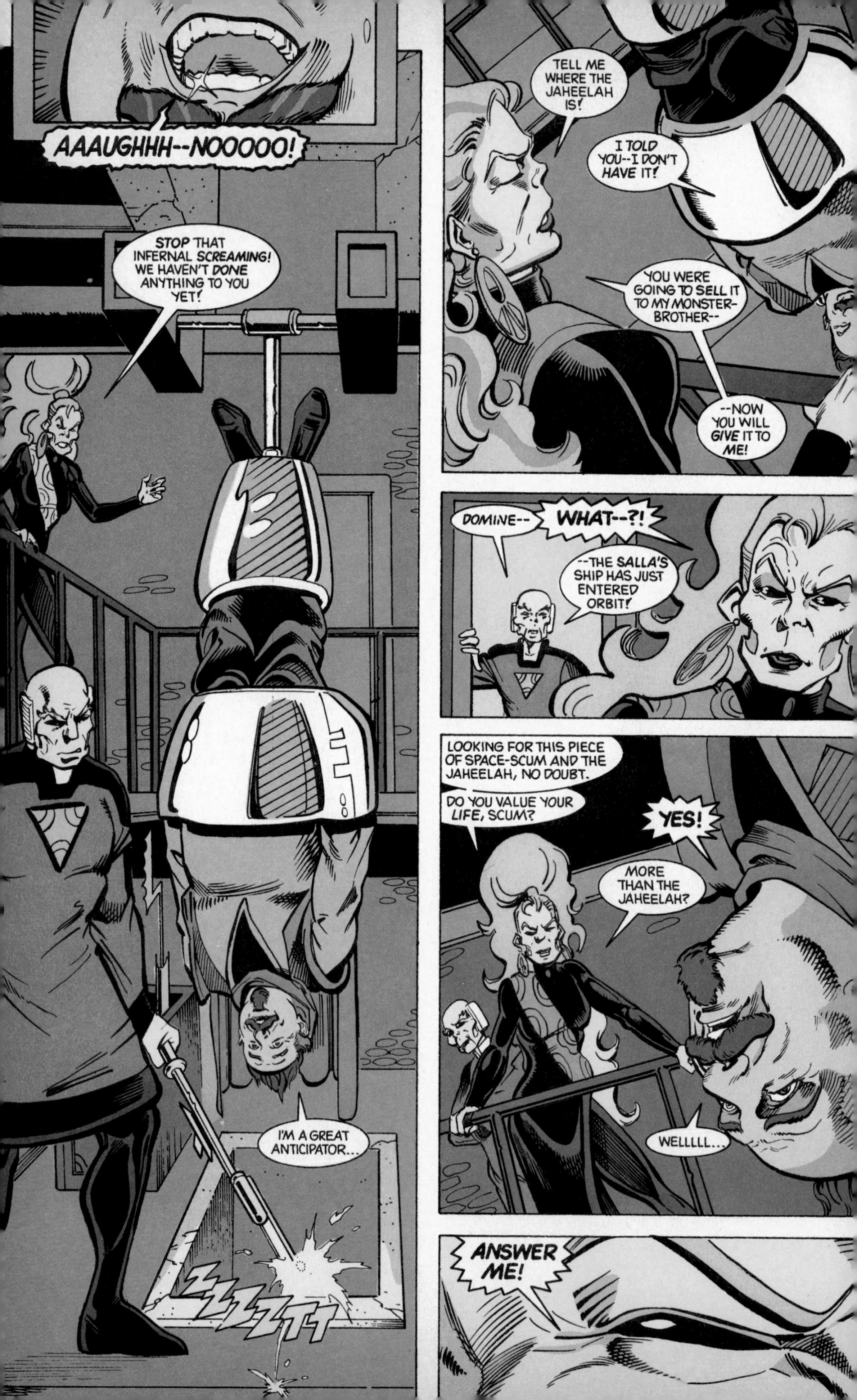
AAAUGHHH--NOOOOO!
STOP THAT INFERNAL SCREAMING! WE HAVEN'T DONE ANYTHING TO YOU YET!
I'M A GREAT ANTICIPATOR...
ZZZZTT
TELL ME WHERE THE JAHEELAH IS!
I TOLD YOU--I DON'T HAVE IT!
YOU WERE GOING TO SELL IT TO MY MONSTER-BROTHER--
--NOW YOU WILL GIVE IT TO ME!
DOMINE--
WHAT--?!
--THE SALLA'S SHIP HAS JUST ENTERED ORBIT!
LOOKING FOR THIS PIECE OF SPACE-SCUM AND THE JAHEELAH, NO DOUBT.
DO YOU VALUE YOUR LIFE, SCUM?
YES!
MORE THAN THE JAHEELAH?
WELLLLL...
ANSWER ME!

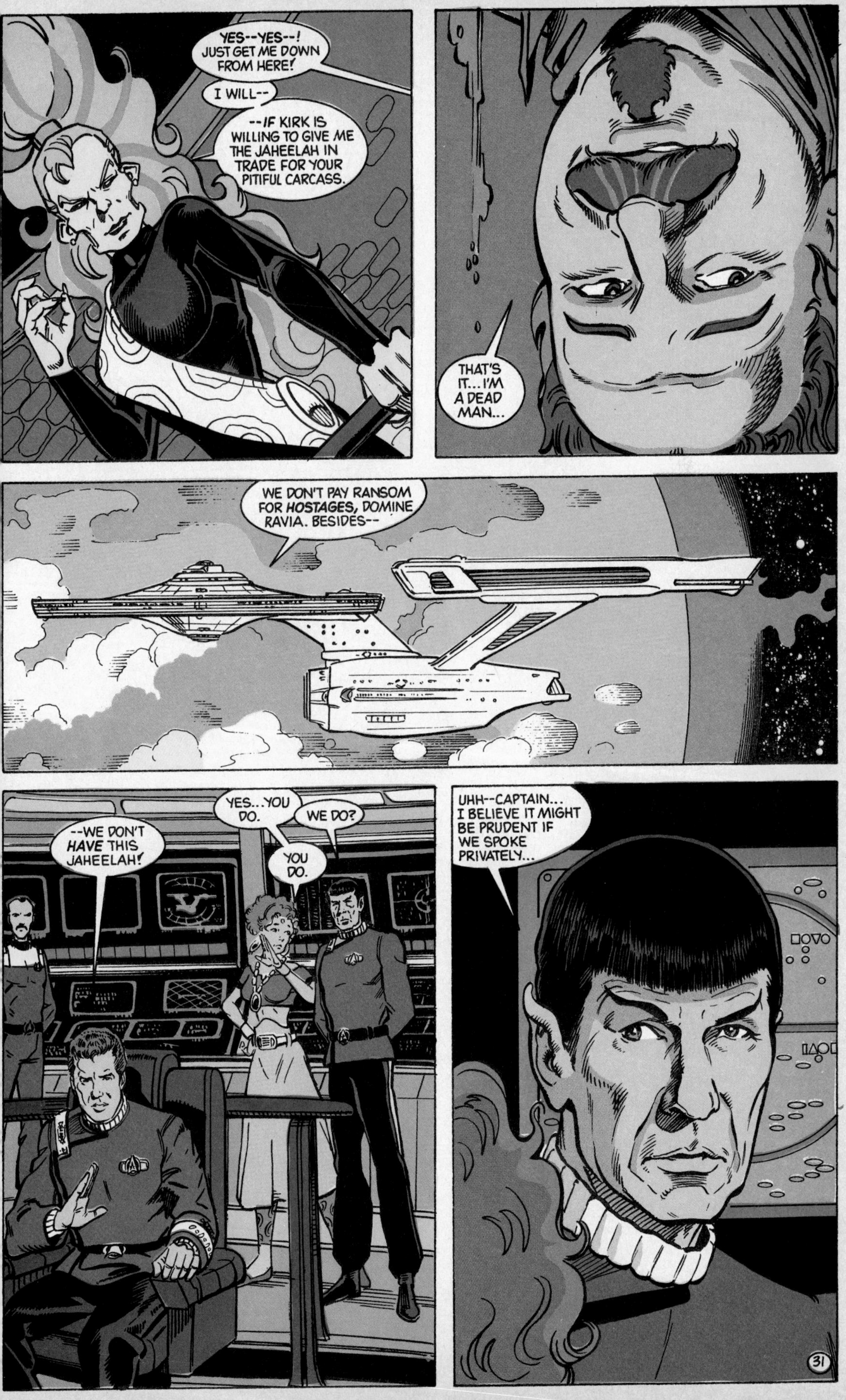
YES--YES--! JUST GET ME DOWN FROM HERE!
I WILL--
--IF KIRK IS WILLING TO GIVE ME THE JAHEELAH IN TRADE FOR YOUR PITIFUL CARCASS.
THAT'S IT... I'M A DEAD MAN...
WE DON'T PAY RANSOM FOR HOSTAGES, DOMINE RAVIA. BESIDES--
--WE DON'T HAVE THIS JAHEELAH!
YES... YOU DO.
WE DO?
YOU DO.
UHH--CAPTAIN... I BELIEVE IT MIGHT BE PRUDENT IF WE SPOKE PRIVATELY...

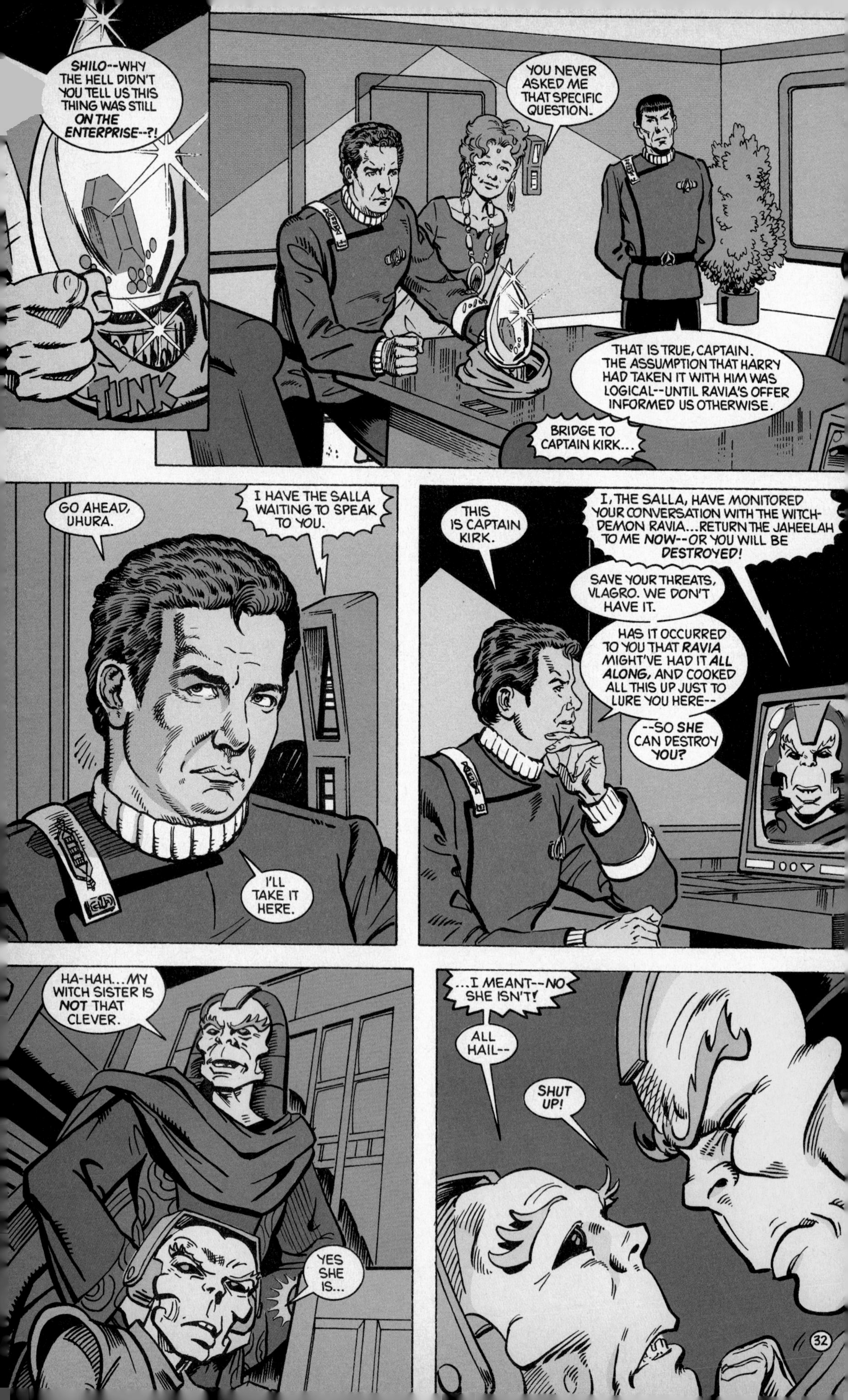

SHILO--WHY THE HELL DIDN'T YOU TELL US THIS THING WAS STILL ON THE ENTERPRISE--?!
TUNK
YOU NEVER ASKED ME THAT SPECIFIC QUESTION.
THAT IS TRUE, CAPTAIN. THE ASSUMPTION THAT HARRY HAD TAKEN IT WITH HIM WAS LOGICAL--UNTIL RAVIA'S OFFER INFORMED US OTHERWISE.
BRIDGE TO CAPTAIN KIRK...
GO AHEAD, UHURA.
I HAVE THE SALLA WAITING TO SPEAK TO YOU.
I'LL TAKE IT HERE.
THIS IS CAPTAIN KIRK.
I, THE SALLA, HAVE MONITORED YOUR CONVERSATION WITH THE WITCH-DEMON RAVIA...RETURN THE JAHEELAH TO ME NOW--OR YOU WILL BE DESTROYED!
SAVE YOUR THREATS, VLAGRO. WE DON'T HAVE IT.
HAS IT OCCURRED TO YOU THAT RAVIA MIGHT'VE HAD IT ALL ALONG, AND COOKED ALL THIS UP JUST TO LURE YOU HERE--
--SO SHE CAN DESTROY YOU?
HA-HAH...MY WITCH SISTER IS NOT THAT CLEVER.
YES SHE IS...
...I MEANT--NO SHE ISN'T!
ALL HAIL--
SHUT UP!

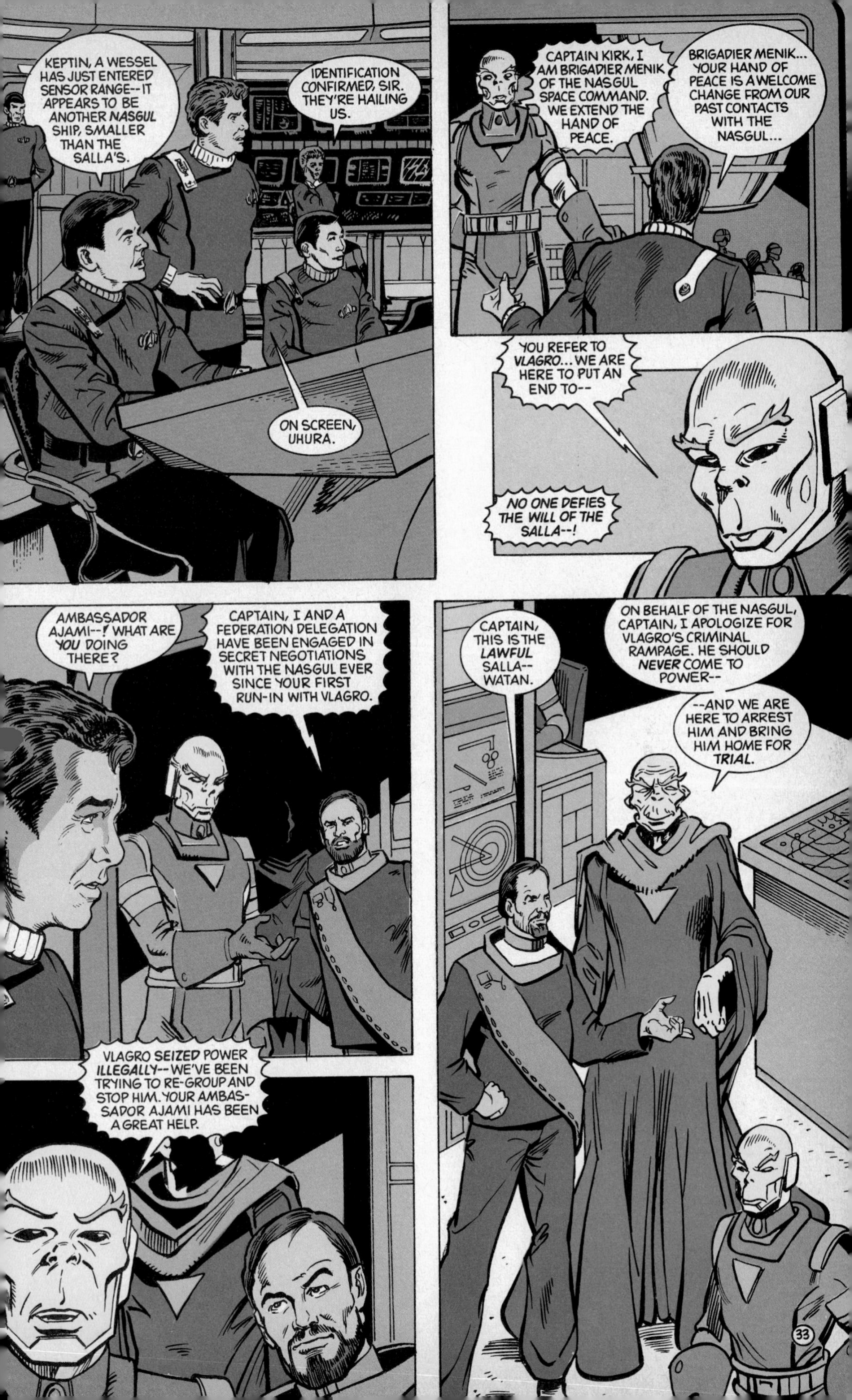
KEPTIN, A WESSEL HAS JUST ENTERED SENSOR RANGE-- IT APPEARS TO BE ANOTHER NASGUL SHIP, SMALLER THAN THE SALLA'S.
IDENTIFICATION CONFIRMED, SIR. THEY'RE HAILING US.
ON SCREEN, UHURA.
CAPTAIN KIRK, I AM BRIGADIER MENIK OF THE NASGUL SPACE COMMAND. WE EXTEND THE HAND OF PEACE.
BRIGADIER MENIK... YOUR HAND OF PEACE IS A WELCOME CHANGE FROM OUR PAST CONTACTS WITH THE NASGUL...
YOU REFER TO VLAGRO... WE ARE HERE TO PUT AN END TO--
NO ONE DEFIES THE WILL OF THE SALLA--!
AMBASSADOR AJAMI--! WHAT ARE YOU DOING THERE?
CAPTAIN, I AND A FEDERATION DELEGATION HAVE BEEN ENGAGED IN SECRET NEGOTIATIONS WITH THE NASGUL EVER SINCE YOUR FIRST RUN-IN WITH VLAGRO.
VLAGRO SEIZED POWER ILLEGALLY-- WE'VE BEEN TRYING TO RE-GROUP AND STOP HIM. YOUR AMBASSADOR AJAMI HAS BEEN A GREAT HELP.
CAPTAIN, THIS IS THE LAWFUL SALLA-- WATAN.
ON BEHALF OF THE NASGUL, CAPTAIN, I APOLOGIZE FOR VLAGRO'S CRIMINAL RAMPAGE. HE SHOULD NEVER COME TO POWER--
--AND WE ARE HERE TO ARREST HIM AND BRING HIM HOME FOR TRIAL.
33

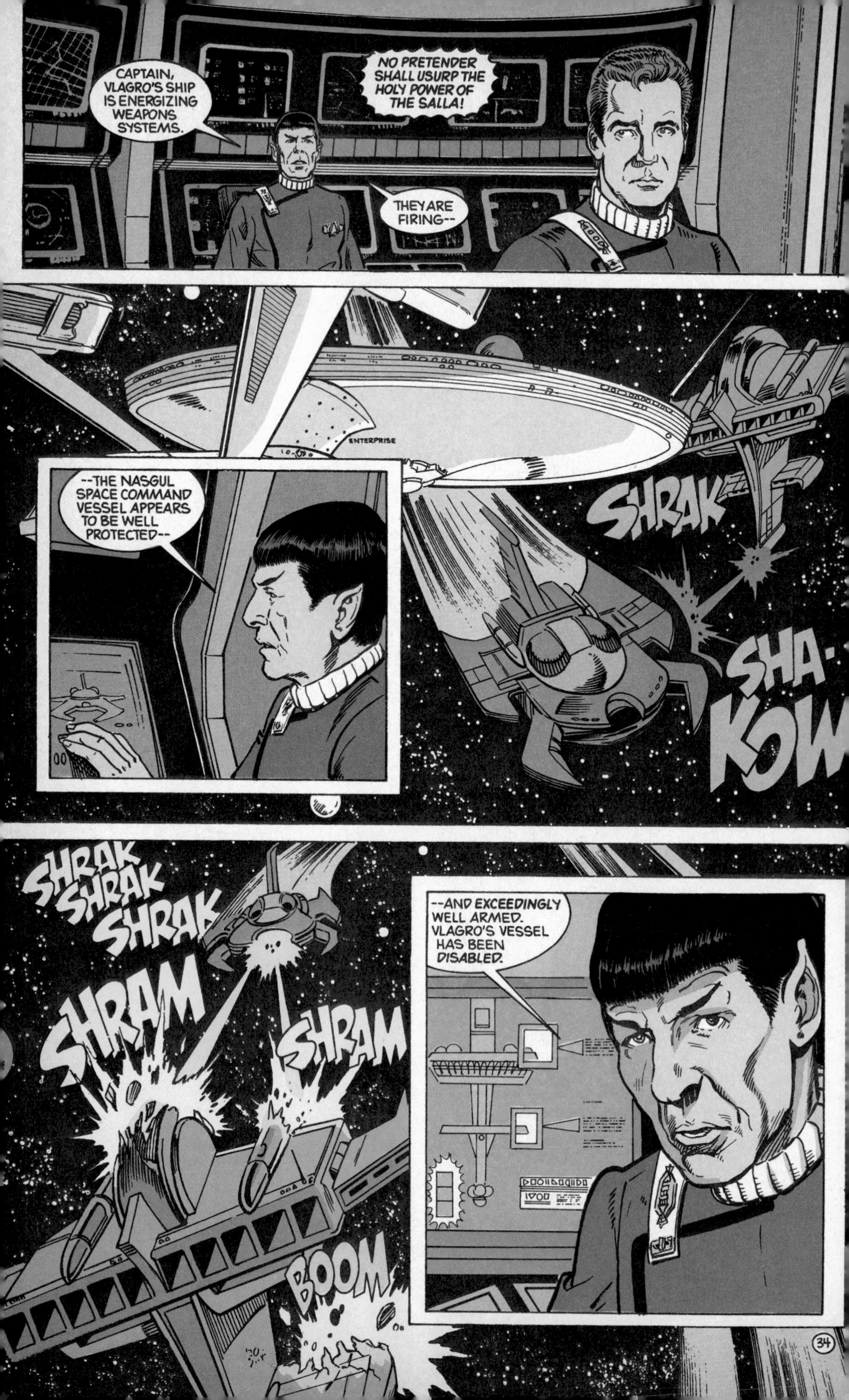

CAPTAIN, VLAGRO'S SHIP IS ENERGIZING WEAPONS SYSTEMS.
NO PRETENDER SHALL USURP THE HOLY POWER OF THE SALLA!
THEY ARE FIRING--
ENTERPRISE
--THE NASGUL SPACE COMMAND VESSEL APPEARS TO BE WELL PROTECTED--
SHRAK
SHA-KOW
SHRAK SHRAK SHRAK
SHRAM
SHRAM
BOOM
--AND EXCEEDINGLY WELL ARMED. VLAGRO'S VESSEL HAS BEEN DISABLED.

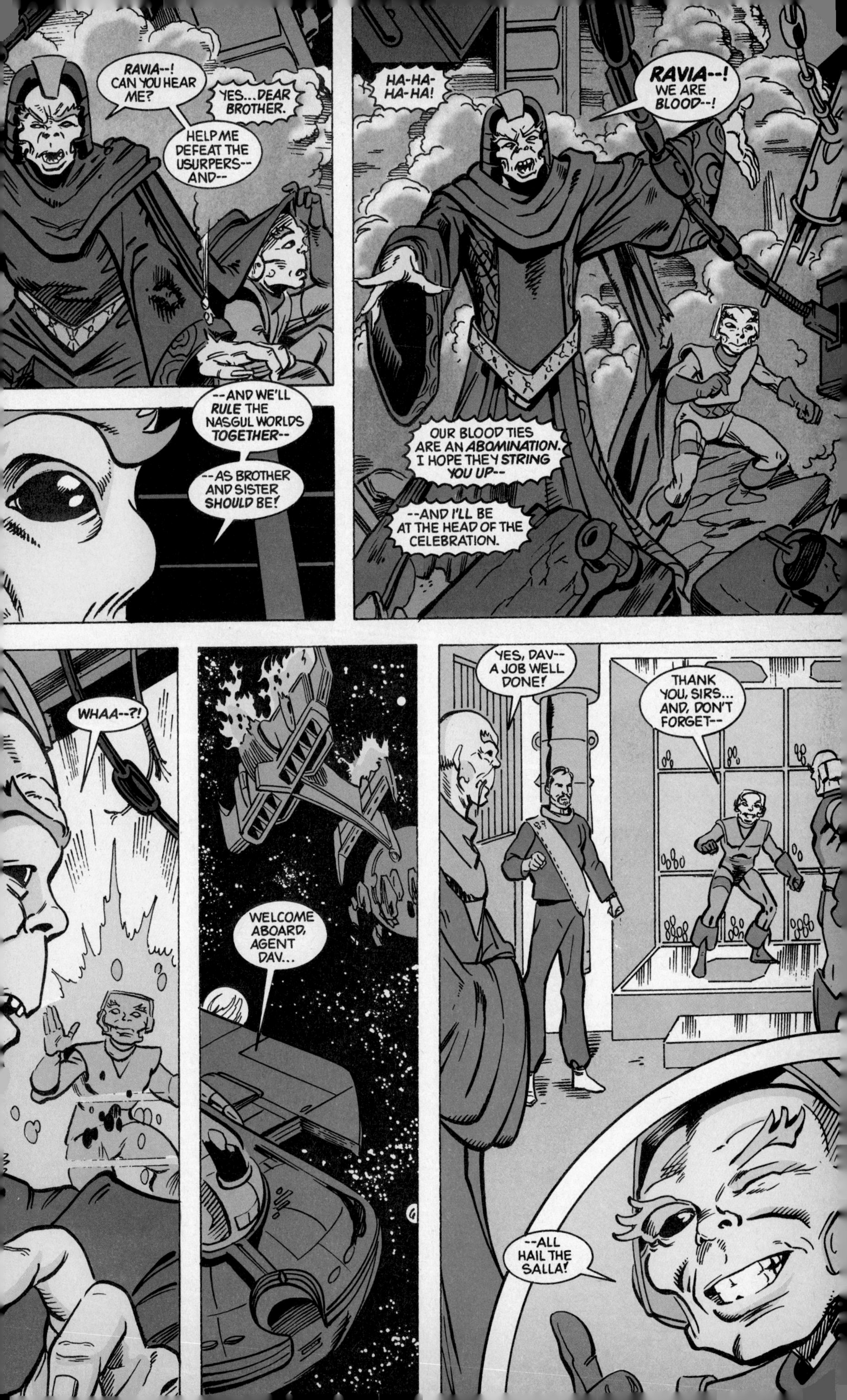
RAVIA--! CAN YOU HEAR ME?
YES...DEAR BROTHER.
HELP ME DEFEAT THE USURPERS-- AND--
HA-HA-HA-HA!
RAVIA--! WE ARE BLOOD--!
--AND WE'LL RULE THE NASGUL WORLDS TOGETHER--
--AS BROTHER AND SISTER SHOULD BE!
OUR BLOOD TIES ARE AN ABOMINATION. I HOPE THEY STRING YOU UP--
--AND I'LL BE AT THE HEAD OF THE CELEBRATION.
WHAA--?!
WELCOME ABOARD, AGENT DAV...
YES, DAV-- A JOB WELL DONE!
THANK YOU, SIRS... AND, DON'T FORGET--
--ALL HAIL THE SALLA!

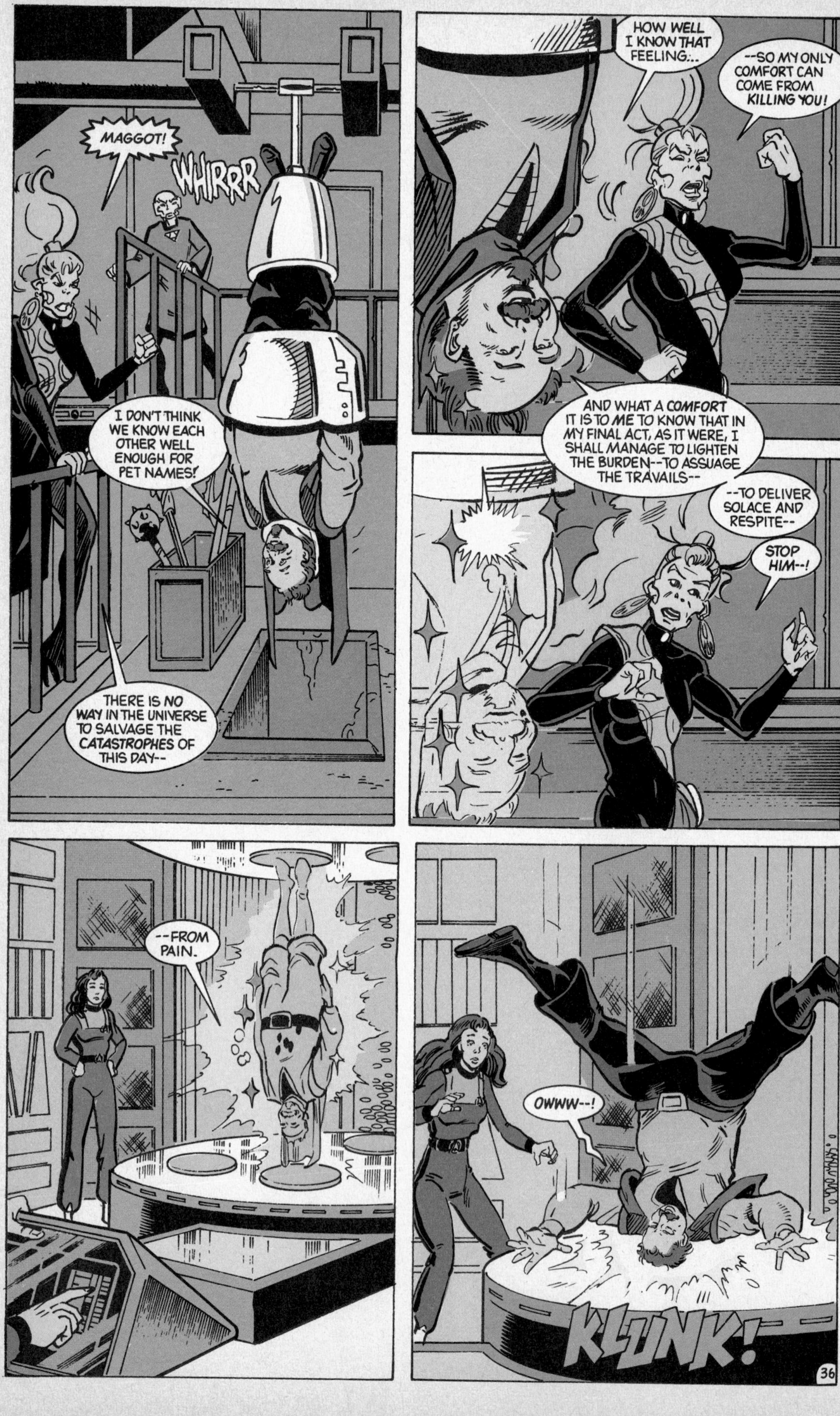

MAGGOT!
WHIRRR
I DON'T THINK WE KNOW EACH OTHER WELL ENOUGH FOR PET NAMES!
THERE IS NO WAY IN THE UNIVERSE TO SALVAGE THE CATASTROPHES OF THIS DAY--
HOW WELL I KNOW THAT FEELING...
--SO MY ONLY COMFORT CAN COME FROM KILLING YOU!
AND WHAT A COMFORT IT IS TO ME TO KNOW THAT IN MY FINAL ACT, AS IT WERE, I SHALL MANAGE TO LIGHTEN THE BURDEN--TO ASSUAGE THE TRAVAILS--
--TO DELIVER SOLACE AND RESPITE--
STOP HIM--!
--FROM PAIN.
OWWW--!
KLUNK!

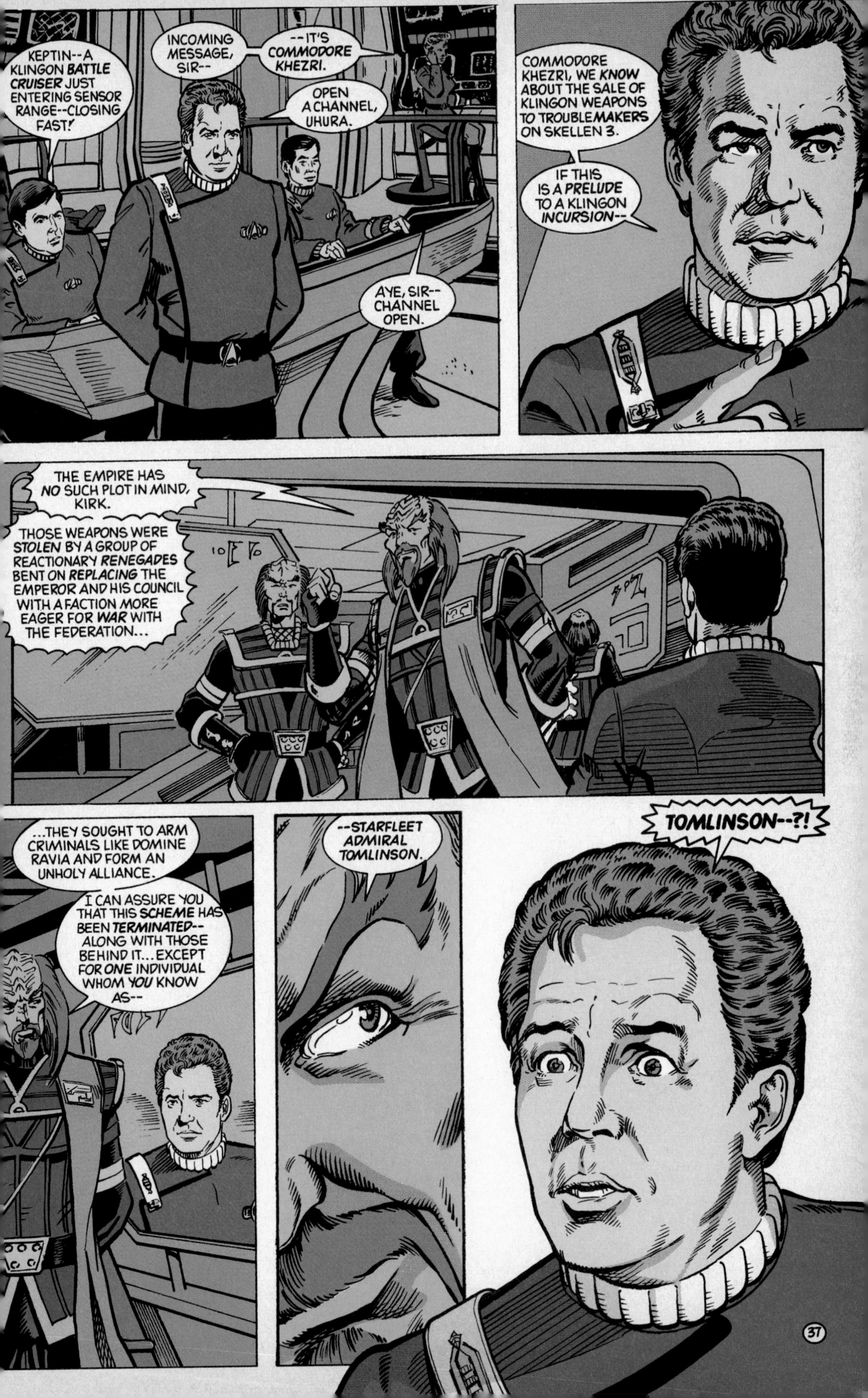
KEPTIN--A KLINGON BATTLE CRUISER JUST ENTERING SENSOR RANGE--CLOSING FAST!
INCOMING MESSAGE, SIR--
--IT'S COMMODORE KHEZRI.
OPEN A CHANNEL, UHURA.
AYE, SIR--CHANNEL OPEN.
COMMODORE KHEZRI, WE KNOW ABOUT THE SALE OF KLINGON WEAPONS TO TROUBLEMAKERS ON SKELLEN 3.
IF THIS IS A PRELUDE TO A KLINGON INCURSION--
THE EMPIRE HAS NO SUCH PLOT IN MIND, KIRK.
THOSE WEAPONS WERE STOLEN BY A GROUP OF REACTIONARY RENEGADES BENT ON REPLACING THE EMPEROR AND HIS COUNCIL WITH A FACTION MORE EAGER FOR WAR WITH THE FEDERATION...
...THEY SOUGHT TO ARM CRIMINALS LIKE DOMINE RAVIA AND FORM AN UNHOLY ALLIANCE.
I CAN ASSURE YOU THAT THIS SCHEME HAS BEEN TERMINATED--ALONG WITH THOSE BEHIND IT... EXCEPT FOR ONE INDIVIDUAL WHOM YOU KNOW AS--
--STARFLEET ADMIRAL TOMLINSON.
TOMLINSON--?!

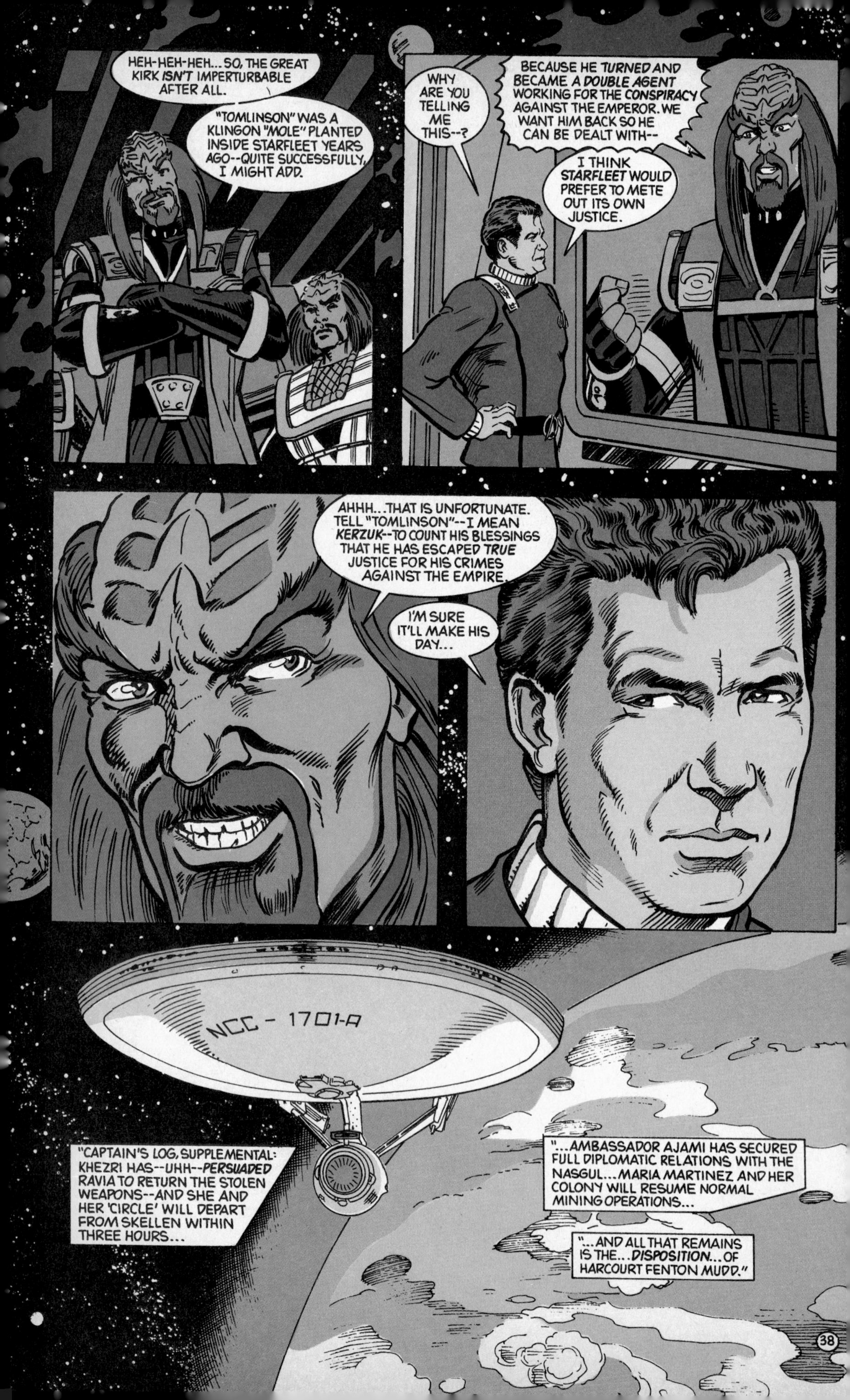
HEH-HEH-HEH... SO, THE GREAT KIRK ISN'T IMPERTURBABLE AFTER ALL.
"TOMLINSON" WAS A KLINGON "MOLE" PLANTED INSIDE STARFLEET YEARS AGO--QUITE SUCCESSFULLY, I MIGHT ADD.
WHY ARE YOU TELLING ME THIS--?
BECAUSE HE TURNED AND BECAME A DOUBLE AGENT WORKING FOR THE CONSPIRACY AGAINST THE EMPEROR. WE WANT HIM BACK SO HE CAN BE DEALT WITH--
I THINK STARFLEET WOULD PREFER TO METE OUT ITS OWN JUSTICE.
AHHH...THAT IS UNFORTUNATE. TELL "TOMLINSON"--I MEAN KERZUK--TO COUNT HIS BLESSINGS THAT HE HAS ESCAPED TRUE JUSTICE FOR HIS CRIMES AGAINST THE EMPIRE.
I'M SURE IT'LL MAKE HIS DAY...
NCC - 1701-A
"CAPTAIN'S LOG, SUPPLEMENTAL: KHEZRI HAS--UHH--PERSUADED RAVIA TO RETURN THE STOLEN WEAPONS--AND SHE AND HER 'CIRCLE' WILL DEPART FROM SKELLEN WITHIN THREE HOURS...
"...AMBASSADOR AJAMI HAS SECURED FULL DIPLOMATIC RELATIONS WITH THE NASGUL... MARIA MARTINEZ AND HER COLONY WILL RESUME NORMAL MINING OPERATIONS...
"...AND ALL THAT REMAINS IS THE... DISPOSITION... OF HARCOURT FENTON MUDD."

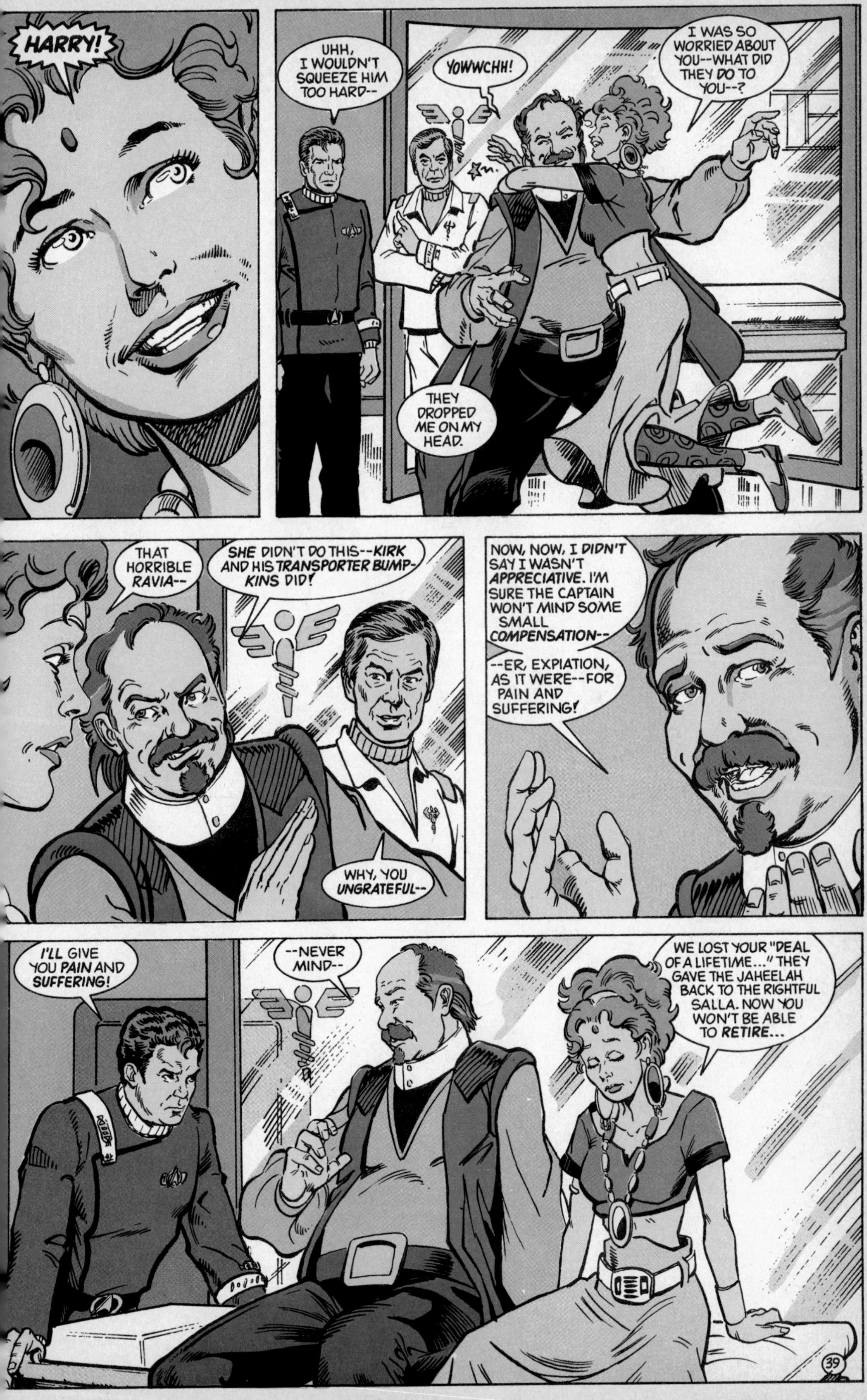
HARRY!
UHH, I WOULDN'T SQUEEZE HIM TOO HARD--
YOWWCHH!
I WAS SO WORRIED ABOUT YOU--WHAT DID THEY DO TO YOU--?
THEY DROPPED ME ON MY HEAD.
THAT HORRIBLE RAVIA--
SHE DIDN'T DO THIS--KIRK AND HIS TRANSPORTER BUMPKINS DID!
WHY, YOU UNGRATEFUL--
NOW, NOW, I DIDN'T SAY I WASN'T APPRECIATIVE. I'M SURE THE CAPTAIN WON'T MIND SOME SMALL COMPENSATION--
--ER, EXPIATION, AS IT WERE--FOR PAIN AND SUFFERING!
I'LL GIVE YOU PAIN AND SUFFERING!
--NEVER MIND--
WE LOST YOUR "DEAL OF A LIFETIME..." THEY GAVE THE JAHEELAH BACK TO THE RIGHTFUL SALLA. NOW YOU WON'T BE ABLE TO RETIRE...

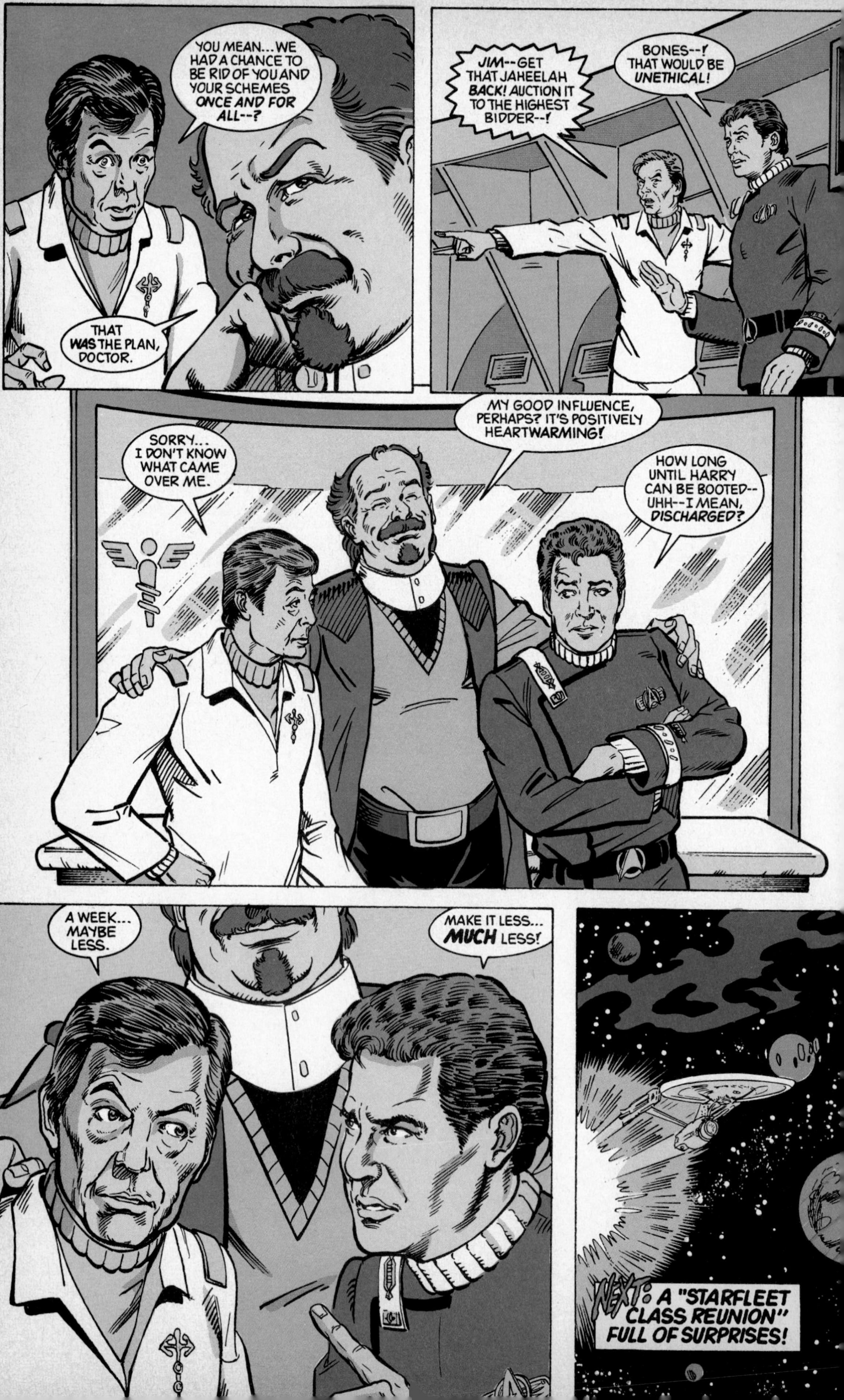
YOU MEAN... WE HAD A CHANCE TO BE RID OF YOU AND YOUR SCHEMES ONCE AND FOR ALL--?
THAT WAS THE PLAN, DOCTOR.
JIM--GET THAT JAHEELAH BACK! AUCTION IT TO THE HIGHEST BIDDER--!
BONES--! THAT WOULD BE UNETHICAL!
SORRY... I DON'T KNOW WHAT CAME OVER ME.
MY GOOD INFLUENCE, PERHAPS? IT'S POSITIVELY HEARTWARMING!
HOW LONG UNTIL HARRY CAN BE BOOTED-- UHH--I MEAN, DISCHARGED?
A WEEK... MAYBE LESS.
MAKE IT LESS... MUCH LESS!
NEXT: A "STARFLEET CLASS REUNION" FULL OF SURPRISES!

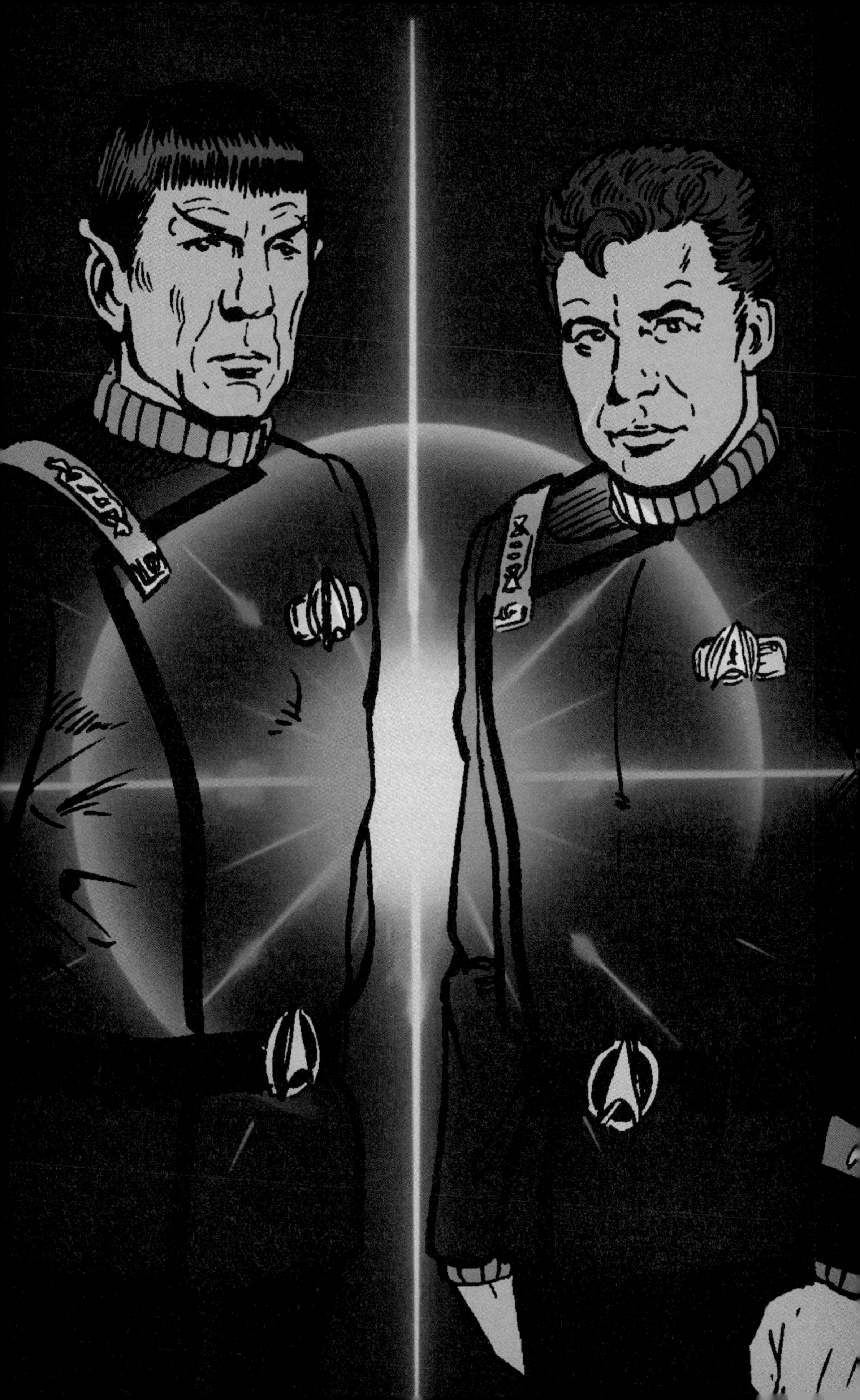

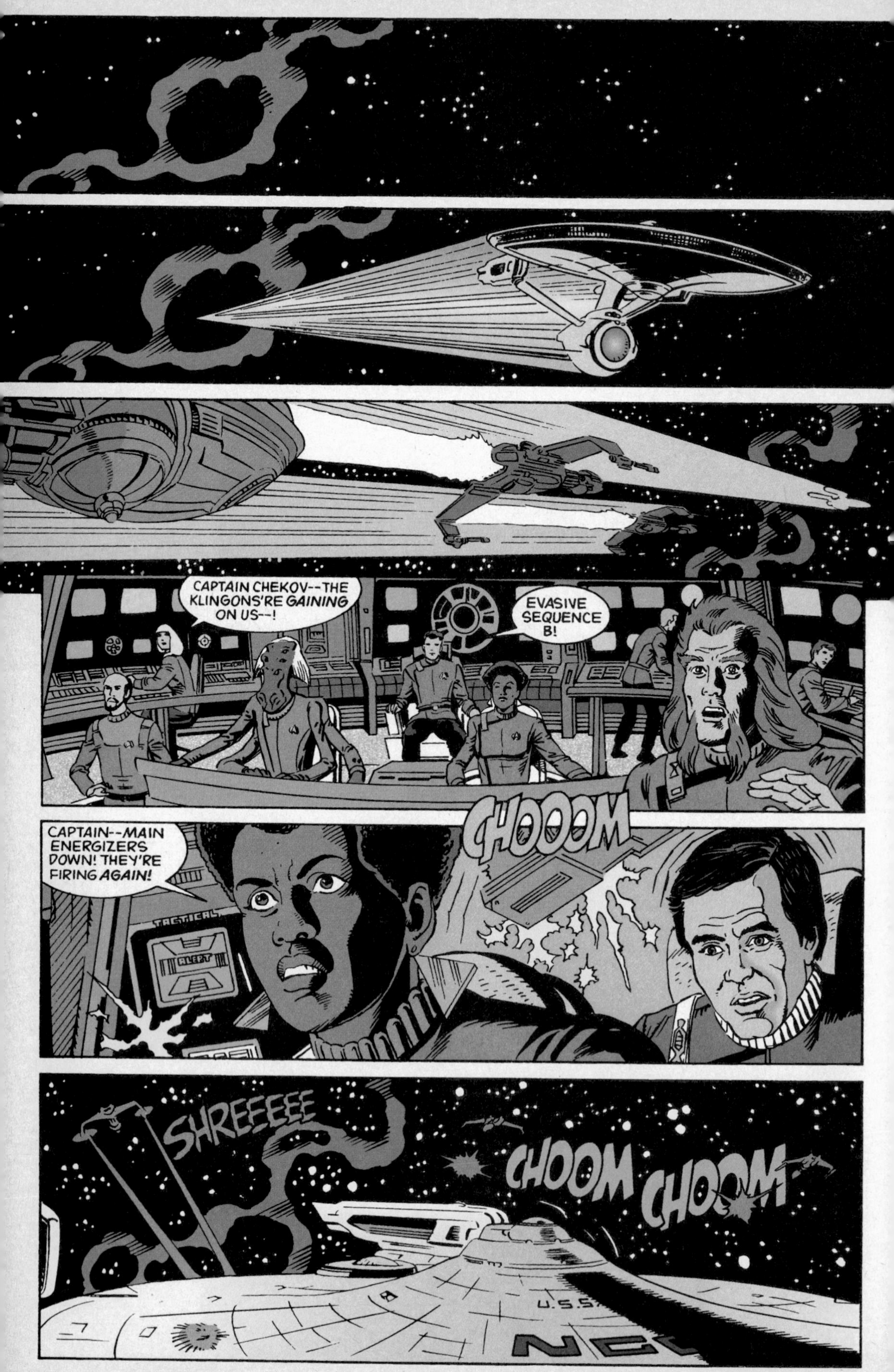
CAPTAIN CHEKOV--THE KLINGONS'RE *GAINING* ON US--!
EVASIVE SEQUENCE B!
CHOOOM
CAPTAIN--MAIN ENERGIZERS DOWN! THEY'RE FIRING *AGAIN!*
TACTICAL
ALERT
SHREEEEE
CHOOM
CHOOM
U.S.S.

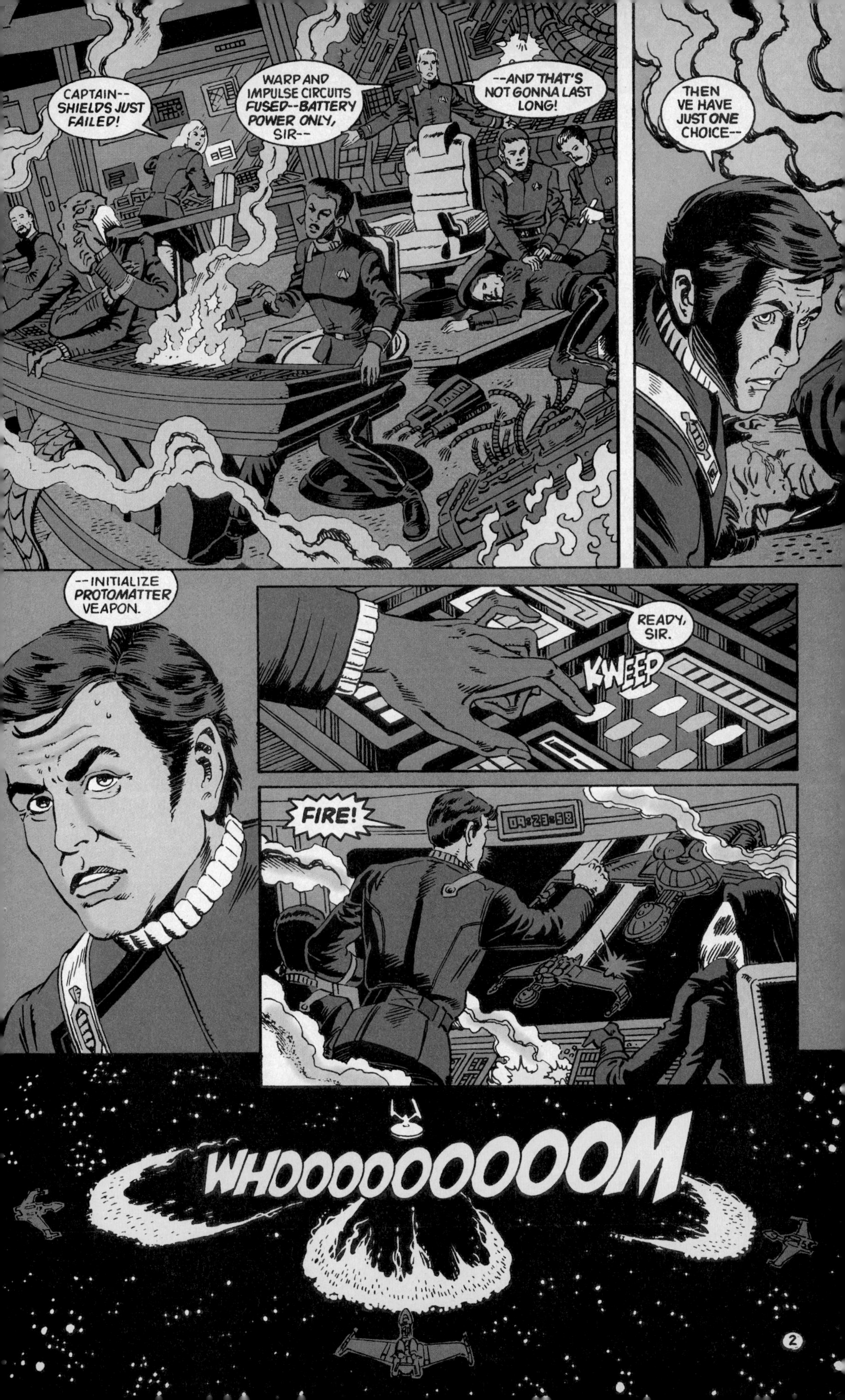
CAPTAIN-- SHIELDS JUST FAILED!
WARP AND IMPULSE CIRCUITS FUSED--BATTERY POWER ONLY, SIR--
--AND THAT'S NOT GONNA LAST LONG!
THEN VE HAVE JUST ONE CHOICE--
--INITIALIZE PROTOMATTER VEAPON.
READY, SIR.
KWEEP
FIRE!
WHOOOOOOOOOOM

THE PEACEKEEPER
PART ONE

HOWARD WEINSTEIN		BOB PINAHA
WRITER		LETTERER
ROD WHIGHAM		TOM McCRAW
PENCILLER		COLORIST
ROMEO TANGHAL		ALAN GOLD
INKER		EDITOR
BASED ON STAR TREK CREATED		BY GENE RODDENBERRY.

3

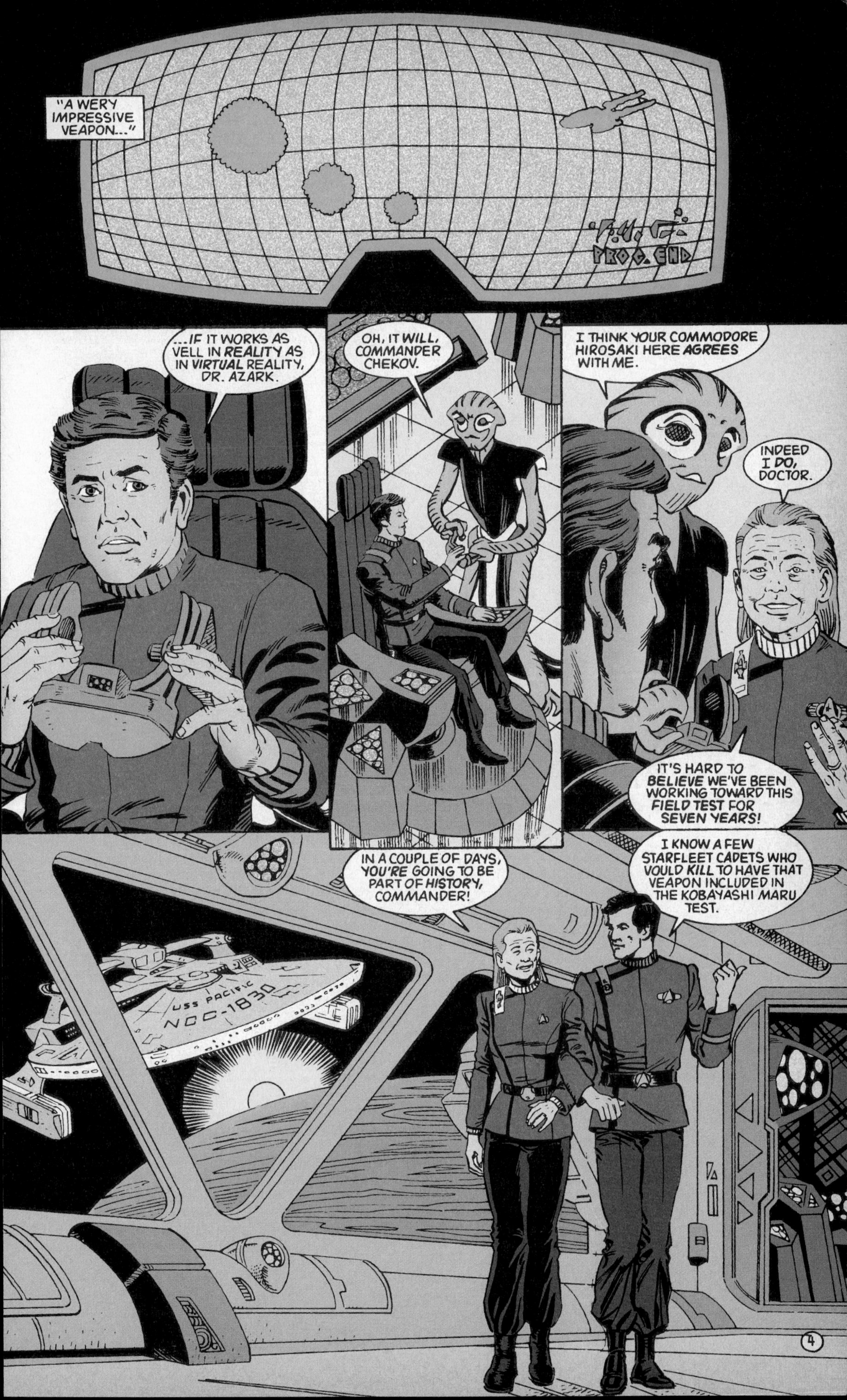
"A WERY IMPRESSIVE VEAPON..."
PROG. END
...IF IT WORKS AS VELL IN REALITY AS IN VIRTUAL REALITY, DR. AZARK.
OH, IT WILL, COMMANDER CHEKOV.
I THINK YOUR COMMODORE HIROSAKI HERE AGREES WITH ME.
INDEED I DO, DOCTOR.
IT'S HARD TO BELIEVE WE'VE BEEN WORKING TOWARD THIS FIELD TEST FOR SEVEN YEARS!
IN A COUPLE OF DAYS, YOU'RE GOING TO BE PART OF HISTORY, COMMANDER!
I KNOW A FEW STARFLEET CADETS WHO VOULD KILL TO HAVE THAT VEAPON INCLUDED IN THE KOBAYASHI MARU TEST.
USS PACIFIC
NCC-1830
4

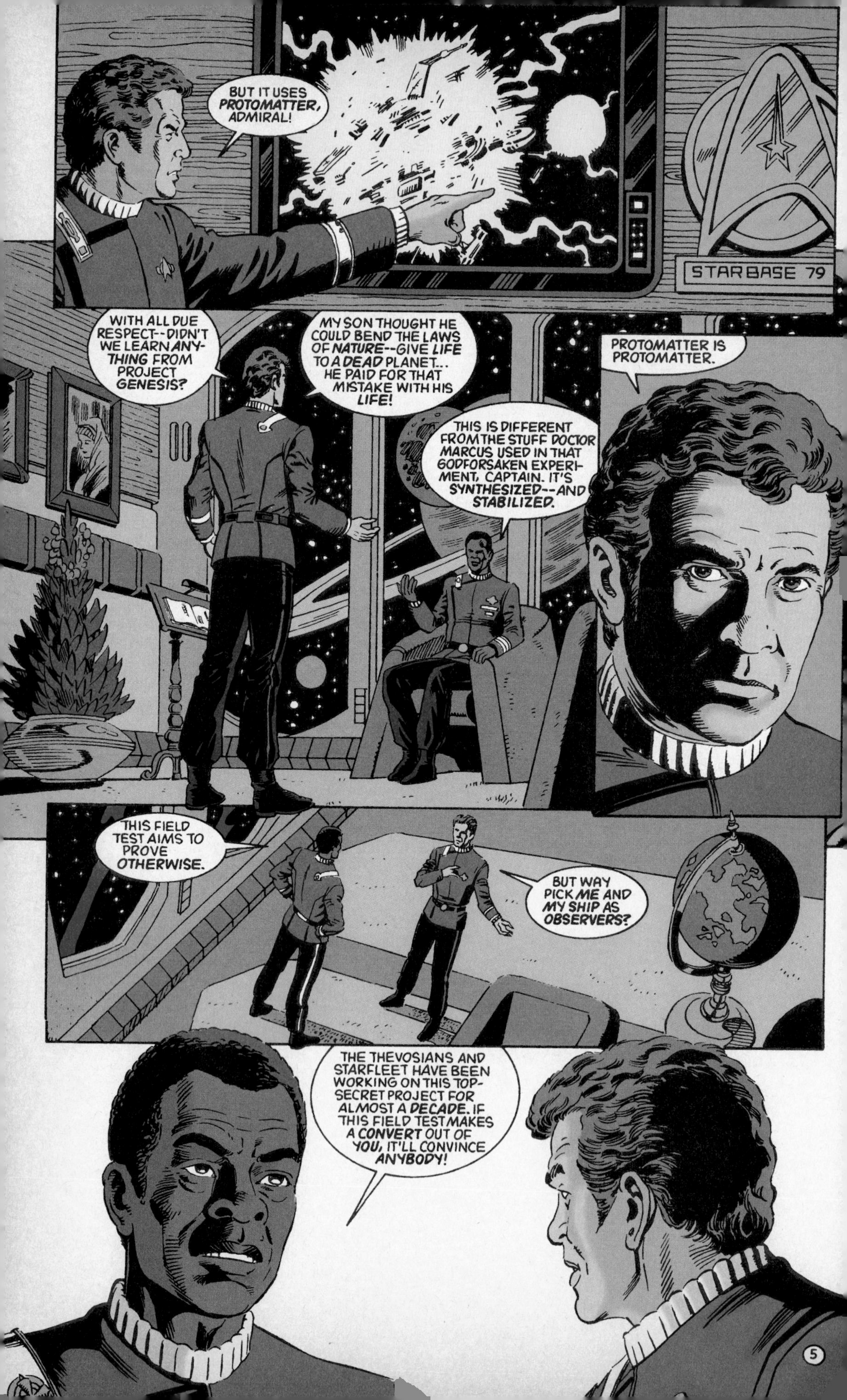
BUT IT USES PROTOMATTER, ADMIRAL!
STARBASE 79
WITH ALL DUE RESPECT--DIDN'T WE LEARN ANYTHING FROM PROJECT GENESIS?
MY SON THOUGHT HE COULD BEND THE LAWS OF NATURE--GIVE LIFE TO A DEAD PLANET... HE PAID FOR THAT MISTAKE WITH HIS LIFE!
THIS IS DIFFERENT FROM THE STUFF DOCTOR MARCUS USED IN THAT GODFORSAKEN EXPERIMENT, CAPTAIN. IT'S SYNTHESIZED--AND STABILIZED.
PROTOMATTER IS PROTOMATTER.
THIS FIELD TEST AIMS TO PROVE OTHERWISE.
BUT WAY PICK ME AND MY SHIP AS OBSERVERS?
THE THEVOSIANS AND STARFLEET HAVE BEEN WORKING ON THIS TOP-SECRET PROJECT FOR ALMOST A DECADE. IF THIS FIELD TEST MAKES A CONVERT OUT OF YOU, IT'LL CONVINCE ANYBODY!

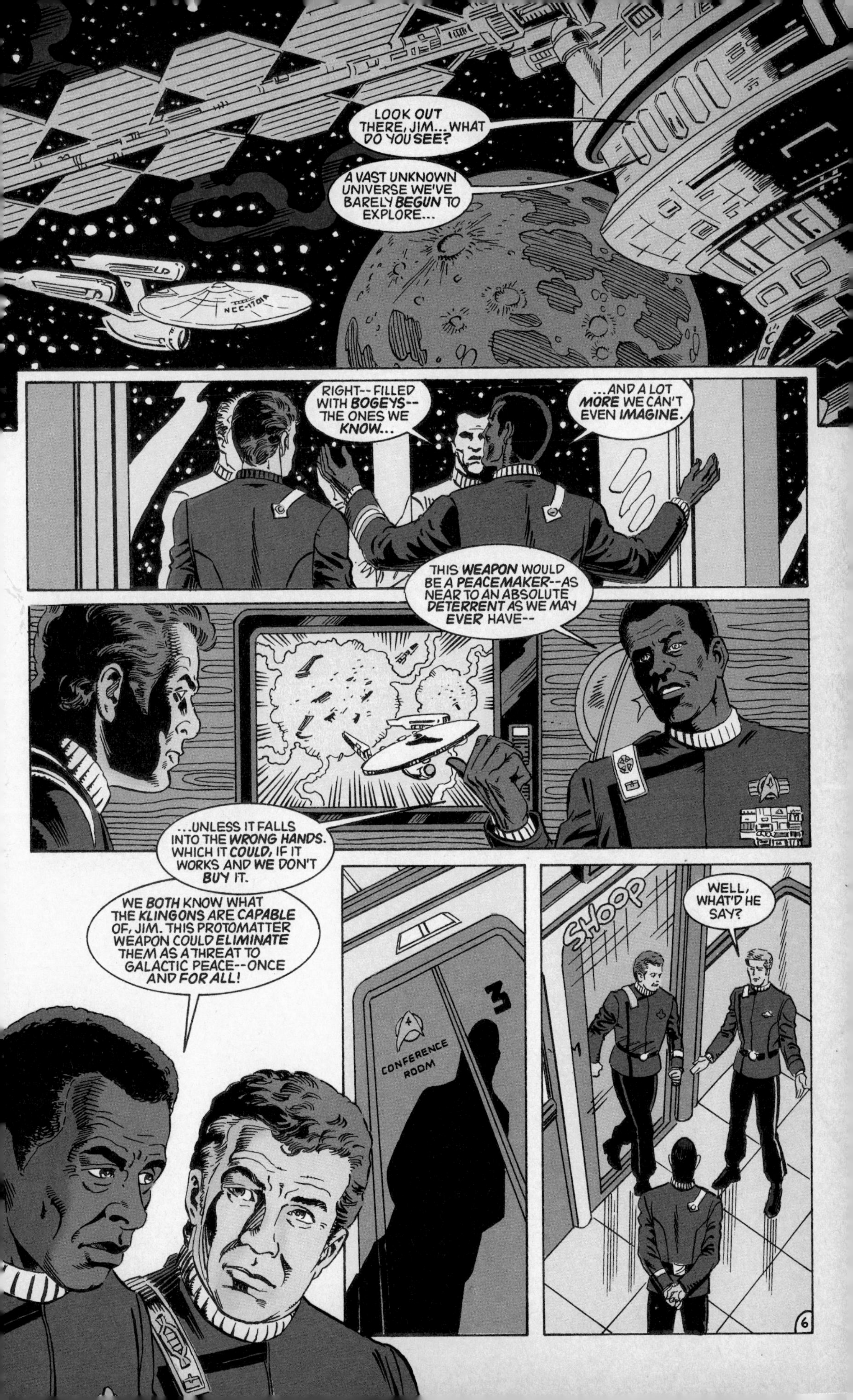

LOOK OUT THERE, JIM... WHAT DO YOU SEE?
A VAST UNKNOWN UNIVERSE WE'VE BARELY BEGUN TO EXPLORE...
NCC-1701A
RIGHT-- FILLED WITH BOGEYS-- THE ONES WE KNOW...
...AND A LOT MORE WE CAN'T EVEN IMAGINE.
THIS WEAPON WOULD BE A PEACEMAKER--AS NEAR TO AN ABSOLUTE DETERRENT AS WE MAY EVER HAVE--
...UNLESS IT FALLS INTO THE WRONG HANDS. WHICH IT COULD, IF IT WORKS AND WE DON'T BUY IT.
WE BOTH KNOW WHAT THE KLINGONS ARE CAPABLE OF, JIM. THIS PROTOMATTER WEAPON COULD ELIMINATE THEM AS A THREAT TO GALACTIC PEACE--ONCE AND FOR ALL!
3
CONFERENCE ROOM
SHOOP
WELL, WHAT'D HE SAY?

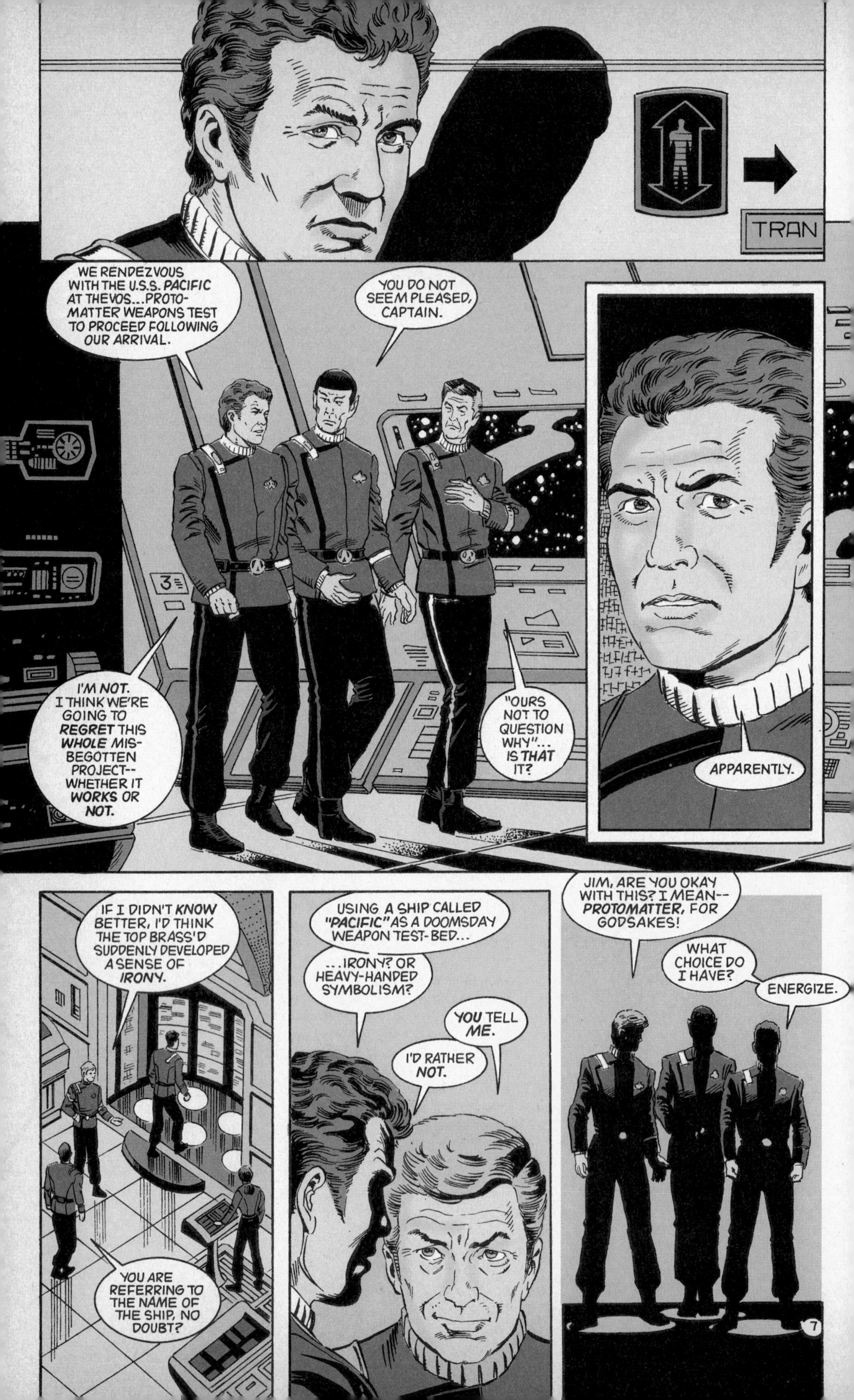

TRAN
WE RENDEZVOUS WITH THE U.S.S. PACIFIC AT THEVOS...PROTO-MATTER WEAPONS TEST TO PROCEED FOLLOWING OUR ARRIVAL.
YOU DO NOT SEEM PLEASED, CAPTAIN.
I'M NOT. I THINK WE'RE GOING TO REGRET THIS WHOLE MIS-BEGOTTEN PROJECT--WHETHER IT WORKS OR NOT.
"OURS NOT TO QUESTION WHY"... IS THAT IT?
APPARENTLY.
IF I DIDN'T KNOW BETTER, I'D THINK THE TOP BRASS'D SUDDENLY DEVELOPED A SENSE OF IRONY.
YOU ARE REFERRING TO THE NAME OF THE SHIP, NO DOUBT?
USING A SHIP CALLED "PACIFIC" AS A DOOMSDAY WEAPON TEST-BED...
...IRONY? OR HEAVY-HANDED SYMBOLISM?
YOU TELL ME.
I'D RATHER NOT.
JIM, ARE YOU OKAY WITH THIS? I MEAN--PROTOMATTER, FOR GODSAKES!
WHAT CHOICE DO I HAVE?
ENERGIZE.
7

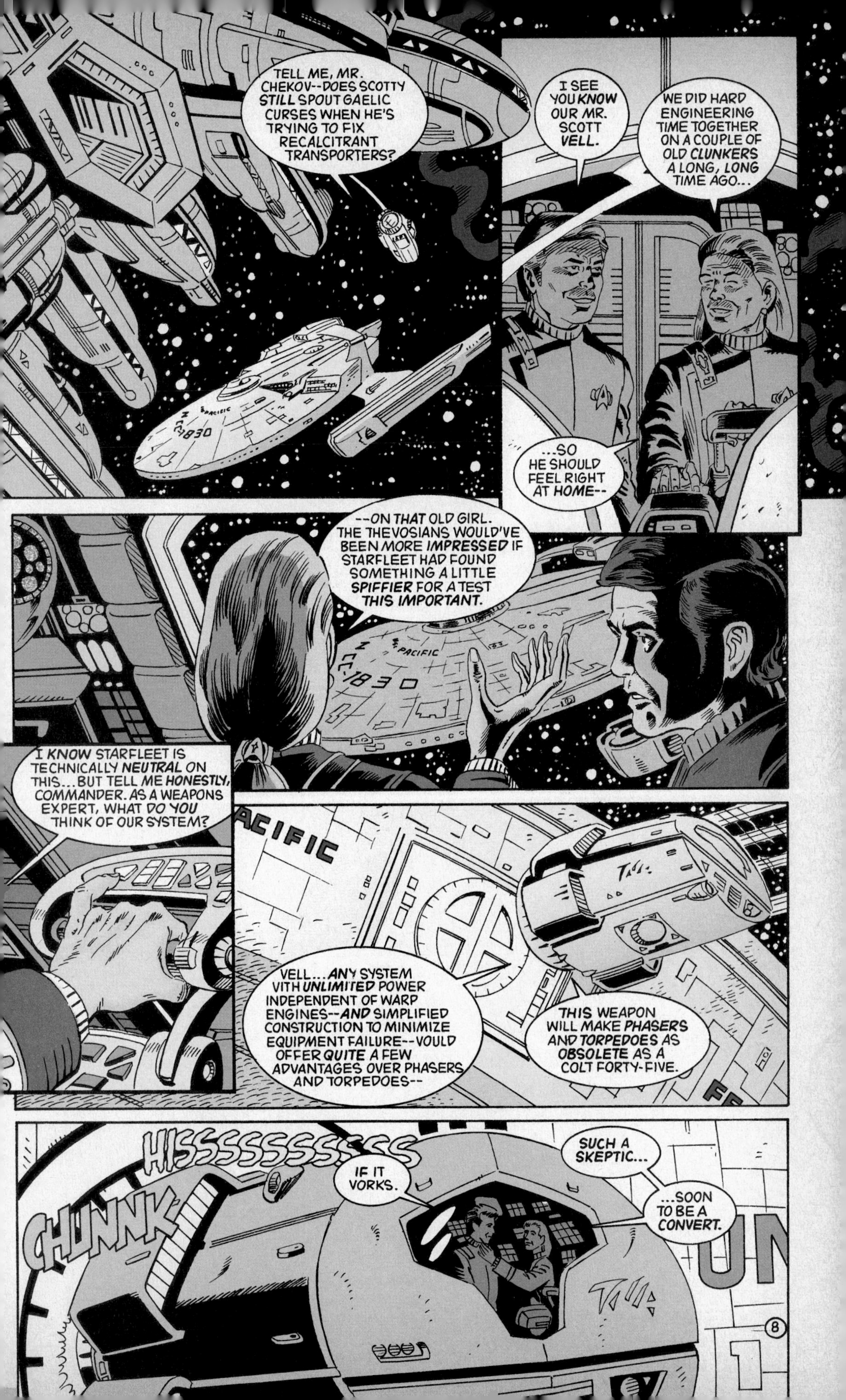
TELL ME, MR. CHEKOV--DOES SCOTTY STILL SPOUT GAELIC CURSES WHEN HE'S TRYING TO FIX RECALCITRANT TRANSPORTERS?
PACIFIC
NCC-1830
I SEE YOU KNOW OUR MR. SCOTT VELL.
WE DID HARD ENGINEERING TIME TOGETHER ON A COUPLE OF OLD CLUNKERS A LONG, LONG TIME AGO...
...SO HE SHOULD FEEL RIGHT AT HOME--
--ON THAT OLD GIRL. THE THEVOSIANS WOULD'VE BEEN MORE IMPRESSED IF STARFLEET HAD FOUND SOMETHING A LITTLE SPIFFIER FOR A TEST THIS IMPORTANT.
I KNOW STARFLEET IS TECHNICALLY NEUTRAL ON THIS... BUT TELL ME HONESTLY, COMMANDER. AS A WEAPONS EXPERT, WHAT DO YOU THINK OF OUR SYSTEM?
ACIFIC
VELL... ANY SYSTEM VITH UNLIMITED POWER INDEPENDENT OF WARP ENGINES--AND SIMPLIFIED CONSTRUCTION TO MINIMIZE EQUIPMENT FAILURE--VOULD OFFER QUITE A FEW ADVANTAGES OVER PHASERS AND TORPEDOES--
THIS WEAPON WILL MAKE PHASERS AND TORPEDOES AS OBSOLETE AS A COLT FORTY-FIVE.
HISSSSSSSSSS
CHUNNK!
IF IT VORKS.
SUCH A SKEPTIC...
...SOON TO BE A CONVERT.
8

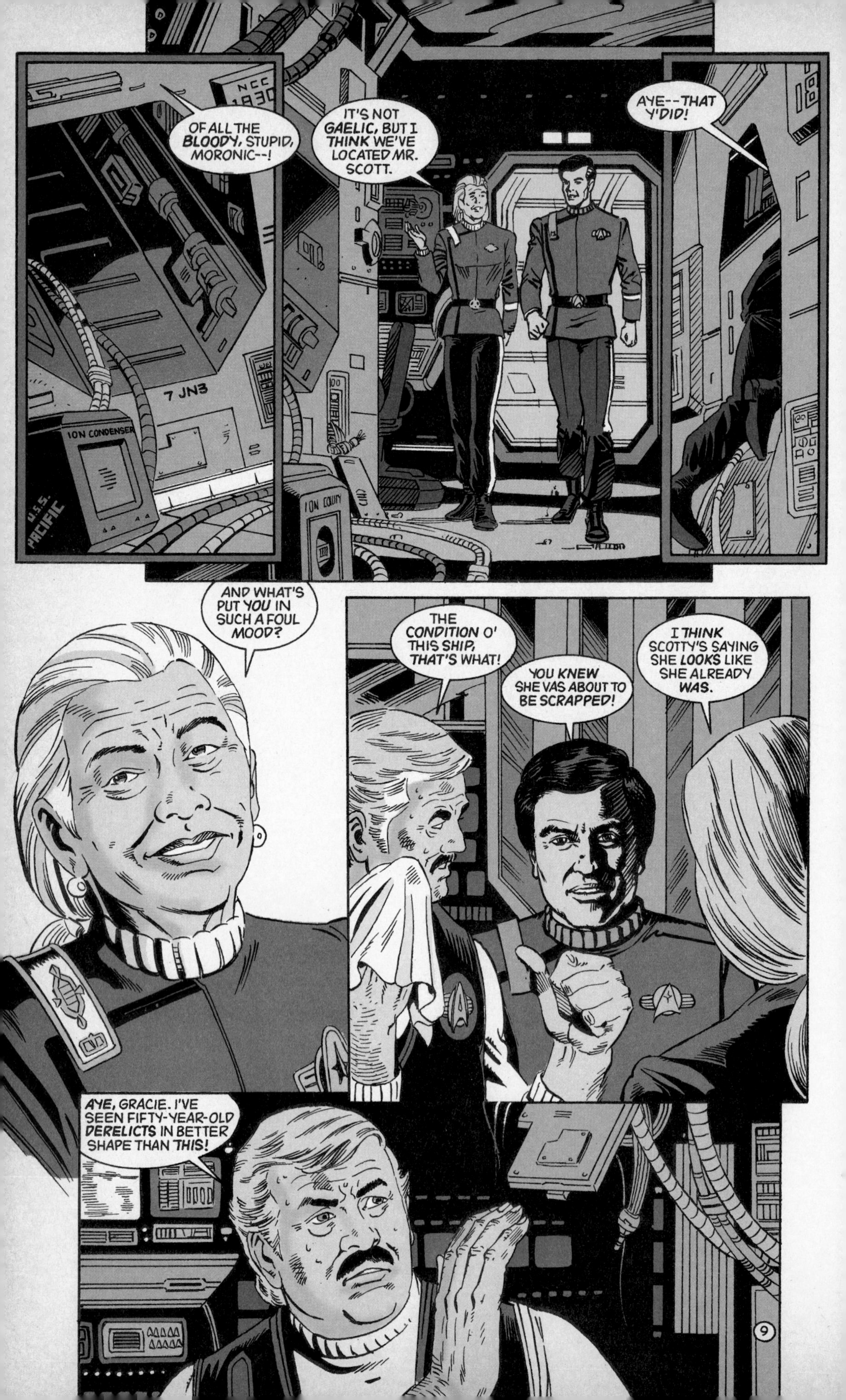

OF ALL THE BLOODY, STUPID, MORONIC--!
IT'S NOT GAELIC, BUT I THINK WE'VE LOCATED MR. SCOTT.
AYE--THAT Y'DID!
NCC 1830
ION CONDENSER
7 JN3
U.S.S. PACIFIC
AND WHAT'S PUT YOU IN SUCH A FOUL MOOD?
THE CONDITION O' THIS SHIP, THAT'S WHAT!
YOU KNEW SHE VAS ABOUT TO BE SCRAPPED!
I THINK SCOTTY'S SAYING SHE LOOKS LIKE SHE ALREADY WAS.
AYE, GRACIE. I'VE SEEN FIFTY-YEAR-OLD DERELICTS IN BETTER SHAPE THAN THIS!

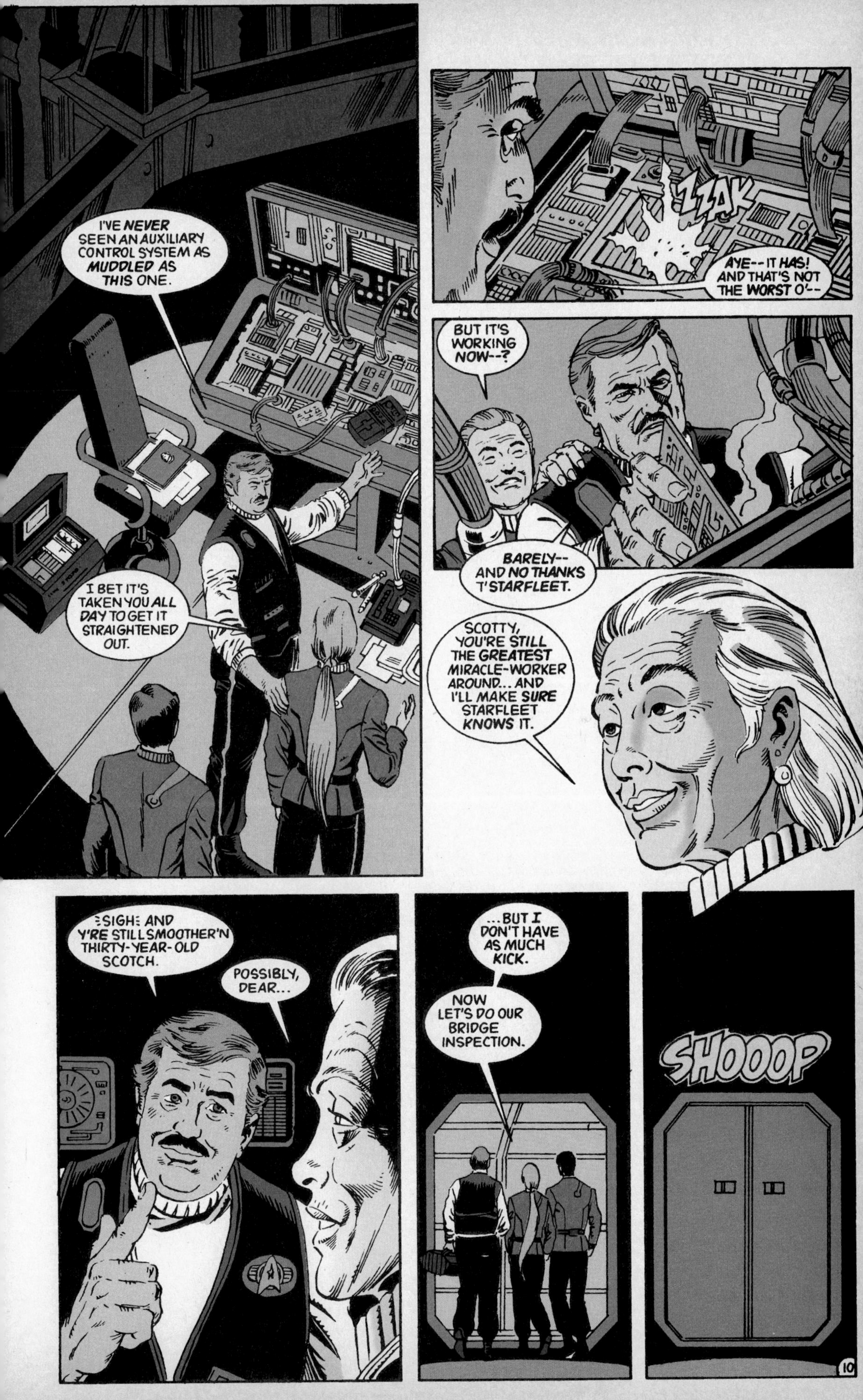
I'VE NEVER SEEN AN AUXILIARY CONTROL SYSTEM AS MUDDLED AS THIS ONE.
I BET IT'S TAKEN YOU ALL DAY TO GET IT STRAIGHTENED OUT.
ZZAK
AYE-- IT HAS! AND THAT'S NOT THE WORST O'--
BUT IT'S WORKING NOW--?
BARELY-- AND NO THANKS T' STARFLEET.
SCOTTY, YOU'RE STILL THE GREATEST MIRACLE-WORKER AROUND... AND I'LL MAKE SURE STARFLEET KNOWS IT.
=SIGH= AND Y'RE STILL SMOOTHER'N THIRTY-YEAR-OLD SCOTCH.
POSSIBLY, DEAR...
...BUT I DON'T HAVE AS MUCH KICK.
NOW LET'S DO OUR BRIDGE INSPECTION.
SHOOOP
10

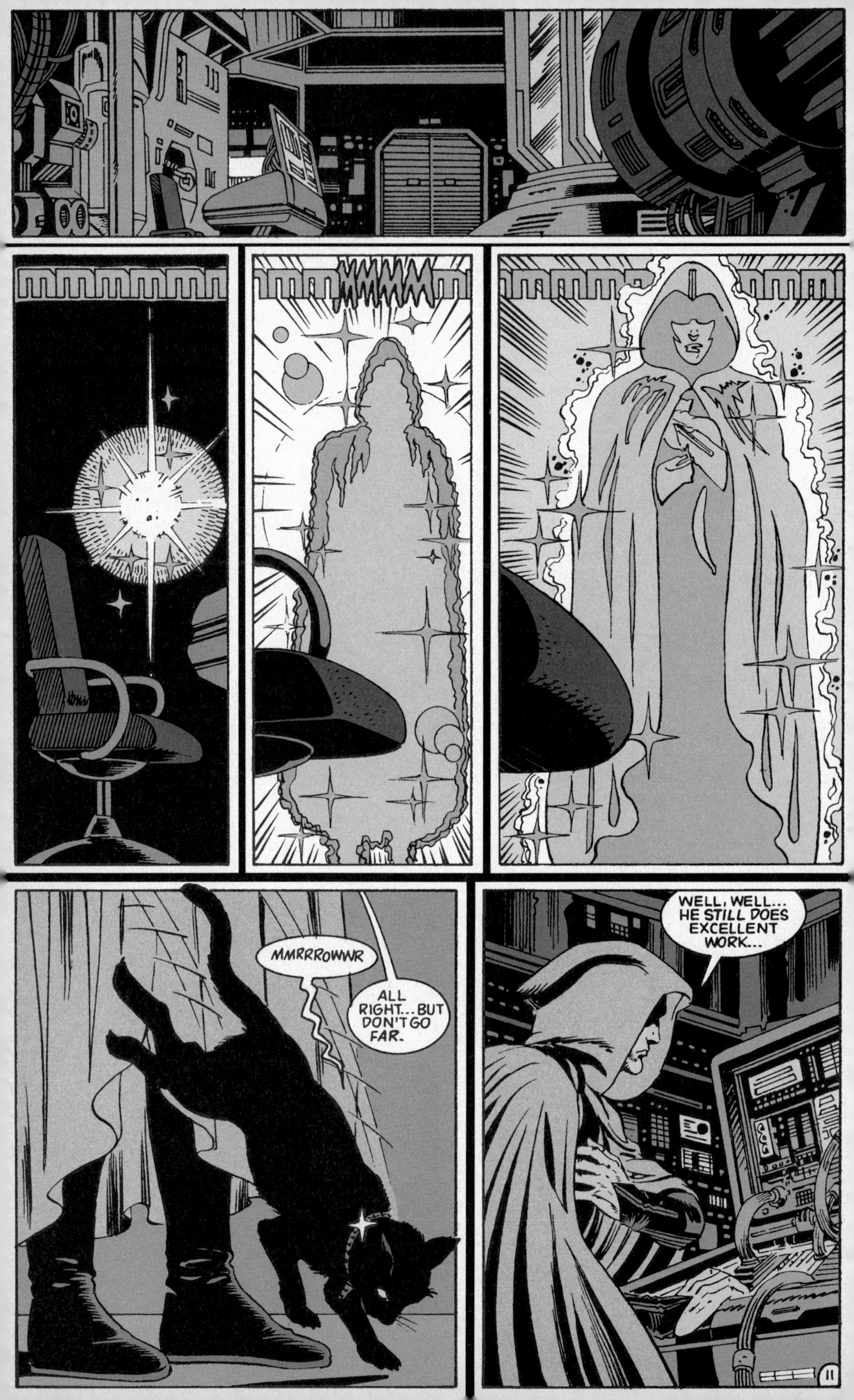
mmmmmmmmmmmmMMMMMmmmmmmmmmmmmm
MMRRROWWR
ALL RIGHT... BUT DON'T GO FAR.
WELL, WELL... HE STILL DOES EXCELLENT WORK...
11

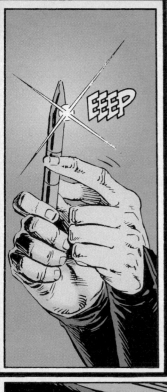

EEP

MMMMRRRR

AN INTRIGUING OBSERVATION... THOUGH I'M NOT SURE I ENTIRELY AGREE.

HOWEVER, WE CAN DEBATE SOME OTHER--

HIIISS!

ARE YOU SURE?

MMROWWR!

YOU'RE RIGHT. I SHOULD KNOW BETTER THAN TO DOUBT YOU.

MMMRROWWR--?

I DON'T THINK SO. I'D BETTER HANDLE IT FROM HERE...

MMMRRRR...

AND YOU'D BETTER BE QUIET.

12

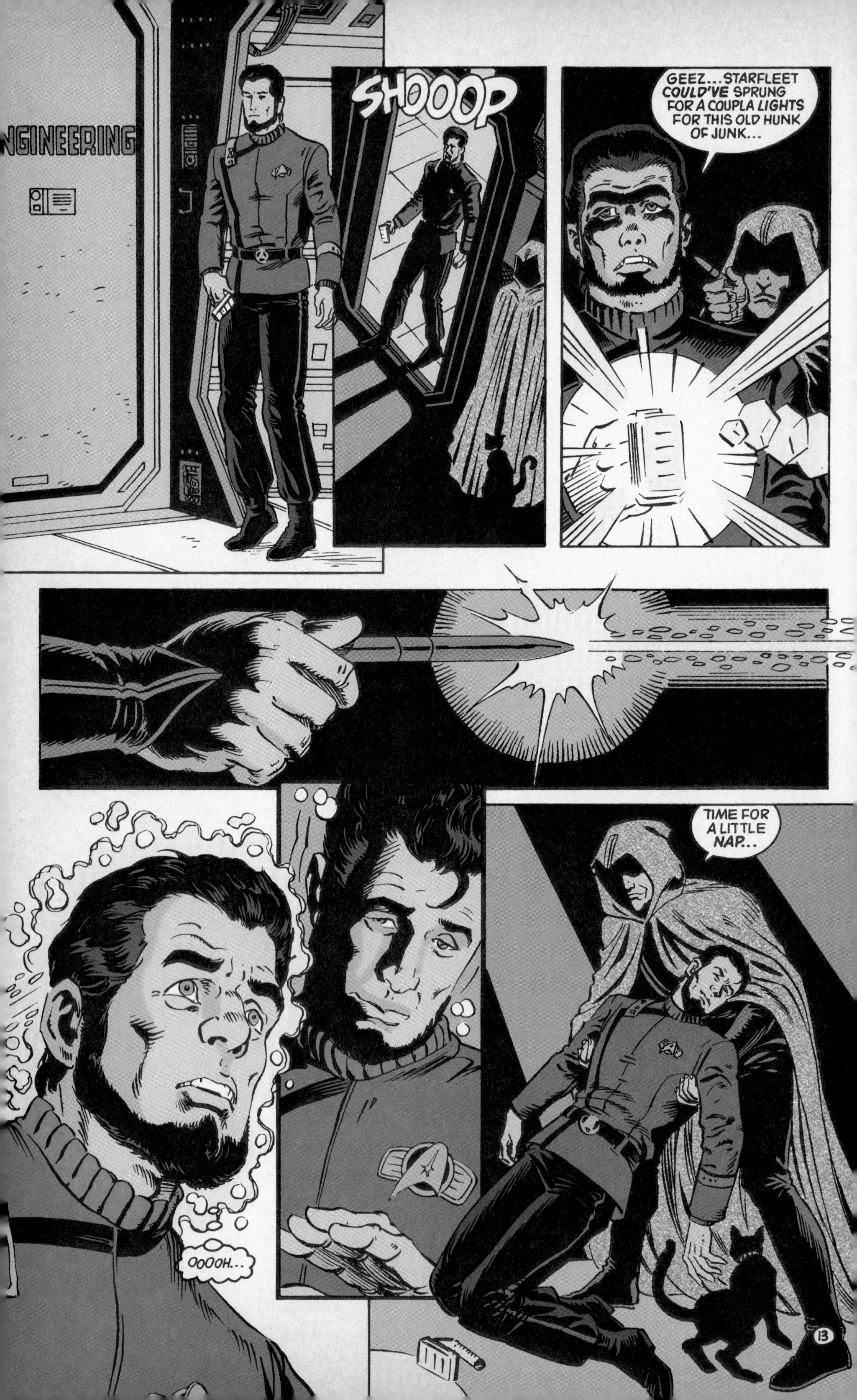
NGINEERING
SHOOOP
GEEZ... STARFLEET COULD'VE SPRUNG FOR A COUPLA LIGHTS FOR THIS OLD HUNK OF JUNK...
TIME FOR A LITTLE NAP...
OOOOH...
13

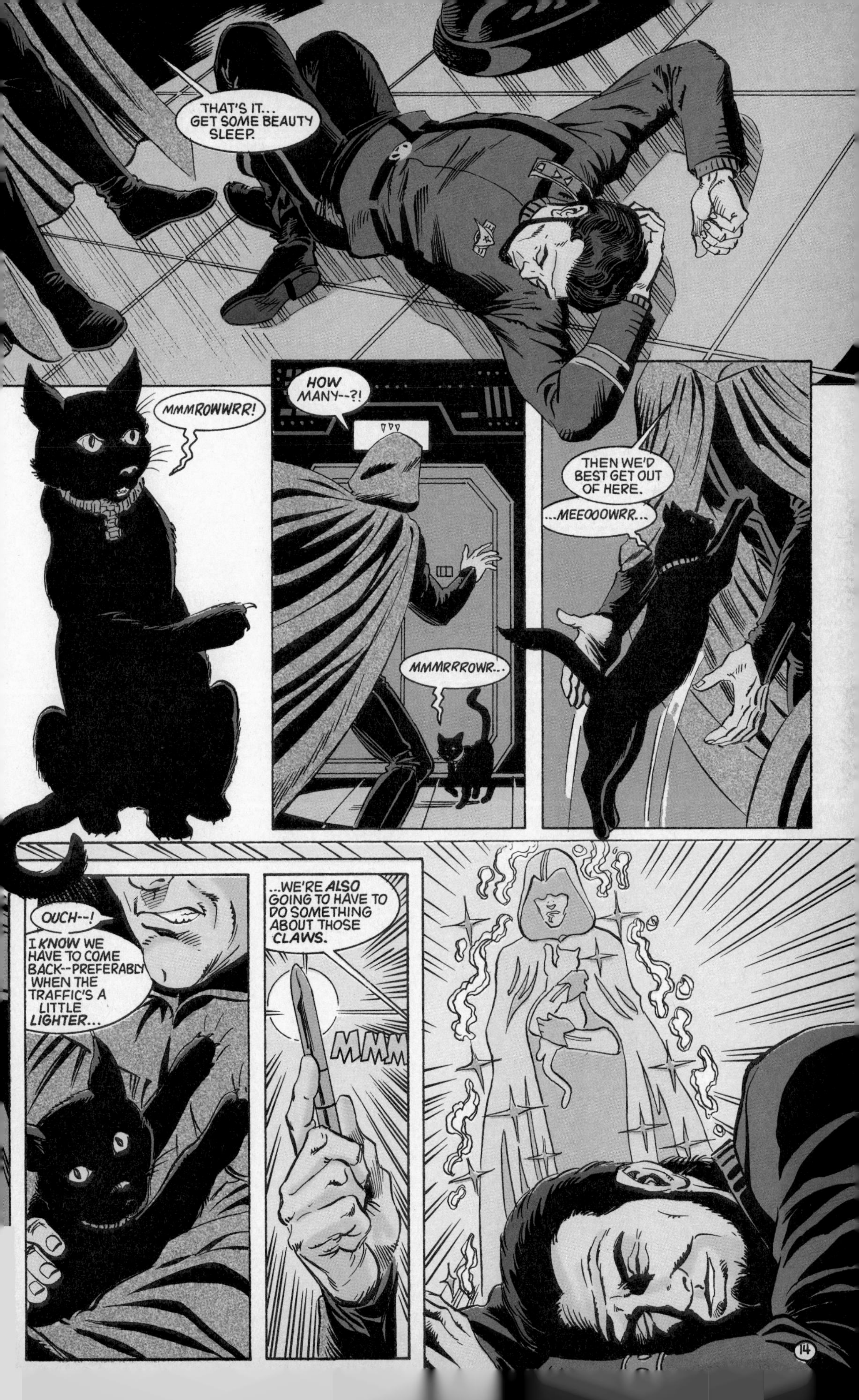
THAT'S IT... GET SOME BEAUTY SLEEP.
MMMROWWRR!
HOW MANY--?!
MMMRRROWR...
THEN WE'D BEST GET OUT OF HERE.
...MEEOOOWRR...
OUCH--!
I KNOW WE HAVE TO COME BACK--PREFERABLY WHEN THE TRAFFIC'S A LITTLE LIGHTER...
...WE'RE ALSO GOING TO HAVE TO DO SOMETHING ABOUT THOSE CLAWS.
MMM

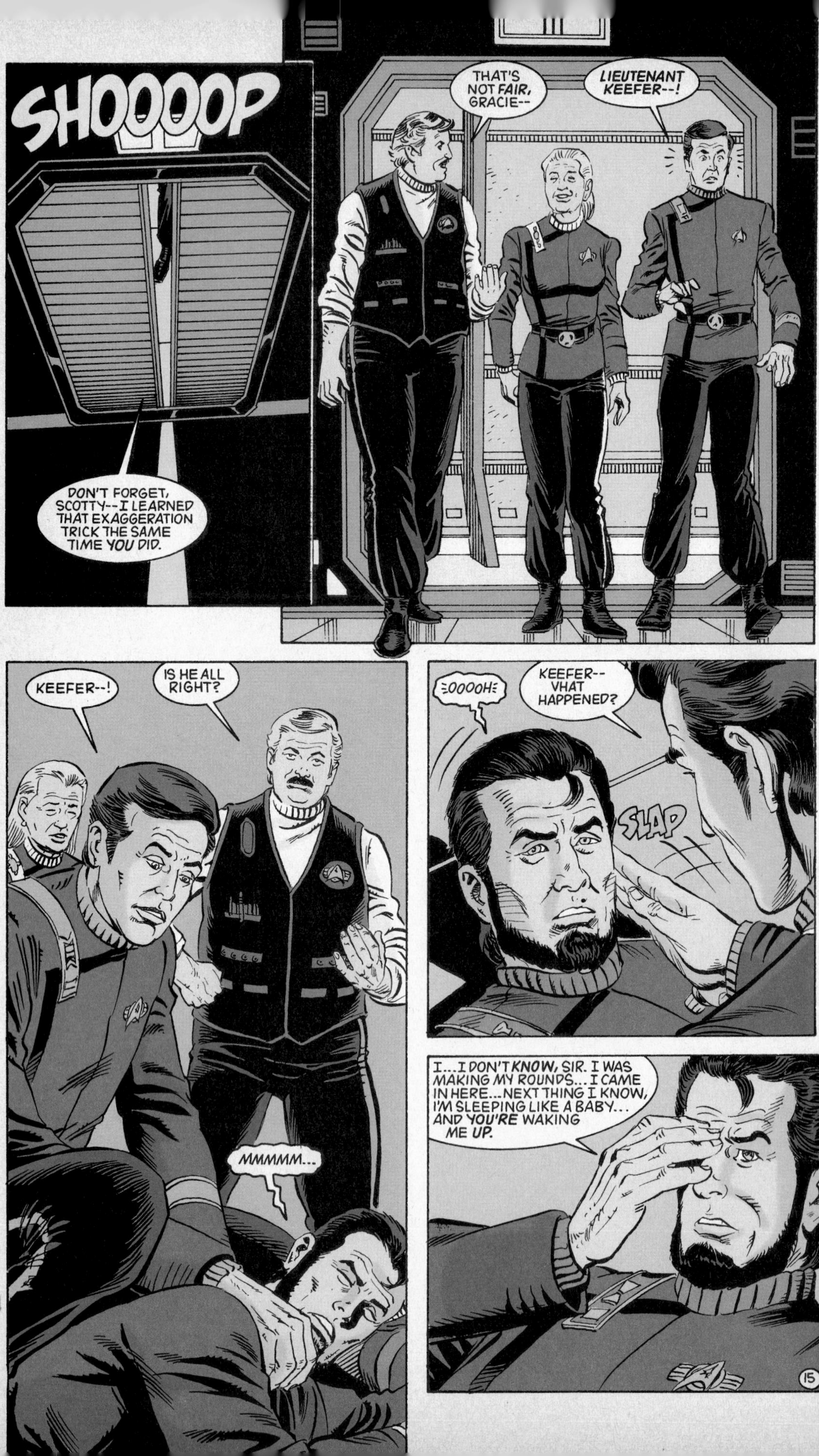
SHOOOOP
DON'T FORGET, SCOTTY--I LEARNED THAT EXAGGERATION TRICK THE SAME TIME YOU DID.
THAT'S NOT FAIR, GRACIE--
LIEUTENANT KEEFER--!
KEEFER--!
IS HE ALL RIGHT?
MMMMM...
OOOOH
KEEFER-- WHAT HAPPENED?
SLAP
I...I DON'T KNOW, SIR. I WAS MAKING MY ROUNDS... I CAME IN HERE...NEXT THING I KNOW, I'M SLEEPING LIKE A BABY... AND YOU'RE WAKING ME UP.
15

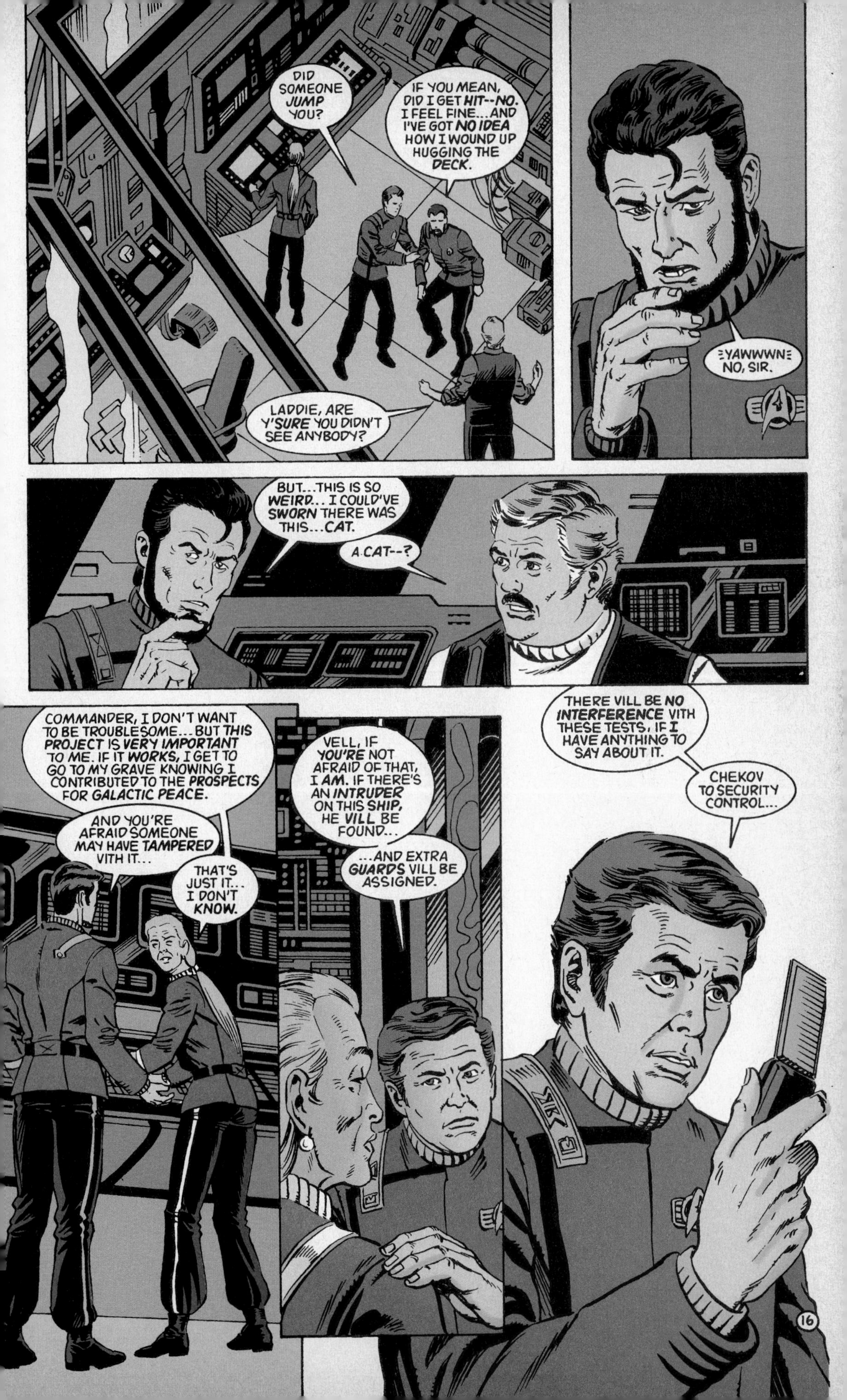
DID SOMEONE JUMP YOU?
IF YOU MEAN, DID I GET HIT--NO. I FEEL FINE...AND I'VE GOT NO IDEA HOW I WOUND UP HUGGING THE DECK.
LADDIE, ARE Y'SURE YOU DIDN'T SEE ANYBODY?
YAWWWN NO, SIR.
BUT...THIS IS SO WEIRD... I COULD'VE SWORN THERE WAS THIS...CAT.
A CAT--?
COMMANDER, I DON'T WANT TO BE TROUBLESOME... BUT THIS PROJECT IS VERY IMPORTANT TO ME. IF IT WORKS, I GET TO GO TO MY GRAVE KNOWING I CONTRIBUTED TO THE PROSPECTS FOR GALACTIC PEACE.
AND YOU'RE AFRAID SOMEONE MAY HAVE TAMPERED VITH IT...
THAT'S JUST IT... I DON'T KNOW.
VELL, IF YOU'RE NOT AFRAID OF THAT, I AM. IF THERE'S AN INTRUDER ON THIS SHIP, HE VILL BE FOUND...
...AND EXTRA GUARDS VILL BE ASSIGNED.
THERE VILL BE NO INTERFERENCE VITH THESE TESTS, IF I HAVE ANYTHING TO SAY ABOUT IT.
CHEKOV TO SECURITY CONTROL...

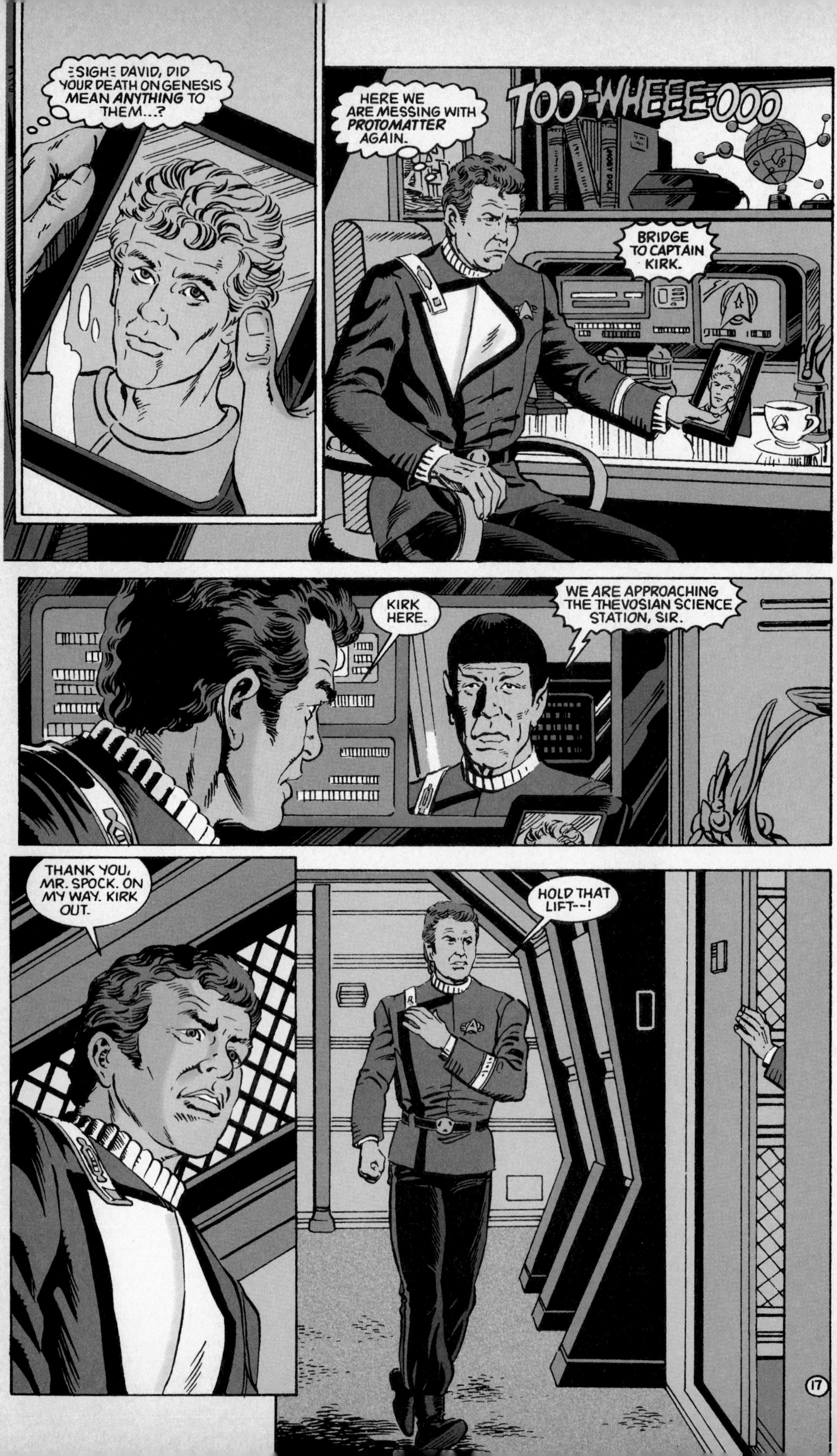

SIGH DAVID, DID YOUR DEATH ON GENESIS MEAN ANYTHING TO THEM...?
HERE WE ARE MESSING WITH PROTOMATTER AGAIN.
TOO-WHEEE-OOO
BRIDGE TO CAPTAIN KIRK.
KIRK HERE.
WE ARE APPROACHING THE THEVOSIAN SCIENCE STATION, SIR.
THANK YOU, MR. SPOCK. ON MY WAY. KIRK OUT.
HOLD THAT LIFT--!

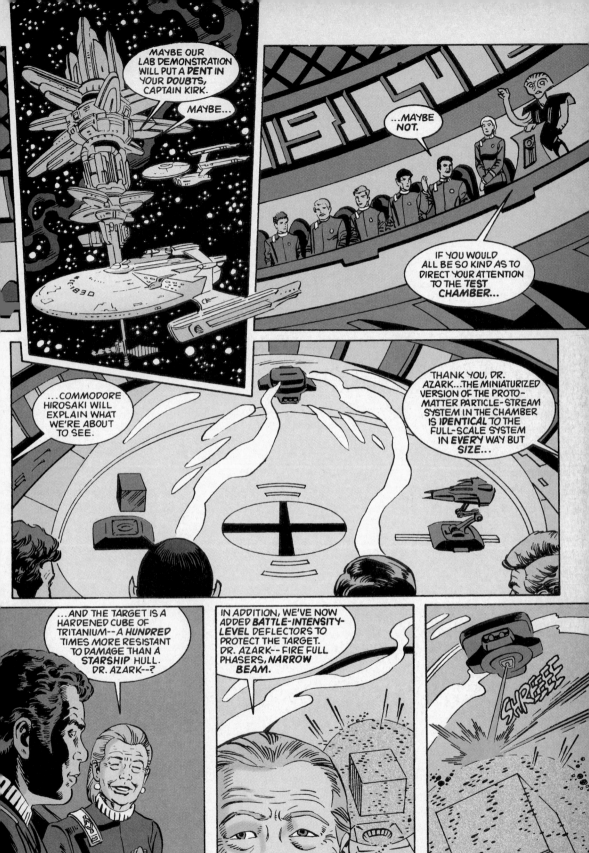

MAYBE OUR LAB DEMONSTRATION WILL PUT A *DENT* IN YOUR *DOUBTS,* CAPTAIN KIRK.

MAYBE...

...MAYBE *NOT.*

IF YOU WOULD ALL BE SO KIND AS TO DIRECT YOUR ATTENTION TO THE *TEST CHAMBER...*

...COMMODORE HIROSAKI WILL EXPLAIN WHAT WE'RE ABOUT TO SEE.

THANK YOU, DR. AZARK...THE MINIATURIZED VERSION OF THE PROTO-MATTER PARTICLE-STREAM SYSTEM IN THE CHAMBER IS *IDENTICAL* TO THE FULL-SCALE SYSTEM IN *EVERY* WAY BUT *SIZE...*

...AND THE TARGET IS A *HARDENED* CUBE OF TRITANIUM-- A *HUNDRED* TIMES MORE RESISTANT TO DAMAGE THAN A STARSHIP HULL. DR. AZARK--?

IN ADDITION, WE'VE NOW ADDED *BATTLE-INTENSITY-LEVEL* DEFLECTORS TO PROTECT THE TARGET. DR. AZARK-- FIRE FULL PHASERS, *NARROW BEAM.*

SHREEE

18

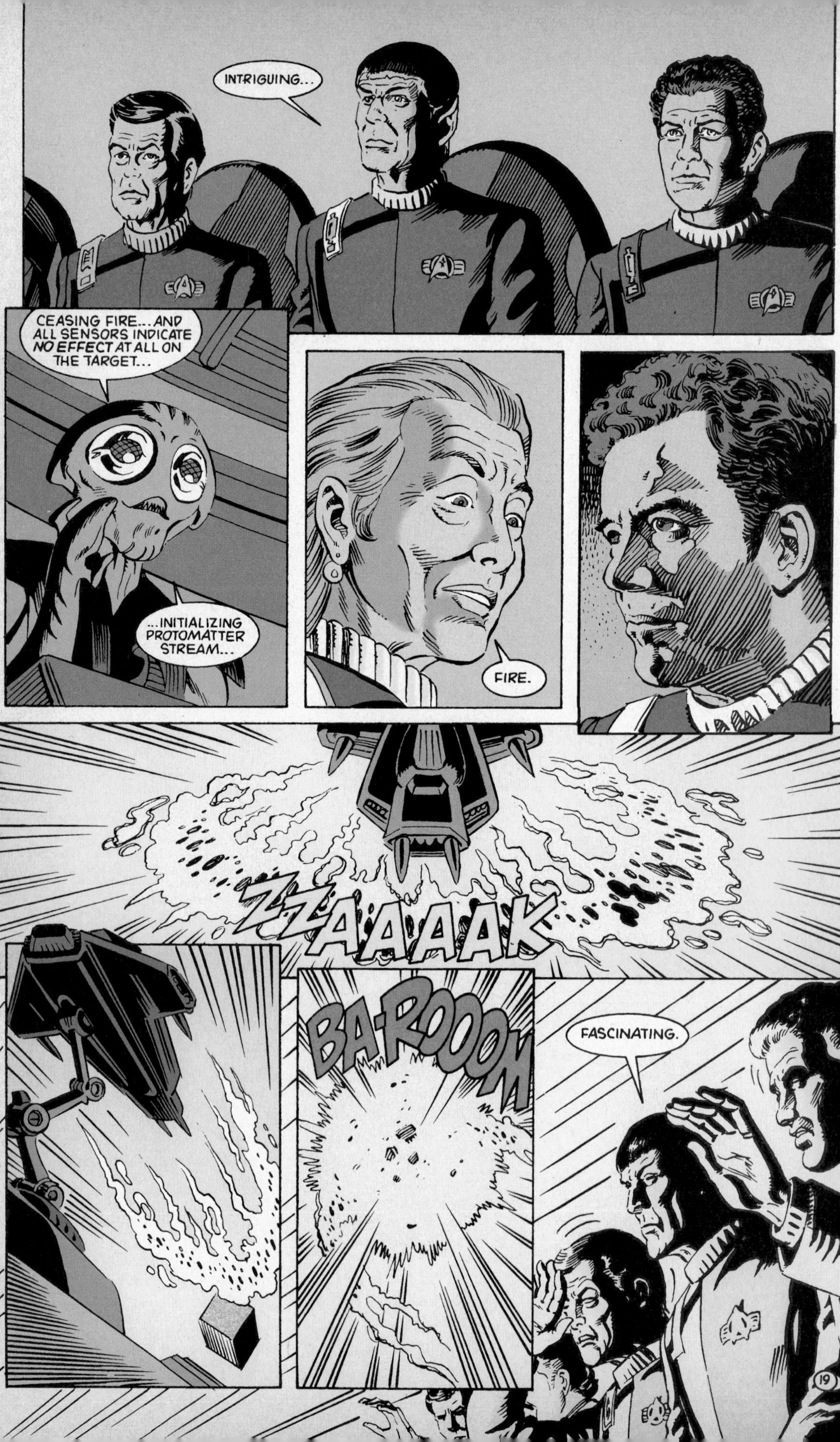

INTRIGUING...
CEASING FIRE... AND ALL SENSORS INDICATE NO EFFECT AT ALL ON THE TARGET...
...INITIALIZING PROTOMATTER STREAM...
FIRE.
ZZAAAAK
BA-ROOOM
FASCINATING.

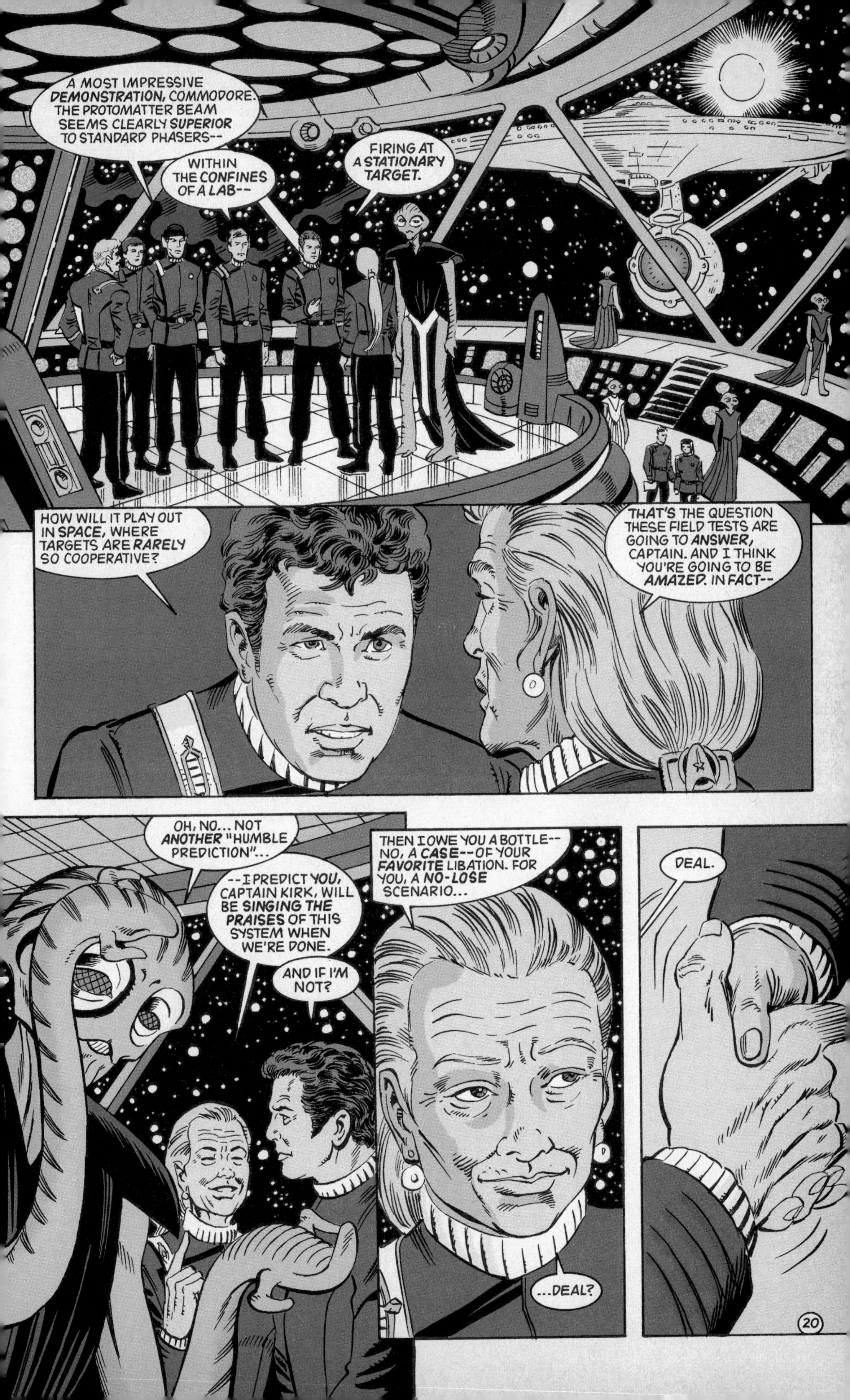
A MOST IMPRESSIVE DEMONSTRATION, COMMODORE. THE PROTOMATTER BEAM SEEMS CLEARLY SUPERIOR TO STANDARD PHASERS--
WITHIN THE CONFINES OF A LAB--
FIRING AT A STATIONARY TARGET.
HOW WILL IT PLAY OUT IN SPACE, WHERE TARGETS ARE RARELY SO COOPERATIVE?
THAT'S THE QUESTION THESE FIELD TESTS ARE GOING TO ANSWER, CAPTAIN. AND I THINK YOU'RE GOING TO BE AMAZED. IN FACT--
OH, NO... NOT ANOTHER "HUMBLE PREDICTION"...
--I PREDICT YOU, CAPTAIN KIRK, WILL BE SINGING THE PRAISES OF THIS SYSTEM WHEN WE'RE DONE.
AND IF I'M NOT?
THEN I OWE YOU A BOTTLE-- NO, A CASE--OF YOUR FAVORITE LIBATION. FOR YOU, A NO-LOSE SCENARIO...
...DEAL?
DEAL.

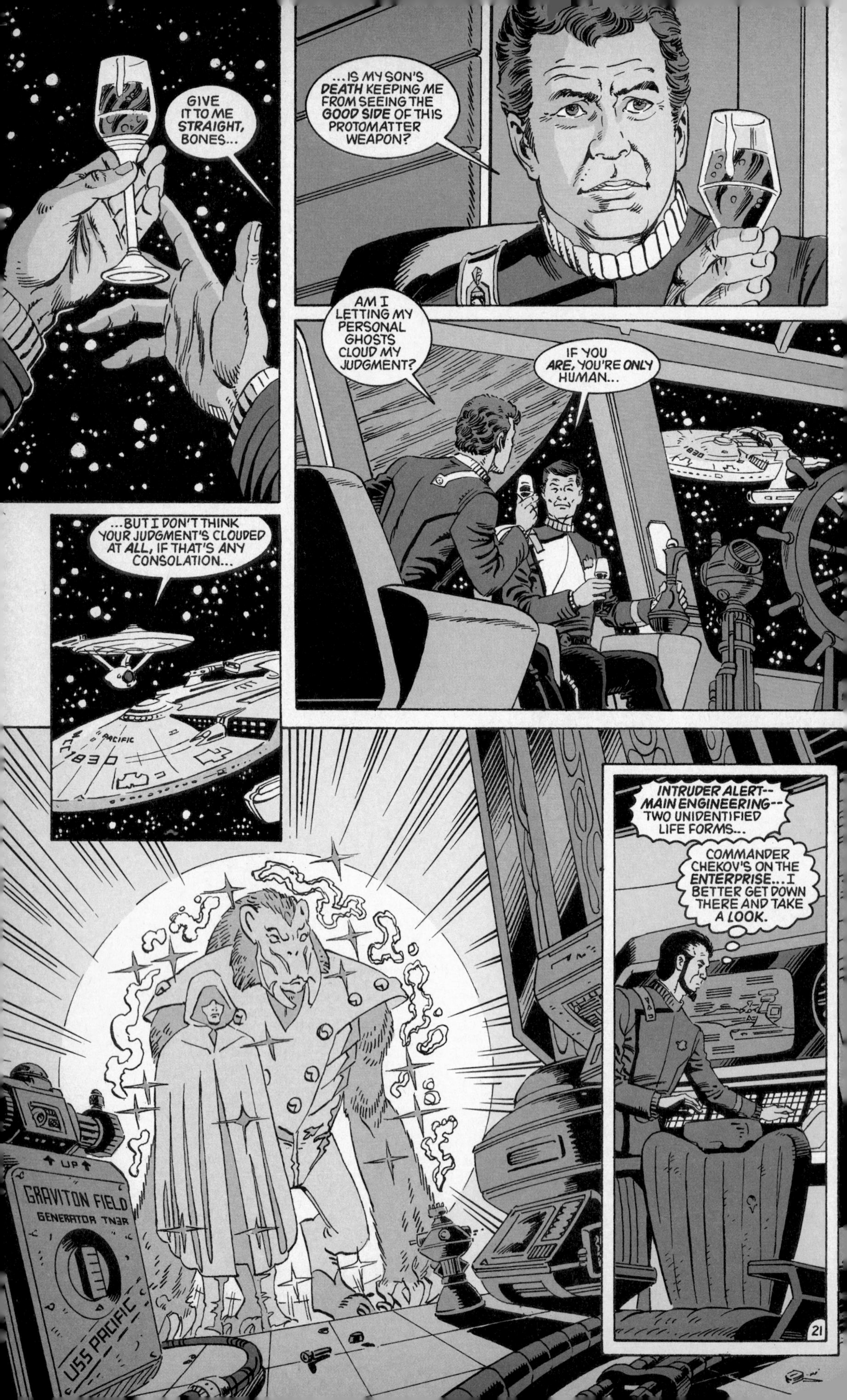
GIVE IT TO ME STRAIGHT, BONES...
...IS MY SON'S DEATH KEEPING ME FROM SEEING THE GOOD SIDE OF THIS PROTOMATTER WEAPON?
AM I LETTING MY PERSONAL GHOSTS CLOUD MY JUDGMENT?
IF YOU ARE, YOU'RE ONLY HUMAN...
NCC-1830
...BUT I DON'T THINK YOUR JUDGMENT'S CLOUDED AT ALL, IF THAT'S ANY CONSOLATION...
PACIFIC
NCC-1830
INTRUDER ALERT-- MAIN ENGINEERING-- TWO UNIDENTIFIED LIFE FORMS...
COMMANDER CHEKOV'S ON THE ENTERPRISE... I BETTER GET DOWN THERE AND TAKE A LOOK.
UP
GRAVITON FIELD
GENERATOR TN3R
USS PACIFIC
21

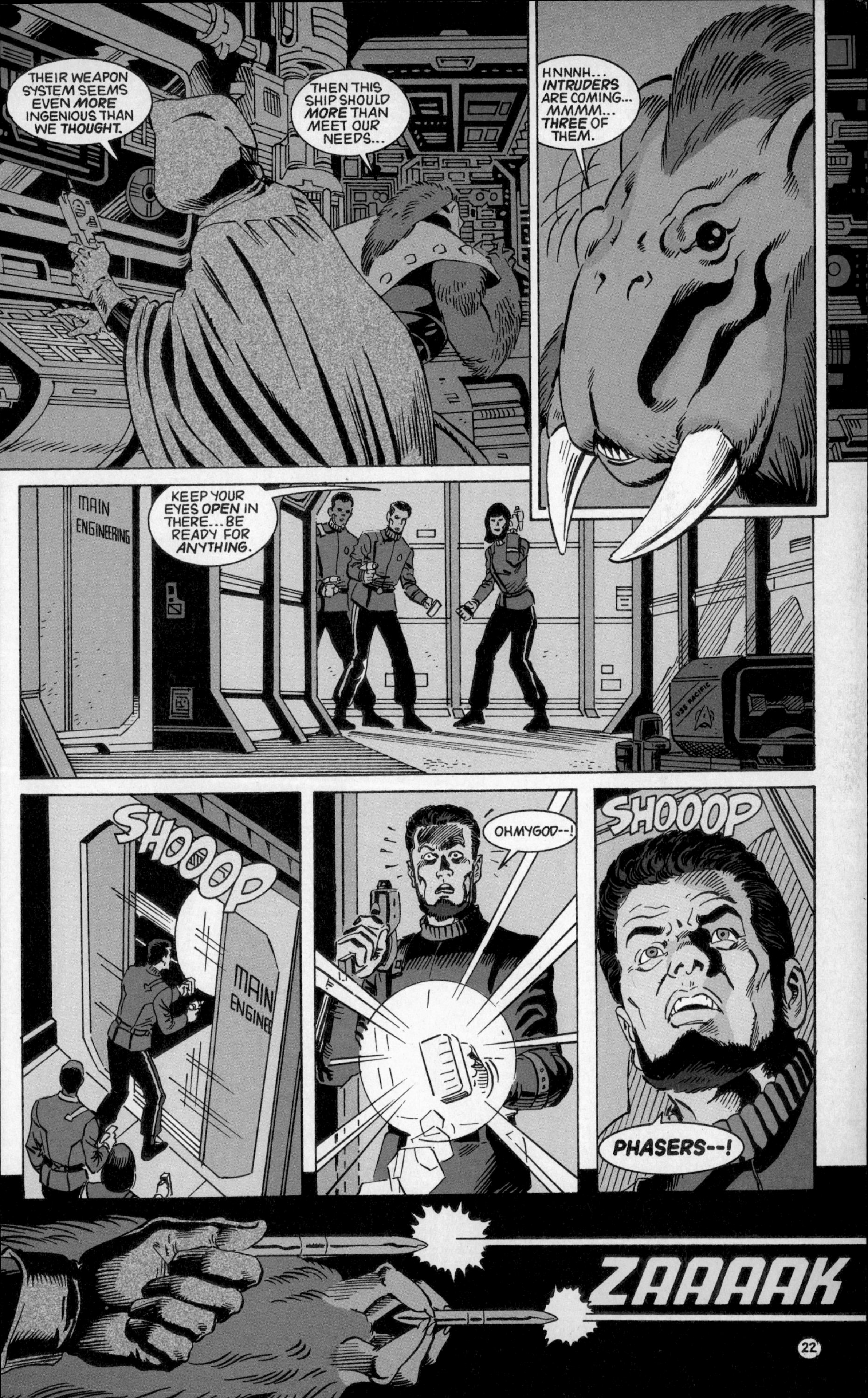
THEIR WEAPON SYSTEM SEEMS EVEN MORE INGENIOUS THAN WE THOUGHT.
THEN THIS SHIP SHOULD MORE THAN MEET OUR NEEDS...
HNNNH... INTRUDERS ARE COMING... MMMM... THREE OF THEM.
MAIN ENGINEERING
KEEP YOUR EYES OPEN IN THERE... BE READY FOR ANYTHING.
USS PACIFIC
SHOOOP
MAIN ENGINEE
OHMYGOD--!
SHOOOP
PHASERS--!
ZAAAAK

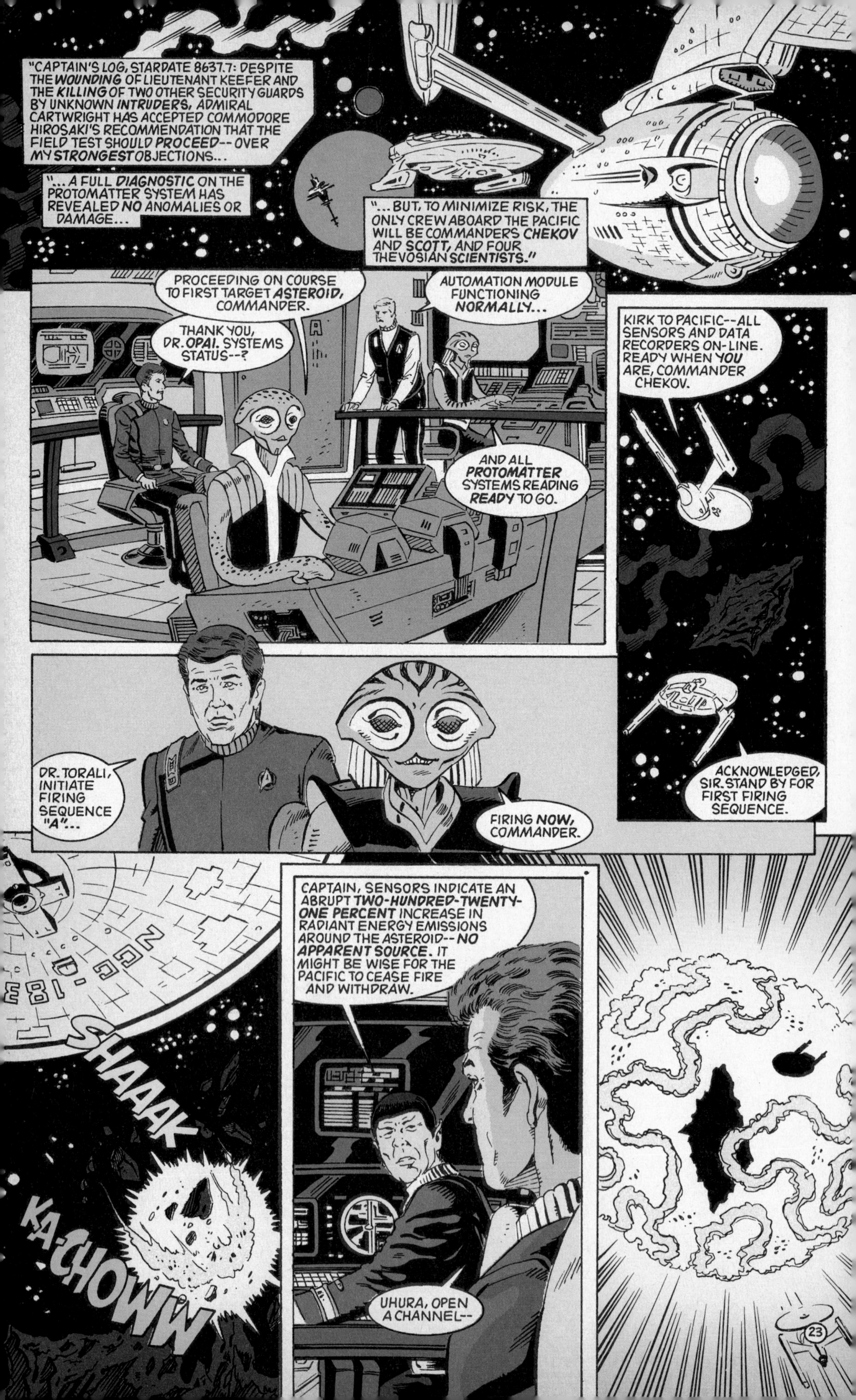
"CAPTAIN'S LOG, STARDATE 8637.7: DESPITE THE WOUNDING OF LIEUTENANT KEEFER AND THE KILLING OF TWO OTHER SECURITY GUARDS BY UNKNOWN INTRUDERS, ADMIRAL CARTWRIGHT HAS ACCEPTED COMMODORE HIROSAKI'S RECOMMENDATION THAT THE FIELD TEST SHOULD PROCEED-- OVER MY STRONGEST OBJECTIONS...
"... A FULL DIAGNOSTIC ON THE PROTOMATTER SYSTEM HAS REVEALED NO ANOMALIES OR DAMAGE...
"... BUT, TO MINIMIZE RISK, THE ONLY CREW ABOARD THE PACIFIC WILL BE COMMANDERS CHEKOV AND SCOTT, AND FOUR THEVOSIAN SCIENTISTS."
PROCEEDING ON COURSE TO FIRST TARGET ASTEROID, COMMANDER.
THANK YOU, DR. OPAI. SYSTEMS STATUS--?
AUTOMATION MODULE FUNCTIONING NORMALLY...
AND ALL PROTOMATTER SYSTEMS READING READY TO GO.
KIRK TO PACIFIC--ALL SENSORS AND DATA RECORDERS ON-LINE. READY WHEN YOU ARE, COMMANDER CHEKOV.
ACKNOWLEDGED, SIR. STAND BY FOR FIRST FIRING SEQUENCE.
DR. TORALI, INITIATE FIRING SEQUENCE "A"...
FIRING NOW, COMMANDER.
NCC-1831
SHAAAK
KA-CHOWW
CAPTAIN, SENSORS INDICATE AN ABRUPT TWO-HUNDRED-TWENTY-ONE PERCENT INCREASE IN RADIANT ENERGY EMISSIONS AROUND THE ASTEROID--NO APPARENT SOURCE. IT MIGHT BE WISE FOR THE PACIFIC TO CEASE FIRE AND WITHDRAW.
UHURA, OPEN A CHANNEL--

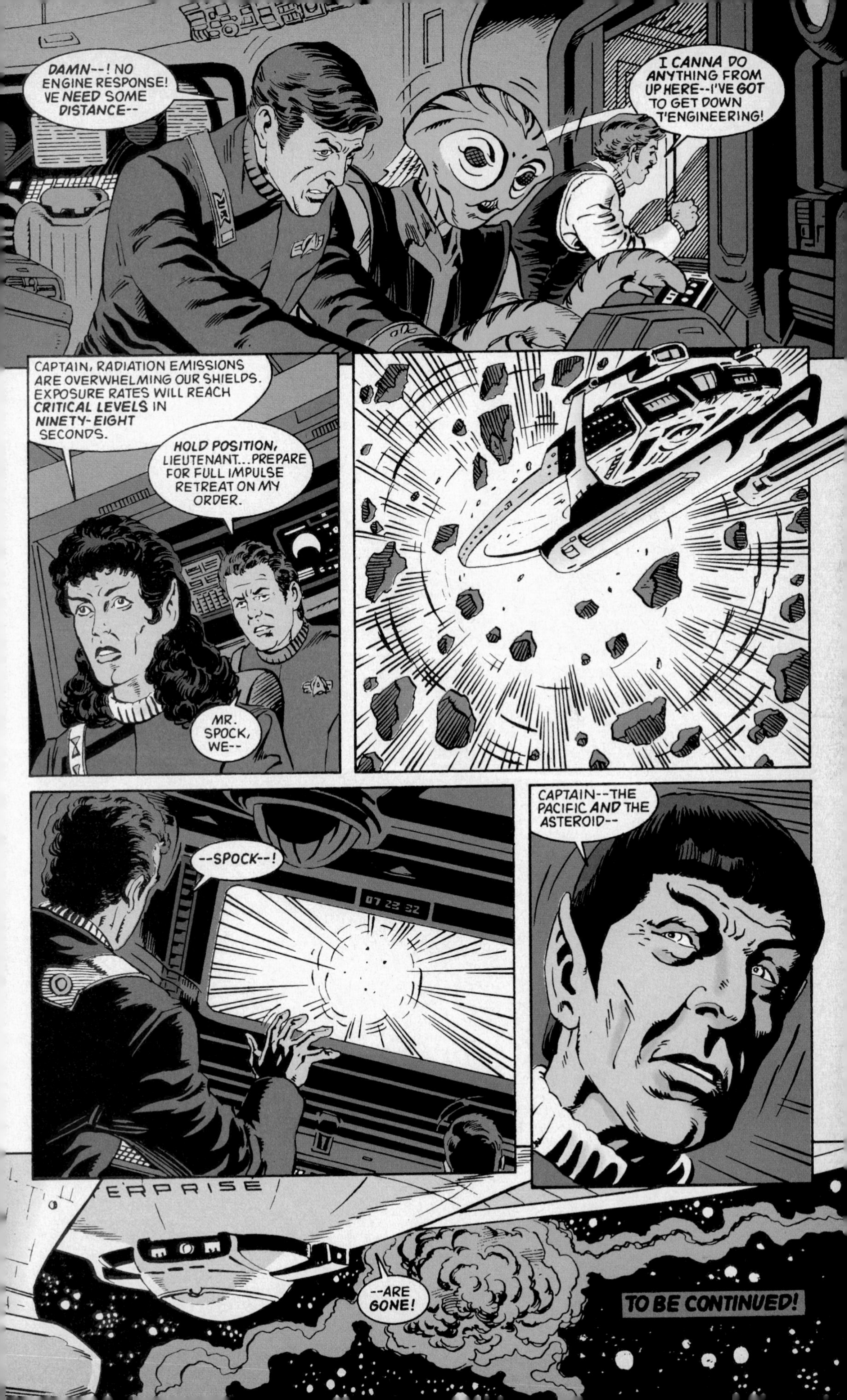
DAMN--! NO ENGINE RESPONSE! VE NEED SOME DISTANCE--
I CANNA DO ANYTHING FROM UP HERE--I'VE GOT TO GET DOWN T'ENGINEERING!
CAPTAIN, RADIATION EMISSIONS ARE OVERWHELMING OUR SHIELDS. EXPOSURE RATES WILL REACH CRITICAL LEVELS IN NINETY-EIGHT SECONDS.
HOLD POSITION, LIEUTENANT... PREPARE FOR FULL IMPULSE RETREAT ON MY ORDER.
MR. SPOCK, WE--
--SPOCK--!
CAPTAIN--THE PACIFIC AND THE ASTEROID--
--ARE GONE!
TO BE CONTINUED!

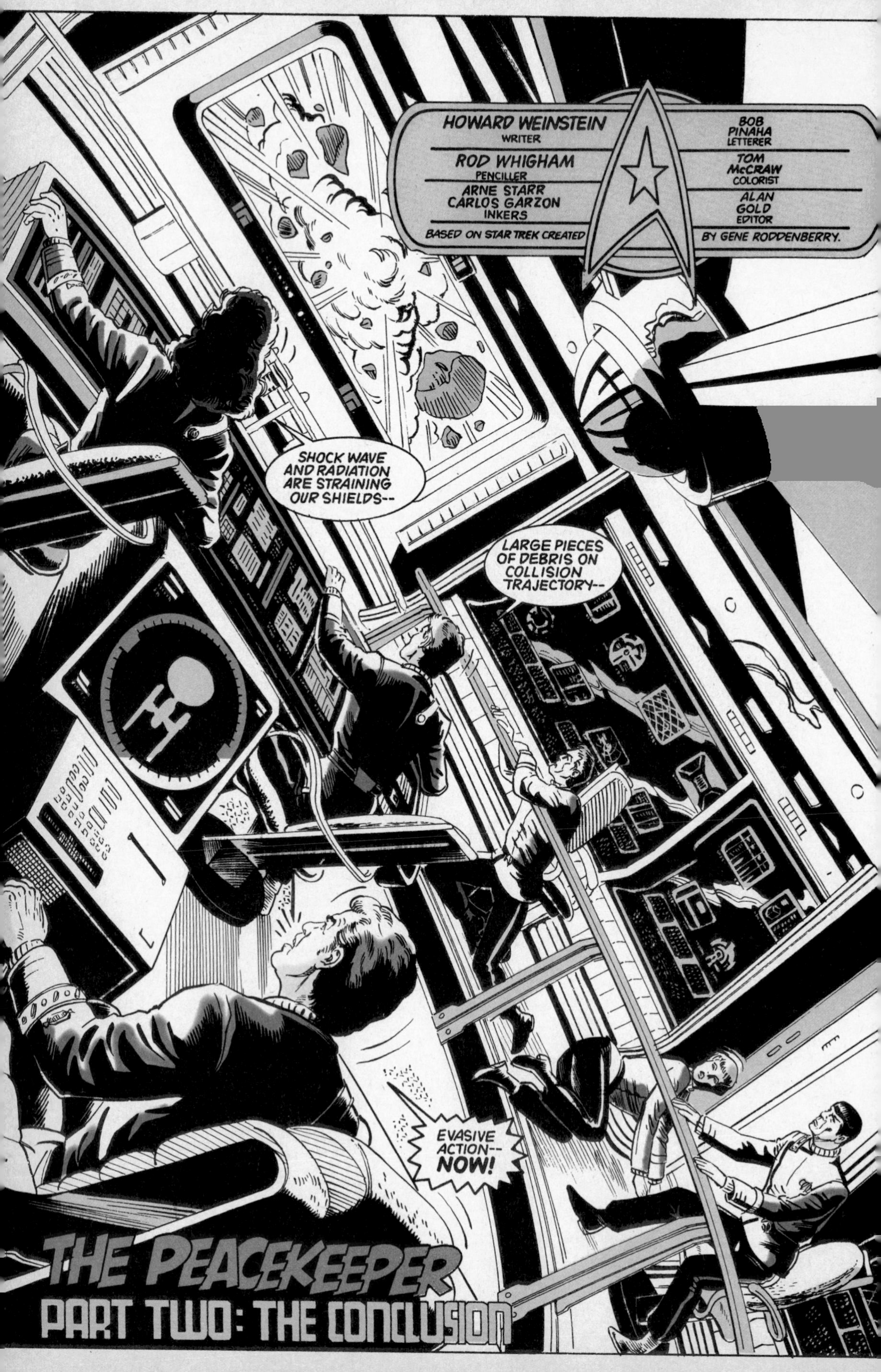

HOWARD WEINSTEIN
WRITER
ROD WHIGHAM
PENCILLER
ARNE STARR
CARLOS GARZON
INKERS
BOB
PINAHA
LETTERER
TOM
McCRAW
COLORIST
ALAN
GOLD
EDITOR
BASED ON STAR TREK CREATED BY GENE RODDENBERRY.
SHOCK WAVE AND RADIATION ARE STRAINING OUR SHIELDS--
LARGE PIECES OF DEBRIS ON COLLISION TRAJECTORY--
EVASIVE ACTION-- NOW!
THE PEACEKEEPER
PART TWO: THE CONCLUSION

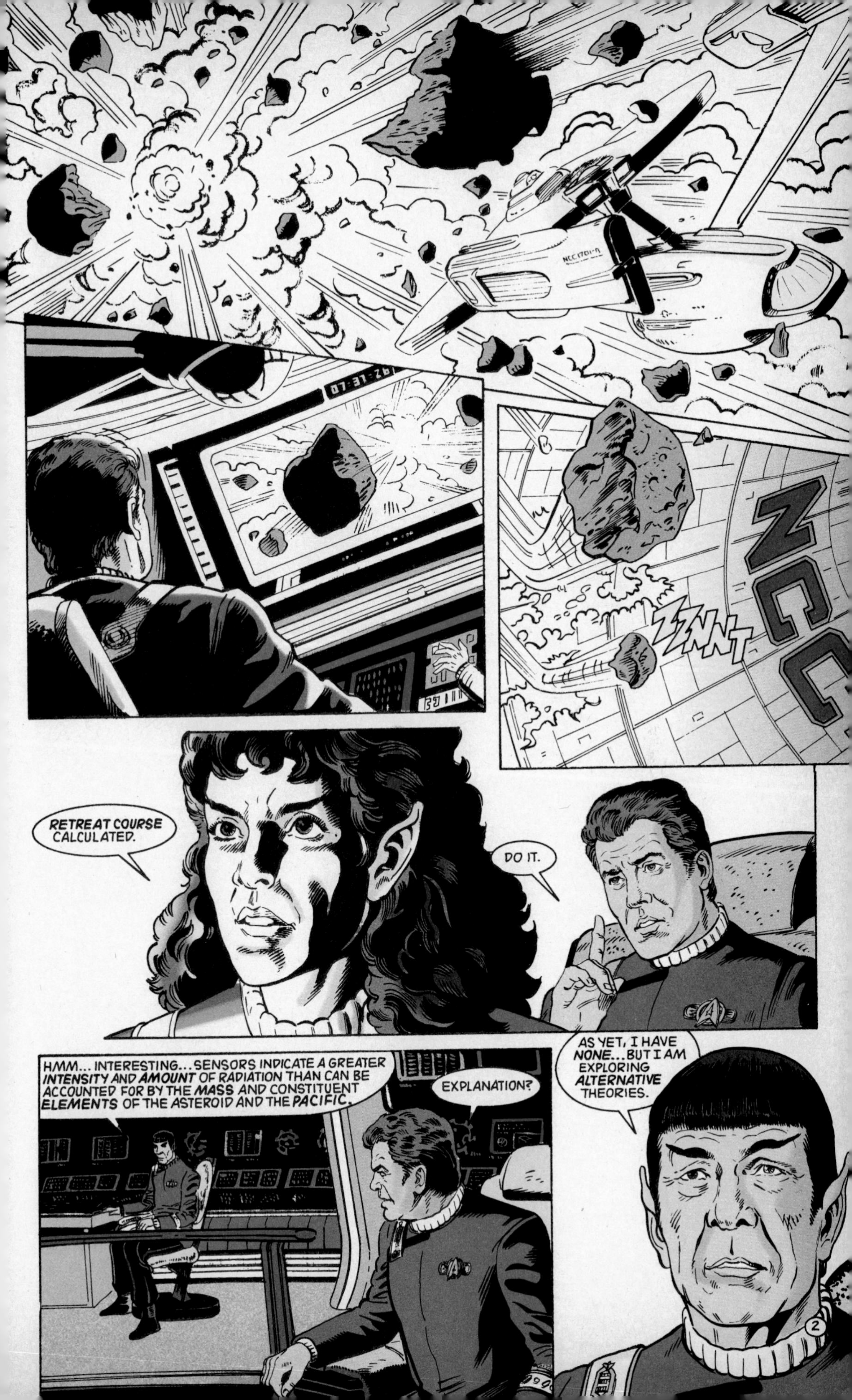
NCC 1701-A
07-31-76
ZZNNT
NCC
RETREAT COURSE CALCULATED.
DO IT.
HMM... INTERESTING... SENSORS INDICATE A GREATER INTENSITY AND AMOUNT OF RADIATION THAN CAN BE ACCOUNTED FOR BY THE MASS AND CONSTITUENT ELEMENTS OF THE ASTEROID AND THE PACIFIC.
EXPLANATION?
AS YET, I HAVE NONE... BUT I AM EXPLORING ALTERNATIVE THEORIES.
2

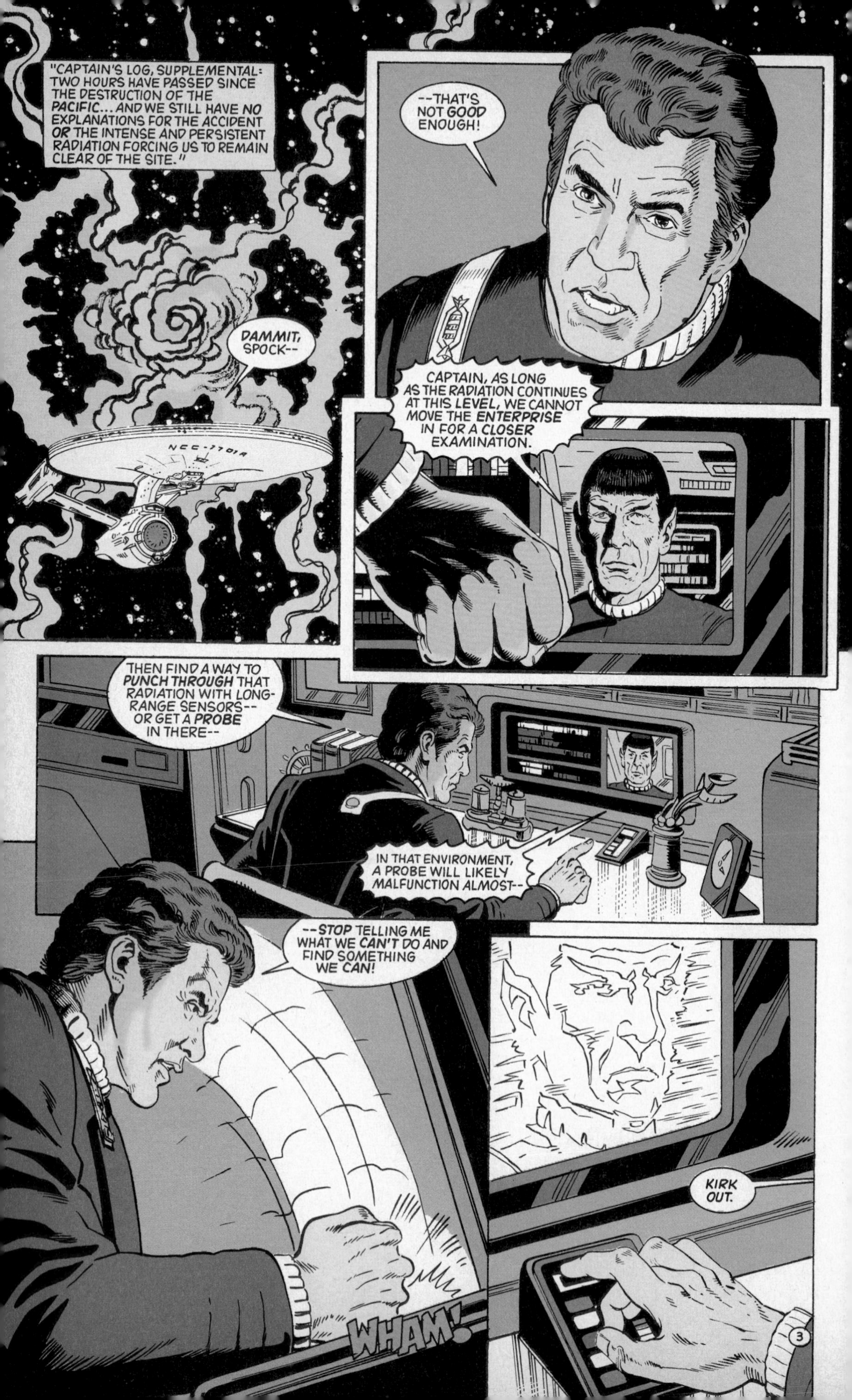
"CAPTAIN'S LOG, SUPPLEMENTAL: TWO HOURS HAVE PASSED SINCE THE DESTRUCTION OF THE PACIFIC... AND WE STILL HAVE NO EXPLANATIONS FOR THE ACCIDENT OR THE INTENSE AND PERSISTENT RADIATION FORCING US TO REMAIN CLEAR OF THE SITE."
NCC-1701A
DAMMIT, SPOCK--
--THAT'S NOT GOOD ENOUGH!
CAPTAIN, AS LONG AS THE RADIATION CONTINUES AT THIS LEVEL, WE CANNOT MOVE THE ENTERPRISE IN FOR A CLOSER EXAMINATION.
THEN FIND A WAY TO PUNCH THROUGH THAT RADIATION WITH LONG-RANGE SENSORS-- OR GET A PROBE IN THERE--
IN THAT ENVIRONMENT, A PROBE WILL LIKELY MALFUNCTION ALMOST--
--STOP TELLING ME WHAT WE CAN'T DO AND FIND SOMETHING WE CAN!
WHAM!
KIRK OUT.

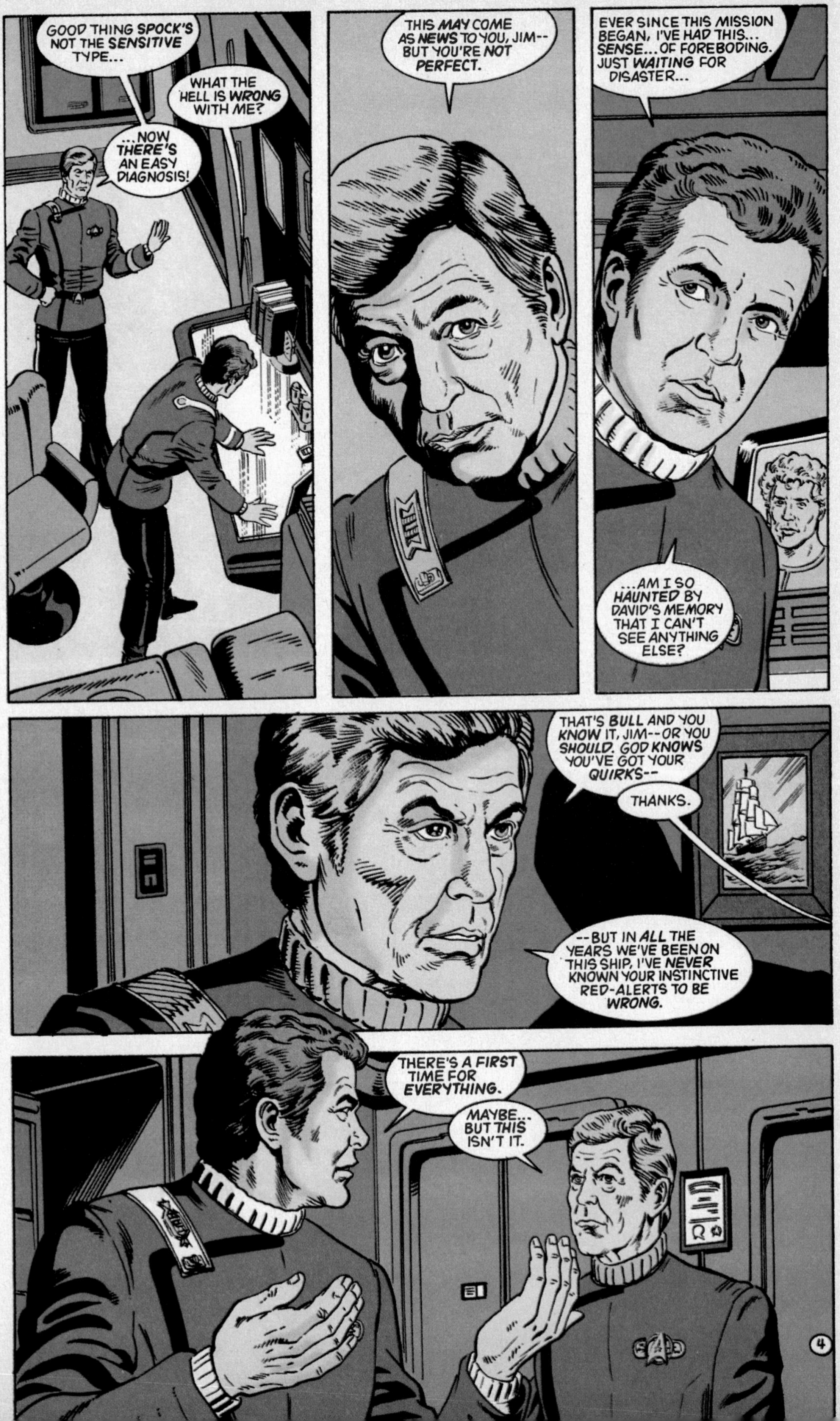
GOOD THING SPOCK'S NOT THE SENSITIVE TYPE...
WHAT THE HELL IS WRONG WITH ME?
...NOW THERE'S AN EASY DIAGNOSIS!
THIS MAY COME AS NEWS TO YOU, JIM-- BUT YOU'RE NOT PERFECT.
EVER SINCE THIS MISSION BEGAN, I'VE HAD THIS... SENSE... OF FOREBODING. JUST WAITING FOR DISASTER...
...AM I SO HAUNTED BY DAVID'S MEMORY THAT I CAN'T SEE ANYTHING ELSE?
THAT'S BULL AND YOU KNOW IT, JIM--OR YOU SHOULD. GOD KNOWS YOU'VE GOT YOUR QUIRKS--
THANKS.
--BUT IN ALL THE YEARS WE'VE BEEN ON THIS SHIP, I'VE NEVER KNOWN YOUR INSTINCTIVE RED-ALERTS TO BE WRONG.
THERE'S A FIRST TIME FOR EVERYTHING.
MAYBE... BUT THIS ISN'T IT.
4

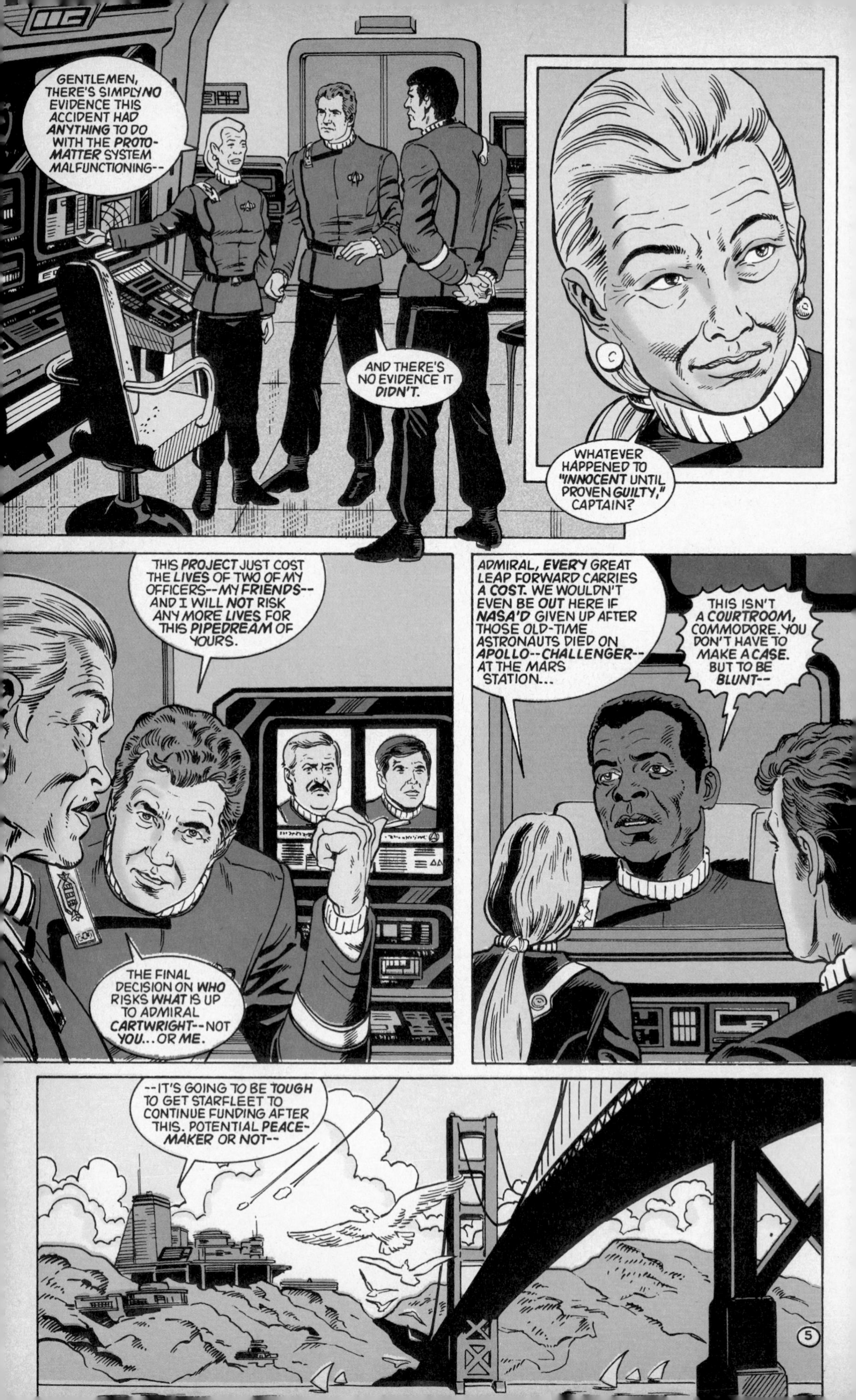
GENTLEMEN, THERE'S SIMPLY NO EVIDENCE THIS ACCIDENT HAD ANYTHING TO DO WITH THE PROTO-MATTER SYSTEM MALFUNCTIONING--
AND THERE'S NO EVIDENCE IT DIDN'T.
WHATEVER HAPPENED TO "INNOCENT UNTIL PROVEN GUILTY," CAPTAIN?
THIS PROJECT JUST COST THE LIVES OF TWO OF MY OFFICERS--MY FRIENDS--AND I WILL NOT RISK ANY MORE LIVES FOR THIS PIPEDREAM OF YOURS.
THE FINAL DECISION ON WHO RISKS WHAT IS UP TO ADMIRAL CARTWRIGHT--NOT YOU...OR ME.
ADMIRAL, EVERY GREAT LEAP FORWARD CARRIES A COST. WE WOULDN'T EVEN BE OUT HERE IF NASA'D GIVEN UP AFTER THOSE OLD-TIME ASTRONAUTS DIED ON APOLLO--CHALLENGER--AT THE MARS STATION...
THIS ISN'T A COURTROOM, COMMODORE. YOU DON'T HAVE TO MAKE A CASE. BUT TO BE BLUNT--
--IT'S GOING TO BE TOUGH TO GET STARFLEET TO CONTINUE FUNDING AFTER THIS. POTENTIAL PEACE-MAKER OR NOT--
5

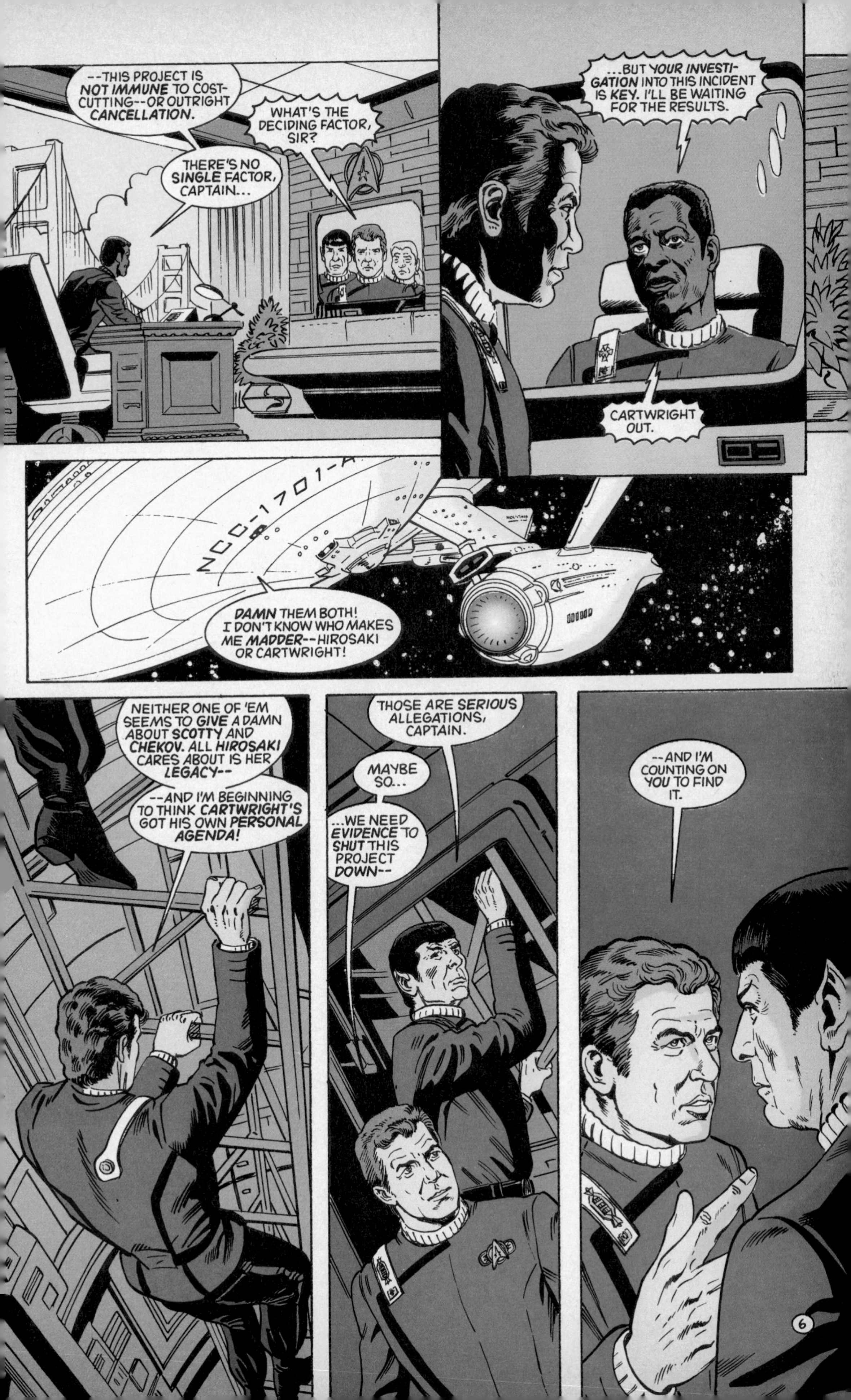
--THIS PROJECT IS NOT IMMUNE TO COST-CUTTING--OR OUTRIGHT CANCELLATION.
WHAT'S THE DECIDING FACTOR, SIR?
THERE'S NO SINGLE FACTOR, CAPTAIN...
...BUT YOUR INVESTIGATION INTO THIS INCIDENT IS KEY. I'LL BE WAITING FOR THE RESULTS.
CARTWRIGHT OUT.
NCC-1701-A
DAMN THEM BOTH! I DON'T KNOW WHO MAKES ME MADDER--HIROSAKI OR CARTWRIGHT!
NEITHER ONE OF 'EM SEEMS TO GIVE A DAMN ABOUT SCOTTY AND CHEKOV. ALL HIROSAKI CARES ABOUT IS HER LEGACY--
--AND I'M BEGINNING TO THINK CARTWRIGHT'S GOT HIS OWN PERSONAL AGENDA!
THOSE ARE SERIOUS ALLEGATIONS, CAPTAIN.
MAYBE SO...
...WE NEED EVIDENCE TO SHUT THIS PROJECT DOWN--
--AND I'M COUNTING ON YOU TO FIND IT.

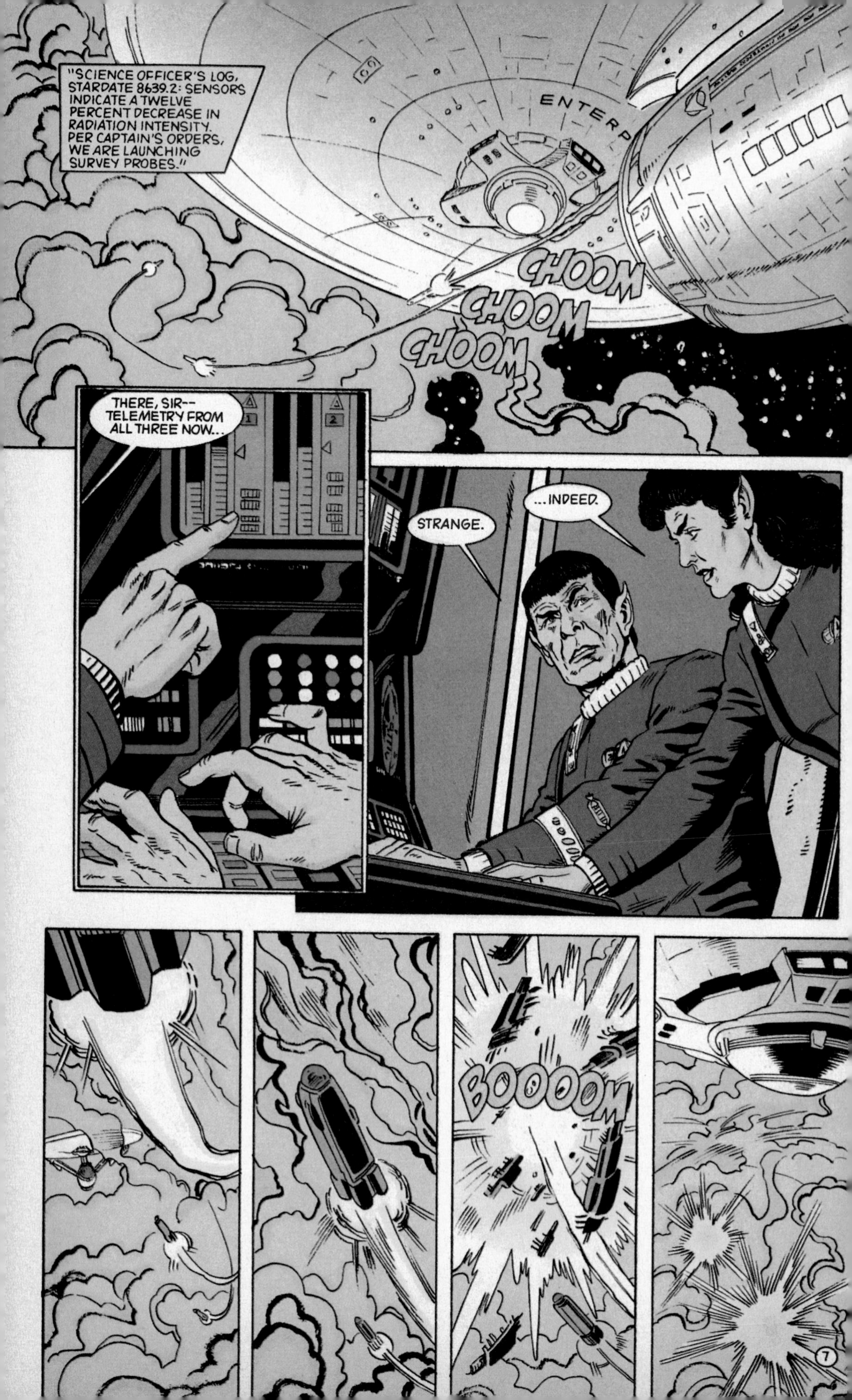
"SCIENCE OFFICER'S LOG, STARDATE 8639.2: SENSORS INDICATE A TWELVE PERCENT DECREASE IN RADIATION INTENSITY. PER CAPTAIN'S ORDERS, WE ARE LAUNCHING SURVEY PROBES."
ENTERP
CHOOM
CHOOM
CHOOM
THERE, SIR-- TELEMETRY FROM ALL THREE NOW...
STRANGE.
...INDEED.
BOOOOM

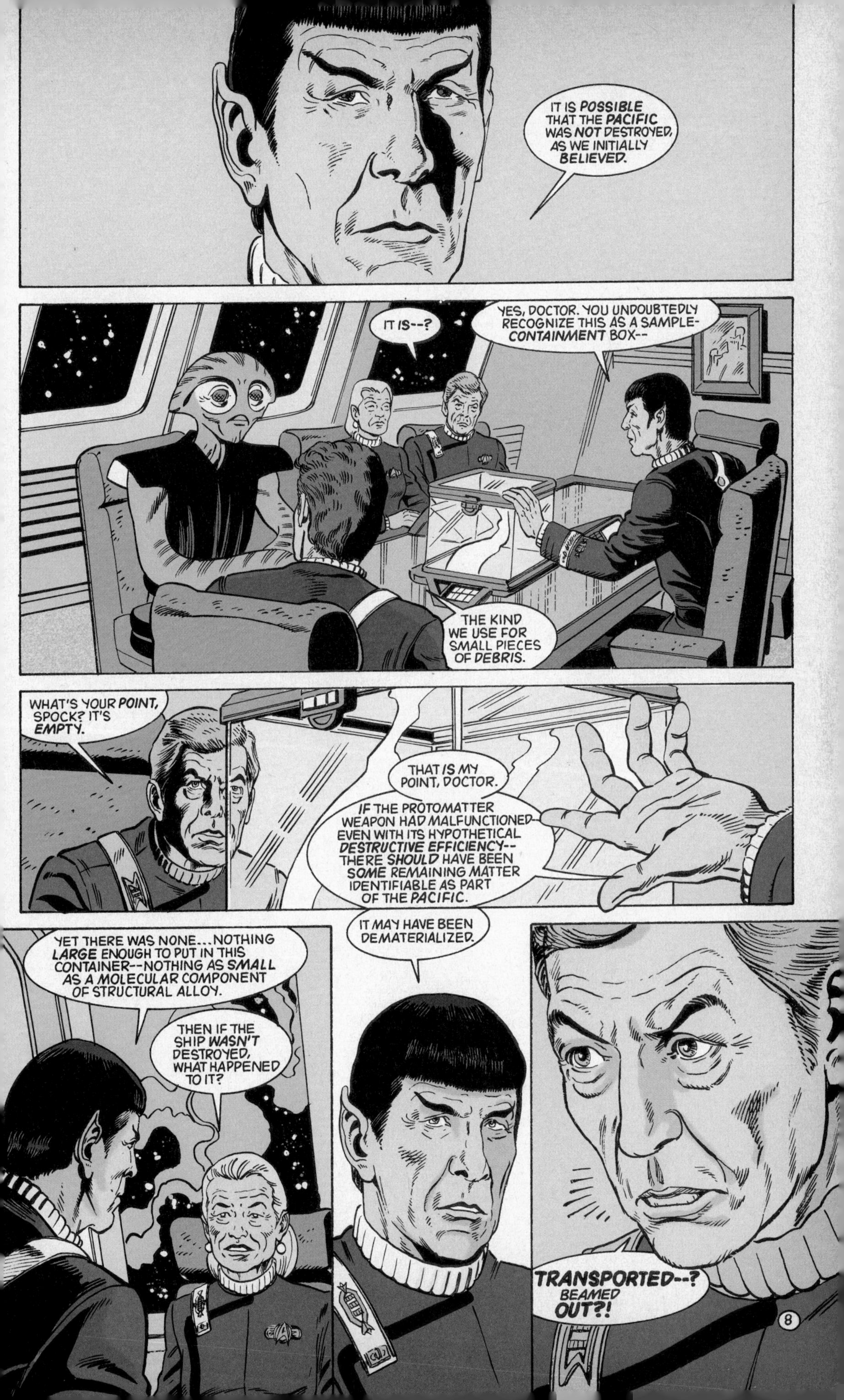
IT IS POSSIBLE THAT THE PACIFIC WAS NOT DESTROYED, AS WE INITIALLY BELIEVED.
IT IS--?
YES, DOCTOR. YOU UNDOUBTEDLY RECOGNIZE THIS AS A SAMPLE-CONTAINMENT BOX--
THE KIND WE USE FOR SMALL PIECES OF DEBRIS.
WHAT'S YOUR POINT, SPOCK? IT'S EMPTY.
THAT IS MY POINT, DOCTOR.
IF THE PROTOMATTER WEAPON HAD MALFUNCTIONED-- EVEN WITH ITS HYPOTHETICAL DESTRUCTIVE EFFICIENCY-- THERE SHOULD HAVE BEEN SOME REMAINING MATTER IDENTIFIABLE AS PART OF THE PACIFIC.
YET THERE WAS NONE... NOTHING LARGE ENOUGH TO PUT IN THIS CONTAINER--NOTHING AS SMALL AS A MOLECULAR COMPONENT OF STRUCTURAL ALLOY.
THEN IF THE SHIP WASN'T DESTROYED, WHAT HAPPENED TO IT?
IT MAY HAVE BEEN DEMATERIALIZED.
TRANSPORTED--? BEAMED OUT?!
8

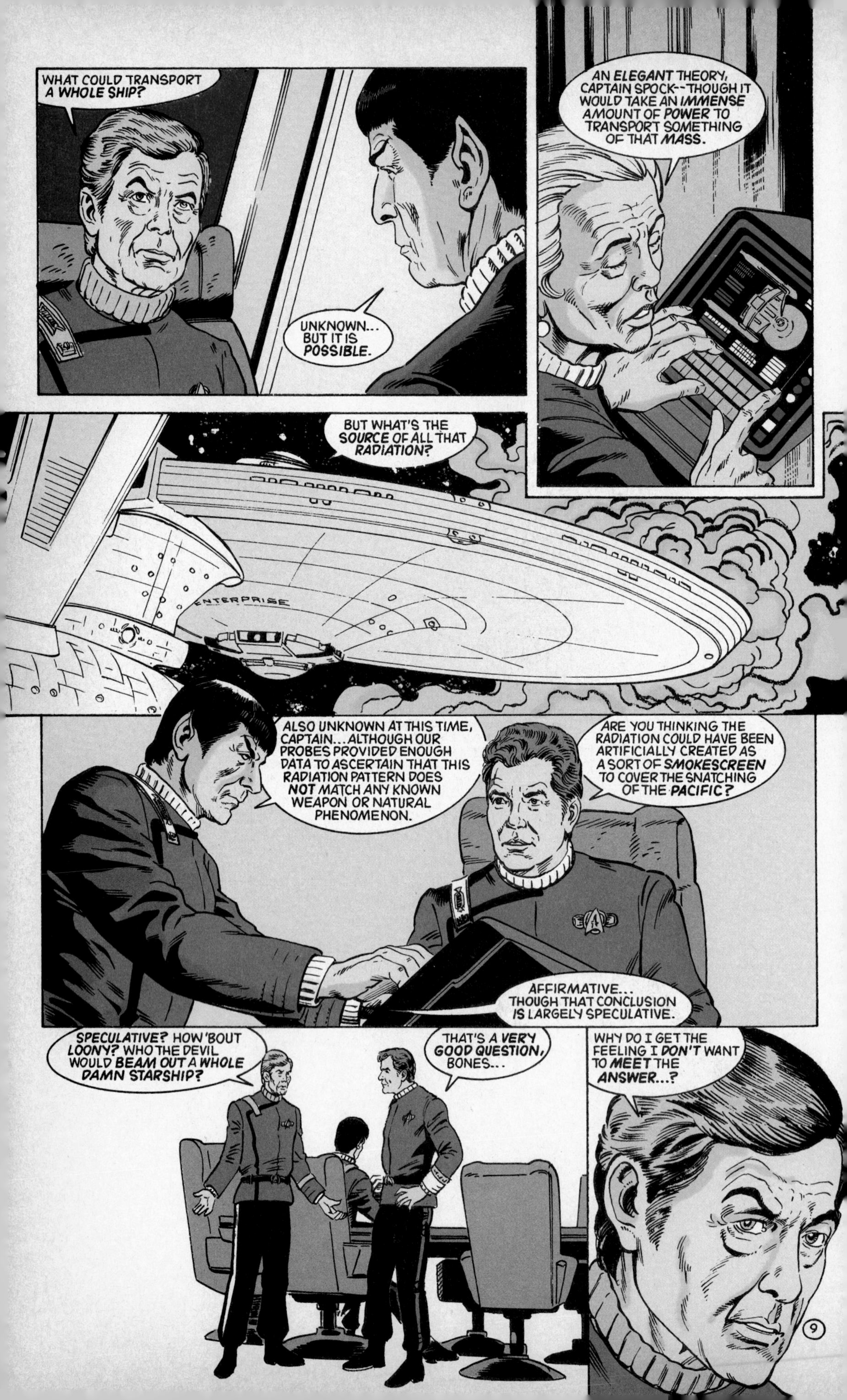
WHAT COULD TRANSPORT A WHOLE SHIP?
UNKNOWN... BUT IT IS POSSIBLE.
AN ELEGANT THEORY, CAPTAIN SPOCK--THOUGH IT WOULD TAKE AN IMMENSE AMOUNT OF POWER TO TRANSPORT SOMETHING OF THAT MASS.
BUT WHAT'S THE SOURCE OF ALL THAT RADIATION?
ENTERPRISE
ALSO UNKNOWN AT THIS TIME, CAPTAIN... ALTHOUGH OUR PROBES PROVIDED ENOUGH DATA TO ASCERTAIN THAT THIS RADIATION PATTERN DOES NOT MATCH ANY KNOWN WEAPON OR NATURAL PHENOMENON.
ARE YOU THINKING THE RADIATION COULD HAVE BEEN ARTIFICIALLY CREATED AS A SORT OF SMOKESCREEN TO COVER THE SNATCHING OF THE PACIFIC?
AFFIRMATIVE... THOUGH THAT CONCLUSION IS LARGELY SPECULATIVE.
SPECULATIVE? HOW 'BOUT LOONY? WHO THE DEVIL WOULD BEAM OUT A WHOLE DAMN STARSHIP?
THAT'S A VERY GOOD QUESTION, BONES...
WHY DO I GET THE FEELING I DON'T WANT TO MEET THE ANSWER...?

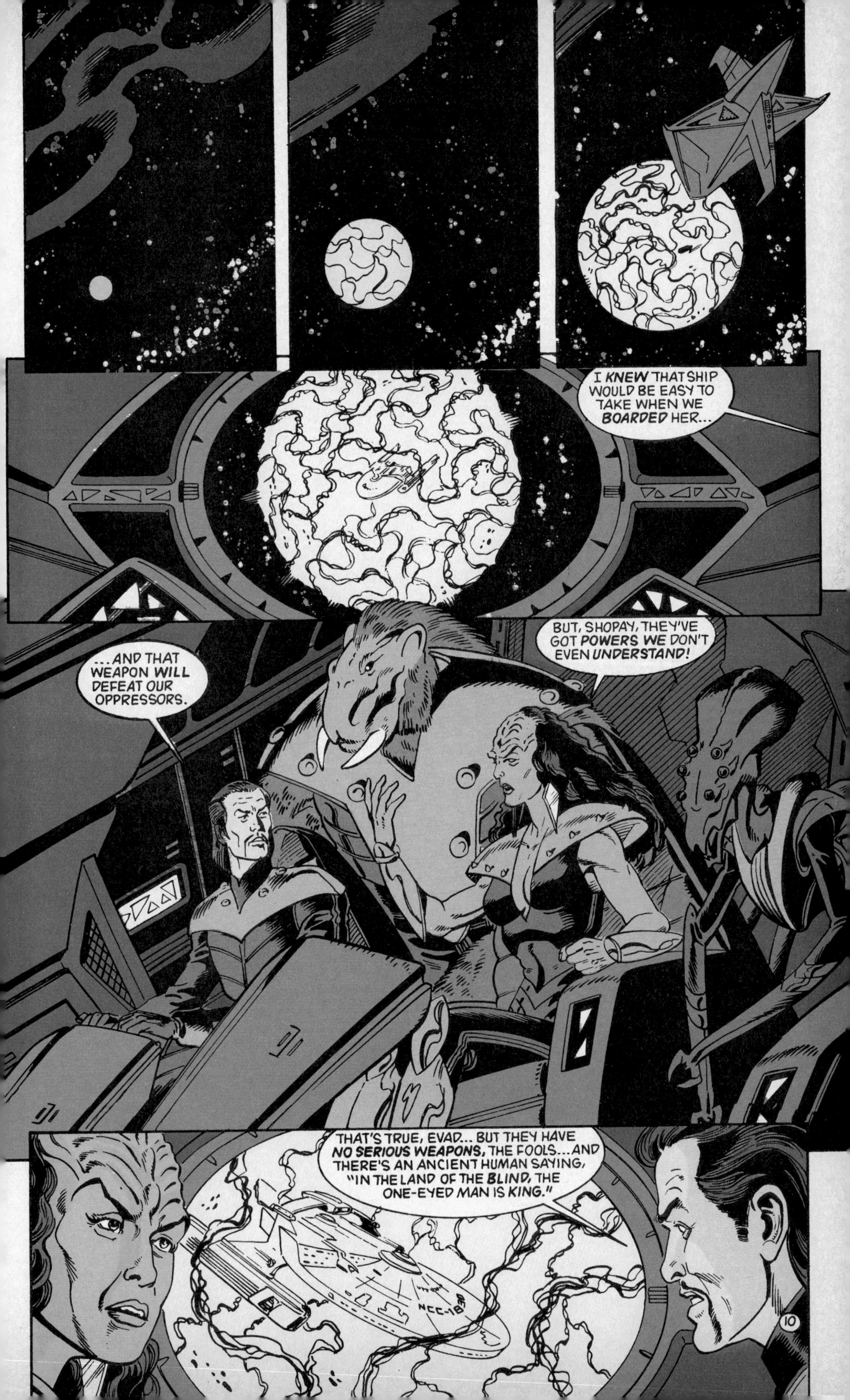
I KNEW THAT SHIP WOULD BE EASY TO TAKE WHEN WE BOARDED HER...
...AND THAT WEAPON WILL DEFEAT OUR OPPRESSORS.
BUT, SHOPAY, THEY'VE GOT POWERS WE DON'T EVEN UNDERSTAND!
THAT'S TRUE, EVAD... BUT THEY HAVE NO SERIOUS WEAPONS, THE FOOLS... AND THERE'S AN ANCIENT HUMAN SAYING, "IN THE LAND OF THE BLIND, THE ONE-EYED MAN IS KING."
NCC-18
10

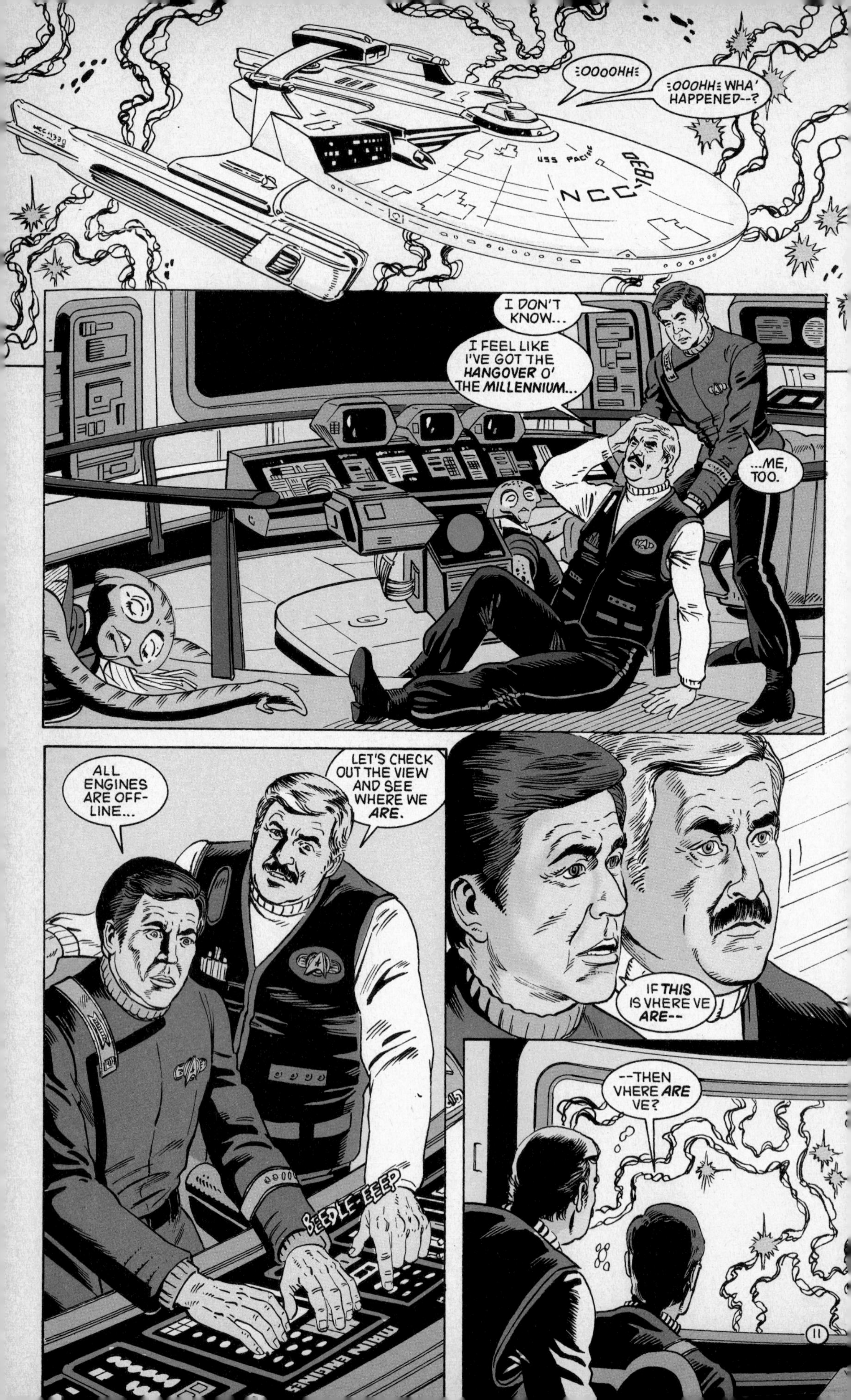
USS PACIFIC
NCC
:OOOOHH:
:OOOHH: WHA' HAPPENED--?
I DON'T KNOW...
I FEEL LIKE I'VE GOT THE HANGOVER O' THE MILLENNIUM...
...ME, TOO.
ALL ENGINES ARE OFF-LINE...
LET'S CHECK OUT THE VIEW AND SEE WHERE WE ARE.
BEEDLE-EEEP
MAIN ENGINES
IF THIS IS VHERE VE ARE--
--THEN VHERE ARE VE?

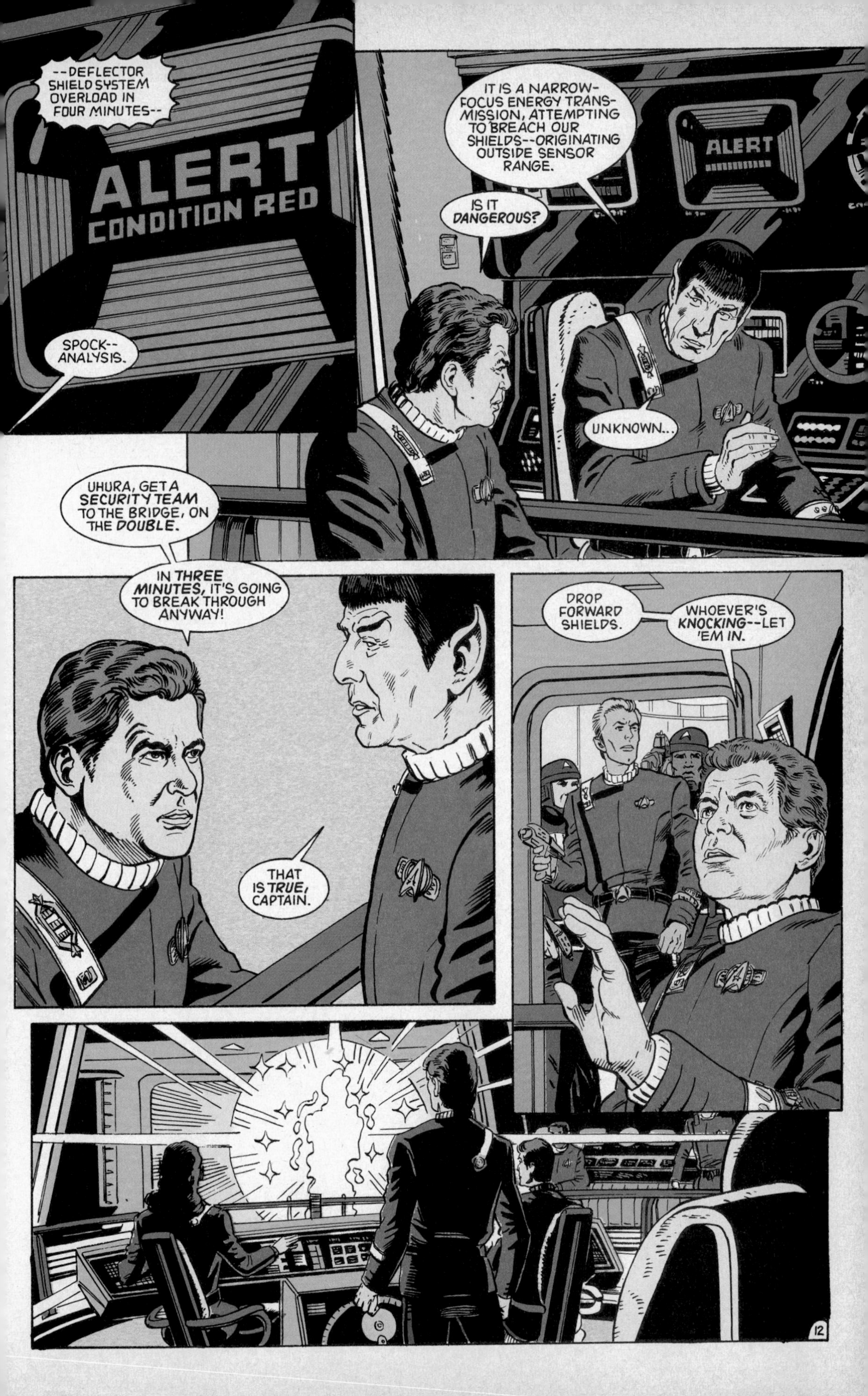
--DEFLECTOR SHIELD SYSTEM OVERLOAD IN FOUR MINUTES--
ALERT
CONDITION RED
SPOCK--ANALYSIS.
ALERT
IT IS A NARROW-FOCUS ENERGY TRANSMISSION, ATTEMPTING TO BREACH OUR SHIELDS--ORIGINATING OUTSIDE SENSOR RANGE.
IS IT DANGEROUS?
UNKNOWN...
UHURA, GET A SECURITY TEAM TO THE BRIDGE, ON THE DOUBLE.
IN THREE MINUTES, IT'S GOING TO BREAK THROUGH ANYWAY!
THAT IS TRUE, CAPTAIN.
DROP FORWARD SHIELDS.
WHOEVER'S KNOCKING--LET 'EM IN.

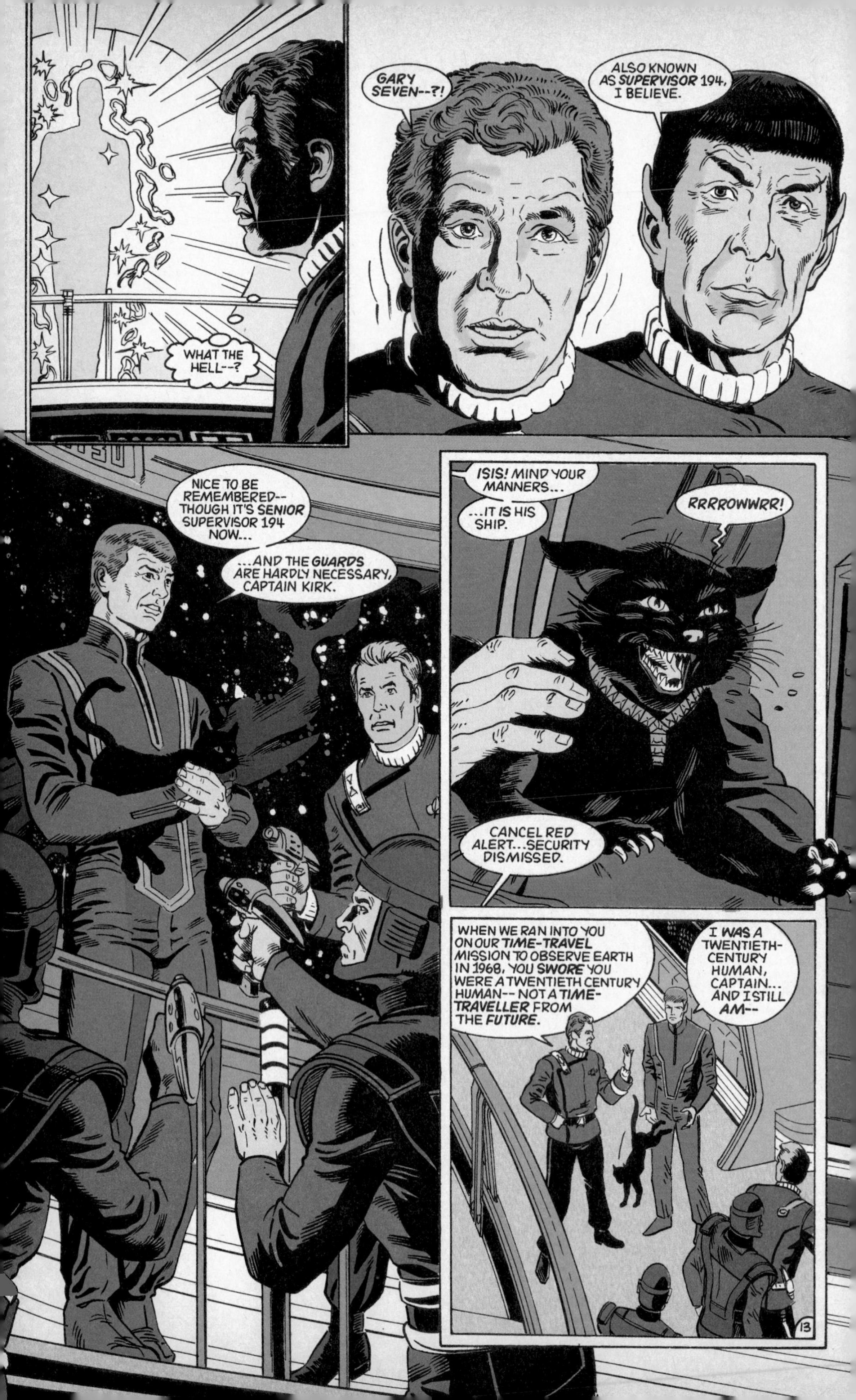
WHAT THE HELL--?
GARY SEVEN--?!
ALSO KNOWN AS SUPERVISOR 194, I BELIEVE.
NICE TO BE REMEMBERED-- THOUGH IT'S SENIOR SUPERVISOR 194 NOW...
...AND THE GUARDS ARE HARDLY NECESSARY, CAPTAIN KIRK.
ISIS! MIND YOUR MANNERS...
...IT IS HIS SHIP.
RRRROWWRR!
CANCEL RED ALERT...SECURITY DISMISSED.
WHEN WE RAN INTO YOU ON OUR TIME-TRAVEL MISSION TO OBSERVE EARTH IN 1968, YOU SWORE YOU WERE A TWENTIETH CENTURY HUMAN-- NOT A TIME-TRAVELLER FROM THE FUTURE.
I WAS A TWENTIETH-CENTURY HUMAN, CAPTAIN... AND I STILL AM--
13

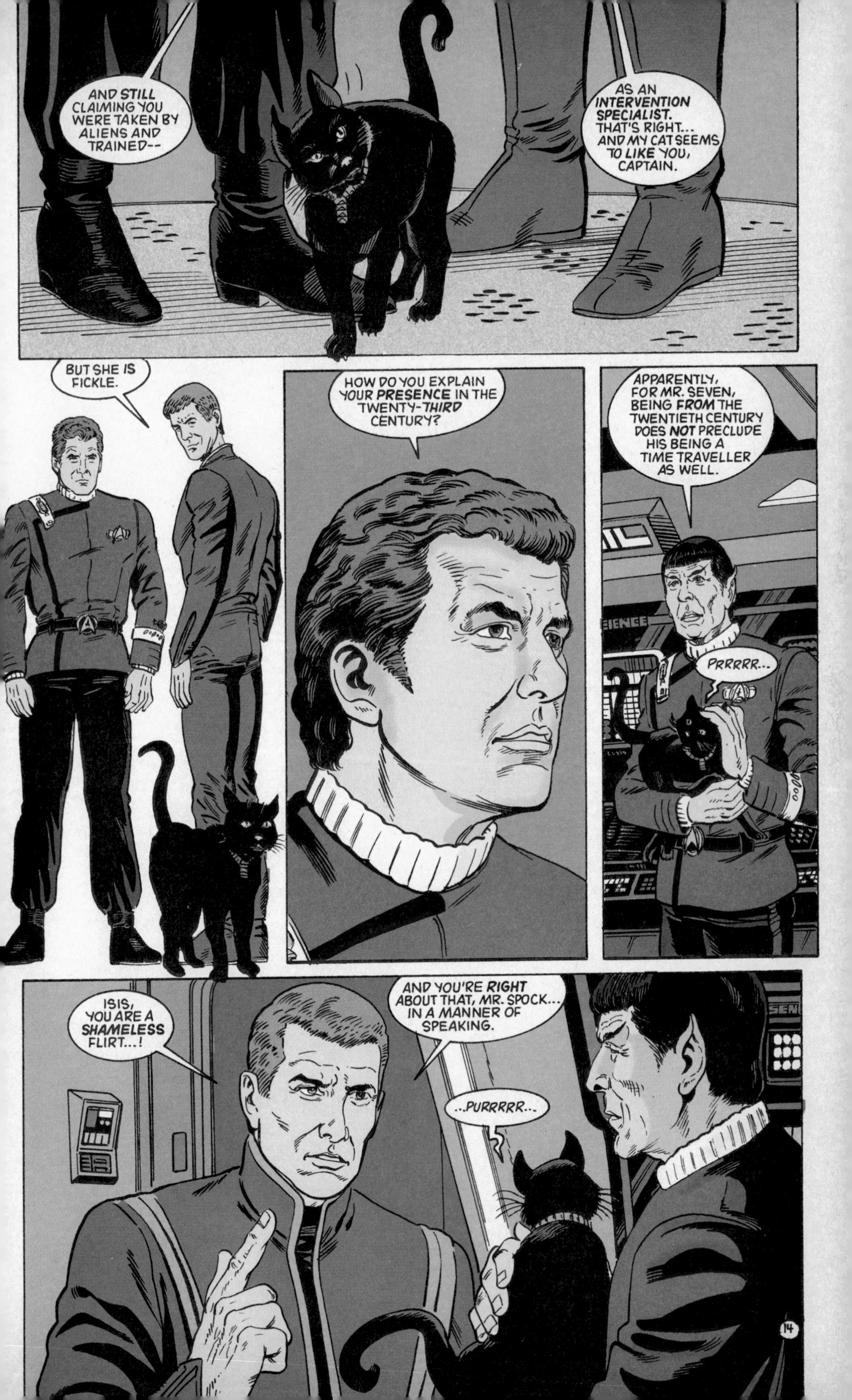
AND STILL CLAIMING YOU WERE TAKEN BY ALIENS AND TRAINED--
AS AN INTERVENTION SPECIALIST. THAT'S RIGHT... AND MY CAT SEEMS TO LIKE YOU, CAPTAIN.
BUT SHE IS FICKLE.
HOW DO YOU EXPLAIN YOUR PRESENCE IN THE TWENTY-THIRD CENTURY?
APPARENTLY, FOR MR. SEVEN, BEING FROM THE TWENTIETH CENTURY DOES NOT PRECLUDE HIS BEING A TIME TRAVELLER AS WELL.
PRRRRR...
ISIS, YOU ARE A SHAMELESS FLIRT...!
AND YOU'RE RIGHT ABOUT THAT, MR. SPOCK... IN A MANNER OF SPEAKING.
...PURRRRR...
14

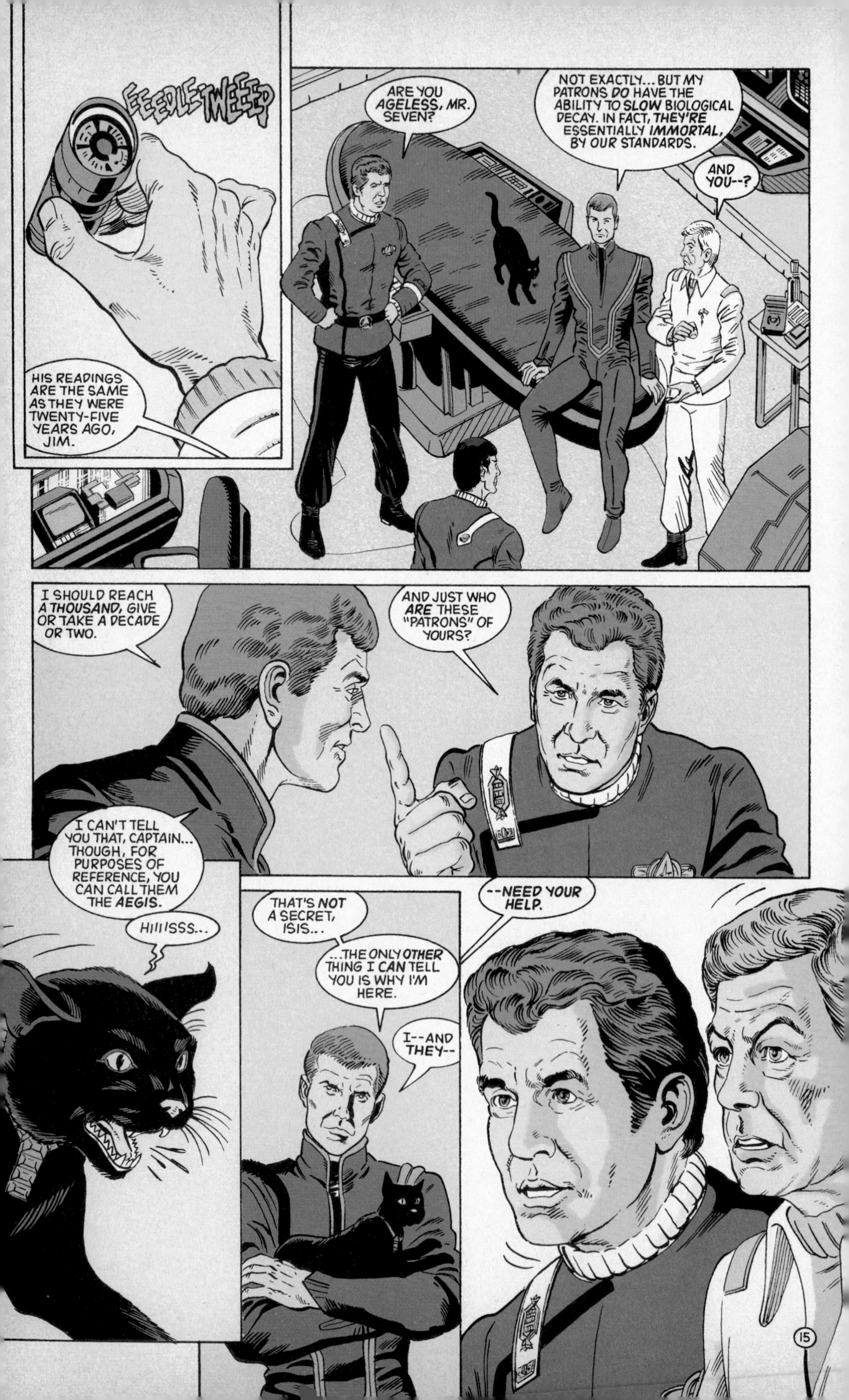
EEEDLE-TWEEEP
HIS READINGS ARE THE SAME AS THEY WERE TWENTY-FIVE YEARS AGO, JIM.
ARE YOU AGELESS, MR. SEVEN?
NOT EXACTLY... BUT MY PATRONS DO HAVE THE ABILITY TO SLOW BIOLOGICAL DECAY. IN FACT, THEY'RE ESSENTIALLY IMMORTAL, BY OUR STANDARDS.
AND YOU--?
I SHOULD REACH A THOUSAND, GIVE OR TAKE A DECADE OR TWO.
AND JUST WHO ARE THESE "PATRONS" OF YOURS?
I CAN'T TELL YOU THAT, CAPTAIN... THOUGH, FOR PURPOSES OF REFERENCE, YOU CAN CALL THEM THE AEGIS.
HIIIISSS...
THAT'S NOT A SECRET, ISIS...
...THE ONLY OTHER THING I CAN TELL YOU IS WHY I'M HERE.
I--AND THEY--
--NEED YOUR HELP.

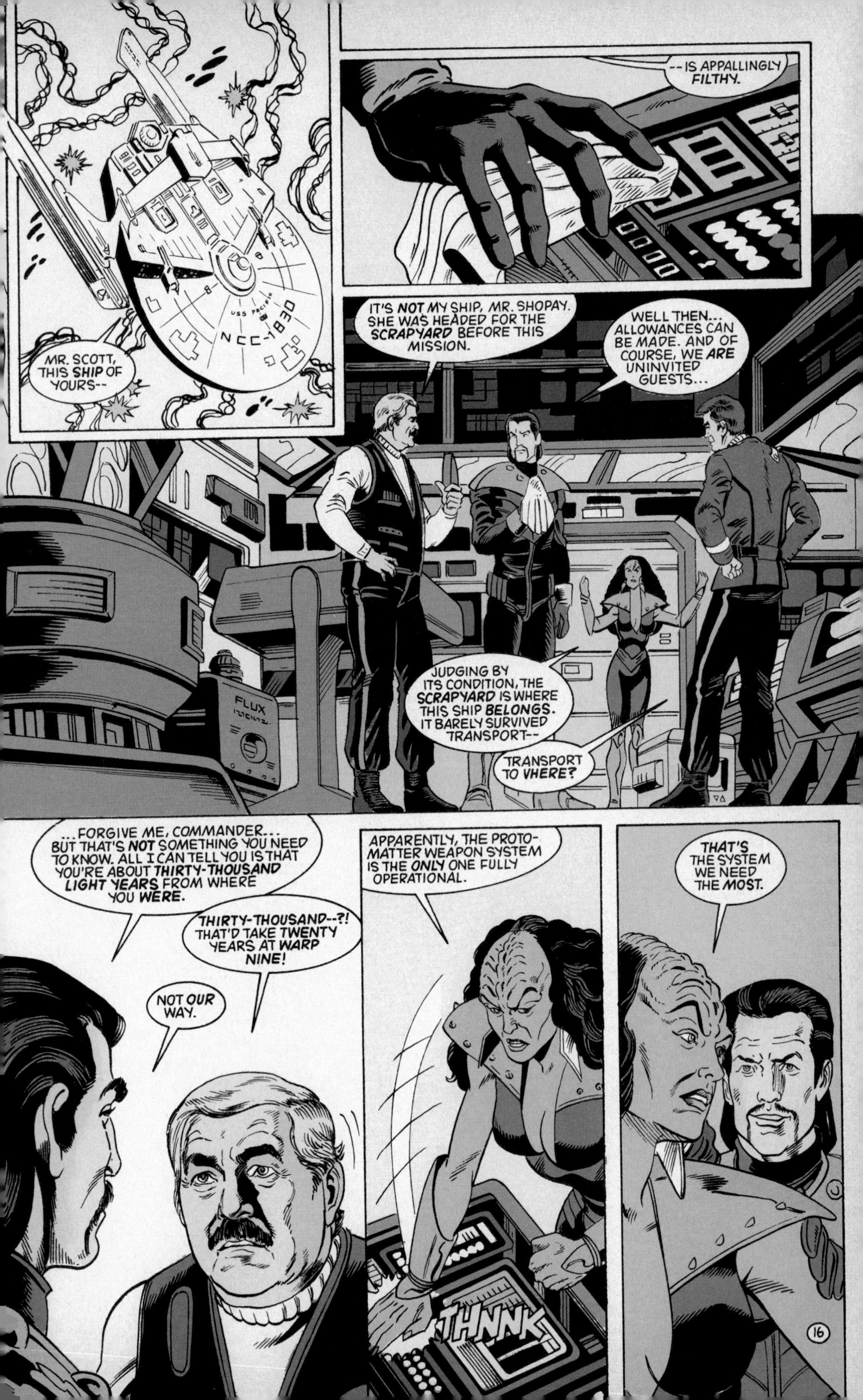
MR. SCOTT, THIS SHIP OF YOURS--
USS PACIFIC
NCC-1830
--IS APPALLINGLY FILTHY.
IT'S NOT MY SHIP, MR. SHOPAY. SHE WAS HEADED FOR THE SCRAPYARD BEFORE THIS MISSION.
WELL THEN... ALLOWANCES CAN BE MADE. AND OF COURSE, WE ARE UNINVITED GUESTS...
FLUX
JUDGING BY ITS CONDITION, THE SCRAPYARD IS WHERE THIS SHIP BELONGS. IT BARELY SURVIVED TRANSPORT--
TRANSPORT TO VHERE?
...FORGIVE ME, COMMANDER... BUT THAT'S NOT SOMETHING YOU NEED TO KNOW. ALL I CAN TELL YOU IS THAT YOU'RE ABOUT THIRTY-THOUSAND LIGHT YEARS FROM WHERE YOU WERE.
THIRTY-THOUSAND--?! THAT'D TAKE TWENTY YEARS AT WARP NINE!
NOT OUR WAY.
APPARENTLY, THE PROTO-MATTER WEAPON SYSTEM IS THE ONLY ONE FULLY OPERATIONAL.
THHNK
THAT'S THE SYSTEM WE NEED THE MOST.
16

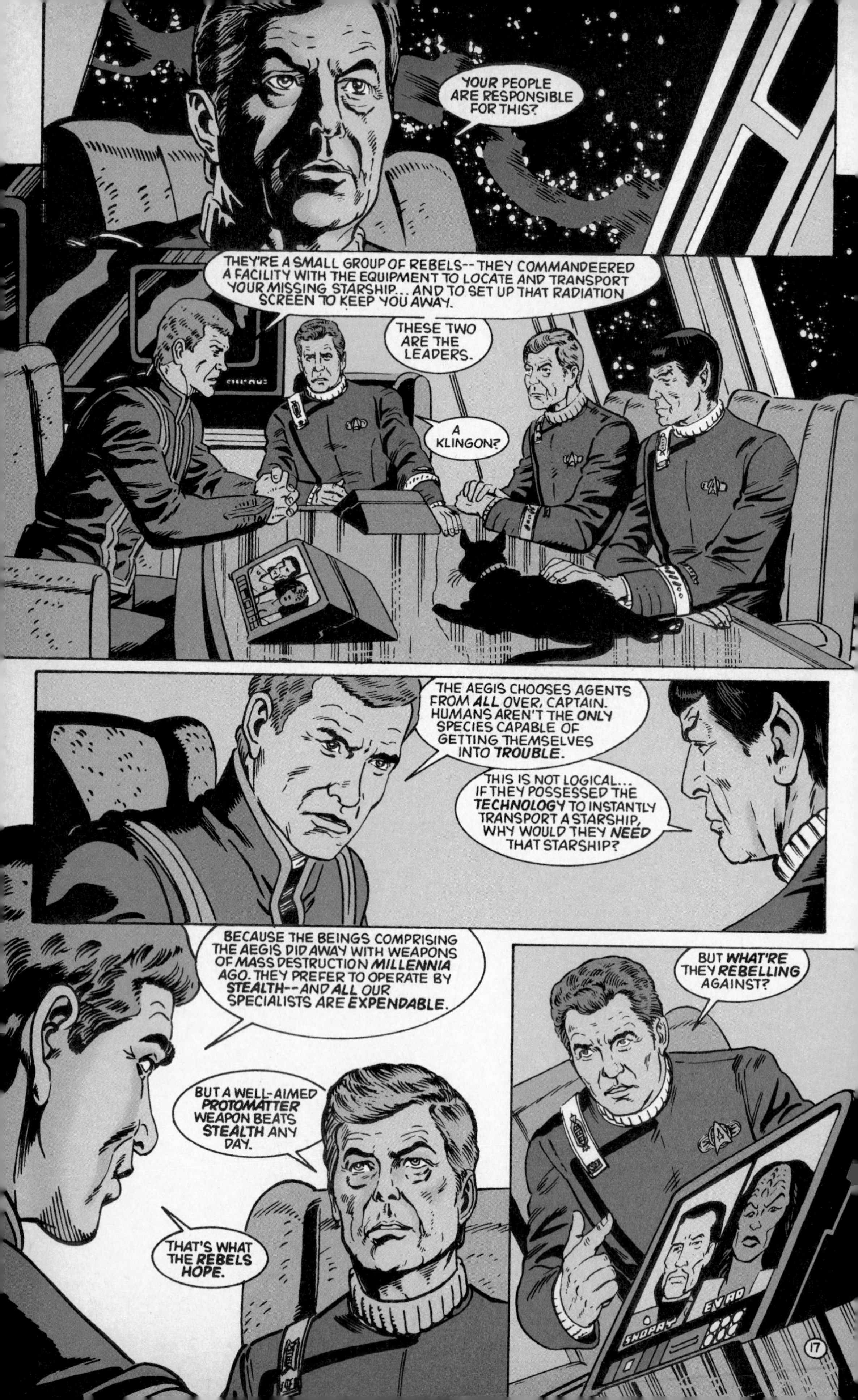
YOUR PEOPLE ARE RESPONSIBLE FOR THIS?
THEY'RE A SMALL GROUP OF REBELS-- THEY COMMANDEERED A FACILITY WITH THE EQUIPMENT TO LOCATE AND TRANSPORT YOUR MISSING STARSHIP... AND TO SET UP THAT RADIATION SCREEN TO KEEP YOU AWAY.
THESE TWO ARE THE LEADERS.
A KLINGON?
THE AEGIS CHOOSES AGENTS FROM ALL OVER, CAPTAIN. HUMANS AREN'T THE ONLY SPECIES CAPABLE OF GETTING THEMSELVES INTO TROUBLE.
THIS IS NOT LOGICAL... IF THEY POSSESSED THE TECHNOLOGY TO INSTANTLY TRANSPORT A STARSHIP, WHY WOULD THEY NEED THAT STARSHIP?
BECAUSE THE BEINGS COMPRISING THE AEGIS DID AWAY WITH WEAPONS OF MASS DESTRUCTION MILLENNIA AGO. THEY PREFER TO OPERATE BY STEALTH-- AND ALL OUR SPECIALISTS ARE EXPENDABLE.
BUT A WELL-AIMED PROTOMATTER WEAPON BEATS STEALTH ANY DAY.
THAT'S WHAT THE REBELS HOPE.
BUT WHAT'RE THEY REBELLING AGAINST?
SNOPAY
EV'AD

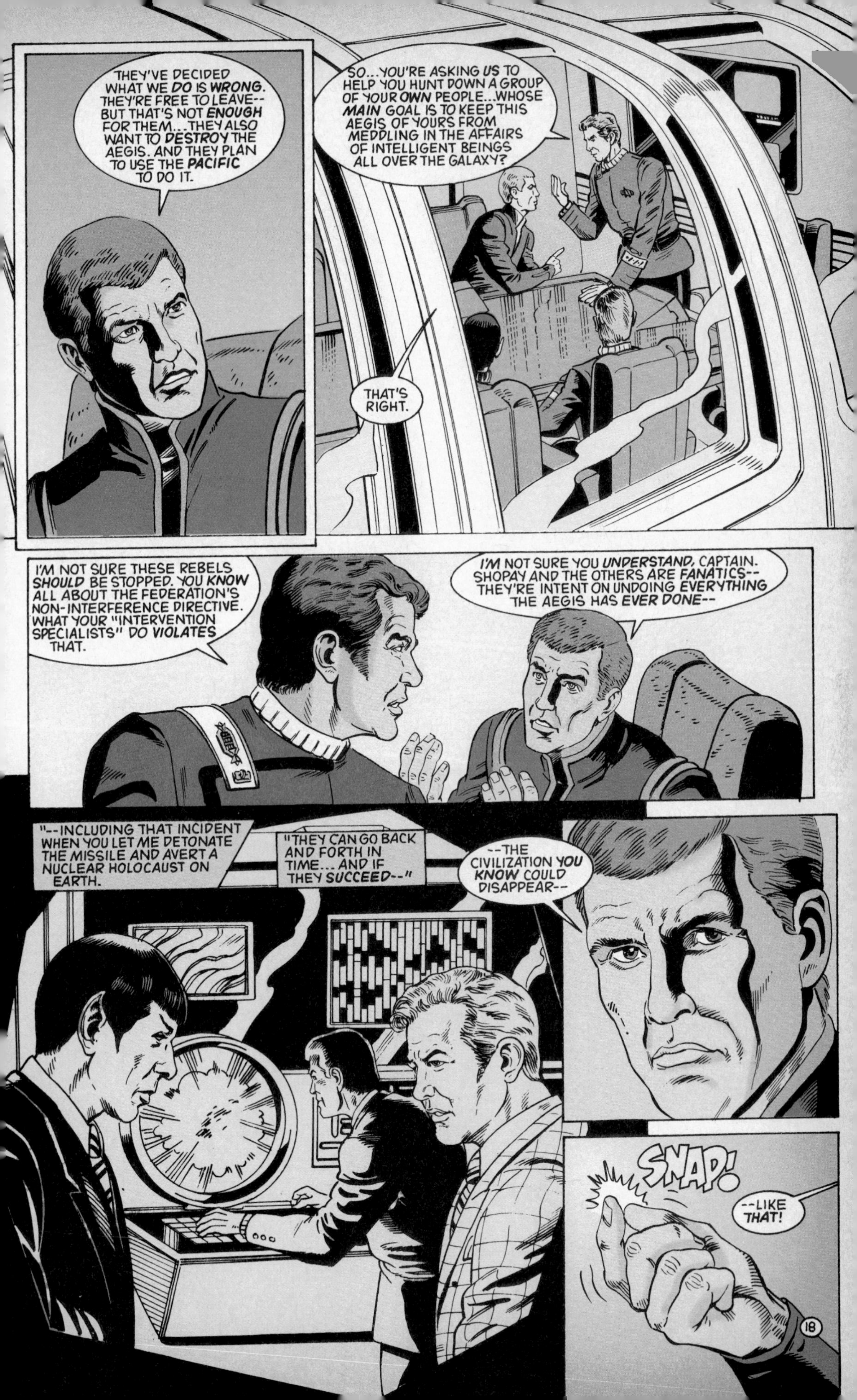
THEY'VE DECIDED WHAT WE DO IS WRONG. THEY'RE FREE TO LEAVE--BUT THAT'S NOT ENOUGH FOR THEM... THEY ALSO WANT TO DESTROY THE AEGIS. AND THEY PLAN TO USE THE PACIFIC TO DO IT.
SO... YOU'RE ASKING US TO HELP YOU HUNT DOWN A GROUP OF YOUR OWN PEOPLE... WHOSE MAIN GOAL IS TO KEEP THIS AEGIS OF YOURS FROM MEDDLING IN THE AFFAIRS OF INTELLIGENT BEINGS ALL OVER THE GALAXY?
THAT'S RIGHT.
I'M NOT SURE THESE REBELS SHOULD BE STOPPED. YOU KNOW ALL ABOUT THE FEDERATION'S NON-INTERFERENCE DIRECTIVE. WHAT YOUR "INTERVENTION SPECIALISTS" DO VIOLATES THAT.
I'M NOT SURE YOU UNDERSTAND, CAPTAIN. SHOPAY AND THE OTHERS ARE FANATICS--THEY'RE INTENT ON UNDOING EVERYTHING THE AEGIS HAS EVER DONE--
"--INCLUDING THAT INCIDENT WHEN YOU LET ME DETONATE THE MISSILE AND AVERT A NUCLEAR HOLOCAUST ON EARTH.
"THEY CAN GO BACK AND FORTH IN TIME... AND IF THEY SUCCEED--"
--THE CIVILIZATION YOU KNOW COULD DISAPPEAR--
SNAP!
--LIKE THAT!
18

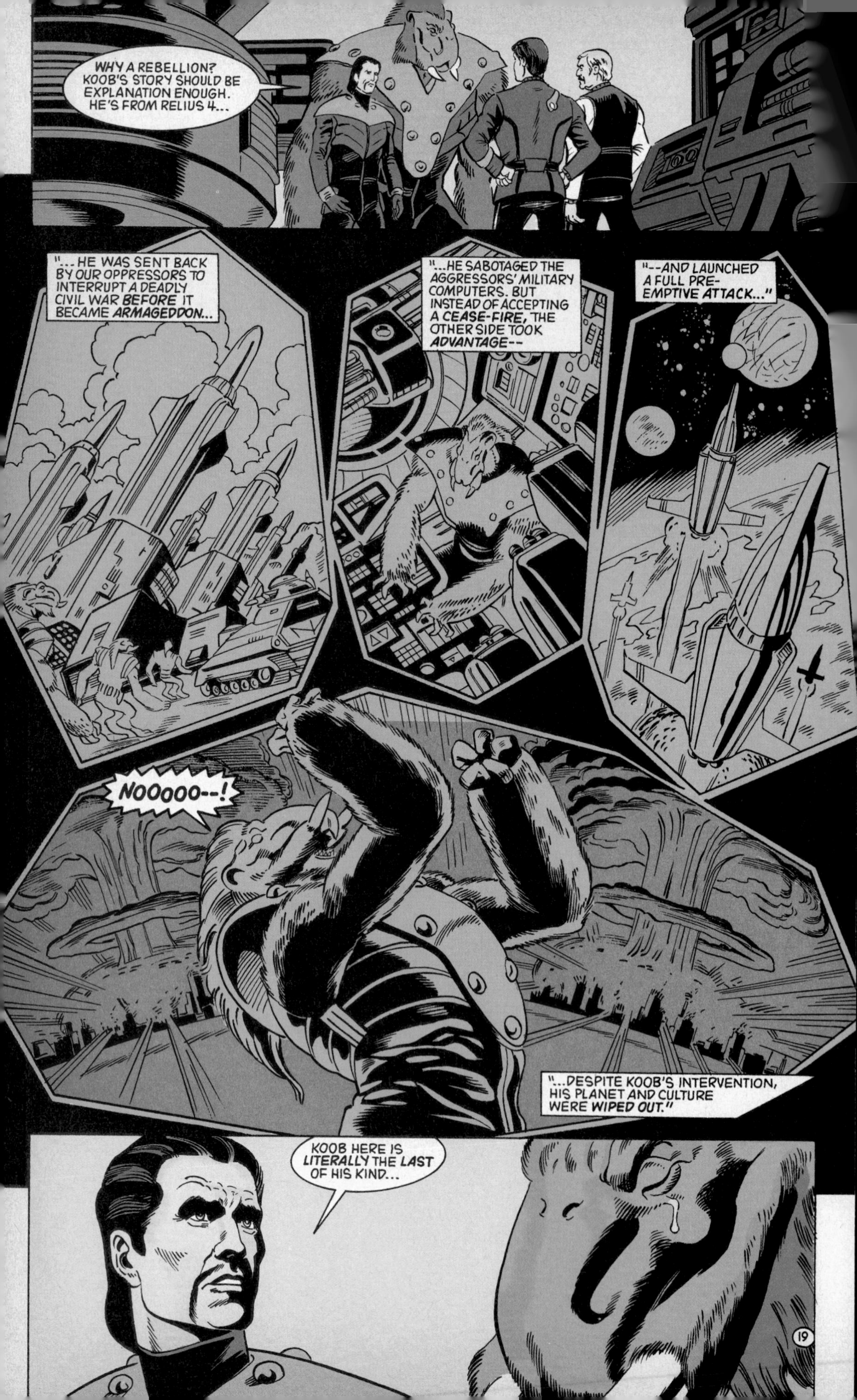
WHY A REBELLION? KOOB'S STORY SHOULD BE EXPLANATION ENOUGH. HE'S FROM RELIUS 4...
"... HE WAS SENT BACK BY OUR OPPRESSORS TO INTERRUPT A DEADLY CIVIL WAR BEFORE IT BECAME ARMAGEDDON...
"...HE SABOTAGED THE AGGRESSORS' MILITARY COMPUTERS. BUT INSTEAD OF ACCEPTING A CEASE-FIRE, THE OTHER SIDE TOOK ADVANTAGE--
"--AND LAUNCHED A FULL PRE-EMPTIVE ATTACK..."
NOOOOO--!
"...DESPITE KOOB'S INTERVENTION, HIS PLANET AND CULTURE WERE WIPED OUT."
KOOB HERE IS LITERALLY THE LAST OF HIS KIND...
19

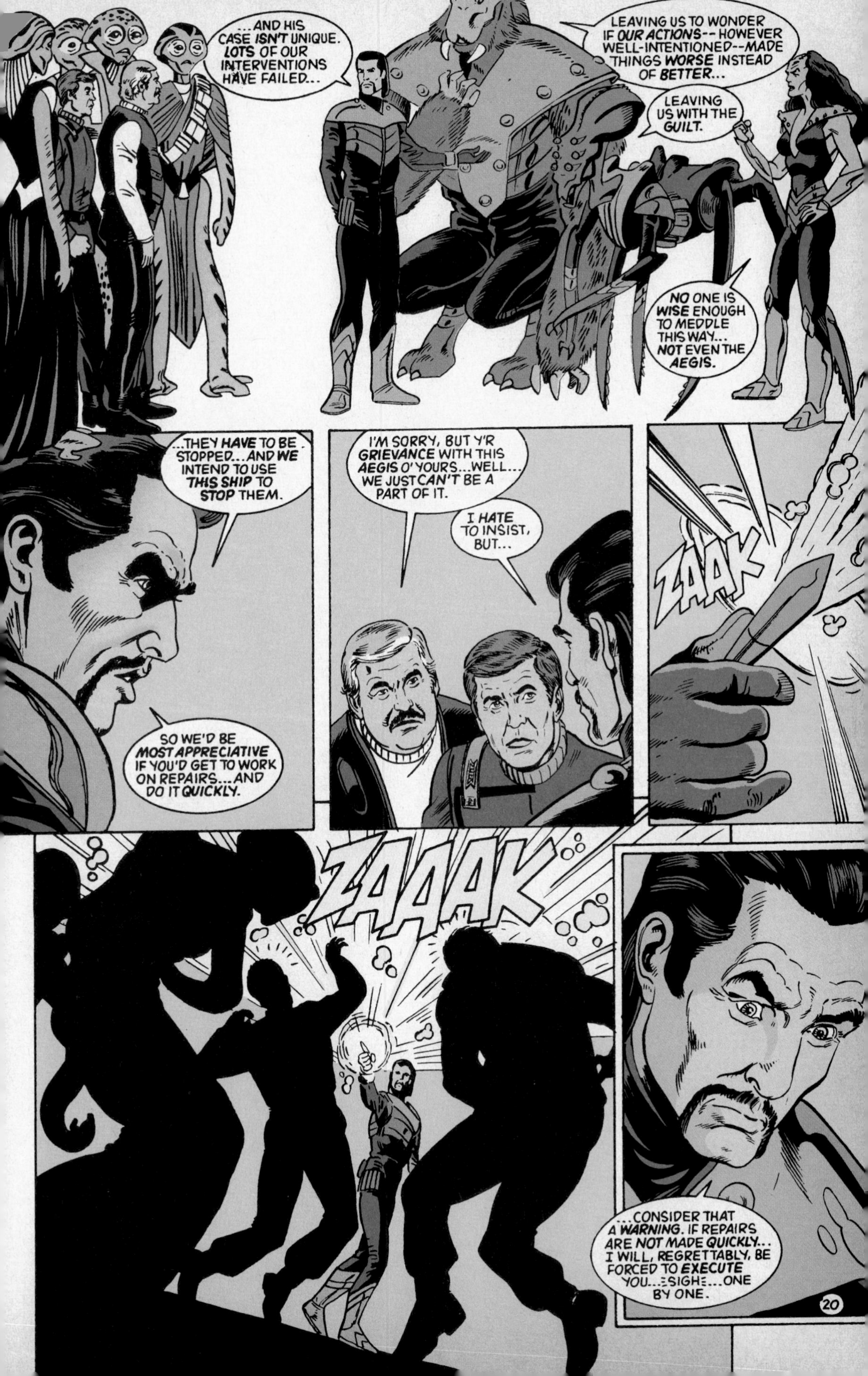
...AND HIS CASE ISN'T UNIQUE. LOTS OF OUR INTERVENTIONS HAVE FAILED...
LEAVING US TO WONDER IF OUR ACTIONS--HOWEVER WELL-INTENTIONED--MADE THINGS WORSE INSTEAD OF BETTER...
LEAVING US WITH THE GUILT.
NO ONE IS WISE ENOUGH TO MEDDLE THIS WAY... NOT EVEN THE AEGIS.
...THEY HAVE TO BE STOPPED... AND WE INTEND TO USE THIS SHIP TO STOP THEM.
SO WE'D BE MOST APPRECIATIVE IF YOU'D GET TO WORK ON REPAIRS... AND DO IT QUICKLY.
I'M SORRY, BUT Y'R GRIEVANCE WITH THIS AEGIS O' YOURS... WELL... WE JUST CAN'T BE A PART OF IT.
I HATE TO INSIST, BUT...
ZAAK
ZAAAK
...CONSIDER THAT A WARNING. IF REPAIRS ARE NOT MADE QUICKLY... I WILL, REGRETTABLY, BE FORCED TO EXECUTE YOU...SIGH...ONE BY ONE.
20

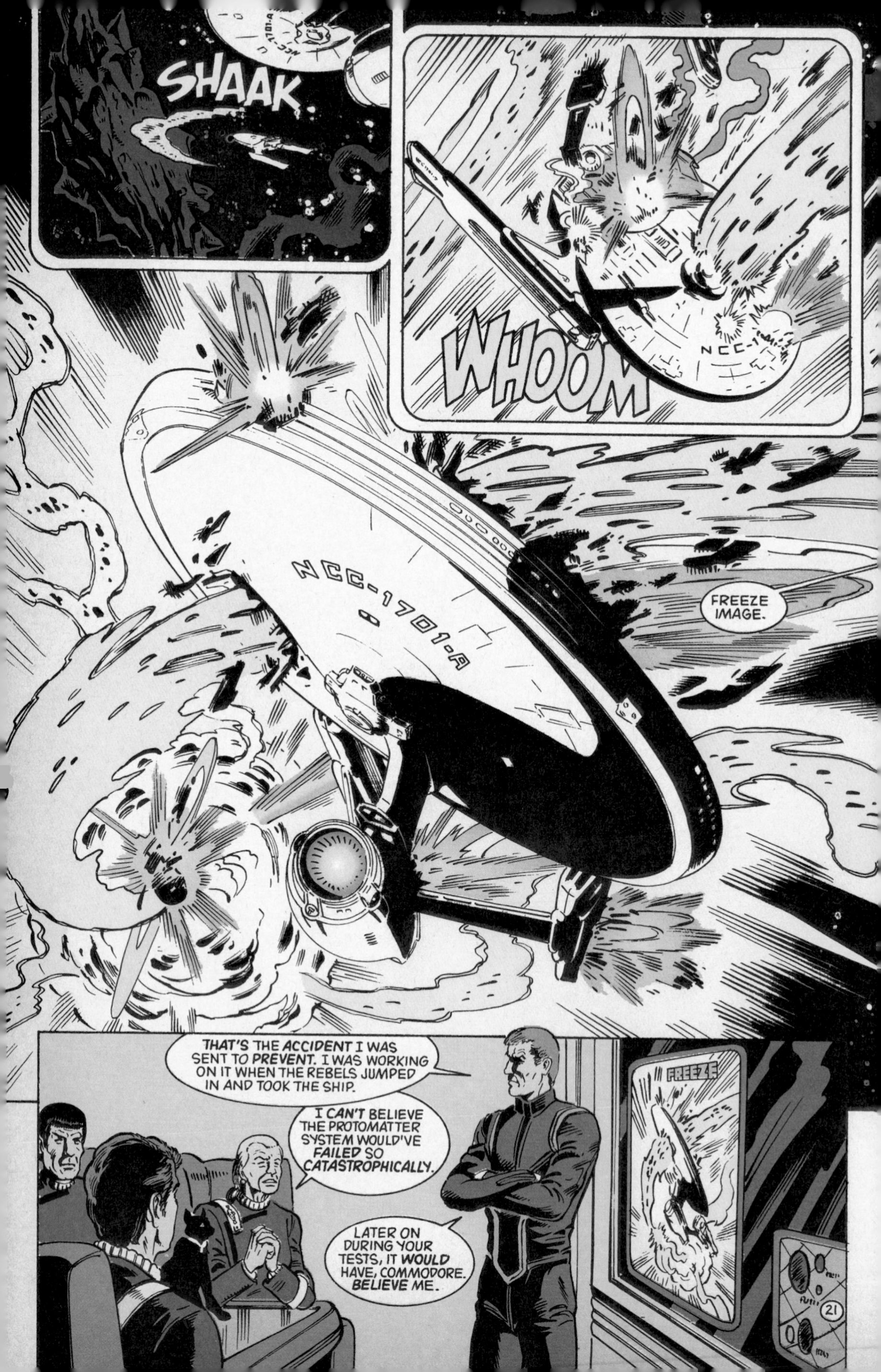
SHAAK
WHOOM
NCC-1701-A
FREEZE IMAGE.
THAT'S THE ACCIDENT I WAS SENT TO PREVENT. I WAS WORKING ON IT WHEN THE REBELS JUMPED IN AND TOOK THE SHIP.
I CAN'T BELIEVE THE PROTOMATTER SYSTEM WOULD'VE FAILED SO CATASTROPHICALLY.
LATER ON DURING YOUR TESTS, IT WOULD HAVE, COMMODORE. BELIEVE ME.
FREEZE
21

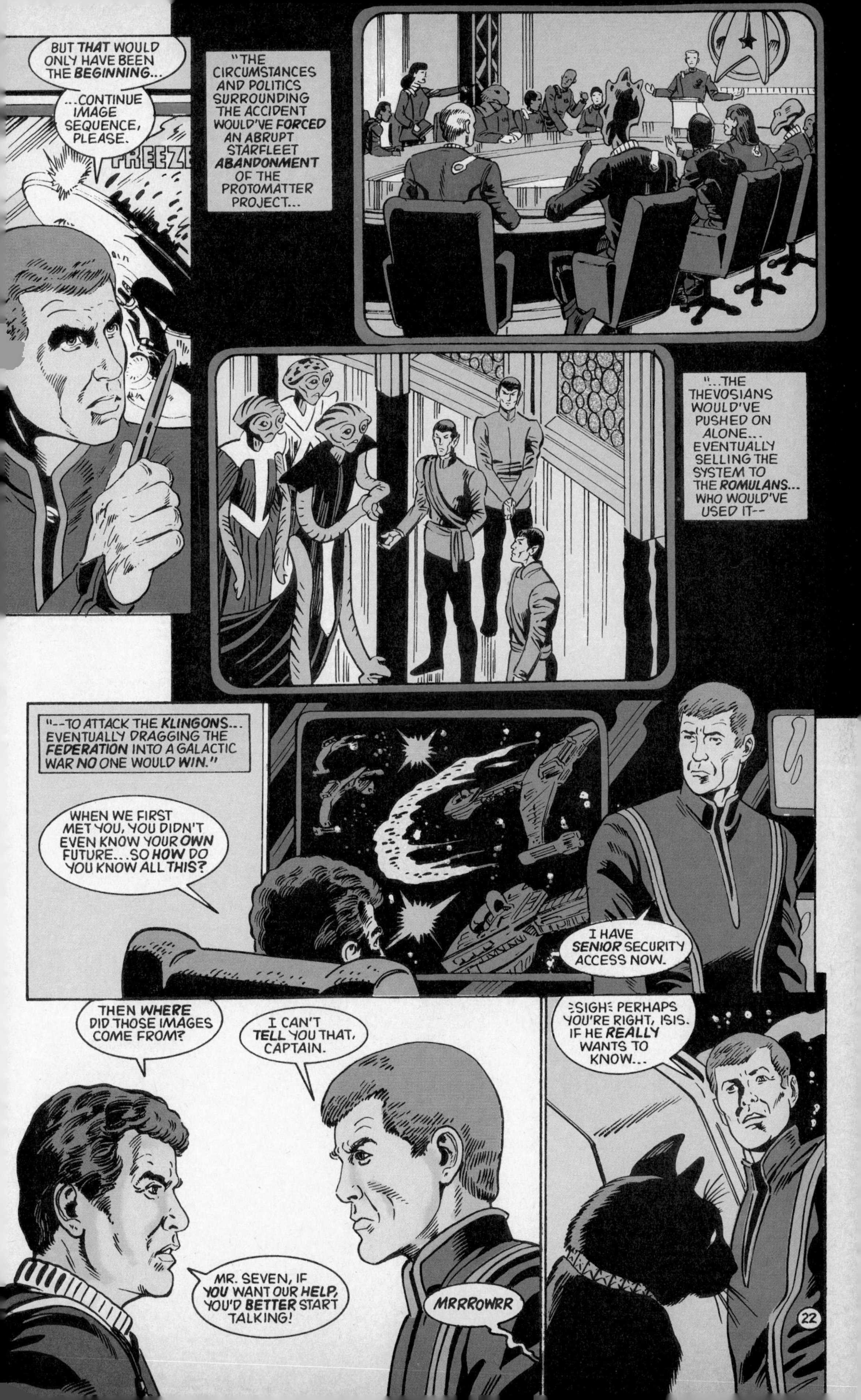
BUT THAT WOULD ONLY HAVE BEEN THE BEGINNING...
...CONTINUE IMAGE SEQUENCE, PLEASE.
FREEZE
"THE CIRCUMSTANCES AND POLITICS SURROUNDING THE ACCIDENT WOULD'VE FORCED AN ABRUPT STARFLEET ABANDONMENT OF THE PROTOMATTER PROJECT...
"...THE THEVOSIANS WOULD'VE PUSHED ON ALONE... EVENTUALLY SELLING THE SYSTEM TO THE ROMULANS... WHO WOULD'VE USED IT--
"--TO ATTACK THE KLINGONS... EVENTUALLY DRAGGING THE FEDERATION INTO A GALACTIC WAR NO ONE WOULD WIN."
WHEN WE FIRST MET YOU, YOU DIDN'T EVEN KNOW YOUR OWN FUTURE...SO HOW DO YOU KNOW ALL THIS?
I HAVE SENIOR SECURITY ACCESS NOW.
THEN WHERE DID THOSE IMAGES COME FROM?
I CAN'T TELL YOU THAT, CAPTAIN.
MR. SEVEN, IF YOU WANT OUR HELP, YOU'D BETTER START TALKING!
MRRROWRR
=SIGH= PERHAPS YOU'RE RIGHT, ISIS. IF HE REALLY WANTS TO KNOW...
22

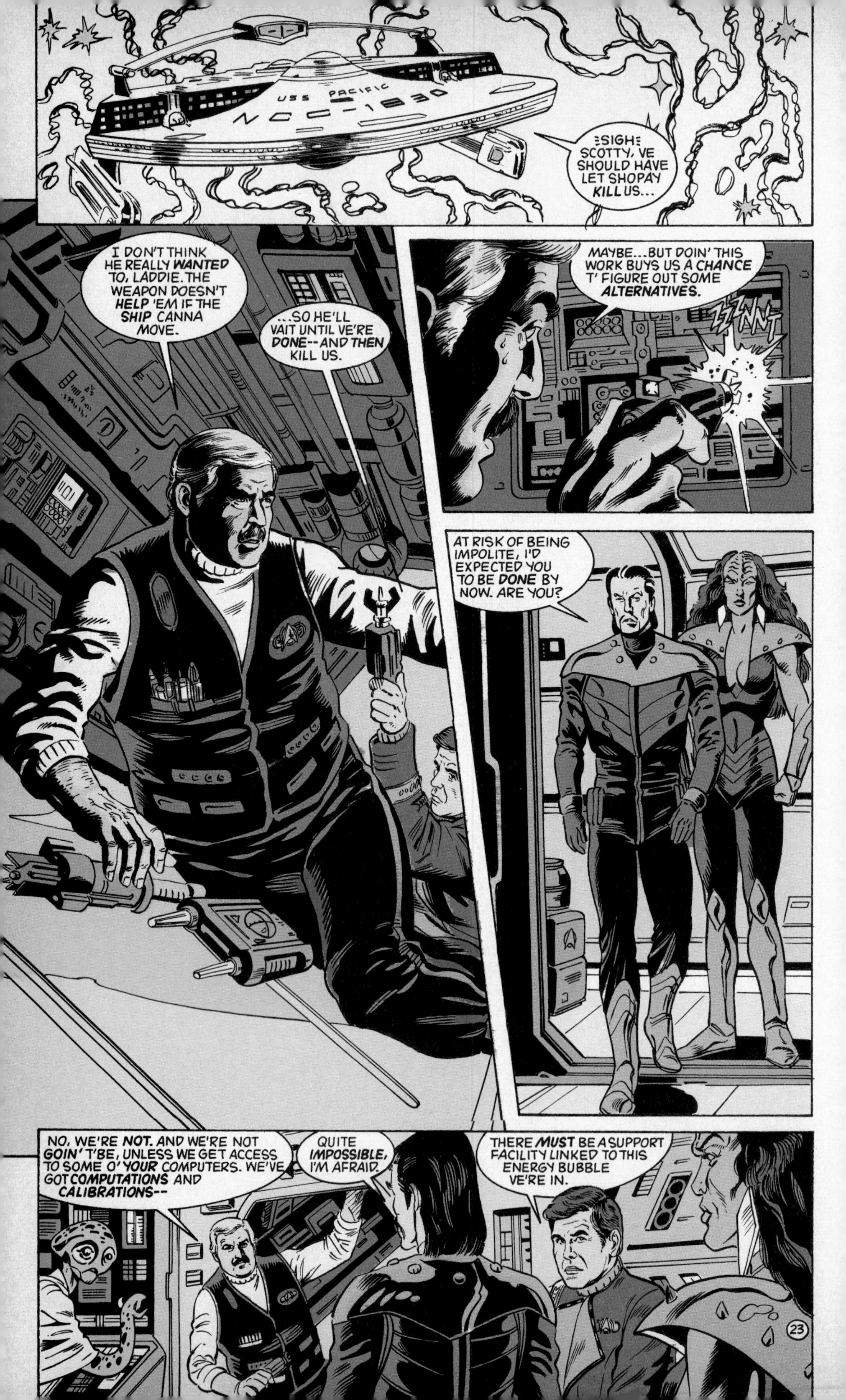
USS PACIFIC
NCC-1830
=SIGH= SCOTTY, VE SHOULD HAVE LET SHOPAY KILL US...
I DON'T THINK HE REALLY WANTED TO, LADDIE. THE WEAPON DOESN'T HELP 'EM IF THE SHIP CANNA MOVE.
...SO HE'LL VAIT UNTIL VE'RE DONE--AND THEN KILL US.
MAYBE...BUT DOIN' THIS WORK BUYS US A CHANCE T' FIGURE OUT SOME ALTERNATIVES.
AT RISK OF BEING IMPOLITE, I'D EXPECTED YOU TO BE DONE BY NOW. ARE YOU?
NO, WE'RE NOT. AND WE'RE NOT GOIN' T'BE, UNLESS WE GET ACCESS TO SOME O' YOUR COMPUTERS. WE'VE GOT COMPUTATIONS AND CALIBRATIONS--
QUITE IMPOSSIBLE, I'M AFRAID.
THERE MUST BE A SUPPORT FACILITY LINKED TO THIS ENERGY BUBBLE VE'RE IN.
23

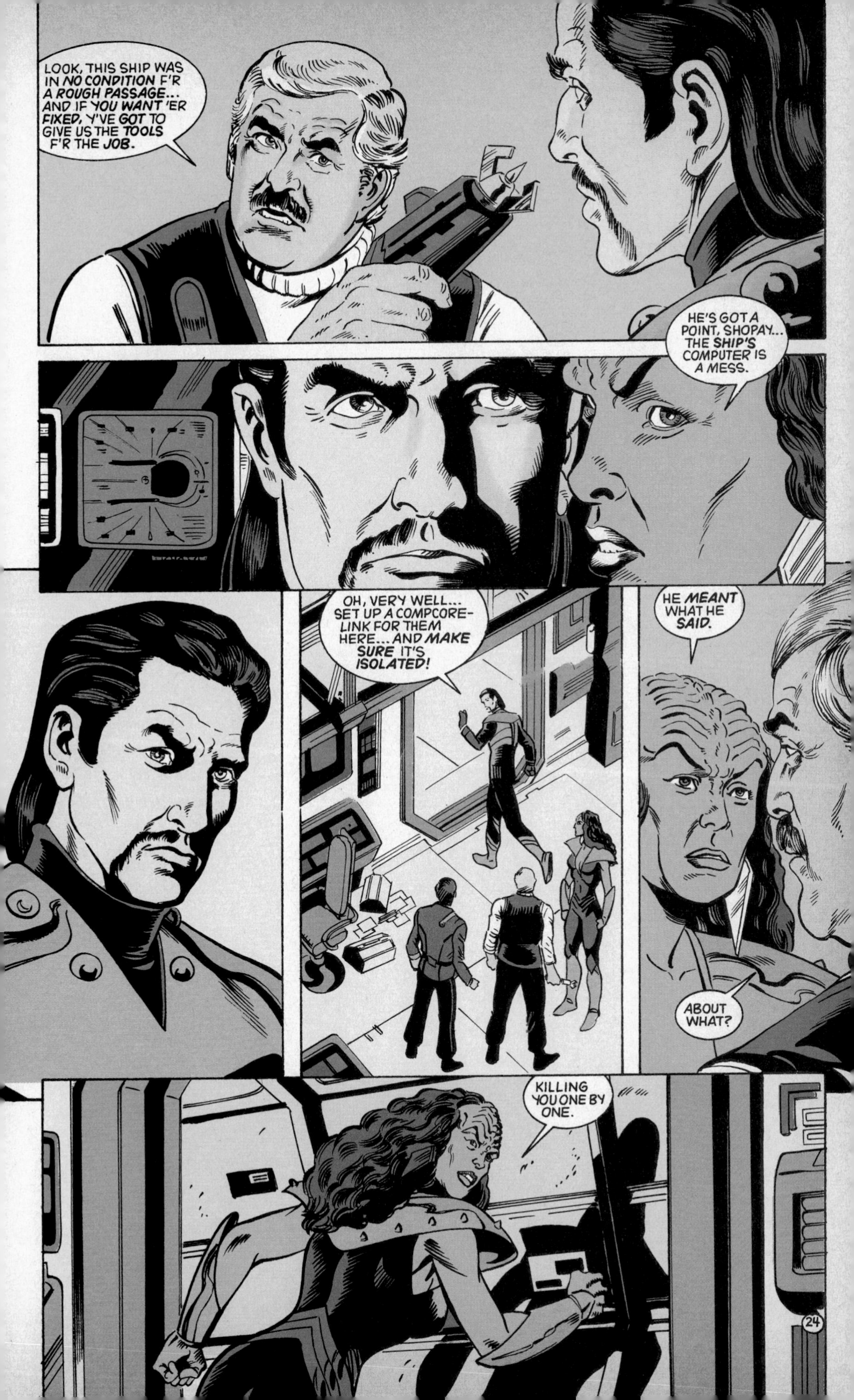

LOOK, THIS SHIP WAS IN NO CONDITION F'R A ROUGH PASSAGE... AND IF YOU WANT 'ER FIXED, Y'VE GOT TO GIVE US THE TOOLS F'R THE JOB.
HE'S GOT A POINT, SHOPAY... THE SHIP'S COMPUTER IS A MESS.
OH, VERY WELL... SET UP A COMPCORE-LINK FOR THEM HERE... AND MAKE SURE IT'S ISOLATED!
HE MEANT WHAT HE SAID.
ABOUT WHAT?
KILLING YOU ONE BY ONE.
24

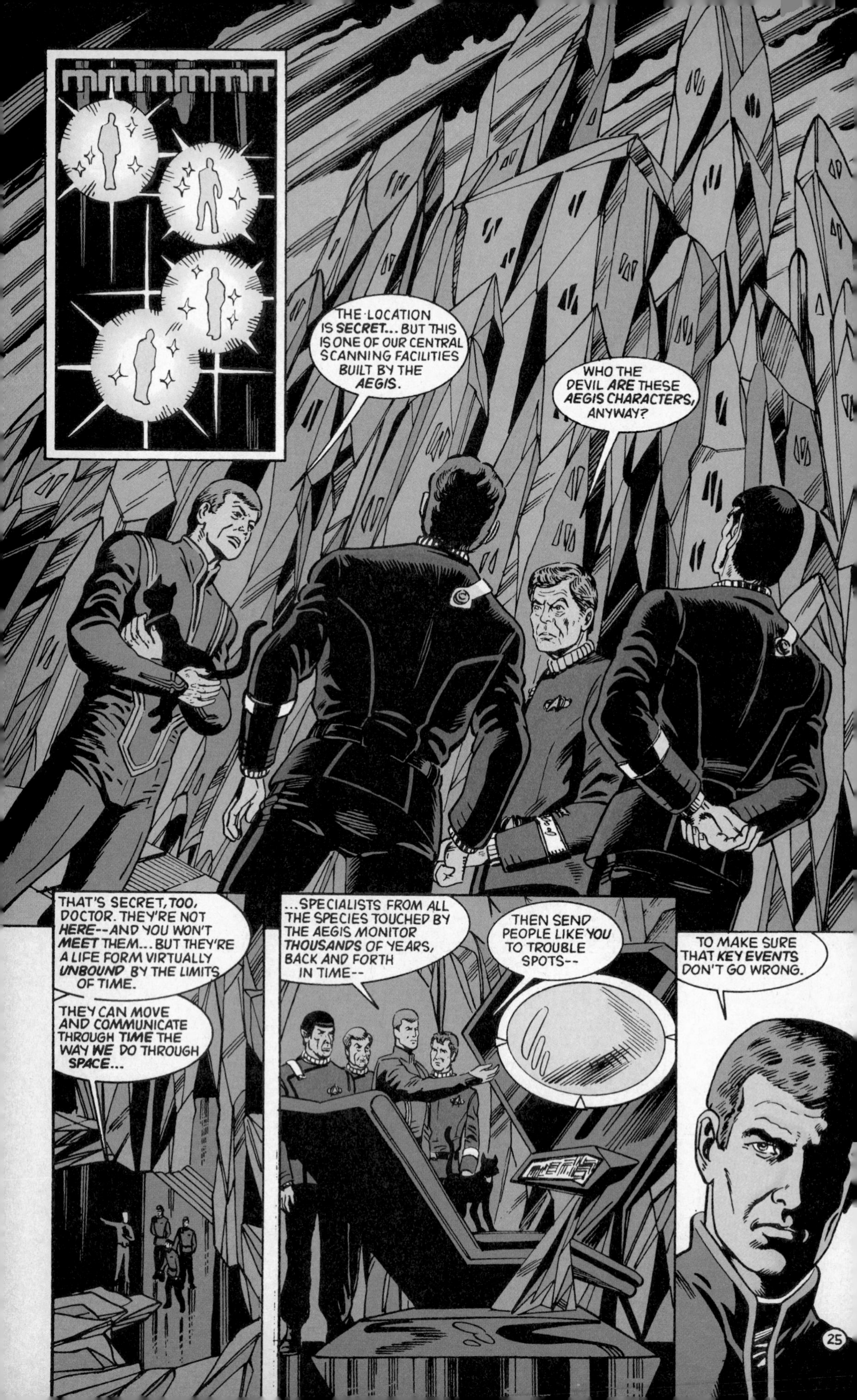
MMMMMM
THE LOCATION IS SECRET... BUT THIS IS ONE OF OUR CENTRAL SCANNING FACILITIES BUILT BY THE AEGIS.
WHO THE DEVIL ARE THESE AEGIS CHARACTERS, ANYWAY?
THAT'S SECRET, TOO, DOCTOR. THEY'RE NOT HERE--AND YOU WON'T MEET THEM... BUT THEY'RE A LIFE FORM VIRTUALLY UNBOUND BY THE LIMITS OF TIME.
THEY CAN MOVE AND COMMUNICATE THROUGH TIME THE WAY WE DO THROUGH SPACE...
...SPECIALISTS FROM ALL THE SPECIES TOUCHED BY THE AEGIS MONITOR THOUSANDS OF YEARS, BACK AND FORTH IN TIME--
THEN SEND PEOPLE LIKE YOU TO TROUBLE SPOTS--
TO MAKE SURE THAT KEY EVENTS DON'T GO WRONG.

WHO'S TO SAY WHAT'S RIGHT AND WRONG? THE WHOLE *IDEA* OF THIS *AEGIS* EXERCISING *THAT* KIND OF *POWER* OVER THE *KNOWN* GALAXY--!

I DON'T MEAN TO BE *CONDESCENDING*... BUT YOUR COMMUNITY OF BEINGS--HOWEVER INTELLIGENT--UNDER- STANDS *FAR LESS* ABOUT THE WAY THINGS *WORK* THAN YOU *THINK.*

DO YOU REALLY BELIEVE *MY SPONSORS* ARE THE *ONLY FORCE* AFFECTING EVENTS?

MEOWRRRR...

NO! THAT'S *PART* OF WHAT *SCARES* ME. THAT'S WHY *WE* ESTABLISHED THE *PRIME DIRECTIVE*-- WE *KNOW* WE DON'T HAVE THE...*WISDOM*...TO PLAY GOD!

WHATEVER HAPPENS IS WHAT WAS *MEANT* TO HAPPEN. THAT'S THE GUIDING PRECEPT BEHIND THE AEGIS. THEY DON'T WASTE TIME WITH FUTILE *PHILOSOPHIZING*-- THEY SIMPLY *ACT*--

--LEAVING THE COSMIC QUESTIONS HUMANS LOVE PONDERING TO WHATEVER FORCE IS *HIGHEST*--A FORCE FAR BEYOND *YOUR* COMPREHENSION... OR *MINE*... OR MY *SPONSORS,* FOR THAT MATTER.

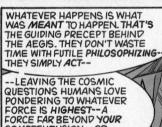

AND WHAT IF THAT *HIGHEST FORCE* DOESN'T EXIST--AND *NOBODY'S* WORRYING ABOUT THOSE "COSMIC QUESTIONS"--?

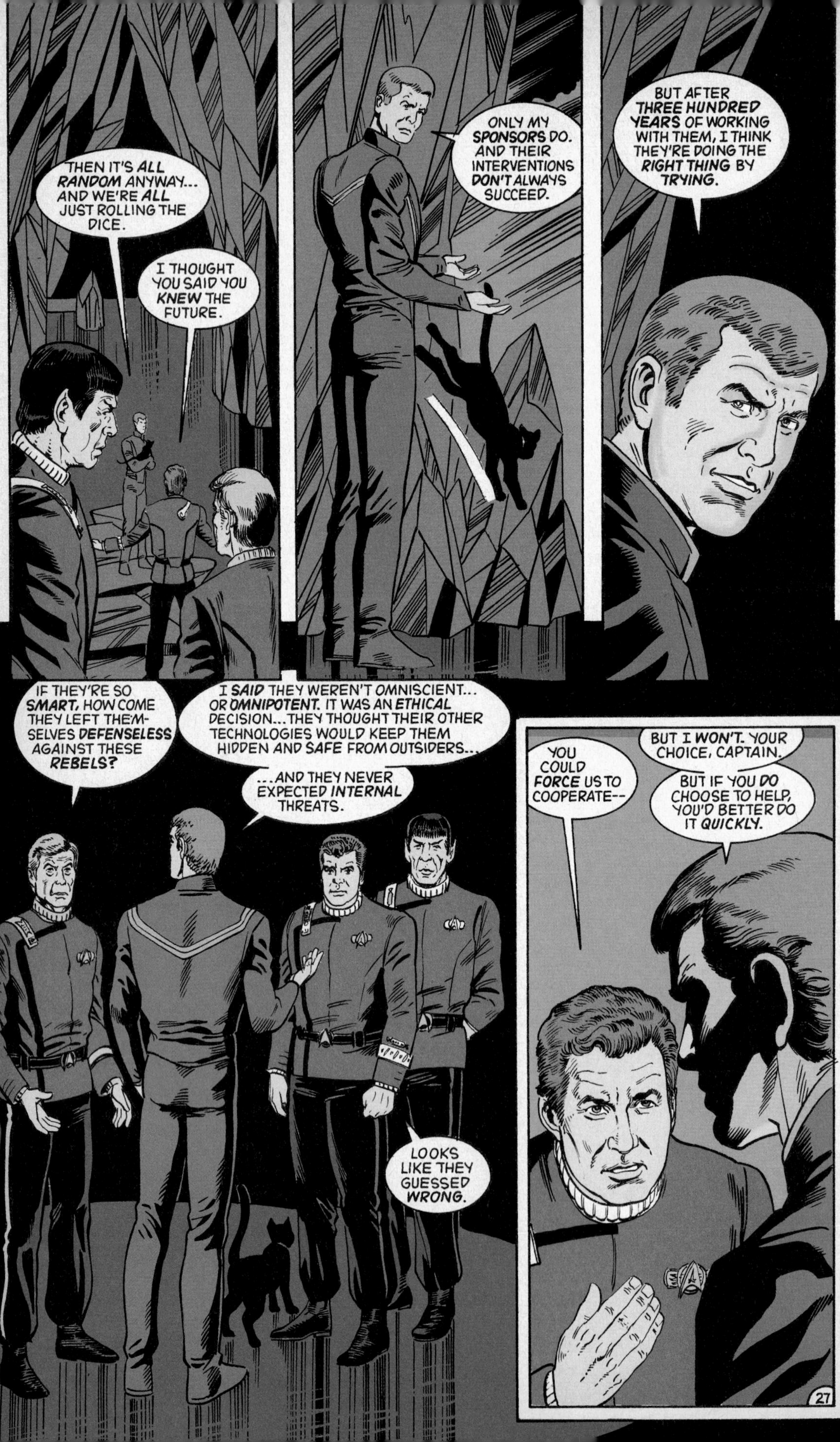
THEN IT'S ALL RANDOM ANYWAY... AND WE'RE ALL JUST ROLLING THE DICE.
I THOUGHT YOU SAID YOU KNEW THE FUTURE.
ONLY MY SPONSORS DO. AND THEIR INTERVENTIONS DON'T ALWAYS SUCCEED.
BUT AFTER THREE HUNDRED YEARS OF WORKING WITH THEM, I THINK THEY'RE DOING THE RIGHT THING BY TRYING.
IF THEY'RE SO SMART, HOW COME THEY LEFT THEMSELVES DEFENSELESS AGAINST THESE REBELS?
I SAID THEY WEREN'T OMNISCIENT... OR OMNIPOTENT. IT WAS AN ETHICAL DECISION... THEY THOUGHT THEIR OTHER TECHNOLOGIES WOULD KEEP THEM HIDDEN AND SAFE FROM OUTSIDERS...
...AND THEY NEVER EXPECTED INTERNAL THREATS.
LOOKS LIKE THEY GUESSED WRONG.
YOU COULD FORCE US TO COOPERATE--
BUT I WON'T. YOUR CHOICE, CAPTAIN.
BUT IF YOU DO CHOOSE TO HELP, YOU'D BETTER DO IT QUICKLY.
27

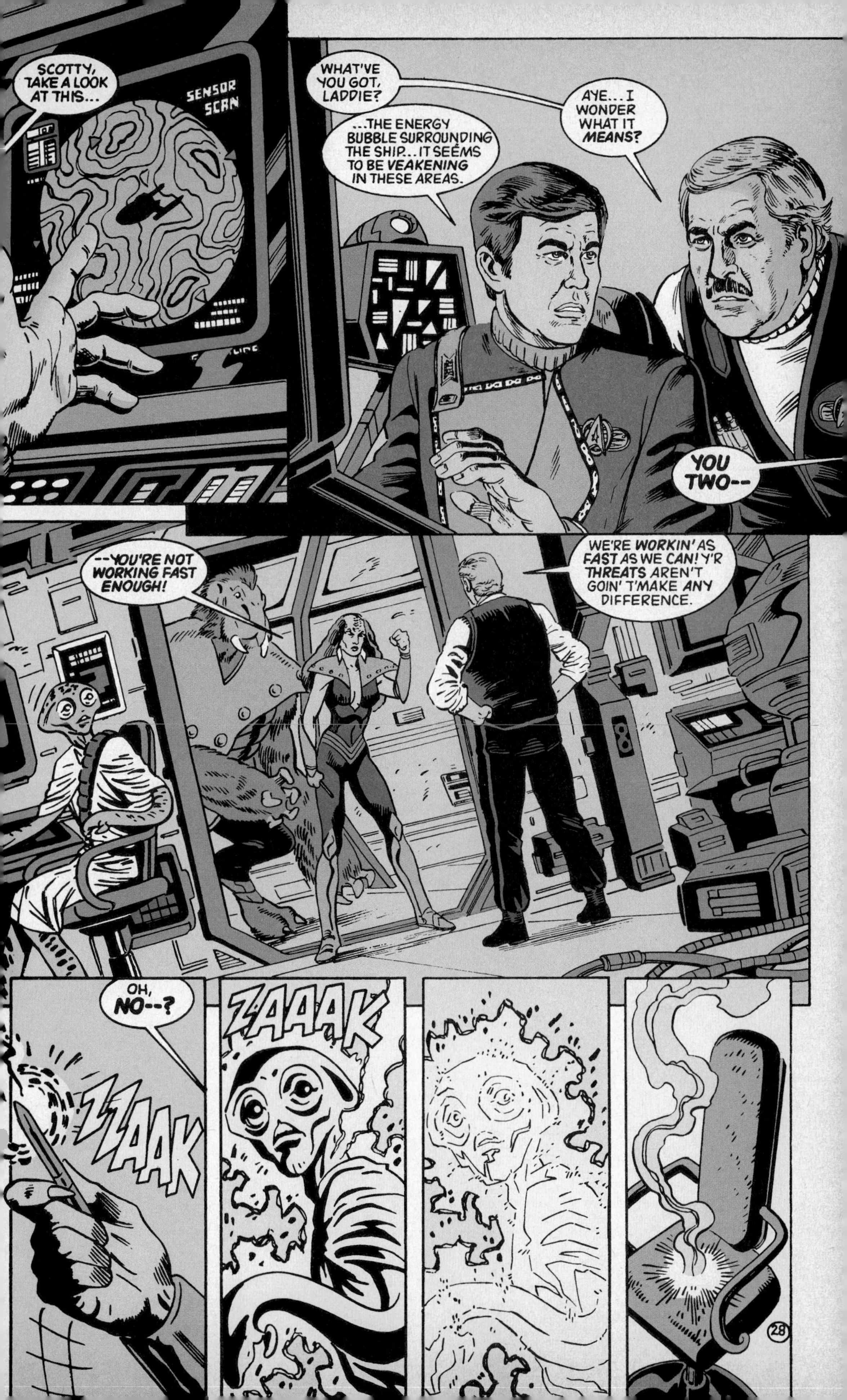
SCOTTY, TAKE A LOOK AT THIS...
SENSOR SCAN
WHAT'VE YOU GOT, LADDIE?
...THE ENERGY BUBBLE SURROUNDING THE SHIP... IT SEEMS TO BE *VEAKENING* IN THESE AREAS.
AYE... I WONDER WHAT IT *MEANS?*
YOU TWO--
--YOU'RE NOT WORKING FAST ENOUGH!
WE'RE *WORKIN'* AS *FAST* AS WE *CAN!* Y'R *THREATS* AREN'T GOIN' T'MAKE *ANY* DIFFERENCE.
OH, *NO--?*
ZZAAK
ZAAAK
28

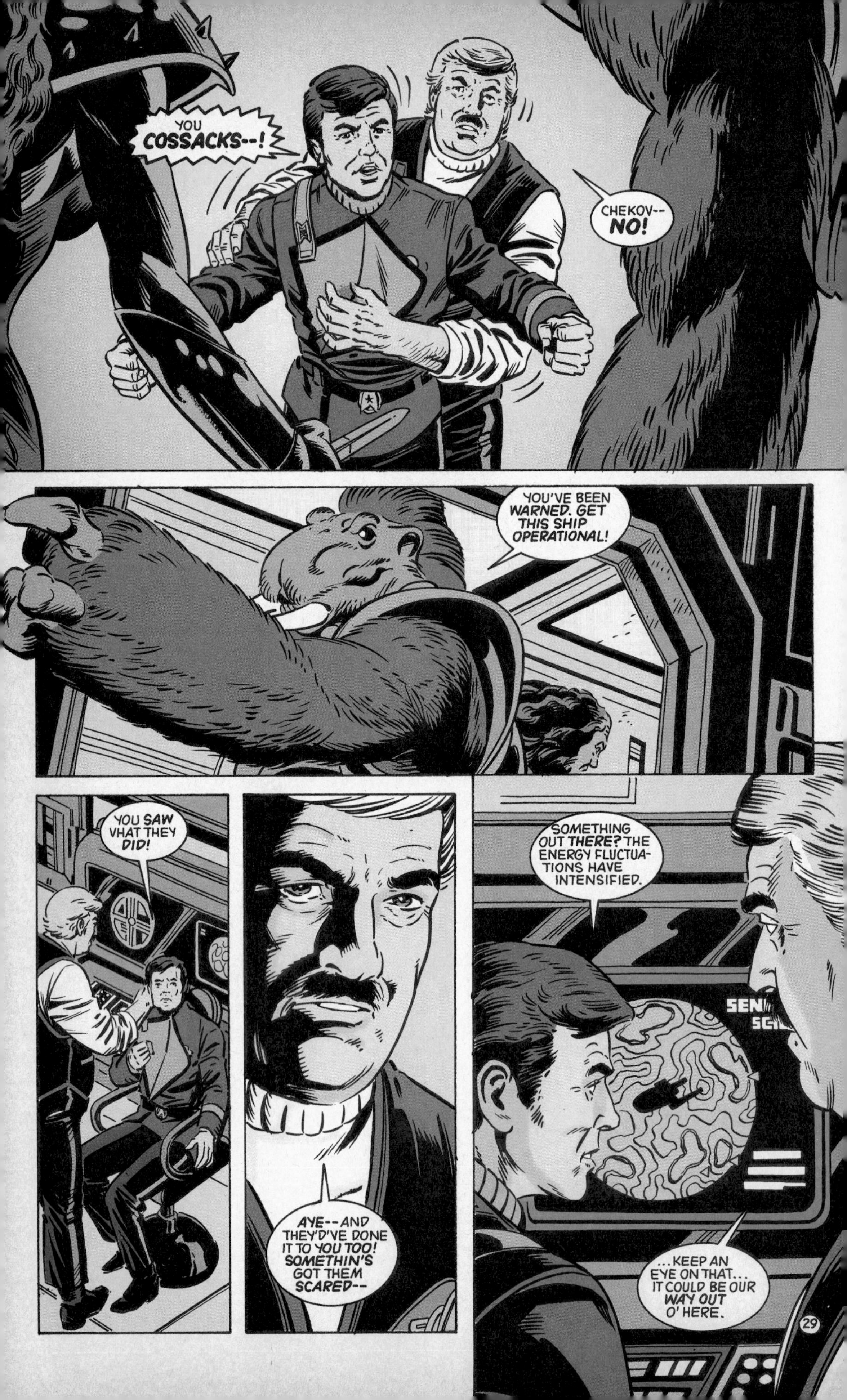

YOU COSSACKS--!
CHEKOV-- NO!
YOU'VE BEEN WARNED. GET THIS SHIP OPERATIONAL!
YOU SAW VHAT THEY DID!
AYE--AND THEY'D'VE DONE IT TO YOU TOO! SOMETHIN'S GOT THEM SCARED--
SOMETHING OUT THERE? THE ENERGY FLUCTUATIONS HAVE INTENSIFIED.
...KEEP AN EYE ON THAT... IT COULD BE OUR WAY OUT O' HERE.

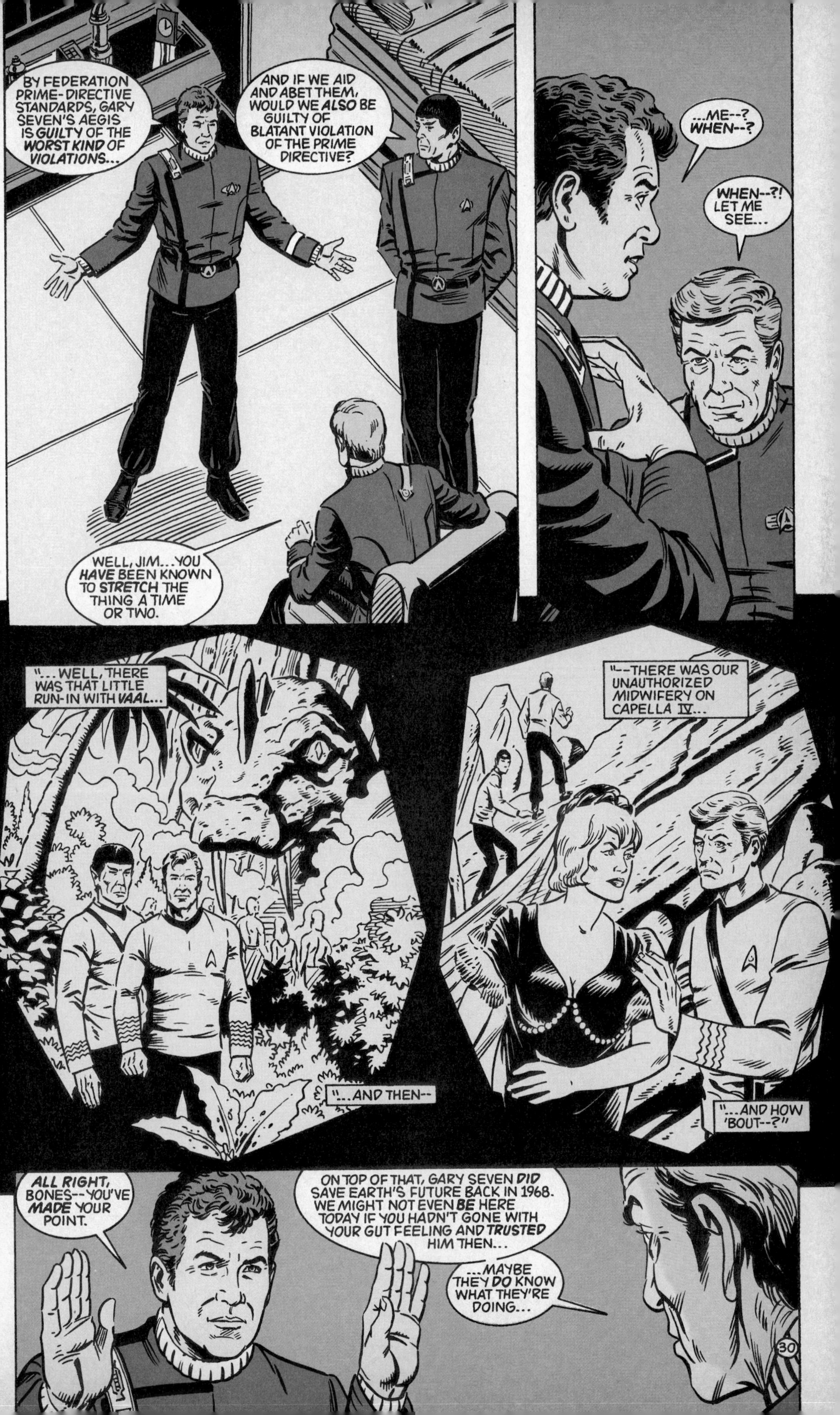
BY FEDERATION PRIME-DIRECTIVE STANDARDS, GARY SEVEN'S AEGIS IS GUILTY OF THE WORST KIND OF VIOLATIONS...
AND IF WE AID AND ABET THEM, WOULD WE ALSO BE GUILTY OF BLATANT VIOLATION OF THE PRIME DIRECTIVE?
WELL, JIM... YOU HAVE BEEN KNOWN TO STRETCH THE THING A TIME OR TWO.
...ME--? WHEN--?
WHEN--?! LET ME SEE...
"...WELL, THERE WAS THAT LITTLE RUN-IN WITH VAAL...
"...AND THEN--
"--THERE WAS OUR UNAUTHORIZED MIDWIFERY ON CAPELLA IV...
"...AND HOW 'BOUT--?"
ALL RIGHT, BONES-- YOU'VE MADE YOUR POINT.
ON TOP OF THAT, GARY SEVEN DID SAVE EARTH'S FUTURE BACK IN 1968. WE MIGHT NOT EVEN BE HERE TODAY IF YOU HADN'T GONE WITH YOUR GUT FEELING AND TRUSTED HIM THEN...
...MAYBE THEY DO KNOW WHAT THEY'RE DOING...
30

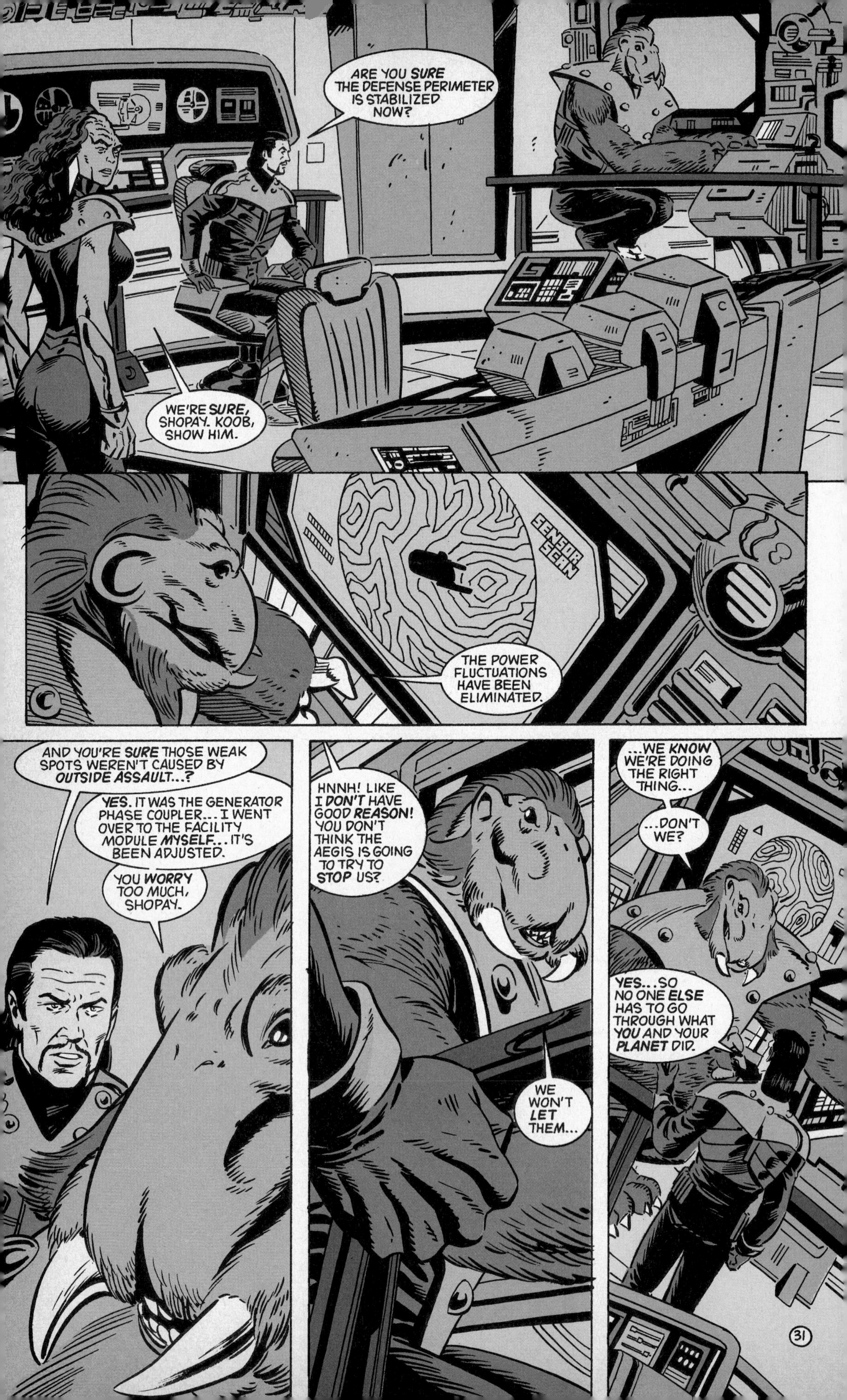
ARE YOU SURE THE DEFENSE PERIMETER IS STABILIZED NOW?
WE'RE SURE, SHOPAY. KOOB, SHOW HIM.
SENSOR SCAN
THE POWER FLUCTUATIONS HAVE BEEN ELIMINATED.
AND YOU'RE SURE THOSE WEAK SPOTS WEREN'T CAUSED BY OUTSIDE ASSAULT...?
YES. IT WAS THE GENERATOR PHASE COUPLER... I WENT OVER TO THE FACILITY MODULE MYSELF... IT'S BEEN ADJUSTED.
YOU WORRY TOO MUCH, SHOPAY.
HNNH! LIKE I DON'T HAVE GOOD REASON! YOU DON'T THINK THE AEGIS IS GOING TO TRY TO STOP US?
WE WON'T LET THEM...
...WE KNOW WE'RE DOING THE RIGHT THING...
...DON'T WE?
YES... SO NO ONE ELSE HAS TO GO THROUGH WHAT YOU AND YOUR PLANET DID.

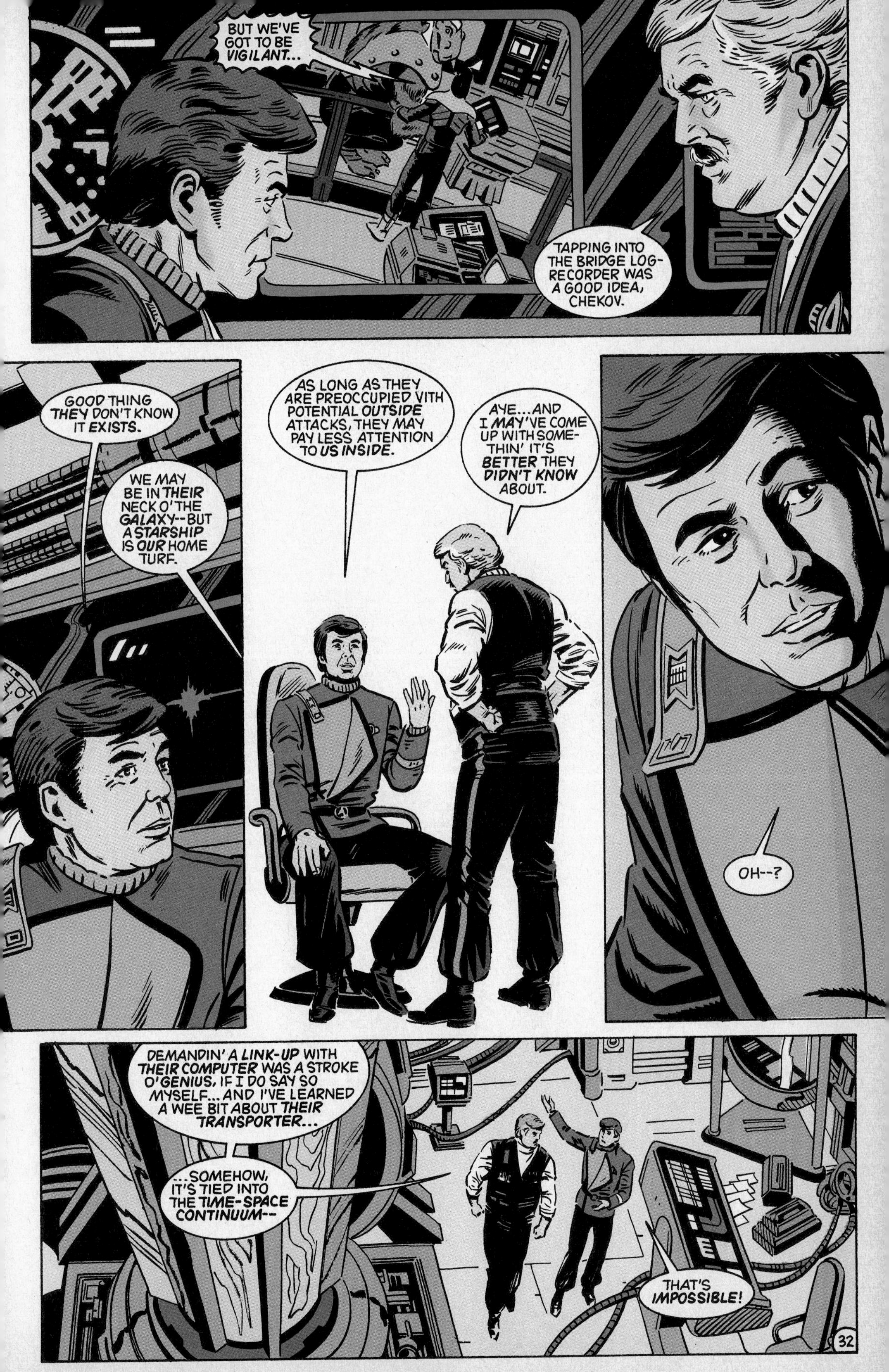
BUT WE'VE GOT TO BE VIGILANT...
TAPPING INTO THE BRIDGE LOG-RECORDER WAS A GOOD IDEA, CHEKOV.
GOOD THING THEY DON'T KNOW IT EXISTS.
WE MAY BE IN THEIR NECK O' THE GALAXY--BUT A STARSHIP IS OUR HOME TURF.
AS LONG AS THEY ARE PREOCCUPIED VITH POTENTIAL OUTSIDE ATTACKS, THEY MAY PAY LESS ATTENTION TO US INSIDE.
AYE...AND I MAY'VE COME UP WITH SOME-THIN' IT'S BETTER THEY DIDN'T KNOW ABOUT.
OH--?
DEMANDIN' A LINK-UP WITH THEIR COMPUTER WAS A STROKE O' GENIUS, IF I DO SAY SO MYSELF... AND I'VE LEARNED A WEE BIT ABOUT THEIR TRANSPORTER...
...SOMEHOW, IT'S TIED INTO THE TIME-SPACE CONTINUUM--
THAT'S IMPOSSIBLE!
32

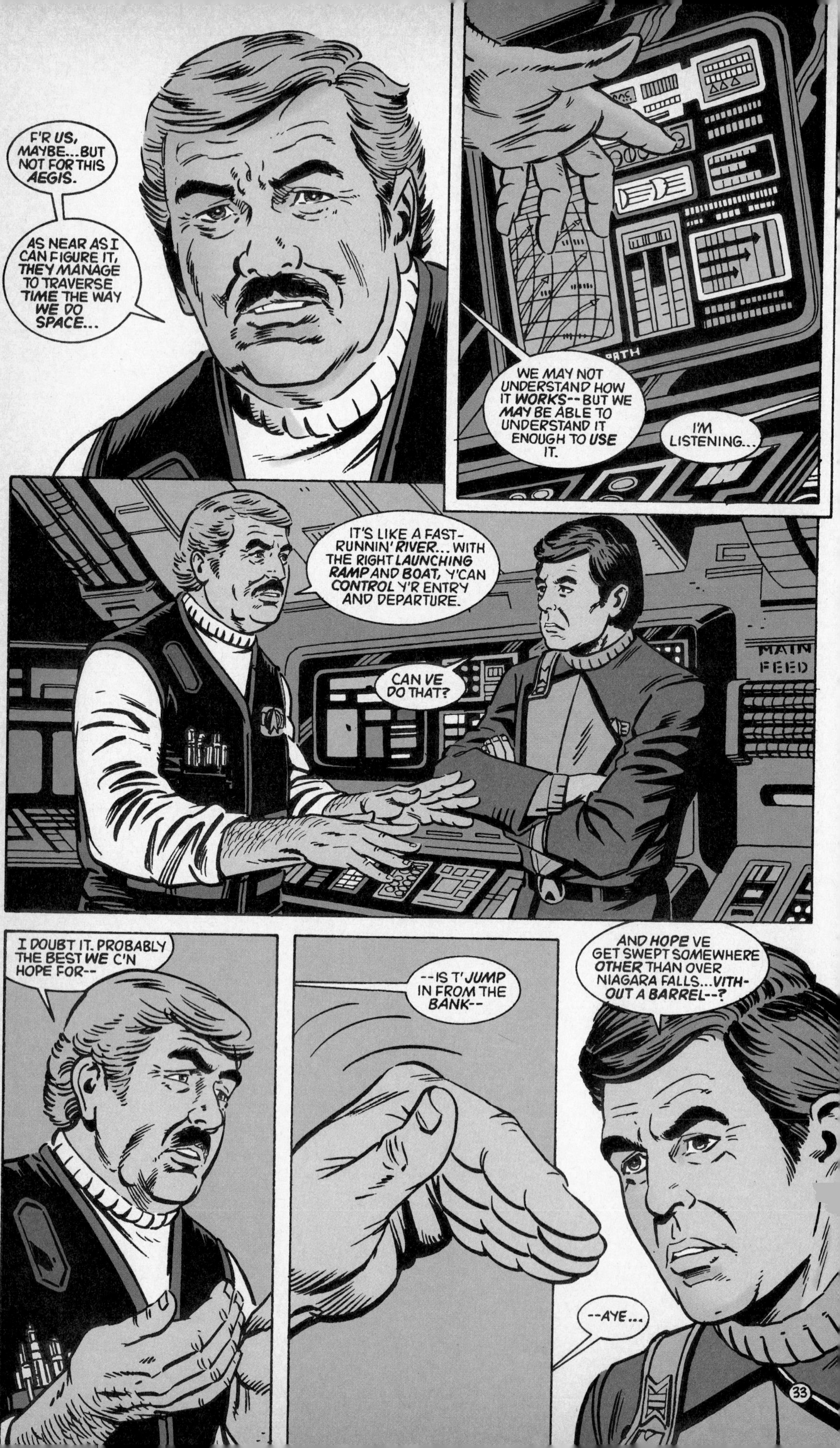
F'R US, MAYBE... BUT NOT FOR THIS AEGIS.
AS NEAR AS I CAN FIGURE IT, THEY MANAGE TO TRAVERSE TIME THE WAY WE DO SPACE...
WE MAY NOT UNDERSTAND HOW IT WORKS-- BUT WE MAY BE ABLE TO UNDERSTAND IT ENOUGH TO USE IT.
I'M LISTENING...
IT'S LIKE A FAST-RUNNIN' RIVER... WITH THE RIGHT LAUNCHING RAMP AND BOAT, Y'CAN CONTROL Y'R ENTRY AND DEPARTURE.
MAIN FEED
CAN VE DO THAT?
I DOUBT IT. PROBABLY THE BEST WE C'N HOPE FOR--
--IS T' JUMP IN FROM THE BANK--
AND HOPE VE GET SWEPT SOMEWHERE OTHER THAN OVER NIAGARA FALLS... VITH-OUT A BARREL--?
--AYE...

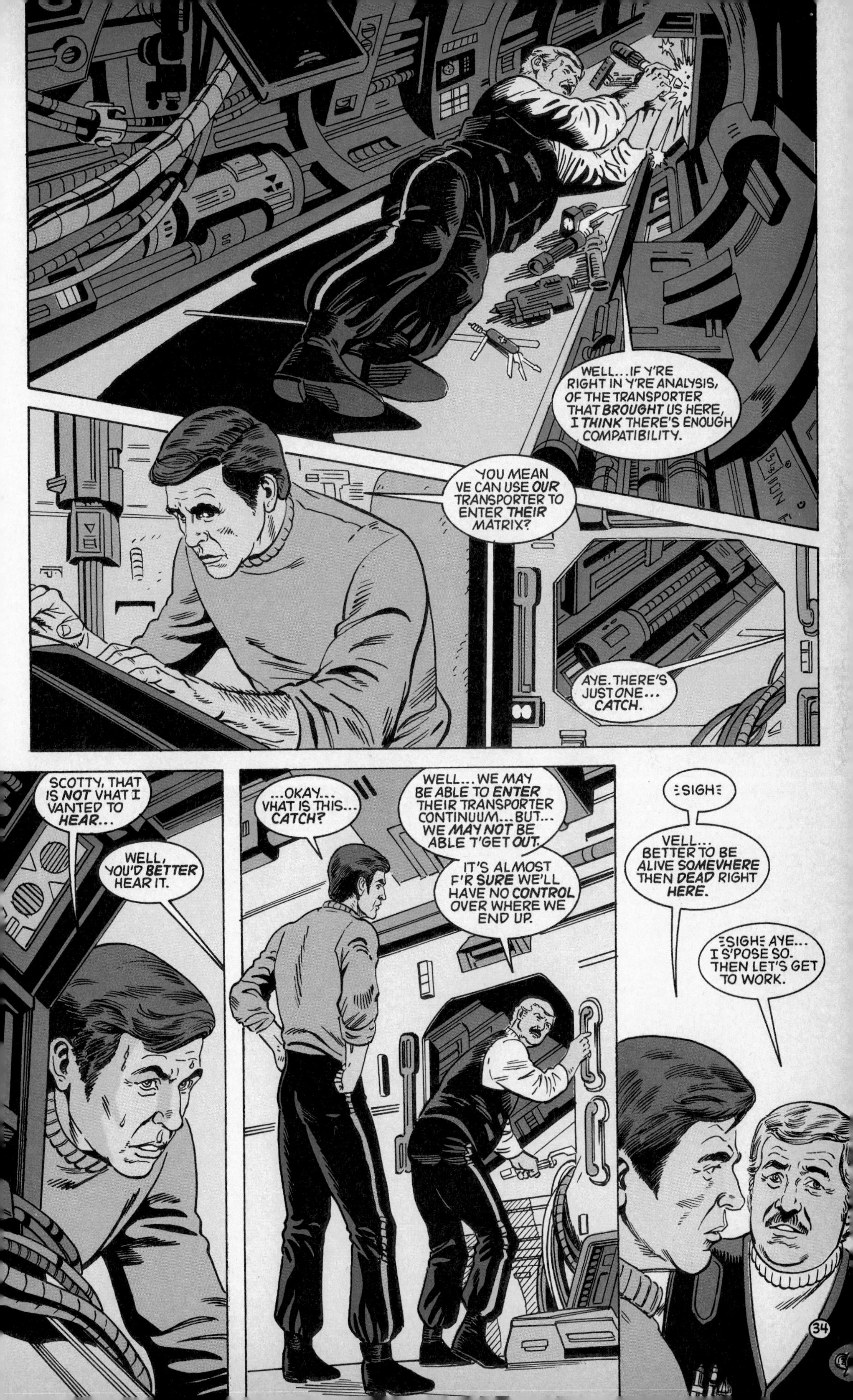
WELL...IF Y'RE RIGHT IN Y'RE ANALYSIS, OF THE TRANSPORTER THAT BROUGHT US HERE, I THINK THERE'S ENOUGH COMPATIBILITY.
YOU MEAN VE CAN USE OUR TRANSPORTER TO ENTER THEIR MATRIX?
AYE. THERE'S JUST ONE... CATCH.
SCOTTY, THAT IS NOT VHAT I VANTED TO HEAR...
WELL, YOU'D BETTER HEAR IT.
...OKAY... VHAT IS THIS... CATCH?
WELL... WE MAY BE ABLE TO ENTER THEIR TRANSPORTER CONTINUUM... BUT... WE MAY NOT BE ABLE T'GET OUT.
IT'S ALMOST F'R SURE WE'LL HAVE NO CONTROL OVER WHERE WE END UP.
SIGH
VELL... BETTER TO BE ALIVE SOMEVHERE THEN DEAD RIGHT HERE.
SIGH AYE... I S'POSE SO. THEN LET'S GET TO WORK.
34

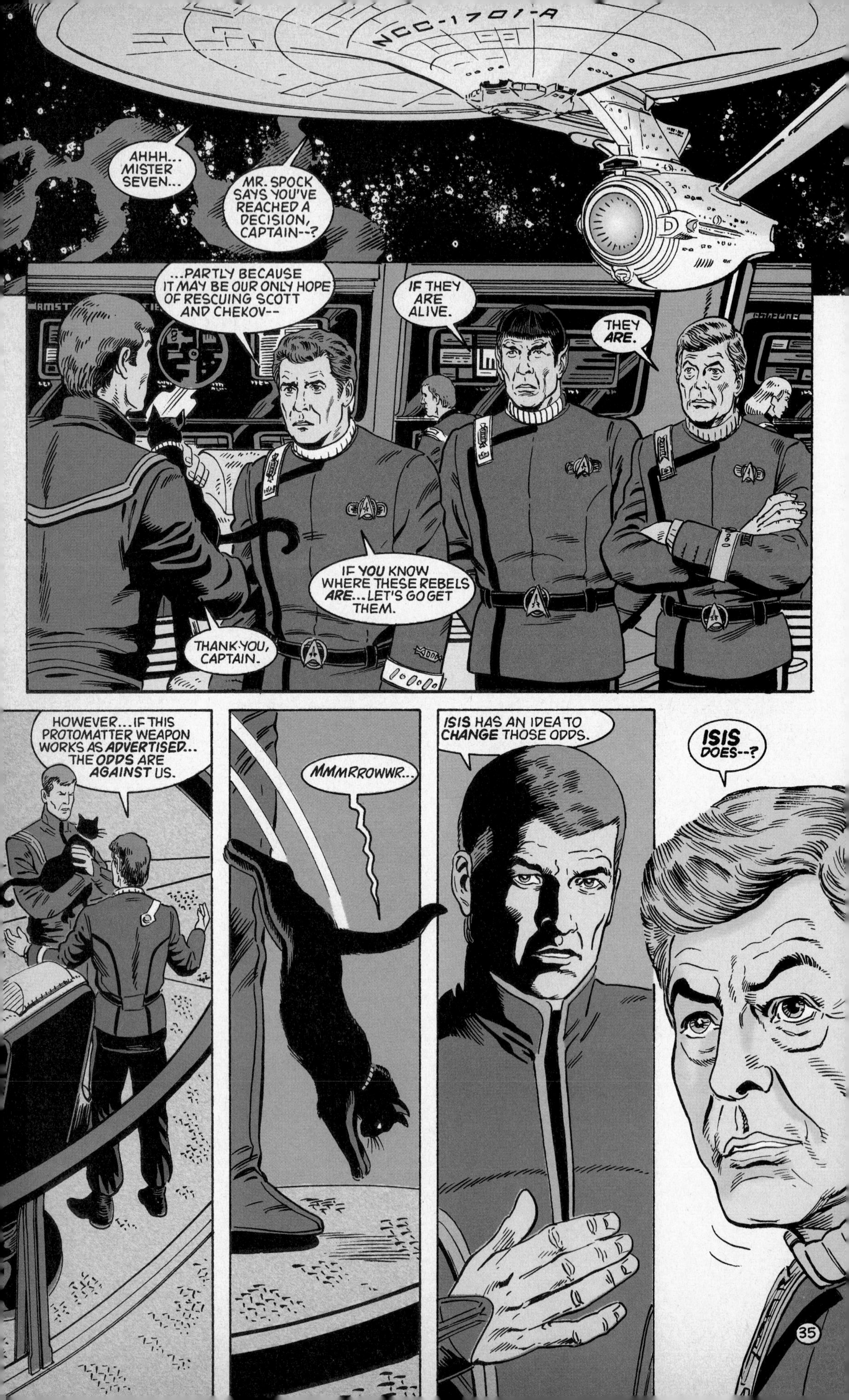
NCC-1701-A
AHHH... MISTER SEVEN...
MR. SPOCK SAYS YOU'VE REACHED A DECISION, CAPTAIN--?
...PARTLY BECAUSE IT MAY BE OUR ONLY HOPE OF RESCUING SCOTT AND CHEKOV--
IF THEY ARE ALIVE.
THEY ARE.
IF YOU KNOW WHERE THESE REBELS ARE... LET'S GO GET THEM.
THANK YOU, CAPTAIN.
HOWEVER... IF THIS PROTOMATTER WEAPON WORKS AS ADVERTISED... THE ODDS ARE AGAINST US.
MMMRROWWR...
ISIS HAS AN IDEA TO CHANGE THOSE ODDS.
ISIS DOES--?

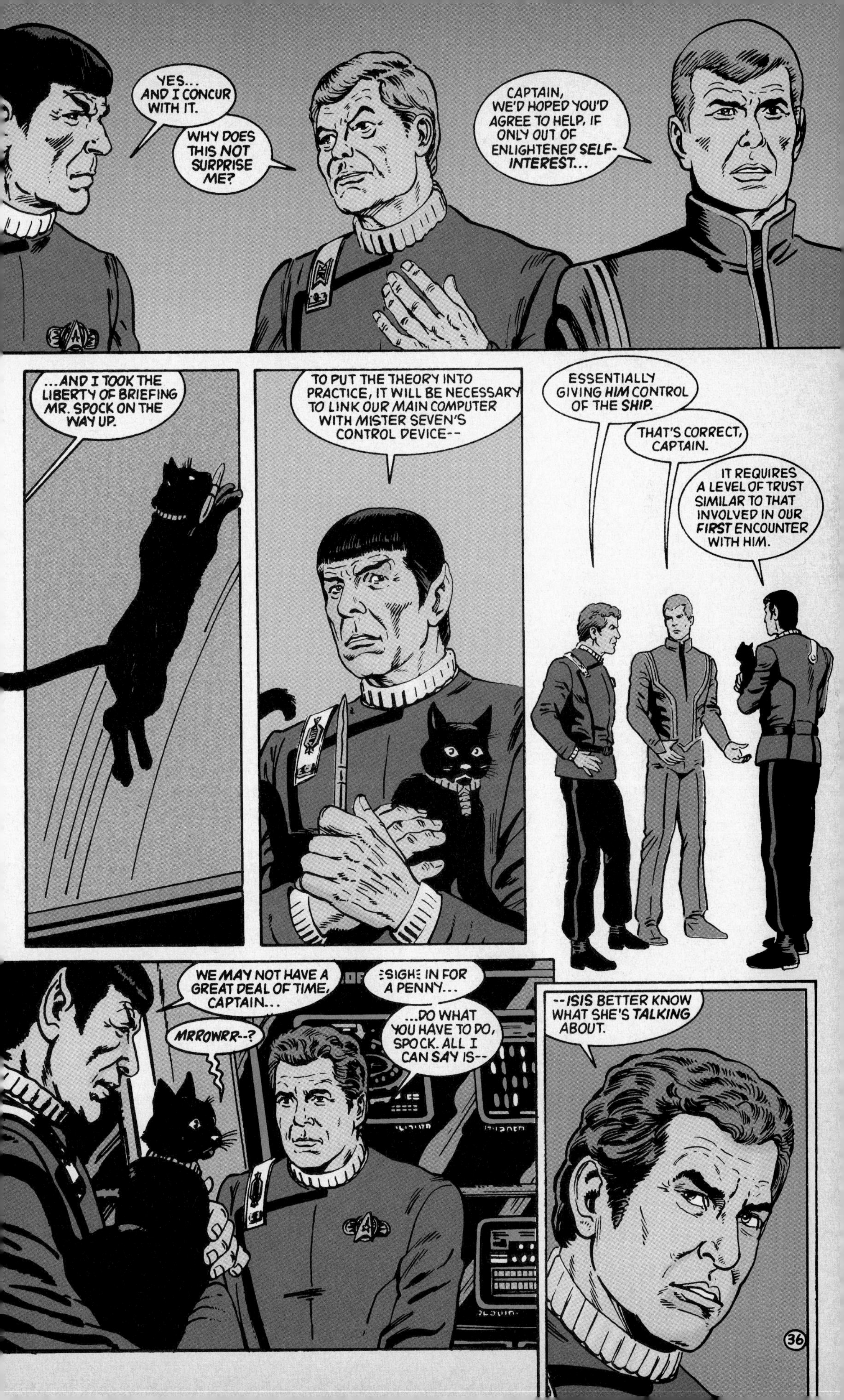
YES... AND I CONCUR WITH IT.
WHY DOES THIS NOT SURPRISE ME?
CAPTAIN, WE'D HOPED YOU'D AGREE TO HELP, IF ONLY OUT OF ENLIGHTENED SELF-INTEREST...
...AND I TOOK THE LIBERTY OF BRIEFING MR. SPOCK ON THE WAY UP.
TO PUT THE THEORY INTO PRACTICE, IT WILL BE NECESSARY TO LINK OUR MAIN COMPUTER WITH MISTER SEVEN'S CONTROL DEVICE--
ESSENTIALLY GIVING HIM CONTROL OF THE SHIP.
THAT'S CORRECT, CAPTAIN.
IT REQUIRES A LEVEL OF TRUST SIMILAR TO THAT INVOLVED IN OUR FIRST ENCOUNTER WITH HIM.
WE MAY NOT HAVE A GREAT DEAL OF TIME, CAPTAIN...
MRROWRR--?
ƐSIGHƎ IN FOR A PENNY...
...DO WHAT YOU HAVE TO DO, SPOCK. ALL I CAN SAY IS--
--ISIS BETTER KNOW WHAT SHE'S TALKING ABOUT.

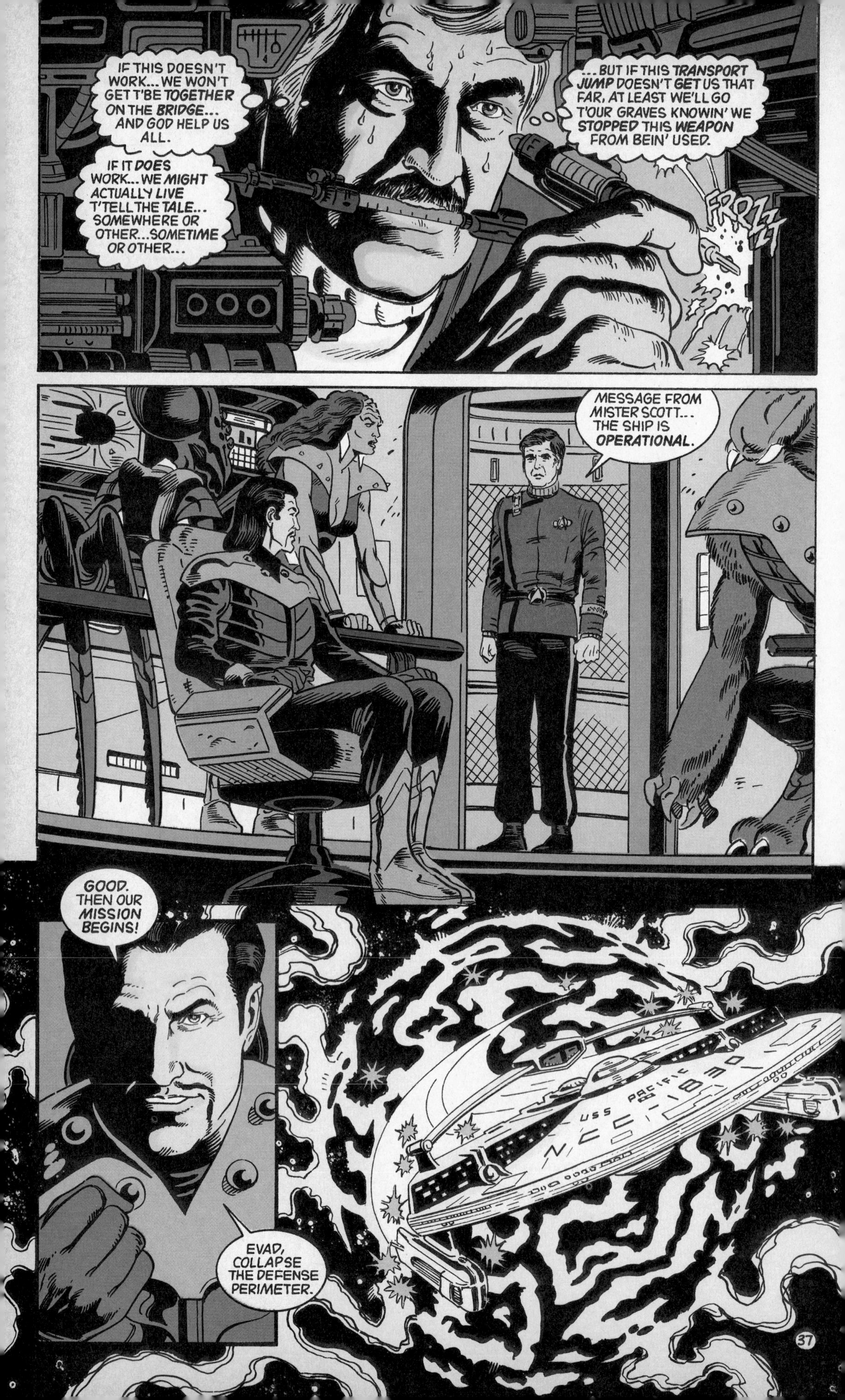
IF THIS DOESN'T WORK... WE WON'T GET T'BE TOGETHER ON THE BRIDGE... AND GOD HELP US ALL.
IF IT DOES WORK... WE MIGHT ACTUALLY LIVE T'TELL THE TALE... SOMEWHERE OR OTHER... SOMETIME OR OTHER...
...BUT IF THIS TRANSPORT JUMP DOESN'T GET US THAT FAR, AT LEAST WE'LL GO T'OUR GRAVES KNOWIN' WE STOPPED THIS WEAPON FROM BEIN' USED.
FRZZZT
MESSAGE FROM MISTER SCOTT... THE SHIP IS OPERATIONAL.
GOOD. THEN OUR MISSION BEGINS!
EVAD, COLLAPSE THE DEFENSE PERIMETER.
USS PACIFIC
NCC-71832

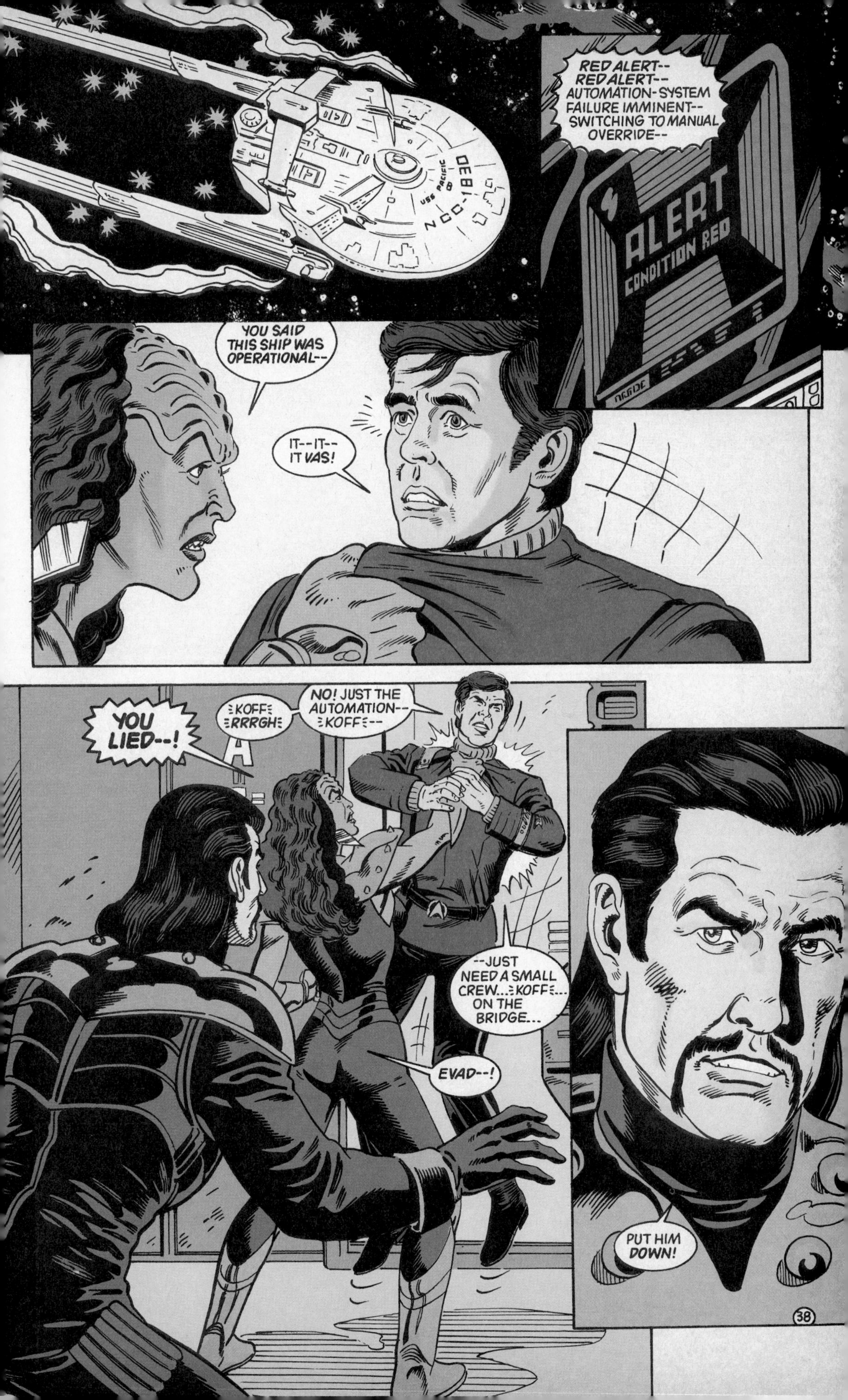

RED ALERT--
RED ALERT--
AUTOMATION-SYSTEM
FAILURE IMMINENT--
SWITCHING TO MANUAL
OVERRIDE--
ALERT
CONDITION RED
YOU SAID THIS SHIP WAS OPERATIONAL--
IT--IT--IT VAS!
YOU LIED--!
KOFF RRRGH
NO! JUST THE AUTOMATION-- KOFF--
--JUST NEED A SMALL CREW... KOFF... ON THE BRIDGE...
EVAD--!
PUT HIM DOWN!
38

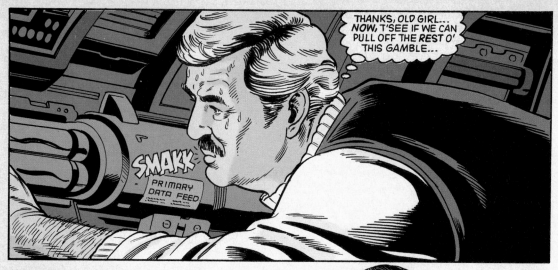

THANKS, OLD GIRL... NOW, T'SEE IF WE CAN PULL OFF THE *REST O'* THIS GAMBLE...

SMAKK

PRIMARY DATA FEED

OOOF!

THUDD

HOW MANY BRIDGE CREW?

...YOU HAVE *FOUR* ARMED PEOPLE TO *VATCH* US--AND YOU'VE ALREADY *SHOWN* US YOU'RE *VILLING* TO KILL. HOW MUCH *DANGER* CAN VE BE?

THE *FIVE* SURVIVING CREW MEMBERS...

ALL RIGHT. GET THEM UP HERE.

39

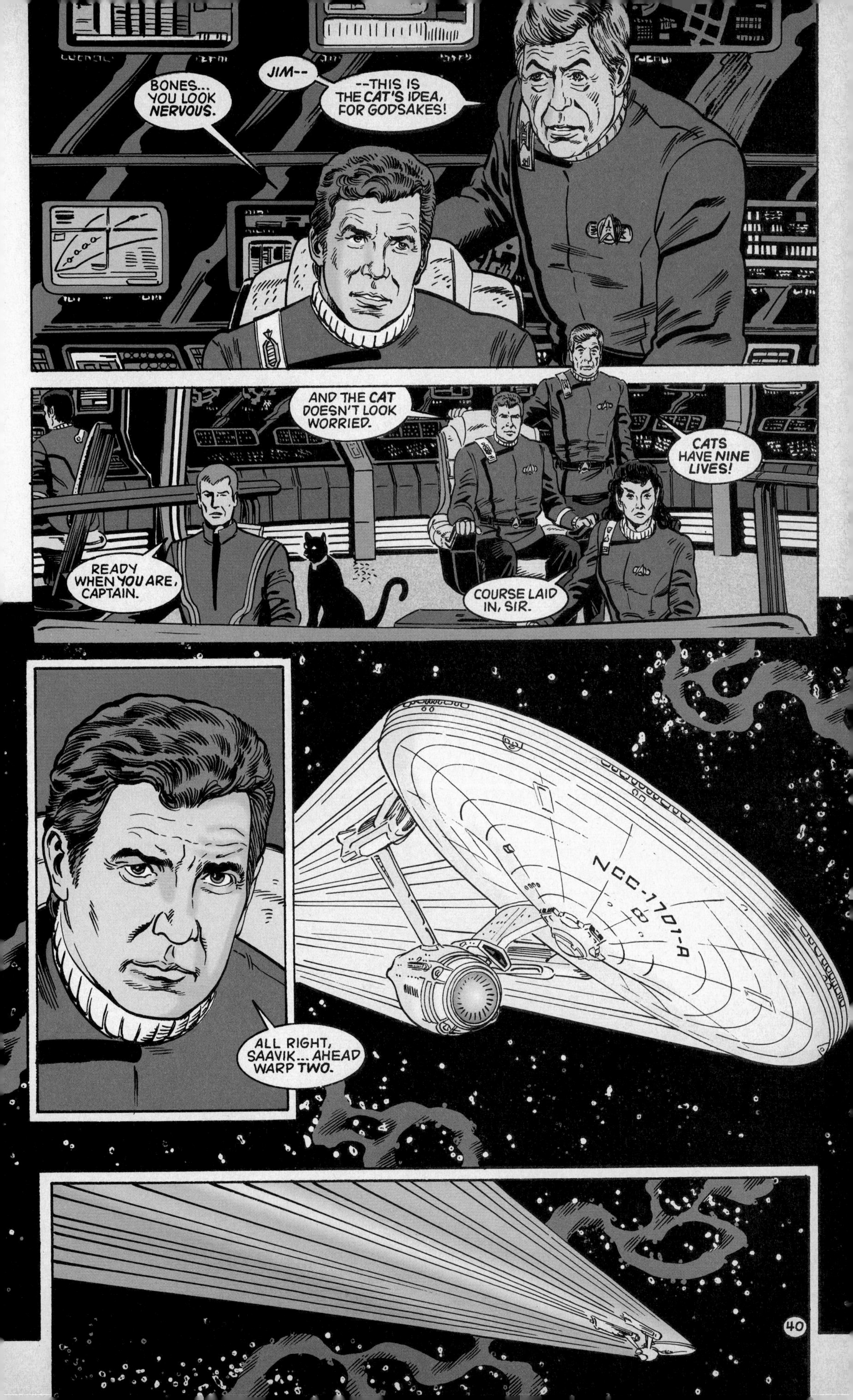
BONES... YOU LOOK NERVOUS.
JIM--
--THIS IS THE CAT'S IDEA, FOR GODSAKES!
AND THE CAT DOESN'T LOOK WORRIED.
CATS HAVE NINE LIVES!
READY WHEN YOU ARE, CAPTAIN.
COURSE LAID IN, SIR.
ALL RIGHT, SAAVIK... AHEAD WARP TWO.
NCC-1701-A

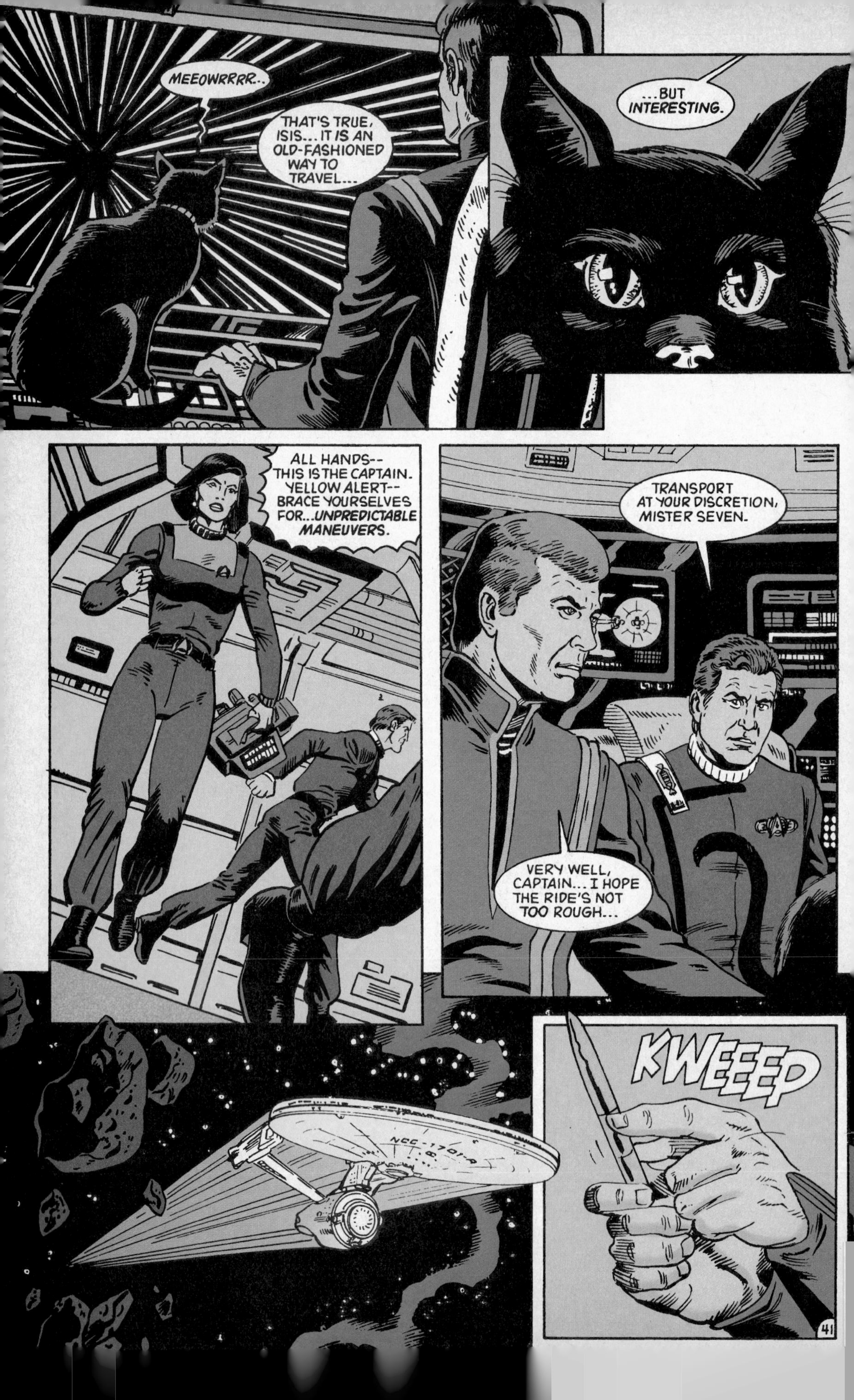

MEEOWRRRR...
THAT'S TRUE, ISIS... IT IS AN OLD-FASHIONED WAY TO TRAVEL...
...BUT INTERESTING.
ALL HANDS-- THIS IS THE CAPTAIN. YELLOW ALERT-- BRACE YOURSELVES FOR...UNPREDICTABLE MANEUVERS.
TRANSPORT AT YOUR DISCRETION, MISTER SEVEN.
VERY WELL, CAPTAIN... I HOPE THE RIDE'S NOT TOO ROUGH...
NCC-1701-A
KWEEEP

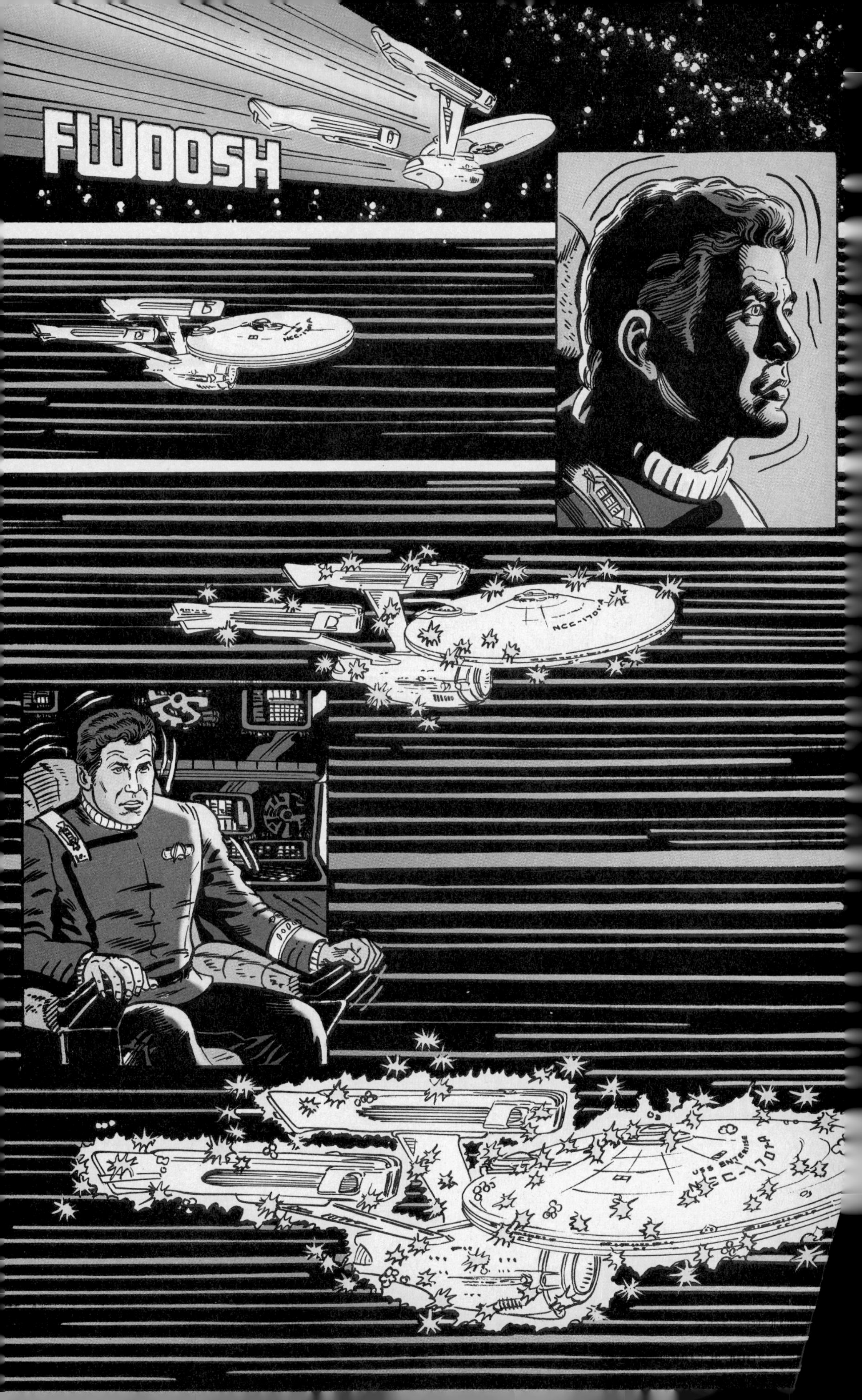
FWOOSH

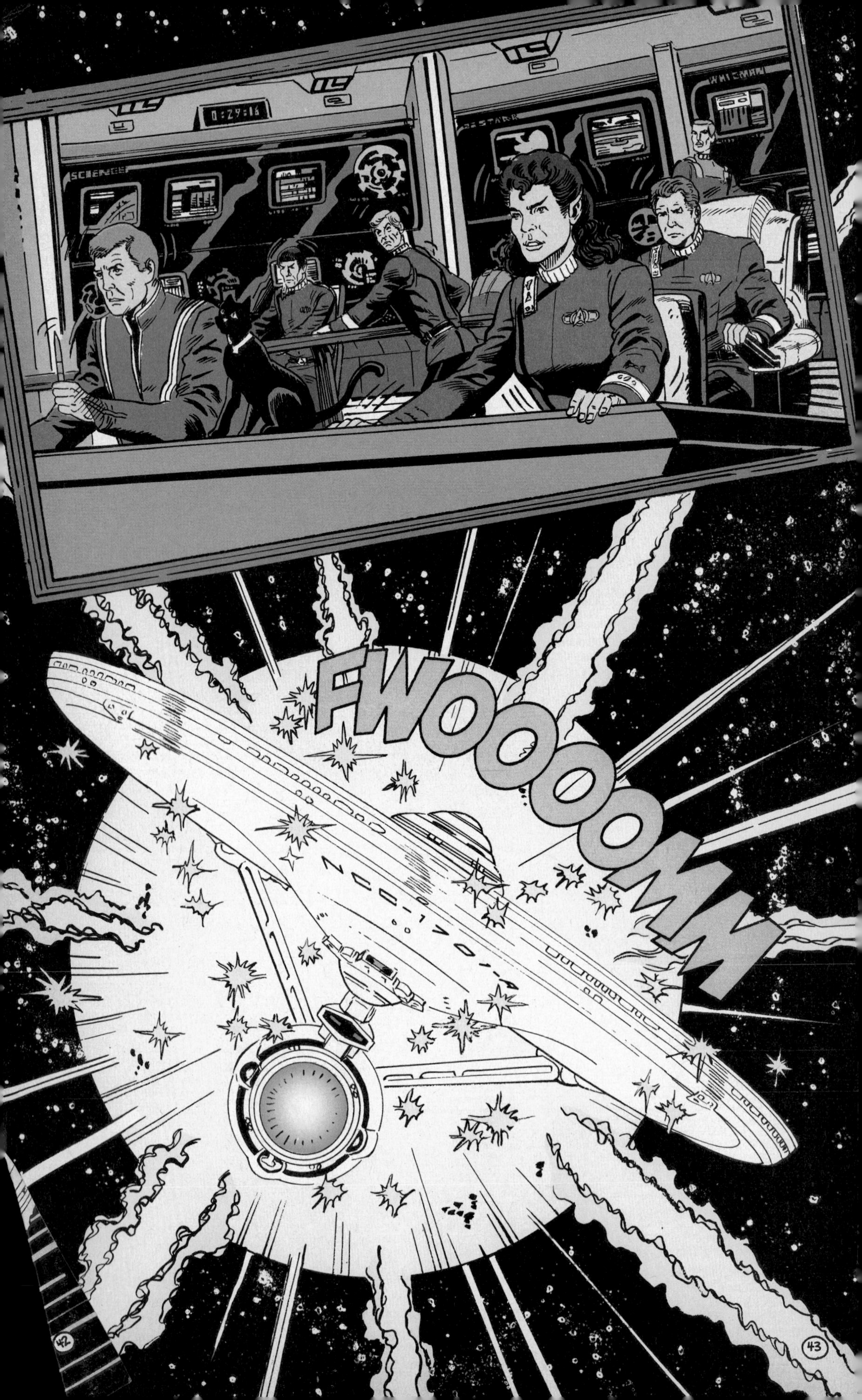

SCIENCE
0:29:16
FWOOOOMM
NCC-1701-A

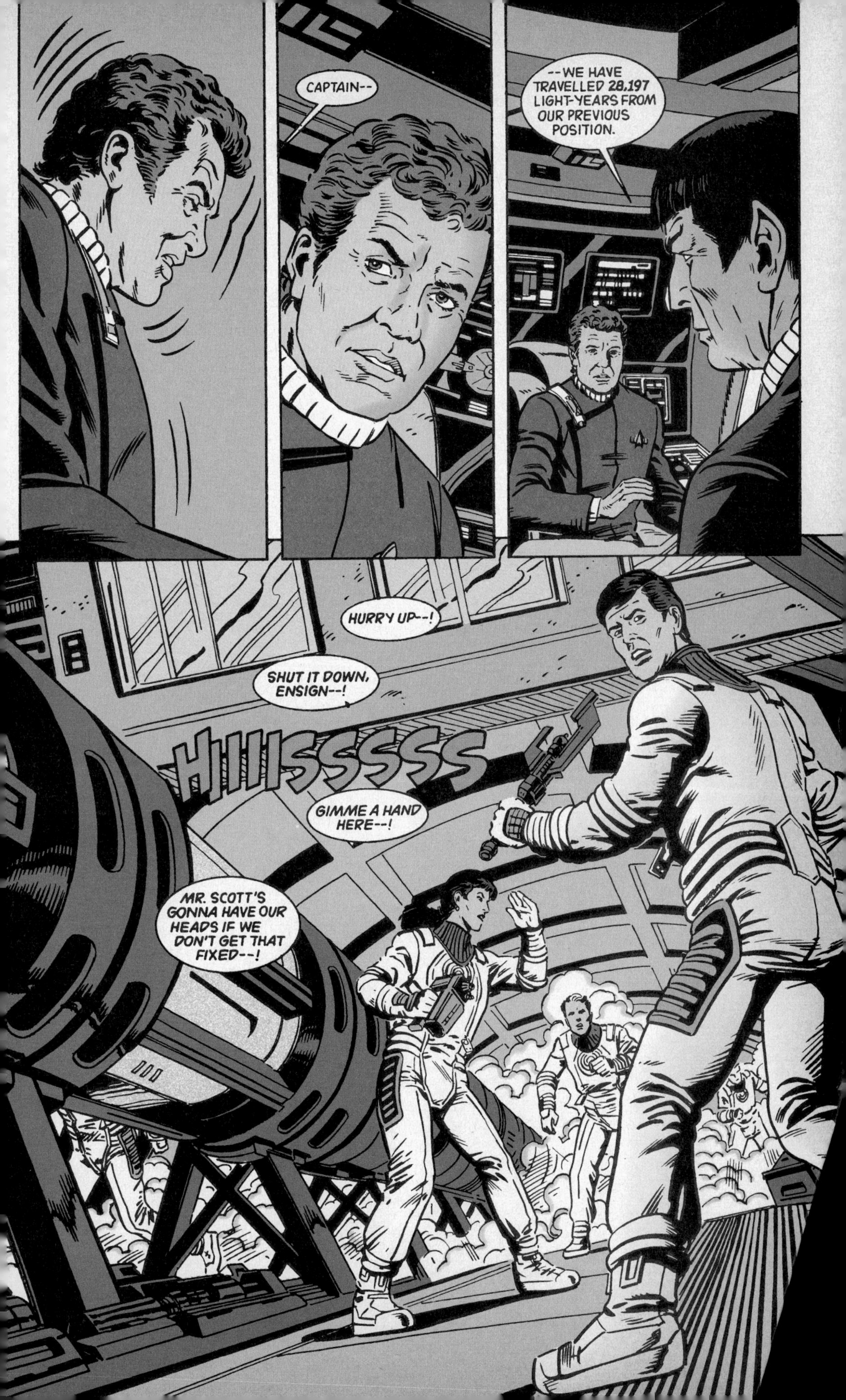
CAPTAIN--
--WE HAVE TRAVELLED 28,197 LIGHT-YEARS FROM OUR PREVIOUS POSITION.
HURRY UP--!
SHUT IT DOWN, ENSIGN--!
HIIISSSSS
GIMME A HAND HERE--!
MR. SCOTT'S GONNA HAVE OUR HEADS IF WE DON'T GET THAT FIXED--!

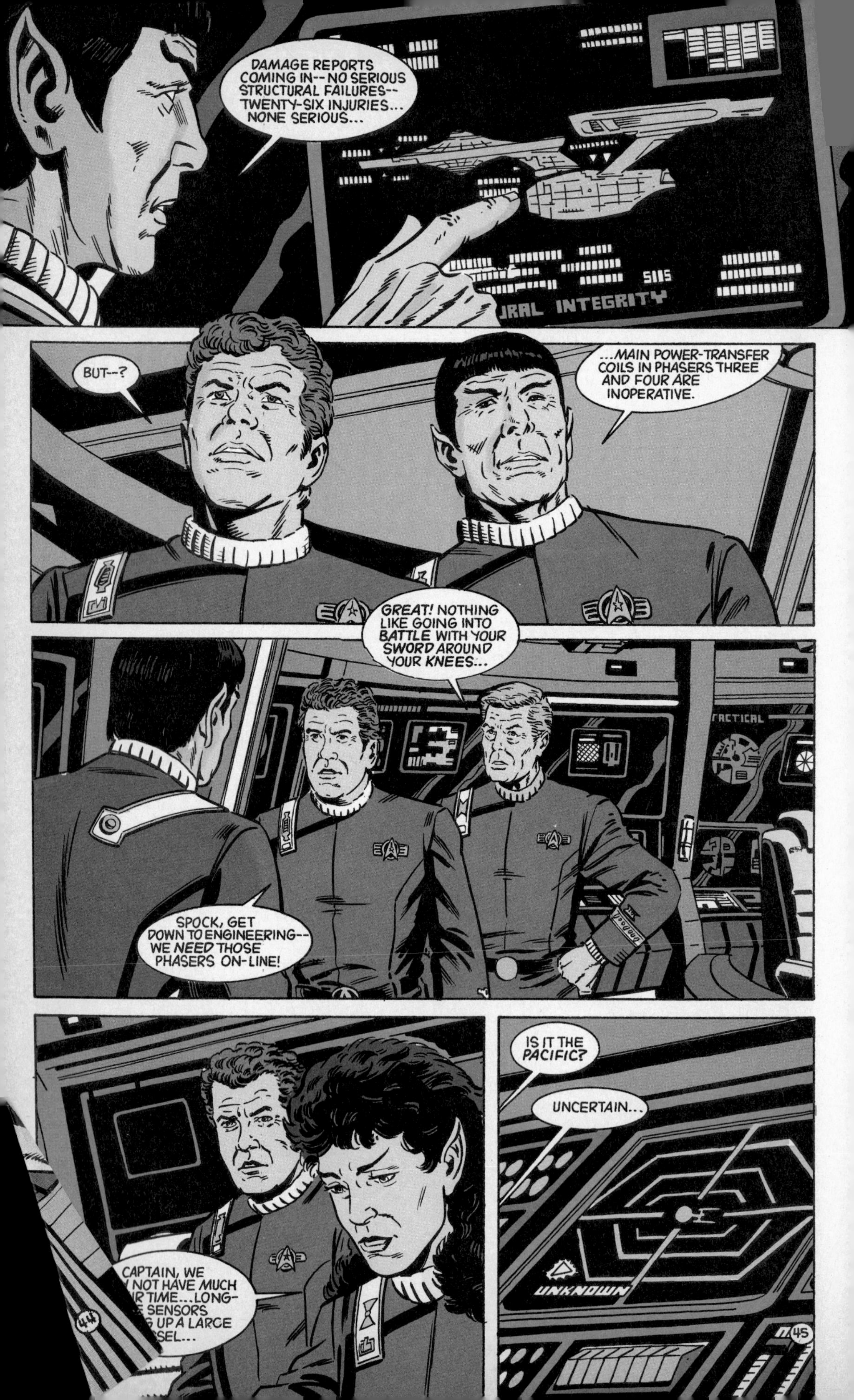
DAMAGE REPORTS COMING IN--NO SERIOUS STRUCTURAL FAILURES--TWENTY-SIX INJURIES... NONE SERIOUS...
SIIS
URAL INTEGRITY
BUT--?
...MAIN POWER-TRANSFER COILS IN PHASERS THREE AND FOUR ARE INOPERATIVE.
GREAT! NOTHING LIKE GOING INTO BATTLE WITH YOUR SWORD AROUND YOUR KNEES...
TACTICAL
SPOCK, GET DOWN TO ENGINEERING--WE NEED THOSE PHASERS ON-LINE!
CAPTAIN, WE
NOT HAVE MUCH
IR TIME...LONG-
E SENSORS
S UP A LARGE
SSEL...
44
IS IT THE PACIFIC?
UNCERTAIN...
UNKNOWN
45

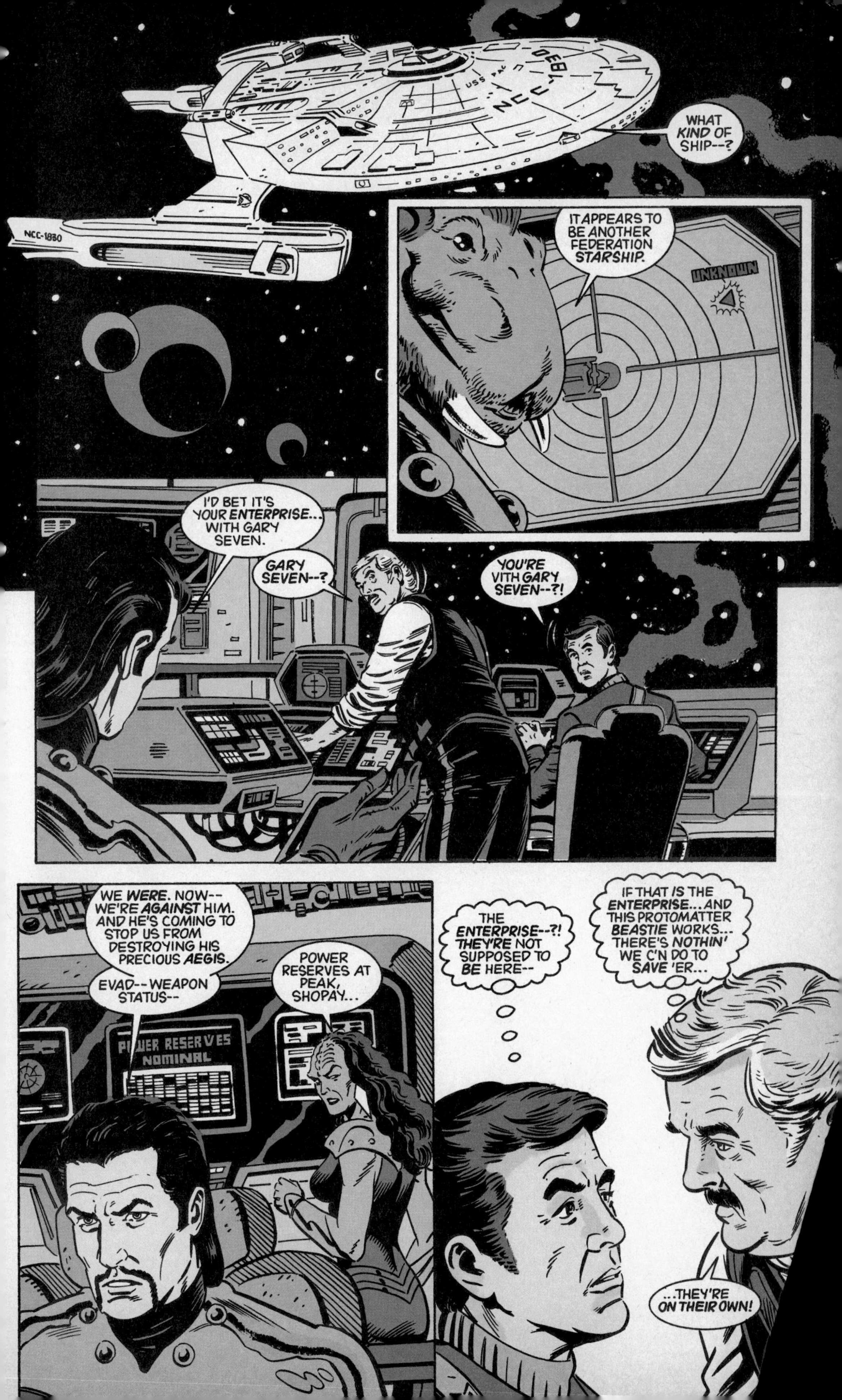
NCC-1830
USS PAC
NCC-1830
WHAT KIND OF SHIP--?
UNKNOWN
IT APPEARS TO BE ANOTHER FEDERATION STARSHIP.
I'D BET IT'S YOUR ENTERPRISE... WITH GARY SEVEN.
GARY SEVEN--?
YOU'RE VITH GARY SEVEN--?!
WE WERE. NOW-- WE'RE AGAINST HIM. AND HE'S COMING TO STOP US FROM DESTROYING HIS PRECIOUS AEGIS.
EVAD-- WEAPON STATUS--
POWER RESERVES AT PEAK, SHOPAY...
POWER RESERVES NOMINAL
THE ENTERPRISE--?! THEY'RE NOT SUPPOSED TO BE HERE--
IF THAT IS THE ENTERPRISE... AND THIS PROTOMATTER BEASTIE WORKS... THERE'S NOTHIN' WE C'N DO TO SAVE 'ER...
...THEY'RE ON THEIR OWN!

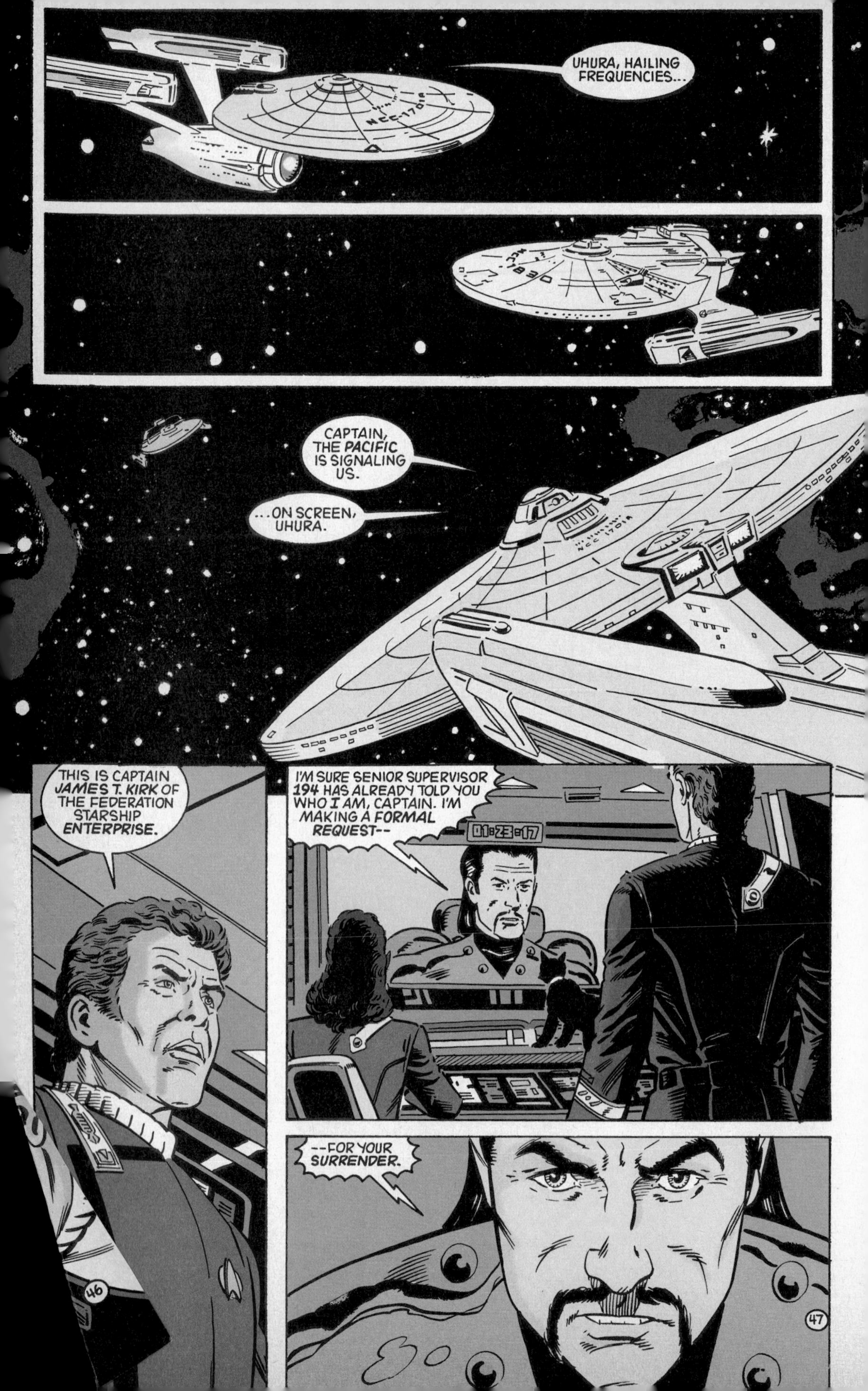
UHURA, HAILING FREQUENCIES...
CAPTAIN, THE PACIFIC IS SIGNALING US.
...ON SCREEN, UHURA.
THIS IS CAPTAIN JAMES T. KIRK OF THE FEDERATION STARSHIP ENTERPRISE.
I'M SURE SENIOR SUPERVISOR 194 HAS ALREADY TOLD YOU WHO I AM, CAPTAIN. I'M MAKING A FORMAL REQUEST--
01:23:17
--FOR YOUR SURRENDER.
46
47

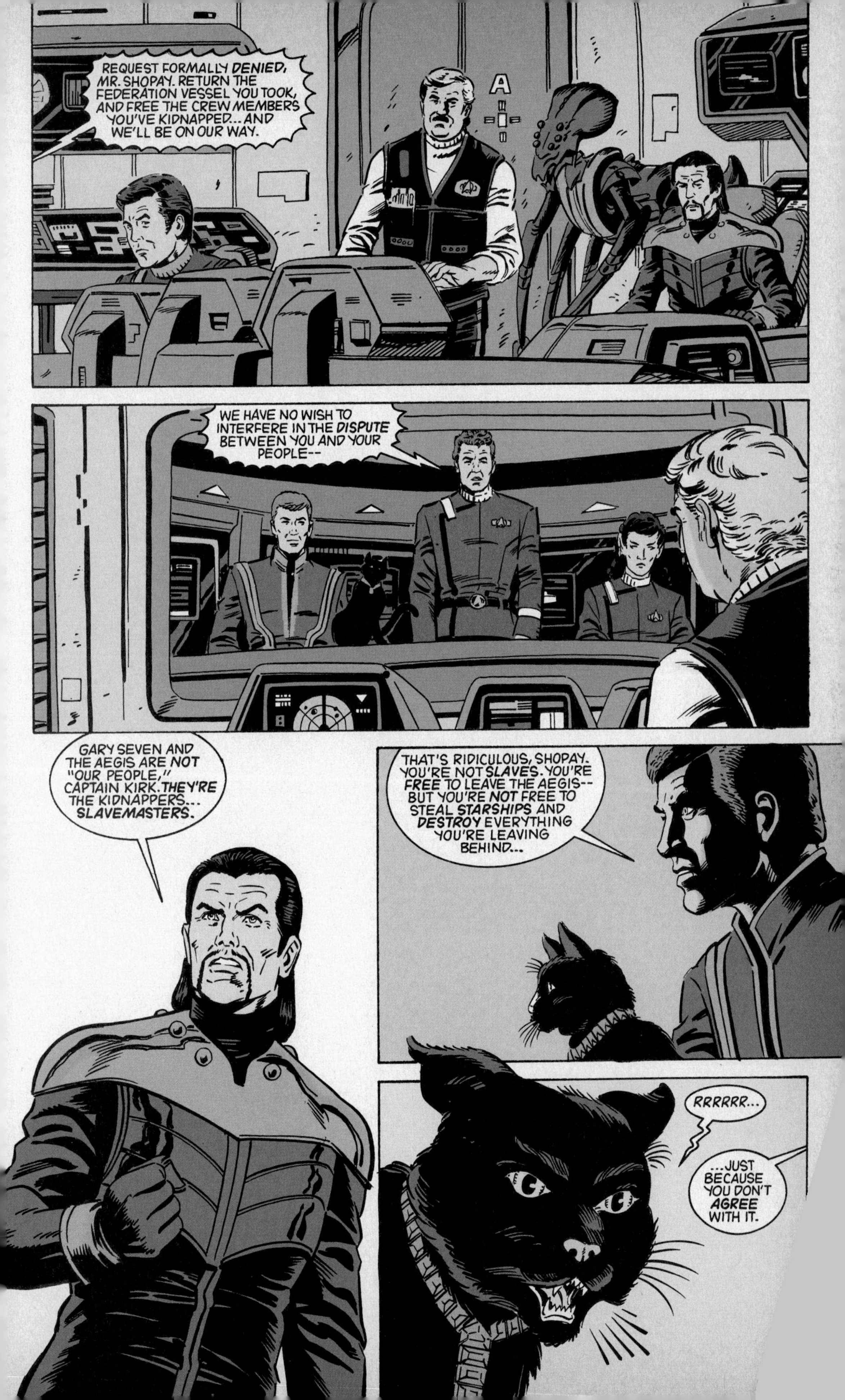
REQUEST FORMALLY DENIED, MR. SHOPAY. RETURN THE FEDERATION VESSEL YOU TOOK, AND FREE THE CREW MEMBERS YOU'VE KIDNAPPED... AND WE'LL BE ON OUR WAY.
WE HAVE NO WISH TO INTERFERE IN THE DISPUTE BETWEEN YOU AND YOUR PEOPLE--
GARY SEVEN AND THE AEGIS ARE NOT "OUR PEOPLE," CAPTAIN KIRK. THEY'RE THE KIDNAPPERS... SLAVEMASTERS.
THAT'S RIDICULOUS, SHOPAY. YOU'RE NOT SLAVES. YOU'RE FREE TO LEAVE THE AEGIS-- BUT YOU'RE NOT FREE TO STEAL STARSHIPS AND DESTROY EVERYTHING YOU'RE LEAVING BEHIND...
RRRRRR...
...JUST BECAUSE YOU DON'T AGREE WITH IT.

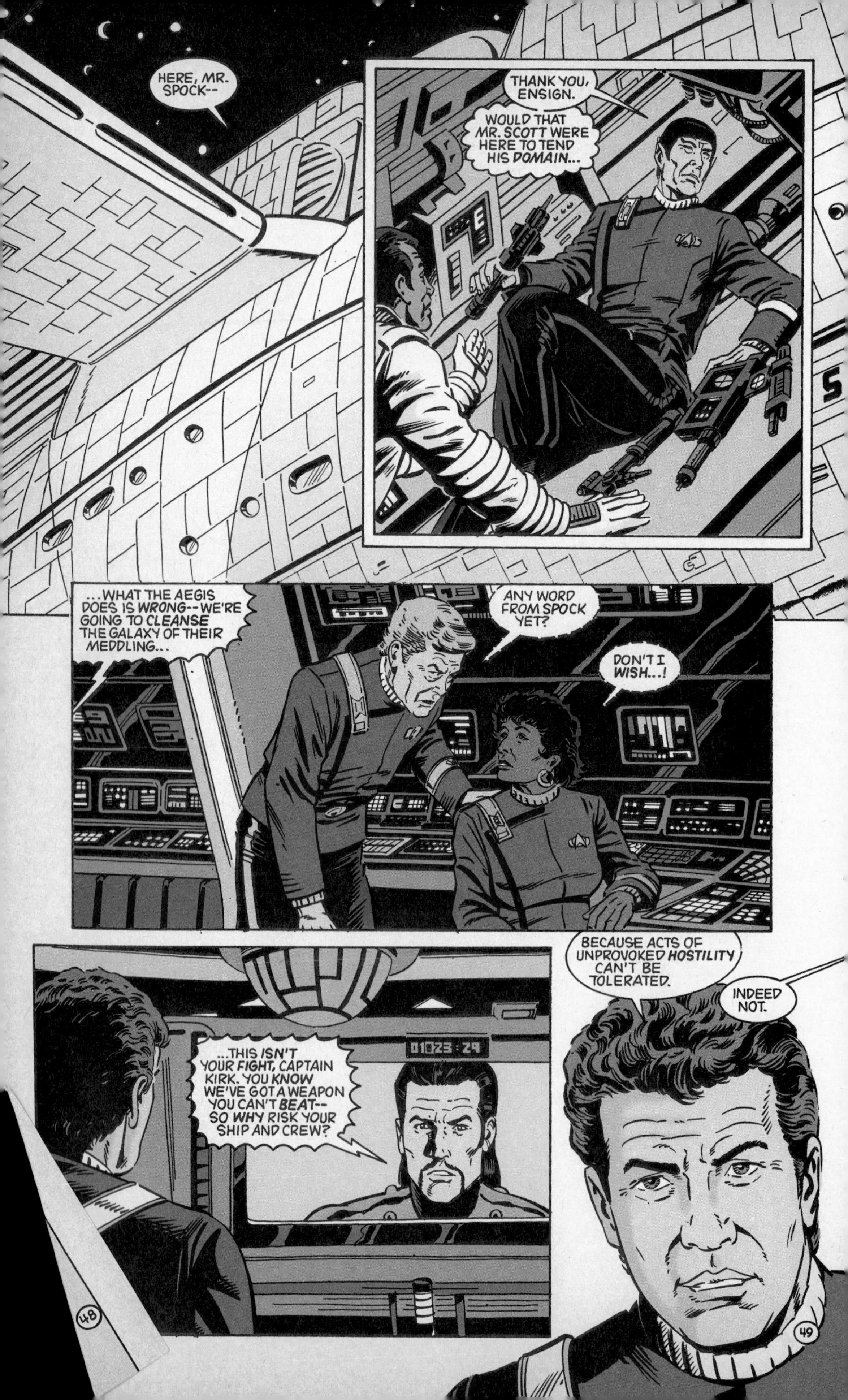
HERE, MR. SPOCK--
THANK YOU, ENSIGN.
WOULD THAT MR. SCOTT WERE HERE TO TEND HIS DOMAIN...
...WHAT THE AEGIS DOES IS WRONG--WE'RE GOING TO CLEANSE THE GALAXY OF THEIR MEDDLING...
ANY WORD FROM SPOCK YET?
DON'T I WISH...!
...THIS ISN'T YOUR FIGHT, CAPTAIN KIRK. YOU KNOW WE'VE GOT A WEAPON YOU CAN'T BEAT--SO WHY RISK YOUR SHIP AND CREW?
01 23 : 29
BECAUSE ACTS OF UNPROVOKED HOSTILITY CAN'T BE TOLERATED.
INDEED NOT.

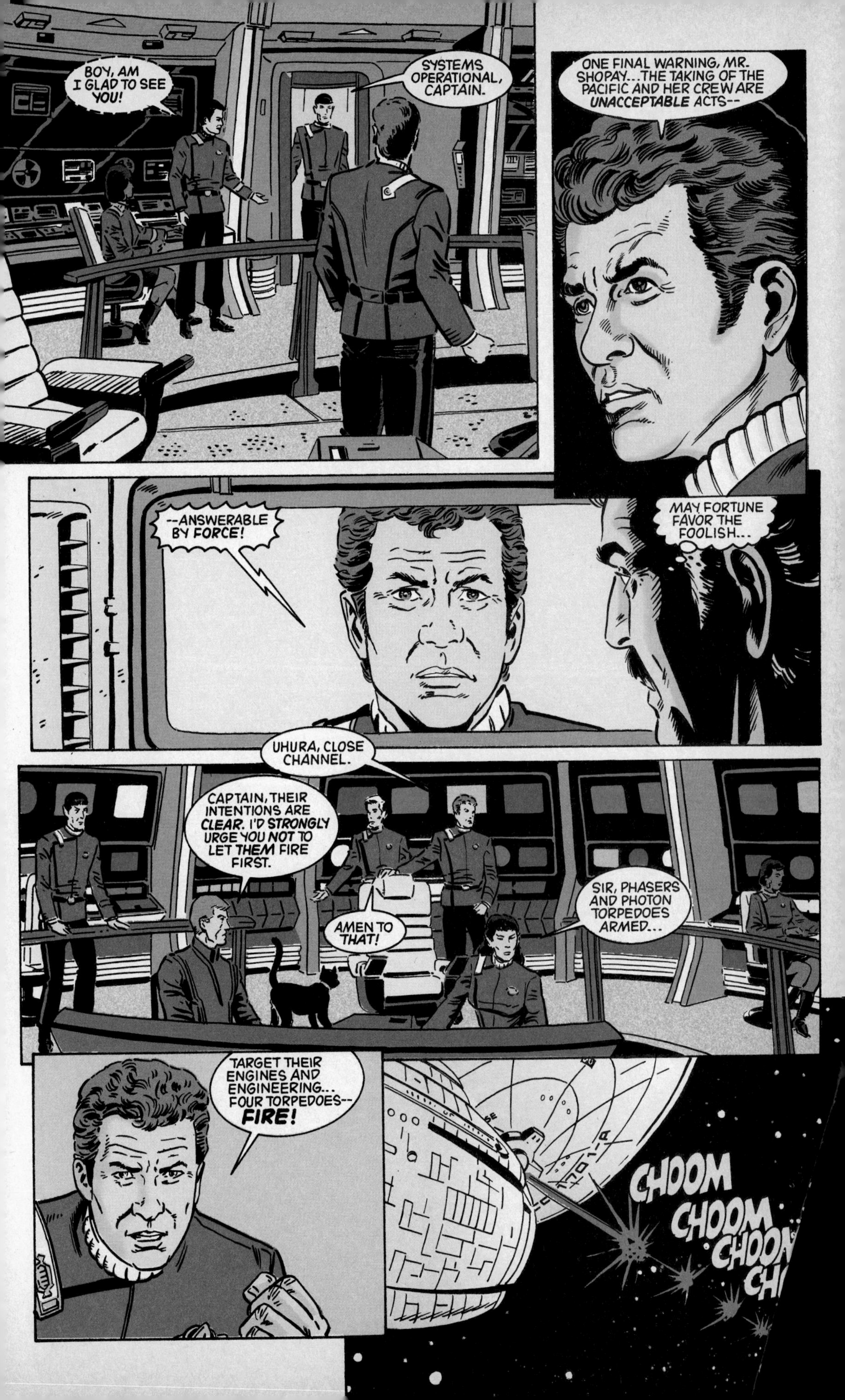
BOY, AM I GLAD TO SEE YOU!
SYSTEMS OPERATIONAL, CAPTAIN.
ONE FINAL WARNING, MR. SHOPAY... THE TAKING OF THE PACIFIC AND HER CREW ARE UNACCEPTABLE ACTS--
--ANSWERABLE BY FORCE!
MAY FORTUNE FAVOR THE FOOLISH...
UHURA, CLOSE CHANNEL.
CAPTAIN, THEIR INTENTIONS ARE CLEAR. I'D STRONGLY URGE YOU NOT TO LET THEM FIRE FIRST.
AMEN TO THAT!
SIR, PHASERS AND PHOTON TORPEDOES ARMED...
TARGET THEIR ENGINES AND ENGINEERING... FOUR TORPEDOES-- FIRE!
CHOOM
CHOOM

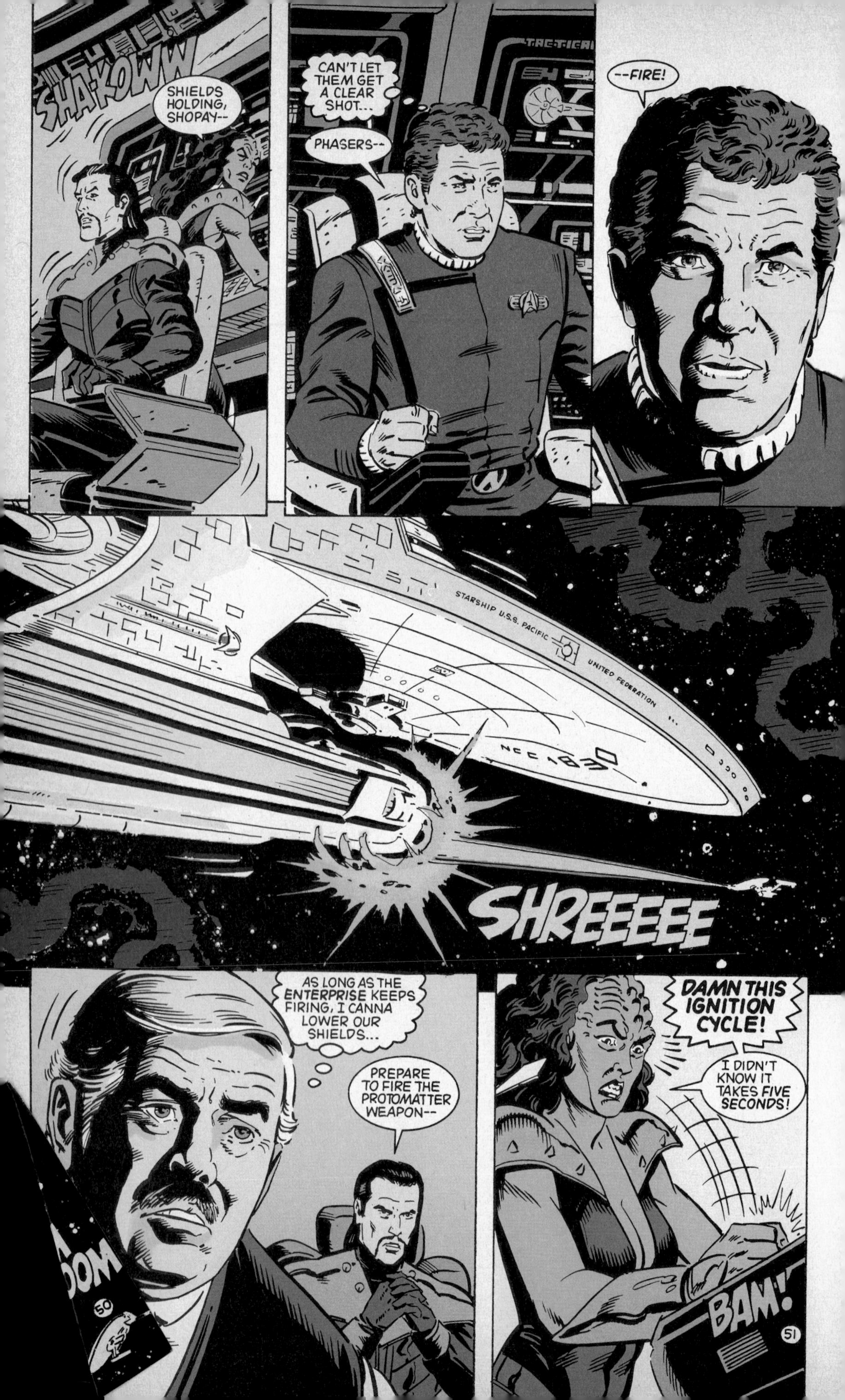

SHA-KOWW
SHIELDS HOLDING, SHOPAY--
CAN'T LET THEM GET A CLEAR SHOT...
PHASERS--
--FIRE!
STARSHIP U.S.S. PACIFIC
UNITED FEDERATION
SHREEEEEE
AS LONG AS THE ENTERPRISE KEEPS FIRING, I CANNA LOWER OUR SHIELDS...
PREPARE TO FIRE THE PROTOMATTER WEAPON--
DAMN THIS IGNITION CYCLE!
I DIDN'T KNOW IT TAKES *FIVE* SECONDS!
BAM!

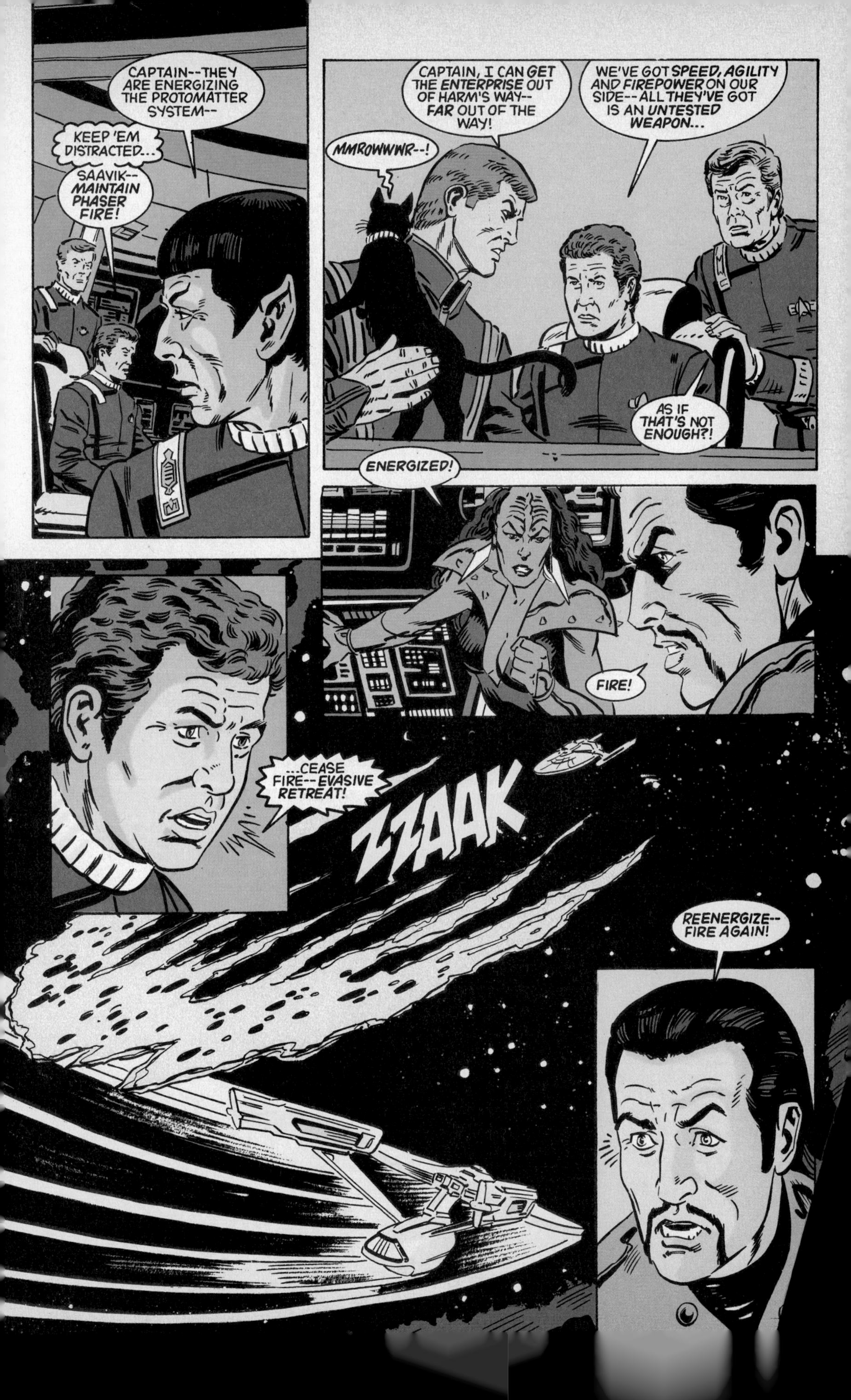
CAPTAIN--THEY ARE ENERGIZING THE PROTOMATTER SYSTEM--
KEEP 'EM DISTRACTED...
SAAVIK--MAINTAIN PHASER FIRE!
CAPTAIN, I CAN GET THE ENTERPRISE OUT OF HARM'S WAY--FAR OUT OF THE WAY!
MMROWWWR--!
WE'VE GOT SPEED, AGILITY AND FIREPOWER ON OUR SIDE--ALL THEY'VE GOT IS AN UNTESTED WEAPON...
AS IF THAT'S NOT ENOUGH?!
ENERGIZED!
FIRE!
...CEASE FIRE--EVASIVE RETREAT!
ZZAAK
REENERGIZE--FIRE AGAIN!

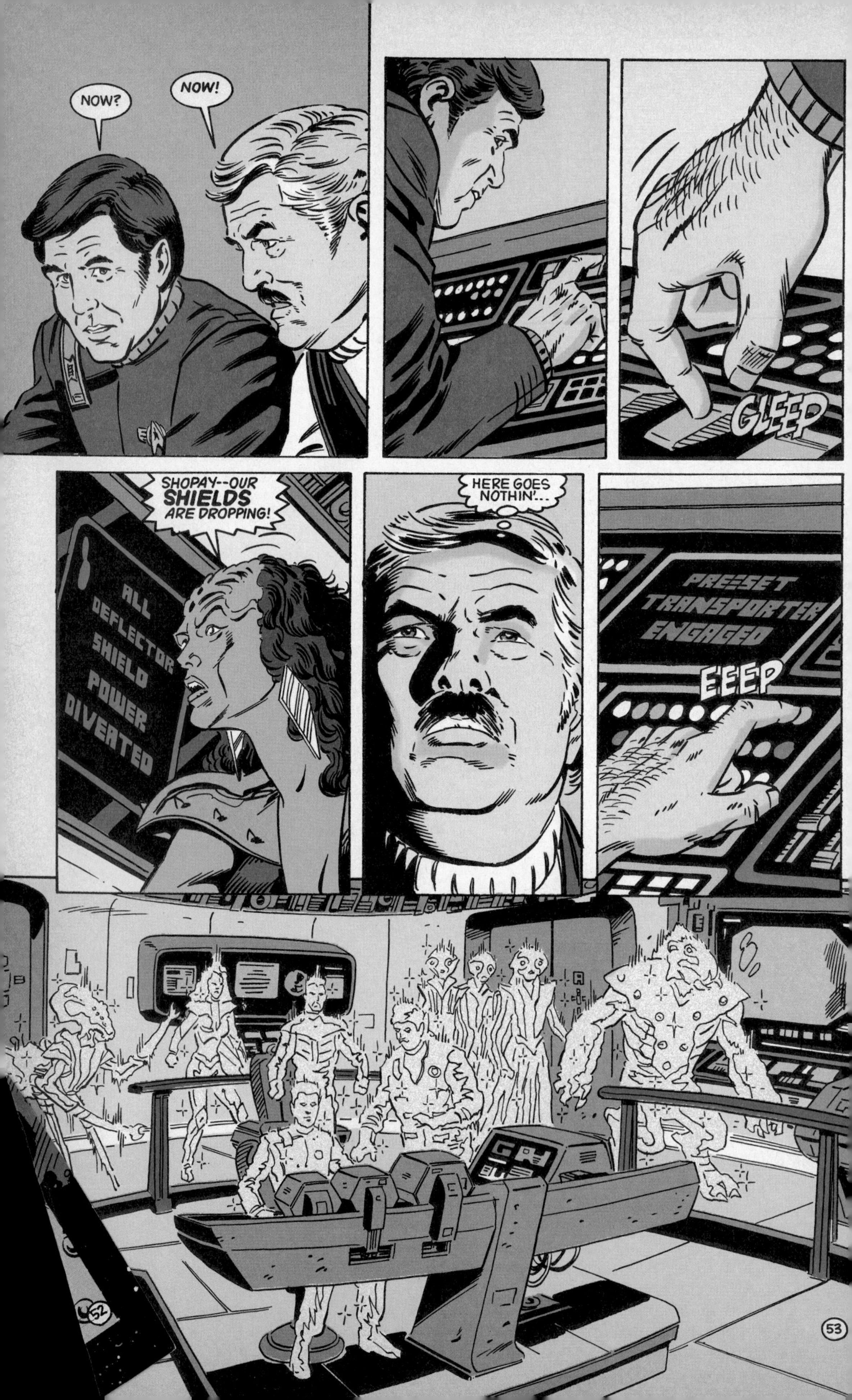
NOW?
NOW!
GLEEP
SHOPAY--OUR SHIELDS ARE DROPPING!
ALL DEFLECTOR SHIELD POWER DIVERTED
HERE GOES NOTHIN'...
PRESET TRANSPORTER ENGAGED
EEEP

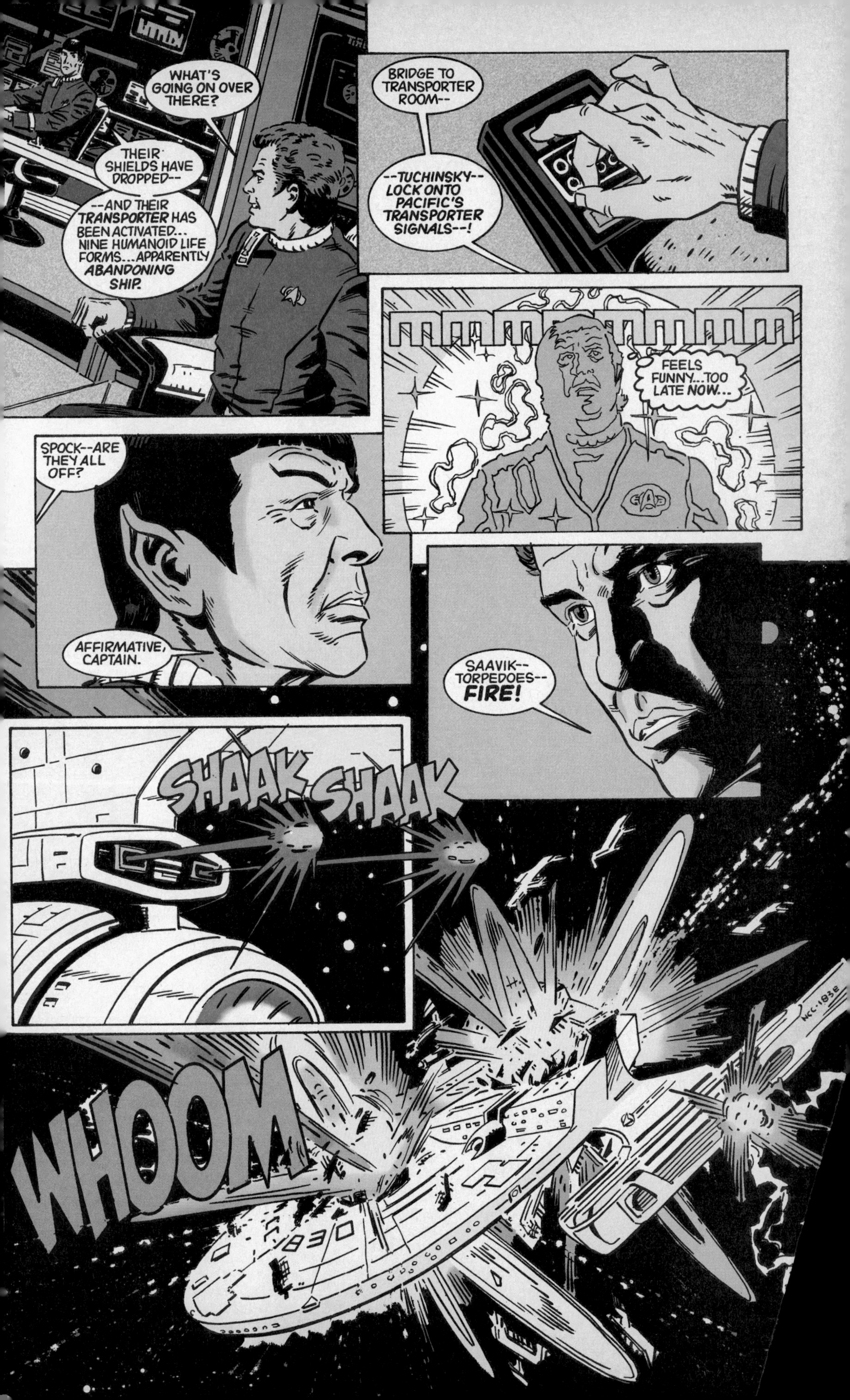
WHAT'S GOING ON OVER THERE?
THEIR SHIELDS HAVE DROPPED--
--AND THEIR TRANSPORTER HAS BEEN ACTIVATED... NINE HUMANOID LIFE FORMS...APPARENTLY ABANDONING SHIP.
BRIDGE TO TRANSPORTER ROOM--
--TUCHINSKY--LOCK ONTO PACIFIC'S TRANSPORTER SIGNALS--!
MMMMMMMMMMM
FEELS FUNNY...TOO LATE NOW...
SPOCK--ARE THEY ALL OFF?
AFFIRMATIVE, CAPTAIN.
SAAVIK--TORPEDOES--FIRE!
SHAAK SHAAK
WHOOM
NCC-1838
1830

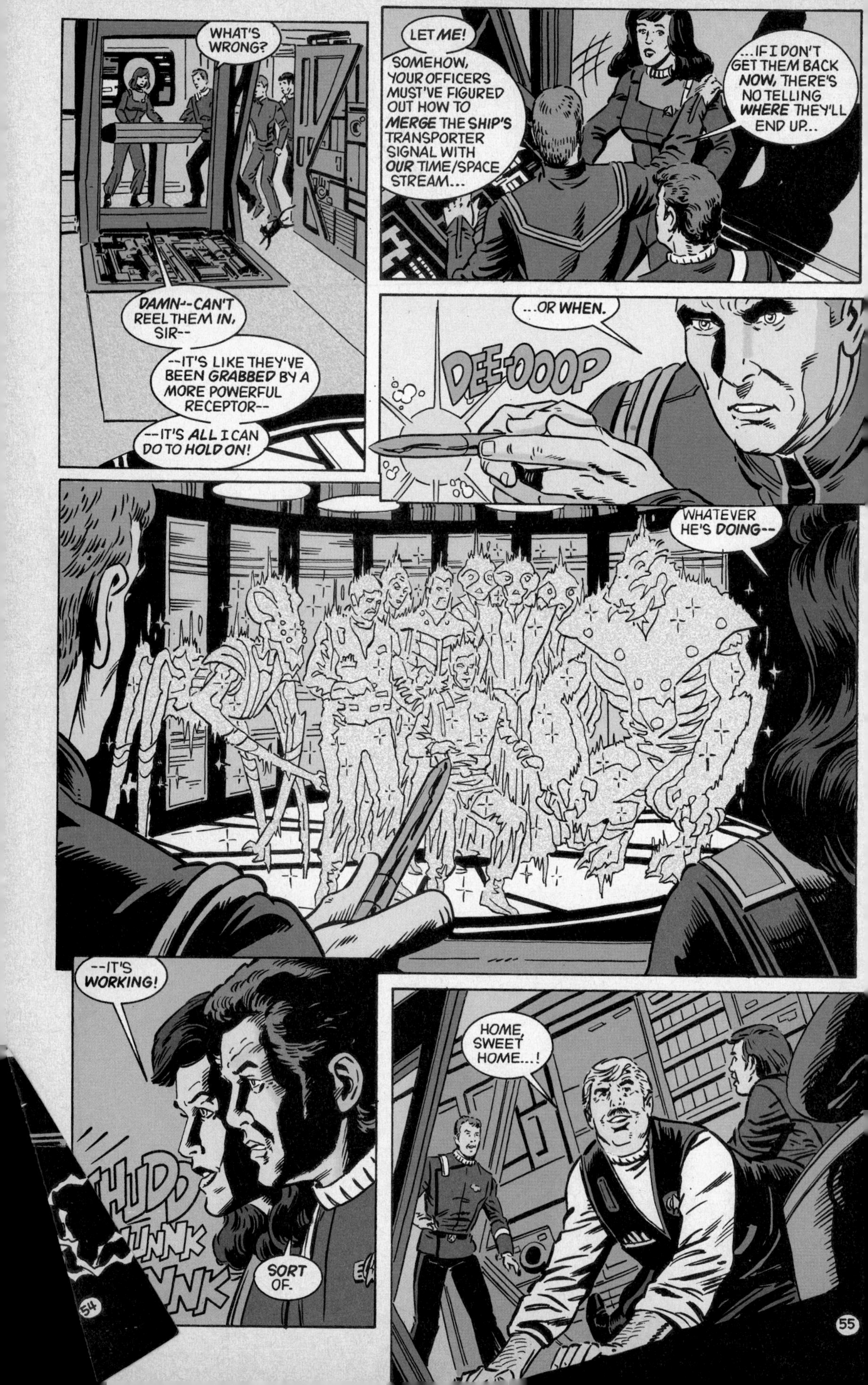
WHAT'S WRONG?
DAMN--CAN'T REEL THEM IN, SIR--
--IT'S LIKE THEY'VE BEEN GRABBED BY A MORE POWERFUL RECEPTOR--
--IT'S ALL I CAN DO TO HOLD ON!
LET ME!
SOMEHOW, YOUR OFFICERS MUST'VE FIGURED OUT HOW TO MERGE THE SHIP'S TRANSPORTER SIGNAL WITH OUR TIME/SPACE STREAM...
...IF I DON'T GET THEM BACK NOW, THERE'S NO TELLING WHERE THEY'LL END UP...
...OR WHEN.
DEE-OOOP
WHATEVER HE'S DOING--
--IT'S WORKING!
SORT OF.
HOME, SWEET HOME...!
54
55

You can find more star-spanning adventures in these books from DC:

STAR TREK: DEBT OF HONOR
Chris Claremont/Adam Hughes/Karl Story

STAR TREK: THE MIRROR UNIVERSE SAGA
Mike Barr/Tom Sutton/Ricardo Villagran

THE BEST OF STAR TREK
Various Writers and Artists

STAR TREK: WHO KILLED CAPTAIN KIRK?
Peter David/Tom Sutton/Gordon Purcell/Ricardo Villagran

STAR TREK: THE NEXT GENERATION—
THE STAR LOST
Michael Jan Friedman/Peter Krause/Pablo Marcos

THE BEST OF STAR TREK:
THE NEXT GENERATION
Various Writers and Artists

STAR TREK: THE NEXT GENERATION—
BEGINNINGS
Mike Carlin/Pablo Marcos/Carlos Garzon/Arne Starr

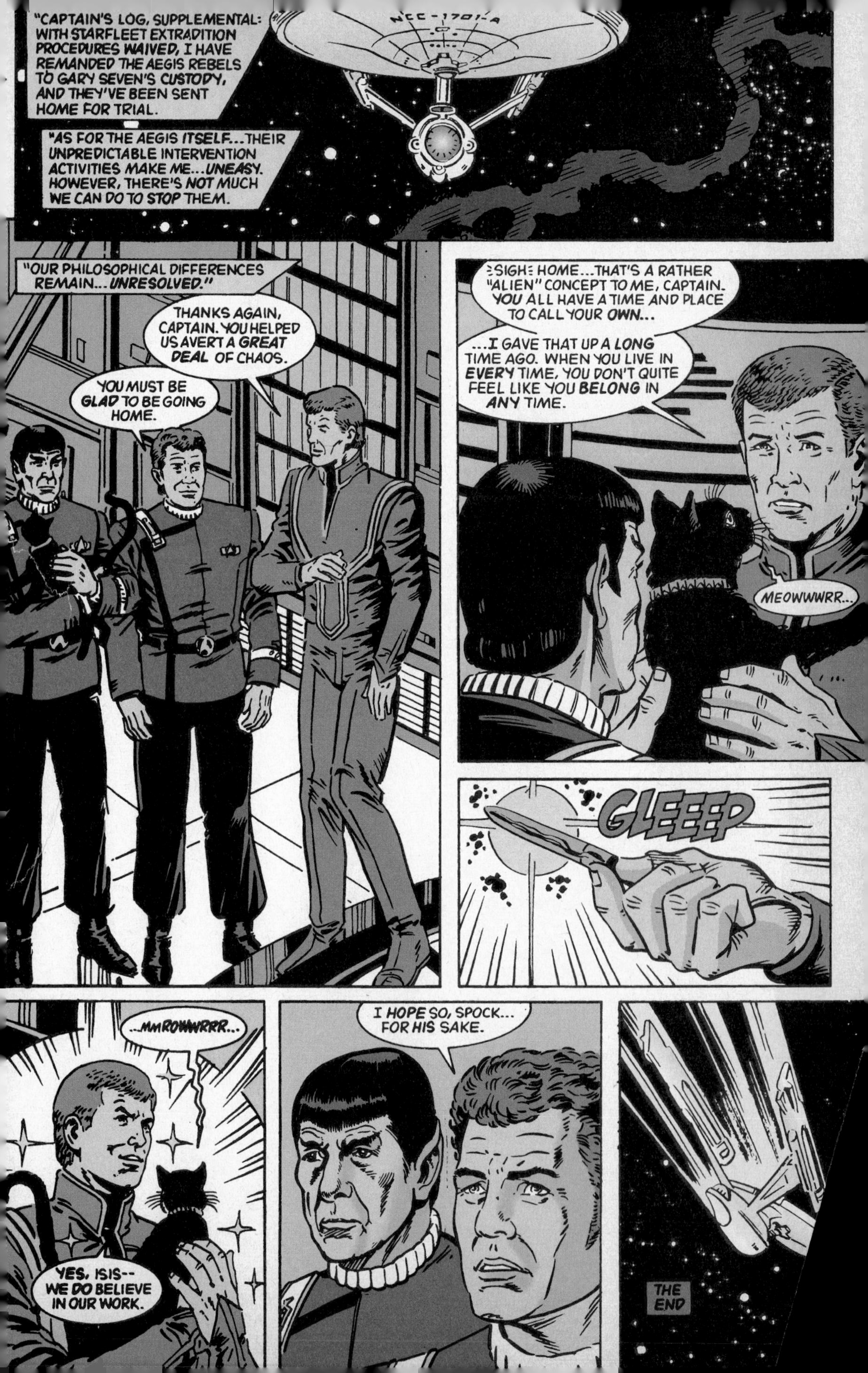
"CAPTAIN'S LOG, SUPPLEMENTAL: WITH STARFLEET EXTRADITION PROCEDURES WAIVED, I HAVE REMANDED THE AEGIS REBELS TO GARY SEVEN'S CUSTODY, AND THEY'VE BEEN SENT HOME FOR TRIAL.
"AS FOR THE AEGIS ITSELF... THEIR UNPREDICTABLE INTERVENTION ACTIVITIES MAKE ME... UNEASY. HOWEVER, THERE'S NOT MUCH WE CAN DO TO STOP THEM.
NCC-1701-A
"OUR PHILOSOPHICAL DIFFERENCES REMAIN... UNRESOLVED."
THANKS AGAIN, CAPTAIN. YOU HELPED US AVERT A GREAT DEAL OF CHAOS.
YOU MUST BE GLAD TO BE GOING HOME.
SIGH HOME... THAT'S A RATHER "ALIEN" CONCEPT TO ME, CAPTAIN. YOU ALL HAVE A TIME AND PLACE TO CALL YOUR OWN...
...I GAVE THAT UP A LONG TIME AGO. WHEN YOU LIVE IN EVERY TIME, YOU DON'T QUITE FEEL LIKE YOU BELONG IN ANY TIME.
MEOWWWRR...
GLEEEP
...MMROWWRRR...
YES, ISIS-- WE DO BELIEVE IN OUR WORK.
I HOPE SO, SPOCK... FOR HIS SAKE.
THE END